PATHS OF PEACE

REDMOND CIVIL WAR ROMANCE SERIES BOOK 2

T. NOVAN

TAYLOR RICKARD

AUSXIP PUBLISHING

www.ausxippublishing.com

Paths of Peace

Cover Design by Mary D. Brooks
Illustrations by Lucia Nobrega
Interior design by AUSXIP Media

Third Edition

ISBN: 978-0-6485709-6-7

Printed in the United States of America

Published by AUSXIP Publishing
Sydney, Australia

PROLOGUE

In the final days of the American Civil War, two very unique people came together to establish what would become a southern dynasty. Colonel Charles Huger Redmond brought his cavalry regiment, the 13th Pennsylvania, to the formerly bustling town of Culpeper, Virginia to establish winter headquarters that would allow for the protection of critical rail lines. In order to support his men and horses until the upcoming spring campaign, their winter encampment also required the taking over of lands owned by Confederate widow Rebecca Gaines.

Over the course of the winter, Charlie and Rebecca's relationship grows from one of cautious, mutual respect to something very different. As their unusual friendship grows, Colonel Redmond finds himself drawn not only to the land, but to the woman as well. He makes a deal with the Widow Gaines to winter his men and horses on her property and she makes a deal for his personal protection during his stay.

Charlie is a charming gentleman, gentle, caring, and very appropriate, a very different kind of man from Rebecca's abusive husband. Though her husband had perished in November of 1863, at the Second Battle of Rappahannock Station, Rebecca finds it extremely difficult to come to terms with her growing feelings for this Union officer.

For his part, Charlie is alarmed to realize he is becoming romantically involved with the lovely Southerner, for he hides a secret that, if discovered, would mean social disgrace and the end of a distinguished military career. Under the carefully crafted and protected military façade, Charlie is a woman.

Over the course of the winter, they find the courage to let their feelings blossom into a deep and abiding love. Before Charlie, who has now been elevated to the rank of Brigadier General, and the 13th Pennsylvania are ordered back into the field of battle, they are married, in part so that Charlie can continue to protect and provide for Rebecca and for the two children, Emily and Andrew, they have taken in and plan to adopt.

The final months of the conflict in Virginia are brutal. Rebecca took in the waves of refugees, women and children who had been made homeless by the ravages of the war. One of these included the infant son of a notorious Washington prostitute and one of the conspirators who orchestrated President Lincoln's assassination, whom she adopted. Charlie and his troops see battle after battle, as General Grant's forces push General Lee's struggling and poorly supplied troops back up the James River from Petersburg to Appomattox. The 13th Pennsylvania Cavalry manages to block trainloads of supplies from reaching General Lee at Appomattox, resulting in Charlie being terribly wounded, and the Army of Virginia being forced to surrender.

With the support of Dr. Elizabeth Walker, his regiment's physician, his batman Jocko Jackson, and medics Albert Samuelson and Walt Whitman, Charlie's life is saved, but he is badly injured, with part of one hand missing and significant muscle loss in his right leg. After a frightening few weeks in the field hospital, they manage to return Charlie to Culpeper, where his recovery is a slow and painful process.

As the town of Culpeper begins to recover after the end of the war, several of Charlie's companions from the 13th Pennsylvania choose to join their leader and settle in the shattered town. Culpeper had once had a thriving population of fifteen hundred, but at the height of the war, after both the Union and Confederate troops had swept through it on multiple occasions, it had been reduced to a burned-out hulk with only 150 residents.

With the end of the war, men and families were slowly returning to their homes or what was left of them and with the support of the handful of Unionists, began the slow process of rebuilding. Elizabeth Walker, who married Charlie's second in command Richard Polk, settles in to be the town's only physician.

Several of Charlie's men had met women, either locals or refugees, and chose to join their former commander in supporting the town. There were a few people in Culpeper who supported the Unionists; others were still angry and resentful. The reconstruction of the South had begun, and for Charlie, Rebecca and the residents of Culpeper, Virginia, the coming years would be an uphill battle.

CHAPTER 1

Monday, December 25, 1865

Charlie wrapped his right arm around Rebecca's waist and snuggled closer under the comforter and blankets that kept the early morning chill from their skin. His wife, as always after sleeping the night through, was warm and soft, her body completely relaxed. This was absolutely his favorite spot in the world. She hummed and curled back into him, carefully grasping the wrist of his injured hand and drawing his arm tighter around her waist.

"Nice," she mumbled and sighed deeply, feeling his warm breath on her ear. She smiled and fell slowly back into a peaceful slumber, warm and content in her husband's arms.

Some changes had been made over the course of the last few months. The first was getting the lock on their bedroom door fixed so it would properly engage. They had discovered very soon after Charlie moved back to their room that Emily always made a beeline for their door first thing in the morning. One very close call of the door flying open while he was only half dressed, made the repair of the lock crucial once the little girl had learned to turn the knob.

Because of the injuries to his body, they also switched sides in the bed. He could no longer lie on his right side without continuous pain waking him through the night. So, she had learned to sleep on the left so he could curl around behind her with less pain.

He was content to hold her as she slept, but he knew it would not last long. Miss Emily would be joining them very soon. Then, of course, the boys would need to be tended.

"Rebecca," he whispered, kissing her ear tenderly.

"No," she mumbled and pulled the covers under her chin.

"Darling, it is time to wake up."

"Just a few more minutes," she rolled over and curled tightly into his chest, tucking her head under his chin. "Please?"

"If we could, Mrs. Redmond, I would be happy to allow you to stay here all day, but I do believe that in a few minutes, we will have company in the form of our daughter."

"Hmm." She slid her hand under his sleep shirt and gently massaged the skin under her hand, careful to avoid the painful and still tender scars. "Then again, General Redmond, perhaps we have time for a little . . ."

"Rebecca . . ." He drew a deep breath as he transformed from man to woman by the simple act of removing the sleeping shirt.

Her hands slowly traveled down Rebecca's body grasping the hem of her nightgown, and without question or hesitation, Charlie slipped it over Rebecca's head and sent it to join the other shirt on the floor.

The banging on the door invaded the happy doze they had both slipped into after the rather intense session of early morning lovemaking.

"Mama. Papa. Merry Chrismas!" The voice of their little daughter called from behind the door. They could hear her dog, a Jack Russell named Papa Puppy, barking excitedly behind her.

Charlie lifted her head to watch as the knob rattled with Emily's attempts to open the door.

"Mama! Papa! It is Chwismas!"

Rebecca chuckled gently, rolling over to face the door. "I suppose we should get up now."

"I am afraid so, darling. Miss Emily is very much like her mama."

"Really? In what way?"

"She will not be denied," Charlie teased, kissing Rebecca's ear.

"You certainly did not seem to mind."

"Not in the least. I always enjoy satisfying your early morning urges."

"Not as much as I enjoy having them satisfied," she said as she tried to snuggle closer.

There was a bang on the door that sounded suspiciously like it was being kicked. "Mama!"

She sighed as she reached to the floor and retrieved their respective sleeping garments. "Here you are, Papa. Put that on and I will fetch your robe."

Rising, Rebecca let her night gown drop over her head.

Charlie watched her get dressed with appreciative eyes. At the same time, she once again donned the attire that made him the proper Papa and gentleman of Redmond Stables.

After placing a log on the embers of the fire to help it flare back to life, Rebecca placed Charlie's robe on the bed, slipped into her own, and then unlocked the door to allow Emily entrance.

The little girl stood for just a moment, looking at Rebecca with brows drawn together as if she were about to have a fit.

"Good morning, sweetheart." She knelt and hugged the child close. "Oooo, you are very chilly. Would you like cuddles with Papa and me while the water heats for tea?"

"Yes." She giggled and then charged the bed where Charlie was waiting to pull her up with his good arm. As soon as she was in bed she burrowed under the covers, laughing and giggling the entire time.

"Good morning, imp. How is Papa's girl this morning?"

"It is Chrismas, Papa." She informed him again in case he missed it the first two times.

7

"I know, but you know what we must do first."

"Yes, Papa. Breakfas firs."

"Very good."

Rebecca dressed first, and then took charge of Em to dress her while Charlie tended to his morning ritual and Tess took care of the boys. Once Emily was dressed, mother and daughter started downstairs toward the breakfast room.

"Mama?"

"Yes, dear?"

"Papa better?"

She looked down into very serious blue eyes and smiled as they started down the staircase hand in hand. "Yes, sweetheart, Papa is getting better each day."

"Good," she said firmly as she tried to take the stairs faster than Rebecca liked.

"Emily Redmond," her mother admonished. "You know better than that. You wait for me."

"Yes, Mama," she sighed and slowed so there was no strain on their joined hands. Her head cocked to one side when she heard a sound all too familiar in the Redmond household. "Andy cries," she said, stating the obvious. "A lot." Rebecca chuckled as she looked up to see Tess and Charlie coming down the hall together. Tess had the crying, squirming child, and Charlie cradled his quieter and far more content older brother against his shoulder.

"Do you want to trade, darling?" She asked, concerned for the strain on Charlie's good arm.

"No. As long as he is still, I should be fine."

Rebecca looked to Andrew, who was still distressed, even though he was in Tess's arms and near the people he loved most. She placed a hand to his forehead. "He has a bit of a fever."

She reached out and took her son, giving Tess charge of Em. Andy looked at her with weary, water eyes, hiccupped, and then laid his head on her shoulder.

"Perhaps we can have Elizabeth look after him when she arrives," Charlie offered as he drew closer to have a look at his sick child. "Do you think it is serious?"

"I do not think so, darling." She pressed her lips to Andy's forehead. "It is just a mild fever. He probably has a touch of the cold that has been going around, keeping Elizabeth so busy."

"My boy," his father whispered, leaning over to give the baby a kiss.

"You take Em and Buddy down to breakfast. I am going to tuck Andy back in." She smiled at Tess. "Would you please bring some oatmeal up for him?"

"Of course, Miss Rebecca."

~

By the time Rebecca had Andy settled and content to remain upstairs with Tess, Richard, Elizabeth, and the other guests had arrived. Rebecca straightened her dress and joined her husband and their guests in the dining room, where breakfast was well under way. All the gentlemen started to rise when she entered, but she waved them off with a smile.

"Good morning, everyone. I am sorry for being late. My youngest son had other ideas this morning." She smiled as she took her seat at the table.

"Charlie said Andy was ill." Elizabeth placed her cup on the saucer. "Would you like me to look in on him?"

"I think it is just a cold, but if you would like to, please do." She smiled gently, knowing it would not do any good to tell her friend not to bother.

"After breakfast." The doctor nodded.

"Yes, there has been a cold going around at the stables in the area," offered Albert. "I have done my best to avoid bringing it home."

Charlie smiled across the table to his wife and sipped his coffee as Em toyed with her eggs. He leaned over to his little girl and whispered a gentle reminder, "Breakfast first."

"Yes, Papa," she sighed and spooned the eggs into her mouth.

Tess handed Charlie the Second, commonly called Buddy, to Rebecca. It was a ritual she had happily settled into, taking one or the other of the boys onto her lap to feed them breakfast. It was a little unusual, but she felt an overwhelming need to mother these children and so she did, sometimes to the great amusement of all those around her.

Duncan smiled at Samantha and nodded to her. In response, Samantha placed her cup and napkin down, and looked intently at the center of the table. "Duncan and I are getting married." She blurted it out in a rush, much to the amusement of all those present.

"Congratulations!" Rebecca reached out, taking Samantha's hand to give it a gentle squeeze.

"Will it be a spring wedding?" Elizabeth asked with a smile.

"It will." Samantha looked to the groom-to-be and managed to blush.

Charlie took a deep breath and sat straight in his chair as he regarded Duncan. He had come to regard the young man as the brother as he never had, and he was truly happy that he was making his life in Culpeper with Samantha and Jeremiah. "Congratulations! Duncan, remind me to tell you where the men hide when the women go into full wedding mode."

"Charles Redmond!" Rebecca laughed from the other end of the table, startling Buddy, who was gumming a piece of bread into submission. "It is possible that Duncan here will want to be involved with his wedding."

He sipped his coffee. "Yes, dear."

He looked at the group of people around the table. His table. All of them were smiling and laughing together. There were Richard Polk, his ex-second in command and Dr. Elizabeth Walker – two of the three people who had become his first friends in the world. Jocko Jackson, once his batman and now the publican in Culpeper, sat with his lady love Esther White. Duncan Nailer, one of his most reliable troopers, who had no one to return to at the end of the war and who chose to stay in Culpeper, mostly because of Samantha Carter and her son Jeremiah, two of the refugees that Rebecca had taken in. The Coopers had become regulars at the Redmond table, and Em called them Uncle Edward and Aunt Grace. Rebecca's cousin Albert, the only member of Charlie and Rebecca's extended family that was actually kin, filled the last seat. Charlie Redmond finally had a home and family.

Breakfast proceeded with the ladies chatting about wedding options and the gentlemen trying to be as inconspicuous as possible. The only man at the table who showed any interest at all was Edward Cooper, no doubt because he could see opportunities for expanding his line of merchandise, since Duncan and Samantha's upcoming wedding was the beginning of what he suspected would be a trend.

Esther White and Samantha held a lively discussion of the current trends in formal dresses, with Rebecca excusing herself for a moment to retrieve the latest copy of Peterson's Magazine of Art, Literature and Fashion. Jocko, Richard, Albert, and Charlie hunkered down in their chairs and focused on their breakfasts. Weddings were just scary. Duncan tried to look interested, but failed miserably, while Jeremiah absorbed his breakfast like a sponge and then fidgeted in his chair, waiting to get to the presents.

As soon as breakfast was over, Em started tugging on her father's coat sleeve. "Papa, pwesents now?"

There were packages under the big spruce tree in the front parlor, and a number of them had come in with the guests. The anticipation was obvious. Jeremiah Carter, who so far this morning had remained absolutely quiet, subdued by the announcement of the marriage of his mother and his best friend, was clearly twitchy and eager to get to the real reason for coming out on a cold morning. "Jeremiah, would you do the honors, sir?"

The boy grinned an eager request to his mother, who nodded. "Yes, sir, General!"

"Then lead the way, lad."

As if rehearsed, all fourteen of them rose from the table, with Rebecca carrying Buddy and Charlie holding Em's hand, and trooped into the front parlor. A huge fire was burning in the fireplace, and the tree was lit with tiny white candles. Colorful packages were laid at the base of the tree. Dutifully, Jeremiah scurried over and started handing out gifts.

～

The day had gone as expected with friends that were more like family joining the Redmonds for the celebration of a quiet Christmas day. Em had managed to make it patiently through breakfast, and then charmed all that had gathered with her not so patient attempts to do as her Papa bid during the opening of the presents.

By the time lunch was ready to be served, the eldest Redmond child was off to bed for her nap with a new doll clutched firmly to her chest. Rebecca had gifted the family with a new Redmond family bible appropriately inscribed with the date of their marriage and the birthdates of all the children. For Charlie, she had found a matching gold watch and pen knife, which were inscribed with his and her initials. She had been over the moon with his gift of a new Singer sewing machine.

Rebecca had been given a reprieve from the presence of Margaret Williams on this particular day, as Reverend Williams had taken ill. The Sunday service on the previous day had even been conducted by Mr. Cooper due to the fact that the minister was too sick to get out of bed. She felt extremely sorry for the poor man, not only for being bed-ridden, but to be subject to his wife for that long of a period was truly an unthinkable torture. In fact, she had decided she would drown herself in her tea rather than have it happen to her.

By evening all the guests were gone, the children were tucked safely into their beds, and they were about to adjourn to the rear parlor where they would have their tea and a game of chess before retiring for the evening.

"Are you sure you do not need any help, darling?" he called even as he loosed his tie and unbuttoned the top button of his shirt.

"I am fine, Charlie," she answered from the morning room,

where Sarah had left a tray of cookies and cake for their evening tea. "I have been making tea every evening for over a year without your help. I am sure I can manage this evening."

He chuckled and sat on a bench in the hall to change his short boots for his carpet slippers. "Yes, but you did not consume as much wine those previous nights as you have tonight."

"Are you suggesting, General Redmond, that your wife is inebriated?"

"No." He put on the warm slippers and remained on the bench so he and Rebecca could continue talking while she retrieved the tea tray. "I am stating flat out that my wife is drunk."

She appeared at that very moment, holding the tray and swaying just slightly. "I am no such thing."

"We shall see." He smiled, standing to join her in the rear parlor. Just as he laid his hand on the knob to open the door, there was a knock on the front door. "Go on in, darling. It is probably just one of our guests having forgotten something. I will be right in."

She watched for a moment as he limped back down the hall on his cane. She could tell he was exhausted and in desperate need of rest, but she also knew that trying to coddle him was a bad idea.

She sighed, silently promising to lose their game as quickly as possible without it being obvious so she could get him up to bed. She knew he would also need his medicine soon and having him in bed would be the best place to give it to him.

She entered the parlor, where Reg had tended to the fire before turning in for the night himself. Charlie and Rebecca treated their staff well, and the little things they did for their employers showed it. Reg certainly did not have to refresh the fire before going up to bed. Either of them could have done it from the logs in the hod, but it made her smile that he had.

Placing the tea service on the small table, she fetched the chessboard table from near the window and placed it in front of the fire between their two chairs. She could hear the rumble of Charlie talking with someone else through the closed door.

Curious as to what was taking him so long, she followed the sound of the voices into the hall. As she approached, Charlie stepped to the side, revealing the person who had interrupted their evening and was now clinging to her husband.

He quickly finished disentangling himself from the woman. Eyeing the guest questioningly, Rebecca moved to his side and wrapped her arm around his waist possessively as he pulled his sleeve from Lizzie's grip. "I see we have a guest. Good evening, Mrs. Armstrong."

∾

Out in the hall, Charlie had opened the door to find Lizzie Armstrong standing on his front stoop, looking tired and worn. A small buggy with a tired looking, non-descript hack between the poles was standing on the drive. Before he could say a word, she threw herself onto his chest.

"Oh, Charlie," she sobbed as she burrowed closer to him. "I did not know where to turn. I remembered your offer. I had nowhere else to go!"

He was nearly knocked backwards by the impact to his chest. He stood there, ineffectually attempting to keep her from crawling into his vest with him. "Lizzie? Um, Lizzie? What are you doing here?"

"I had to leave Washington. I had nowhere else to go. You have to help me, Charlie! Please?"

He stood there, helpless in the face of a beautiful, sobbing woman clinging to his lapels, and throwing herself on his mercy to help her. The fact that he felt he owed a debt of gratitude to her did nothing to ease the situation.

Once again he was General Redmond, the man to whom all turned to solve their problems. He felt decidedly uncomfortable with her clinging to him like this. He grimaced, trying to figure out how to handle this turn of events, and gently patted her shoulder, trying to calm her down. "There, there. It cannot be so bad. Come in, and we will work this out."

"Oh, Charlie." She wormed her way under his arm, delighting in feeling it wrap around her shoulder. He thought this was better than the lapel clinging and tears on his good silk vest, but still not very comfortable. "There is trouble in Washington, and I am afraid that I have done some horrible things that have me caught up in the middle of it. I know you are the only one I can trust."

"It is all right, Lizzie. We will work it out. Come on now." He managed to disengage from her clutching hands. From the sound of Rebecca's footsteps behind him, he had not managed to disengage from her grasp quickly enough.

He hastily pulled away from Lizzie's grip. "Yes, dear. Mrs. Armstrong has a problem and has turned to us. Could you take her into the parlor while I call Reg to get her bags and take her buggy around to the stable?"

"Of course." His wife's personal temperature dropped about ten degrees as she forced a smile and offered, "Good evening, Mrs. Armstrong."

Lizzie forced a tear-streaked smile. "Good evening, Mrs. Redmond. I am so sorry to bother you and the General so late and on Christmas, but I am in trouble, and had nowhere else to turn."

Charlie, grateful to be relieved of the sobbing, clinging woman, limped over to the bell pull and rang Reg's night bell. "I am sure Reg will be here in a moment." The look in Rebecca's eyes and the tone of her voice told him that life would be interesting later that night.

"Right this way." As she gestured Lizzie toward the parlor, she glared at her husband. "You let Reg handle those bags, Charles Redmond. Do not try to be gallant and lift them."

"I promise, my darling, I will. My leg is already bothering me." He pulled the bell cord again, this time a little more vigorously. "I will join the two of you as soon as Reg gets here."

"Yes, dear. I will do my best to tend to her until you are free." Rebecca turned on her heel, walking in a manner that he had learned meant his wife's mood had just gone south. Very south. Perhaps to Patagonia. Antarctica was also possible. Not to mention she had trotted out Charles; if she had added Huger, he had already concluded sleeping in the barn with Jack would be a safer option for the rest of the night.

As the two women disappeared through the parlor door, he sagged against the wall, waiting impatiently for Reg to appear. It occurred to him that it was probably safer to be in the hall right then. The frigid air from opening the front door was nothing compared to what he was pretty sure Rebecca was radiating. He was certain that if being disturbed at ten in the evening on Christmas day was bad, and finding him standing in the hall with another woman in his arms was very bad, then finding him with Lizzie Armstrong was catastrophic.

If Lizzie was in enough trouble that she had driven by herself all the way down to Culpeper from Washington in a one-horse buggy, a drive he knew from experience would have taken all afternoon and the vast majority of the evening, he was very certain things were about to become exceptionally bad in his household.

Reg stumped down the back stairs into the hall and saw his employer propped against the wall. "Yes, Gen'l? Are you all right, sir?"

"No, Reg, I am not, but there is nothing you can do to help me personally. We have an unexpected guest. Her buggy is out front, so would you bring her bags in and put them in the room at the far end of the upstairs hall, then take care of the horse? I am sorry to get you out so late, but there is naught to be done about it."

"Yes, sir. And I will tell Beulah to get upstairs and get the room ready."

"Thank you, Reg." The General heaved himself off the wall he was holding up. He slipped his hand into his vest pocket and pulled out a small brown bottle, tipped it to his lips and sipped the last of the mixture down quickly, cursing that he had already used most of what the bottle had held that morning. Then he resolutely limped to the back parlor.

Rebecca poured the distressed woman a small brandy and handed it to her. She accepted it with a nod and a smile. "I am sorry for just turning up at your home like this. I just did not know where else to go."

Charlie stood by the fire, smoking a cigar, eyeing his old friend, and wishing for more of his medicine. His hip was killing him tonight. The weather had suddenly turned colder, and he felt as if he had a shard of ice sticking in his side.

"So, Lizzie. I know I said that if you ever needed help, you could call on me. But appearing in the middle of the night on Christmas suggests that you are in serious trouble. What can we do to help?" He wished he could just go lie down. Until then, standing was actually less painful than sitting. *Please, make this short.*

"Oh, Charlie, they were going to arrest me if I stayed in Washington," she sobbed, a tear making its way down her cheek. "The only way to prevent it was to leave the city. As quickly as possible. And the only person I have ever truly trusted was you."

"Why were they going to arrest you?"

Rebecca sat in her chair listening. She had been swirling her brandy in the heavy glass until Lizzie's last comment, then she knocked it back. Louder than she meant to, she muttered, "I can give you one guess."

She had not intended to say it, but having Lizzie show up this late, unexpectedly, on Christmas, put her hackles up just a bit. When she had extended herself to her husband's former courtesan just after their marriage, the possibility of a situation like this had never occurred to her.

"I am very sure it was not for the reason you think, Charlie." Lizzie lowered her head, demurely unable to meet her friend's eyes and ignoring Rebecca's comment completely. "I have done something," she paused and looked up at him through tear-drenched lashes, "dishonorable."

His eyes slid over to the chair by the fireplace where his wife sat when he distinctly heard, "Oh there is a shock," as she poured herself another brandy. When she glanced over and saw him, she did manage a sweet, but non-apologetic smile.

He stared into the fire for a moment, and then turned back to their guest. "If it did not affect me, if you swear to me that nothing you ever did with me was dishonorable, you do not have to tell me anything you do not want to. I promised, and you know I will honor my word."

"Oh, thank you, Charlie." The tone of Lizzie's voice was heartfelt and somehow very intimate, which annoyed his wife to no end.

"I am afraid I cannot be as trusting as my loving husband." Rebecca's tone was curt and businesslike. Lizzie did not miss the emphasis on the word husband. "I have a home and a family to protect. What is it that you have done that has run you out of Washington and to our doorstep?"

Lizzie slumped in her chair. Dealing with Rebecca was not the same as Charlie. She finished her brandy in one gulp, and silently held the snifter out for more. He limped over and poured her one, then took one himself and waited.

"It began a little less than two years ago. There was a man—a charming man—who asked me to do a favor for him. As time went by, he asked for other little favors, to hold a note for a friend to pick up, this and that—nothing I thought was terribly important." She paused and sipped her brandy. "His name was Payne. He was hanged this summer as part of the conspiracy to assassinate President Lincoln."

The General cleared his throat then asked, "So, you have been charged with spying. How far behind you are they?"

"No, I have not. I made a concession to Seward and McClellan. If I told them the names of everyone I knew and then left the city right away, they would not come for me." She looked back and forth between these two people who were the only ones she believed she could trust. "I promise you both, nothing I ever did for him put you in harm's way." She looked away again and added softly, "I could not do that to you, Charlie."

His face stiffened into a perfectly neutral mask. "I know, I never told you anything, but any information you passed for Payne could have harmed me, or my troops. Lizzie, how could you?"

He turned to throw his cigar into the fireplace, and to get a grip on his own emotions. How in god's name could she do such a thing? After a moment he turned back to her, his voice cold and flat. "So. You are here. I gave you my word, and I take it that Lizzie Armstrong needs to disappear." He looked back and forth between the women. "Ladies, do either of you have any suggestions?"

"Lizzie," Rebecca warned, "I know why Charlie is keeping his word to you. It is because his honor is more important to him than almost anything else, but I want you to know that I have no such loyalty of promise to you. If the things you have done bring any harm to my children or to my husband, I will protect them with the last breath in my body."

"I promise you I would rather be incarcerated than bring harm to you or yours. Seward and McClellan told me to disappear and promised they would not charge me." She hung her head. McClellan had been absolutely revolting when he told her that her real crime was being stupid–and obsessed with tall, blue-eyed, black-haired pretty boys.

"Then," Rebecca sighed as she rubbed the bridge of her nose. "A nice extended trip to Europe?"

"Unfortunately, the agreement I made requires me to remain available in the event that I am called to testify. I cannot leave the country."

The blonde nodded. "All right." She looked to her husband. "Have you any ideas, my love?"

"Well, we could find one of our single gentlemen friends and marry her off, but I fear that would take at least a little time." He grimaced. "On the other hand, there are so many displaced people, especially now, perhaps we simply need to create a new identity for her. I certainly understand that process."

Rebecca looked between them. "Yes, yes you do." Slowly she walked over to Lizzie, appraising her carefully. "Of course. It is perfect."

In harmony, Lizzie and Charlie looked at her and said, "What?"

The blonde laid her hand on Lizzie's shoulder and smiled at her husband. "Why, Charles Redmond is that any way to greet your long-lost cousin? Charlotte Redmond, from Charleston, South Carolina."

Charlie froze. Lizzie blanched. Rebecca went on blithely, pleased with the cleverness of her own solution.

"It is perfect. Absolutely perfect. With a little hair dye and some tutoring by you," she raised her brows at him, waiting for his nodded agreement before continuing. "Charlotte Redmond can be the newest resident of Culpeper. Home after being abroad for several years."

"Staying with either Scottish or French cousins during the war to avoid the unpleasantness?" His voice was oddly subdued, but he was game to explore the story.

"Of course," his wife agreed, nodding as she considered her strategy. "Having gone there to study art before the war. After Charleston was blockaded, she stayed there where it was safe."

Lizzie nodded. "Charlotte Redmond." She thought for a moment. "Charlie? Are you all right with this? Can you accept me taking over that identity?"

"Yes. There is a certain ironic justice in having Charlotte come back to life after all these years." He finished his brandy. "And I am certainly not going to use it again. Yes, this will work. And now, ladies, it is very late, and I am very tired. Perhaps we can talk further about this tomorrow." *And I need my medicine now.*

"Charlie, you go on up to bed. I will show her to her room for the night and then we will get her properly settled in tomorrow."

"Thank you, darling. I asked Reg to take her bags to the blue guest room at the far end of the hall." He kissed her softly on the lips, and then turned to the door, where he paused and turned to his unexpected, and to be perfectly honest, unwelcome guest. "I bid you good night, Lizzie."

Rebecca watched the exchange with hooded eyes. "You know, it occurs to me that if this is going to work, from this moment on she must be Charlotte. We cannot afford to make any errors."

Charlie nodded, with a slight smile. "Then, good night, Cousin Charlotte." He turned and walked out of the room, the slump of his shoulders and the slow, strained limp showing just how much pain he was in. Rebecca wondered which was worse, the physical pain or the emotions associated with Charlotte's rebirth.

His hands were shaking and a fine sheen of sweat moistened his forehead by the time he got up the stairs to the safety of the bedroom and could pour out his dose of laudanum.

The bitter fluid was as sweet on his tongue as a blessing, for within minutes the pain would ease. Rapidly, he stripped, got dressed in a nightshirt that was one of Rebecca's favorites, and eased into bed, waiting for the pain to subside and his wife to join him.

He was anxious to see what she would have to say about the newest member of their household. Between the pain and the very real annoyance of having Lizzie appear on their doorstep so soon after they had gotten rid of the refugees and finally had the house to themselves, he was sure that she would have a few choice comments.

She eased the door open, not wanting to disturb the entire household. She had already decided that if Lizzie had awakened any of the children, she would pack the woman up and send her right back to Washington. Slipping inside, she saw Charlie was already lying in bed, his good hand resting behind his head. Taking a deep breath, she crossed the room and opened her wardrobe to retrieve a nightgown. "This is an interesting development."

He just stared at her for a moment, and then barked a short laugh. "My love, you are, as ever, a master of understatement."

She sighed, trying to undress without tearing the clothes from her body in her frustration. "You sound as if you are amused by the fact that your former lover has just turned up on our doorstep in the middle of the night."

"Not at all, dear. I am far from amused at having her here under these circumstances. But I was amused at how you expressed it." He watched her struggling with her laces and buttons, and rose up from the bed, trying to hide the wince as his hip complained. "Would you like some help?"

"No. No, I am fine." She managed to remove the bodice and began working on the skirt. "Think about it. Obviously, they know

21

where she has gone. She said she has to be available to them. That means they know she is here. If they know, then you may certainly rest assured that others know as well. Perhaps people that we would rather not have around our home or children."

He sighed, and gently shifted her fingers away from the ties on the skirt. "Whether she stays or goes at this point, it is too late. She is here. From one point of view, it may be better for us politically to keep her here–where we can keep an eye on her. I will wire Grant and Seward in the morning. That may help considerably."

"The only thing that will help considerably is having her out of my home and away from my children and you. I know I told her that she was welcome to visit. Firstly, I was being polite. Second, I did not expect that would mean she would just show up here unannounced and in trouble."

"Nor did I, dear. There are times when I wish I could simply go back on my word, but…" He finally managed to untie the knot that the ties on her overskirt had formed and eased it down over her hips.

"I know. I understand." She stepped out of her skirts, grabbing up the nightgown as she moved across the room to her dresser. "You make sure, Charles Redmond, that she keeps her distance from you."

He stood looking at her with his jaw hanging open for a moment. "Rebecca." He cleared his throat. Jealousy was not exactly what he had expected from her, but somehow it gave him a warm little glow. No one had ever been possessive of him before. "Of course, darling, I am entirely yours. I should hope by now you know that."

"Just so you know, she was making eyes at you tonight. She was displaying all her feminine wiles for you to notice. Just because you did not, does not mean she will not keep trying."

He wrapped his good arm around her waist from behind, nuzzling her neck and ear as he whispered, "I did not notice because as far as I am concerned, there are no other women in the world except you. The rest are just friends."

CHAPTER 2

Tuesday, December 26, 1865

Lizzie considered throwing her pillow at the solicitous servant who had entered her room at what felt like the crack of dawn.

"Miss Charlotte, Miss Rebecca asked me to serve as your lady's maid until . . . um, I am Beulah, and I am the housekeeper here at Redmond Stables." She threw open the curtains, flooding the room with bright, morning light.

"Dear God, what unearthly time is it?" Lizzie was not a morning person and this woman, who seemed to think her name was Charlotte, was not helping with her bright and cheery attitude.

"Why, Miss Charlotte, it is very late. It is almost eight o'clock, and if you do not hurry and get dressed, you will completely miss breakfast."

With a groan, she rolled out of the bed and allowed Beulah to assist her into her simplest day dress. Breakfast was waiting. Perhaps she could manage to force down a cup of tea and a piece of toast without getting nauseous or falling asleep at the table.

Lizzie, or more precisely Charlotte floated down the stairs and into the morning room with all of the grace of a misdirected haunt. Rebecca was right there to greet her and get her settled with the rest of the family. The odor of sausages made her faintly queasy.

"Good morning. I am glad to see you could join us." Rebecca paused briefly and smiled. "Charlotte." The blonde settled Emily at the table and then handed Buddy to Charlie before settling down to try and get some cereal into Andy. "How did you sleep, dear cousin?"

"Um, fine, thank you, Cousin Rebecca, what little sleep I got." The scene of these three rambunctious children, all in various stages of disarray as a result of their applying their food to their faces, and in the case of the two boys, their hands, chests, and hair in disgusting globs, offended her sense of morning order.

Mornings were for sleeping, then quietly and slowly emerging into the real world after applying a perfect façade, not for rolling around in bowls of gruel and plates of half masticated eggs.

Charlie watched as his friend paled a bit. He gave Buddy a piece of biscuit. "Well, Charlotte, I am sure you will get accustomed to the routine of the house in short order. We are usually up and about by five thirty, with the children fed and off to Tess by seven. We decided to get a delayed start today because of your late arrival last night."

"Five-thirty?" *Oh, my God, these people are heathens. No one who is anyone rises at five-thirty.* "Ah, well, I see that I shall have to adjust my schedule accordingly. We normally kept rather different hours when I was in, um, Paris."

Rebecca managed to hold her coffee in her mouth, even though she choked a bit on her suppressed laugh. "I am sure of it. It really is not that difficult. Once you are adjusted to the schedule of the farm, I will be happy to take you down and show you the horses and how things run. We have several mares who should foal within the next month or so. When they do, you should come down and watch one of the births. It is a fascinating procedure."

The thought of a mare dropping her foal, with all of the blood, and secretions, and miscellaneous membranes made Lizzie's stomach churn. She looked at the coffee and decided that it was not what was needed for her stomach right now. Instead she took a sip of water to steady herself. "Thank you, I am sure it is . . . intriguing."

Charlie gave his wife a look that screamed 'be nice,' and then he gently cleared his throat. "Charlotte, once you are settled, I think you should go into town and meet some of the locals."

Her shoulders slumped. The local yokels, more likely. What would a small town like Culpeper have to offer when compared to the cities where she had lived in her various career moves? What did they discuss in a town like this? Probably crops and weather and how many babies were born and what cow had dropped its calf. And the women here probably had the fashion sense of a toadstool, to judge from the plain blouse, vest, and skirt that Rebecca was wearing. "Yes, Cousin Charlie, I would, no doubt, enjoy making the acquaintance of the local residents. But perhaps it is a bit early for me to be introduced to them?"

"Nonsense. If you are going to make a life here, it is important that you get to know everyone." He picked a piece of mashed biscuit from his shirt, noticing the way Charlotte's eye had fallen on Rebecca with some disdain. "Of course, you could take my wife up on her offer. I am sure that you could get accustomed to mucking stalls and tossing hay, like she does nearly every day to make this farm what it is. No one around here refuses to do what needs to be done to be successful. Do you understand me?"

Rebecca looked at her husband with a smile. It was clear that he was going to be just as rigorous about getting Charlotte to fit in as she was.

Lizzie looked from one determined face to the other. Obviously, if she was going to create a new life here, she had to abide by these two schemers' rules. "Why, yes, of course. I was simply thinking that it would be more useful if I had at least the basics of that history we discussed last night before I made my first forays into local society."

He tried not to growl when he offered, "The basics are this, Charlotte. You are my cousin from Charleston. You have been in Paris; you stayed there during the war but have returned home and are visiting here while you decide where to settle, because I am one of your last living relatives. The rest we will put together as we go along. Until then, you will mingle, you will be polite, and you will get to know these people, and the way this house is run."

She recognized that her circumstances were such that adjusting to the schedule of the household was in her best interest. "Certainly, Cousin." She took a sip of coffee, surprised to find it to be as good as any she had ever had. "Perhaps, Cousin Rebecca, you could introduce me to the children and the household today? I expect my trunks to arrive sometime this afternoon, and then I will be prepared to dress properly to meet your friends and neighbors."

"Of course," she nodded. "Emily?"

Em had been watching this exchange with fascination. This lady who looked a little like Papa clearly was very different from all the other grownups that had visited her home. It was very clear that Mama did not like this lady very much. She knew she needed to be on her very best behavior. "Yes, Mama?"

"This is your Cousin Charlotte. She will be staying with us for a while. Do you have anything you would like to say to her?"

She turned to the new woman and thought for a moment, then climbed down from her chair beside Papa's and curtsied. "Pleased to meet you, Cousin Charlotte." Em reached out a hand still sticky with strawberry jam to shake the lady's hand, but the lady ignored it. At least she ignored it until the sticky hand dropped to her skirted knee.

"Get your nasty hand off my dress!" Charlotte grabbed a napkin and proceeded to try and wipe the bright red jam off her delicate lavender silk skirt. Em retreated to her father's side.

He glared at Charlotte while he placed his hand on his daughter's back to reassure her. "Well done, my little imp. You are quite the little lady. You did very well," he said gently. He helped her back into her chair and then turned back to Charlotte. "This," he gestured to the baby in the crook of his good arm, "is Charlie the second. We call him Buddy. And that is Andy, Andrew Richard."

Rebecca was holding Andy, and the other two children were present. It was the only reason that Charlotte was still alive. The look on her face made that quite clear to anyone paying attention. Charlie was definitely paying attention.

"Quite a family you two have acquired. They are all handsome children. And Andy looks so like you, Rebecca, while the other two both have a striking resemblance to Charlie." This was a side of him that Lizzie had never seen. It was obvious that he was immensely proud of his children, and especially of the little girl with the black hair and blue eyes who looked so much like him that she could be the daughter of his body. Her thoughts traveled to a letter she had received from Rebecca some nine months before explaining the arrival of Charlie the second and warning her of impending dangers associated with the tarred brush she was now trying to flee. *Why in the name of God, did I not pay attention then?*

"We are very lucky to have them." Rebecca sipped her coffee before adding, "And each other."

Em continued to look back and forth between her mother and the new lady. She decided that she agreed with her mother. She did not like Cousin Charlotte, either.

Lizzie looked at the two of them, surrounded by their little family, and realized this was what Charlie always needed and had always wanted–and that she could never have given him this kind of life. A small, bittersweet smile crossed her features. At that minute, a discreet knock on the door announced the entrance of the children's nurse.

Rebecca smiled at her right hand with the children. "Ah, Tess, as usual, your timing is perfect. The children have finished their breakfast."

"Yes, Ma'am. Bath time for the boys." The nanny turned to the eldest child. "Will you help me with your brothers before your lessons, Miss Em?"

She crinkled her nose. She would because she had to. "Yes, Tess."

Charlie stood with the children. "I must be going as well. He bent and kissed Em on her forehead. "You be good today, imp. Remember to keep your shoes on, or your mama will yell at both of us." He kissed the two boys, and then bent to kiss Rebecca gently on the lips. "Have a good morning, darling. I will be home for lunch." He nodded to Charlotte and made his way out the door after Tess and the children.

Rebecca carefully and very skillfully folded her napkin. She took a deep breath. "All right, you are here. You need our help, and as I promised Charlie, we will help you as best we can. You will not be turned away from our home or our protection, but let us get two things very clear, shall we?"

"Yes, Rebecca?"

"Charlie is mine."

Lizzie looked directly into her hostess's eyes. "I know. I know that better than I think you imagine. And I have no intention of trying to change that situation. But you must know that I do feel a bit... wistful about it."

"And if you talk to any of my children again as you did to Em, I will have your head on a silver platter."

Charlotte took a deep breath, nodding her acknowledgement. She took a sip of her coffee. "Now, my most gracious hostess, shall I meet the rest of the staff, or shall we do something about making my hair a bit darker?"

Rebecca escorted Charlotte to her sitting room upstairs, then rang for Beulah. When the servant entered the room, she made a snap decision–to bring her trusted servant into the deception. Otherwise, there would be too many questions that would be asked behind their backs. This way, Beulah would be able to handle the other servants, and assist in sustaining the deception.

The housekeeper entered the sitting room looking a bit concerned. Normally, Miss Rebecca met with her in the rear parlor if she wanted to discuss a household issue. This area was more normally Lizbet's domain.

"Beulah, I am about to ask you a very important question and I would like you to answer me honestly. Can I trust you?"

The servant was startled, and, to be honest, a bit offended at the question. She had shown her loyalty to her employers over and over and she considered herself to be a woman of honor. "Miz 'Becca, how can you even ask me that question? Of course, you can trust me. You and Gen'l Charlie gave me a home, a good job, a place when there was no place for anyone like me anymore. You can trust me with your life!"

"I am glad to hear that, because that is exactly what it may come down to. This woman–" She gestured to Lizzie. "–is not General Redmond's cousin. She is a friend from Washington who has run into a bit of trouble. She has asked for our help, and the General and I are offering her our protection. However, she will be taking the identity of the General's cousin. In order for that to happen, we have to make some changes, starting with her hair. So please go fetch the things we will need to dye it a dark brown or even black."

Beulah looked from Rebecca to Lizzie and back again. She raised her eyebrow, recognizing the expression on Rebecca's face as one of guarded concern. Whatever this woman meant to Gen'l Charlie, clearly Miz 'Becca was very wary. She would be too.

She walked over to the beautiful woman sitting quietly by the fire, and carefully examined her hair, evaluating the color, the texture and feeling the strands between her fingers to judge how healthy the hair was. She thought for a few minutes, then turned to both of them. "Ma'am, I cannot make her hair that blue-black that Gen'l Charlie has, but I can make it a reddish dark brown–almost black–that will be most realistic."

"Then so be it, Beulah. Thank you. We will do this up here, well out of the view of the rest of the house." She moved to the woman that she really did regard as a friend regardless of her status as a servant. "Your assistance is greatly appreciated. I will not forget this."

"Miss 'Becca, it will take me at least an hour to gather up the things I need, and to prepare the dye–more likely an hour and a half. But I will hurry."

"Thank you. We will wait here, as we have some things to discuss."

The housekeeper bustled out of the room as Rebecca turned to her guest. She stooped down to put the kettle on the hob and pulled her tea set closer to her. Then she sat and looked directly at Lizzie. "So, Charlie may not want to know, but I do. If there is any risk to either him or my children, I need to know and be prepared for it."

She sighed, knowing that she would have to tell Rebecca, and further, that her hostess's perceptiveness would require that she be brutally honest. "It began because a man came into my life."

"And this man was Lewis Payne? The same man who attacked Mr. Seward the night that Mr. Lincoln was shot?" She wanted the whole story. She did not want to be caught by surprise by anything.

Lizzie looked at the fire burning cheerfully in this cozy room. "He said his name was Lewis Payne. I found out later that it was really Lewis Payne Powell. He was tall and slender with black hair and blue eyes, a soft southern accent, and lovely manners. Unfortunately, he was also a spy, though I did not know that until much later."

"I see." Rebecca looked into the bedroom she and Charlie shared, and then she sighed. "He looked like my husband?"

"Very much," she nodded. There was that word again. Rebecca was making sure to drive the point home. "It may have been part of why I trusted him so easily–because he reminded me of Charlie. At first, he simply called on me, like so many other men. Then he started asking me for favors–little things, like holding a package for him, letting him leave letters at my place for his friends to pick up. I did not think much of it; he was so casual and natural about it. It was several months before I even asked him why he did not use his own address. By then, I was so deeply implicated in the southern spy network, with their couriers coming and going and using my home as their post box, it was hopeless."

Rebecca was trying to stay calm but she was finding it more difficult than she had anticipated. "So you helped a man who helped assassinate President Lincoln. You helped a man who may have passed on information that could have gotten Charlie killed. You profess to love him. How could you do that?"

Lizzie buried her face in her hands, quiet tears streaming down her face. "I honestly did not know until I was so deeply involved that I could not see a way out. He was young and gentle and unassuming and," she cried softly and looked up, a hopeless, lost look in her eyes, "he reminded me of another lost young man."

Rebecca drew a deep breath and let it out slowly. "Let me make something perfectly clear to you. I had hoped we could be friends because Charlie thinks so much of you, but what you have done is despicable. I will offer you everything I can because it is what my husband wants. He has apparently decided not to dwell on what your crimes may or may not be, and he wants to afford you the benefit of the doubt. I cannot and will not do the same. I will help you. I will be polite to you. But unless you can prove yourself by doing, without question, anything and everything Charlie and I tell you, we will not be friends."

She hung her head. "You are entirely right. I should have called in the authorities as soon as I realized what he was doing, but I just could not do that to him. He was so sweet. Eventually, I stopped it. And I never gave away any information I had. But, if you had met him, you would understand, I think. I still cannot believe that he actually climbed the steps and tried to kill Secretary Seward." Lizzie cried quietly for a moment or two, then looked directly in Rebecca's eyes. "I will do whatever you ask, be whoever you need me to be. I swear I will do nothing to harm you, your family, or Charlie."

Rebecca stood and paced the room for a moment. "I will give you the chance that he seems to think you deserve. Let me tell you now that if any harm comes to my children, or if any further harm comes to my husband because of your presence here, I will take the steps necessary to protect my family. I swear to you, I will kill if I must to see them safe."

Charlotte nodded. "I understand entirely. You have my word that I will be the very image of propriety. I have made my deals with the powers in Washington. General McClellan himself was the one who made it possible for me to retire quietly. I cannot go back, but I can go forward, and in doing so, I will do everything in my power to make sure that you and Charlie and the children are not tarred with the same brush I have been touched by."

"Fine. Then I will do everything in my power to make sure that you get a fair chance and a fresh start."

She sat, looking at Rebecca's determined features. *I will have to walk gently with her, regardless of what she says. And I will have to hide my feelings for Charlie even better than before.* "Thank you. It is far more than I could ever reasonably expect from anyone, and especially from Charlie's wife."

∼

Sunday, December 31, 1865

He looked up and then down while standing in the main hallway, tapping his cane impatiently, waiting for the rest of his family to gather for the trip into town and church. Reverend Williams was feeling better and would be back in the pulpit after four weeks of being abed.

Charlotte had gone up after breakfast to get her wraps, Rebecca and Tess had hauled the boys up to swaddle them in more wooly blankets, and to get Em a clean handkerchief. Albert had decided to change his coat, which earned him a raised eyebrow from Charlie and a smirk from Rebecca. Albert was, of course, doing his best to impress Cousin Charlotte. Charlotte was having none of it but enjoyed leading the young man on.

He glanced outside. The family coach was there, waiting. He continued to tap his cane.

Rebecca descended the stairs, her youngest son tucked in the loving cradle of her arms. She stopped about halfway down the stairs and looked at her husband questioningly. "What are you thinking about?"

He smiled at his wife and son, easing the furrow that had been brewing between his brows. "Who, me? Just waiting, dear."

"Oh no, I know better than that. Your brows are drawn together; you are chewing a hole in your bottom lip. It is more than waiting for me."

"Well, I was considering what kind of reaction the biddy brigade would have to my cousin." He grinned ruefully. "And what kind of reaction she would have to them. Not to mention the spectacle your cousin is making of himself, drooling in her footsteps. It should be an interesting morning."

"Albert is a young man. He is allowed to make a fool of himself over a beautiful woman." She smiled and winked at him. "As for the biddy brigade, they will only know what we tell them. Have they any reason to doubt your cousin?"

He looked at her with one eyebrow raised. "Doubt my cousin? You have to ask? No, I do not doubt that she will make an appropriate impression on them. I know that she is a snob, a flirt, a tease, and a woman with absolutely no patience for fools, even though she can be one herself. I expect the first encounter between Charlotte and Mrs. Williams will be downright pyrotechnical."

"So I have something to look forward to then?"

"No doubt," he said wryly.

Just then, the rest of the entourage started clambering down the stairs. Em scrambled ahead of Tess, who was holding Buddy and trying to catch up to the little girl without either falling or dropping the baby. Charlotte, in her best Washington day dress, was attempting to sail down the stairs like an elegant clipper, while Albert stumbled alongside of her like an ungainly tug. If he had been wearing a sword, he would have fallen over it.

"Ah. Here at last. Shall we get on with it then?" The General attempted to herd his mismatched flock out to the carriage.

Rebecca did her best not to laugh out loud at the scene before her. One thing was for certain, she would have to find a way to calm his nerves if this ruse was going to succeed.

After an appropriate level of fussing, and tugging, and shifting, the small horde was settled into the coach–rather snuggly, to be sure, but settled. Albert had been relegated to the box alongside Reg, as there simply was not enough space inside for him. Charlotte found herself with Buddy thrust into her arms, and she was holding him gingerly, as if he might break if she were careless. But she went on gamely. "Tell me, cousins, whom I will be meeting today."

Charlie sat quietly, holding Em on his good knee, and waited for Rebecca to take the lead. It was her town, after all.

"You certainly will meet Reverend and Mrs. Williams. The good Reverend is a kind and generous man and deserves nothing but respect. Mrs. Williams is a shrew, and you have full permission to loathe her as much as I do."

Charlie cleared his throat and scowled at his wife. "My dear, please . . . it is Sunday, and the children . . ." He turned to Charlotte. "Mrs. Williams is strongly committed to the Confederacy and I fear that the outcome of the war has left her bitter. It is a sad thing, I think."

"Ever the gallant officer and diplomat." Rebecca smiled at her husband. "You will also meet the Coopers. They own the mercantile here in town and have served as surrogate parents for me since mine passed. Of course, there will be Richard and Elizabeth Polk . . . ."

"Richard Polk? Major Richard Polk?" She faced Charlie. "Your Major Polk? My God, Charlie . . ."

"Colonel Polk now, and, yes, one and the same. I will have a word with him, and with Dr. Walker, as soon as we arrive."

Rebecca did feel a bit sorry for Lizzie and tried to reassure her. "You know, Charlotte, Charlie trusts Elizabeth and Richard implicitly. I am sure that you will have no worries."

She looked back and forth between them. "Are you saying that Dr. Walker married Major, um, Colonel Polk? Richard Polk is married–and to that outrageous woman doctor?"

"If I were you, I would be very careful about who I call outrageous," Rebecca warned. It was bad enough that her family was being thrust into this drama. She certainly would not allow her to make insulting comments about a woman she regarded a true sister, and the woman who had saved Charlie's life.

She looked into Rebecca's stormy eyes and realized she had just made a major error. "No, no, I did not mean anything by it. I simply never expected Richard Polk to marry, especially to someone who was so, um, unconventional."

"I am afraid that if you are to remain here, Charlotte, you may have to become accustomed to the unconventional. Not everyone has managed to have the propriety in life that you have." Rebecca literally oozed sarcasm with that comment.

Charlotte looked down into her lap meekly. Anything she said right now would only manage to drive her foot deeper into her mouth, and the taste of shoe leather was not to her liking.

Charlie jumped into the rather tense chasm that had opened miraculously in the middle of his carriage. "You may run into my old batman, Sergeant Jackson, as well. He has taken up wooing the local midwife, Esther White."

"Tell me, Cousin Charlie, did any of your men return home after the war?"

He laughed. "Actually, most of them. But a few stayed here in Culpeper. Jocko, our farrier Tarent, Duncan Nailer, Richard Polk. Are there any others who stayed with us, Rebecca?"

"You ask me? How would I know? I can barely keep track of you and the children on a good day," she teased as she gave his hand a gentle pat. She was going to have to learn to keep her temper, or she could foresee her husband having a breakdown trying to keep the peace.

"I believe that is the limit of the Yankee transplants into Culpeper. Oh, you will meet our fair city's mayor, Horace Frazier, and his wife Missy, a lovely lady. Mr. Frazier is a right proper old curmudgeon, he is, would you agree, my dear?"

"He is indeed. Mumbles most of the time. I believe that is because he is always cursing someone or something." Andy took this opportunity to make a huge ruckus, taking Rebecca's attention from her husband and his cousin to the wailing child in her arms.

Wisely, Em piped up. "Andy is doing it again."

The coach pulled into the churchyard. Normally, people gathered under the trees to chat a bit before the service, but today people hurried into the church to escape the cold wind which could go through all but the most tightly woven woolens. A small boy, no more than ten, was the only person who stayed out in the cold. He was scrambling to lead peoples' horses and buggies over to the shelter of the newly built horse shed behind the church for a penny or two.

"Here we are." When Charlie was uncomfortable, he would state the obvious, usually with a rather forced joviality.

Rebecca left him to tend to Charlotte, and with Tess, took the children inside right away to get them out of the cold. As she entered the church, Elizabeth was at the door, ready to relieve Tess of Buddy. One look at Rebecca and she knew something was definitely amiss.

"What is wrong?"

"Elizabeth, do you remember telling me once that nothing Charlie and I did would shock you?"

"Yessss…" She looked askance at her friend. "So what have you two done this time?"

"Something very stupid, I am afraid." She looked around the area, spying a quiet corner where they could talk. Taking Elizabeth by the arm, she led her over and gave her the briefest details of what had transpired at Redmond Stables over the past week. "So there it is. I am insane."

Elizabeth drew a deep breath. "Charlie's ex-lover is living in your house, and passing herself off as Cousin Charlotte Redmond, newly returned from avoiding the war by living in Paris?" She nodded, reflectively. "Yes. You have lost your mind. I recommend several months in quiet seclusion in the country." She grinned. "Oh, yes, well, you are already in the country. So I suppose we will have to work something else out for you, my dear."

The doctor looked over to the door as Lizzie Armstrong, in her role as Charlotte Redmond, made her entrance. It was quite an event. Every male in the building, with the exception of Mayor Frazier, stopped to admire the picture of feminine fashion and elegance that had graced their little church. Every woman also stopped, especially the younger ones like the Misses Reynolds and Simms, clearly appraising the competition. The results were not good. Charlie and Rebecca had just introduced a massive source of stress to the social fabric of this small town.

"Elizabeth, when we return home for supper after services, do you think you could just slip a bit of arsenic into my plate?"

"No, dear, I will not. And I shall not do it for her, either. With our fortune, all it would do is make her skin even more luminous than it is." She sighed. Even Richard considered looking twice as she walked in but found the tips of his boots far more interesting. "The only thing we can do is get her married off and pregnant–as quickly as we possibly can."

"It is nice to have an ally. I do not mind telling you that having her under Charlie's nose makes me very nervous. There she is looking beautiful, while I am either covered in muck from the barns or something one of the children has opted to spit back up."

"Dear Lord. You and me both. How long is she going to stay? Because I swear, if either Charlie or Richard looks at her twice, I may personally kill them."

"She is going to stay until we find a way to be rid of her. I suggest we have a planning meeting as soon as possible. I am not terribly thrilled with the thought of having to hide their bodies," Rebecca teased. Elizabeth joined her in the humor of the situation.

"Well, your house this afternoon will not do–she could walk in on us at any time. And tomorrow is the New Year's Day party. Would you care to come into town for luncheon with me next week? Something needs to be done."

Elizabeth looked surreptitiously over at the woman, whose hand was now being bowed over by her own husband. "Soon. Charlotte Redmond could be as socially lethal as Lizzie Armstrong. Perhaps even more so."

Rebecca emitted a high-pitched squeak, which she tried to suppress, but only succeeded in swallowing the wrong way. That sent her into a coughing fit, which drew the attention of those around her. "No, no, I am fine," she gasped as Grace Cooper and Samantha Carter hurried over to check on her.

Richard glanced up as Rebecca hurried in with the children, and ambled over toward the door, expecting to see Charlie come in right behind her. Instead, he was blessed with the view of Lizzie Armstrong with her hair dyed a gleaming red-black, dressed to the nines, though entirely appropriately for a Sunday service, on Charlie's arm. Young Albert, his nose red and eyes watering from the cold, was trailing along like a lost puppy, and it appeared there were several other puppies gravitating in their general direction among the newly returned southern boys.

He hurried over to his old friend, and growled in a harsh whisper, all the while smiling at Charlie and the lady on his arm, "Have you lost your mind!"

He turned, and smiled at Lizzie, though the smile did not come close to making it to his eyes. In a voice too low for anyone but Lizzie and Charlie to hear, he hissed, "What in the hell are you doing here of all places? I thought you had better sense than to try and pursue Charlie once he was married."

The General cleared his throat loudly and grabbed Richard by the arm. "We need to talk," he growled as he pulled his old friend to the side, offering very quickly and quietly, "It is not what you think. Her name is Charlotte Redmond. She is my cousin from Charleston who has been abroad during the war." The look in Charlie's eyes was one he hoped Richard remembered. They had used this silent communication many times during the war, when it was important for them to get a message across without actually saying anything.

Richard nodded, and then looked back at the waiting woman. "We will have to discuss this, but for now, I suppose I can play along." He bowed over her hand, and rather more loudly than was absolutely necessary, said, "Good morning, Miss Redmond. It is a pleasure to see you again after so many years. I believe we met just before you left for Europe. Was it '58?"

Her heart pounded with the rampant beating that had started when she had first entered the church. It was bad enough that Charlie and Rebecca, who were devout Christians, insisted that she come into a church, but to be face to face with men who had been in her house in Washington more than once was just plain nerve-wracking. She plastered a smile on her face and said simply. "Yes, I believe it was."

In a lower voice, Richard continued. "Time has treated you well, ma'am. I am surprised that you would exchange the sophistication of your life abroad for the quiet of Culpeper, especially to come into the home of your newly-wed cousin."

In a subdued voice, she answered with more truth than he knew. "Sir, the aftermath of the war has changed the circumstances for many people, myself among them. Had I any other alternative than to throw myself on the generosity of my cousin and his wife, I assure you, I would have taken it."

He bowed again, a little stiffly. "Well I hope your stay is peaceful."

Margaret Williams watched these little exchanges from behind her organ keyboard with some interest, absently fingering the notes of the day's prelude as people filed into the church. She muttered to herself as she watched with interest. "Who is this Jezebel? How dare that damned Yankee drag some fancy woman into my church? Poor Rebecca. I warned her, but would she listen to me? No, she never listens to me. The little tart thinks herself above me, always has, first married to Mr. Gaines, may he rest in peace, and now to that disgusting excuse for a man, that turncoat."

She looked over to where Rebecca and that Dr. Walker, who Mrs. Williams had publicly declared to be no proper woman since she would not take her husband's name, were talking intently. "Oh, ho, there is trouble in paradise, I would say. Rebecca is clearly not happy. Perhaps this woman is not so much a Jezebel as a Lilith. Either way, she is not one for my church, I shall see to that!" She struck a loud chord on the organ, as if to emphasize her muttered declaration.

Meanwhile, Charlie had abandoned his cousin to Albert's care, and the younger man was earnestly introducing her to anyone and everyone he could, which was basically every young man in the church, and a few of the older ones. Mrs. Williams noticed with some degree of malicious amusement that not a single woman stepped forward to meet the newcomer. Charlie caught Edward Cooper by the elbow and had a few words with him. "Oh, good. Mr. Cooper will introduce her to the congregation. Well, we shall see who this woman is, I suppose."

With that, Mrs. Williams started into the processional for the service, and people scrambled to take their seats. She watched her husband shuffle out from the side door, and walk slowly to the altar, haltingly bow and cross himself, and proceed to the pulpit. Reverend Williams cleared his throat, and the service began.

The service proceeded normally, with the first reading, a prayer, the first hymn, and then, as usual, Reverend Williams called on Mr. Cooper, in his role as senior church elder, to read the list of those who were missing because of illness or other reasons, and to welcome any new members or guests. "Ah, now we will find out the name of this paragon."

He went through a list of people who were home ill that was longer than the one the previous week. Mrs. Williams was just thankful that her husband was no longer on that doleful list. Then he got to the important information--the name of this interloper.

He cleared his throat and continued. "Now, on a lighter note, I would like you to join me in welcoming a guest to our congregation. Miss Charlotte Redmond, the cousin of our General Redmond, is visiting after spending several years abroad. If we are fortunate, Miss Redmond will be with us for a while."

Margaret watched as Miss Redmond blushed and tried to look demure. "It would be that man's cousin. Another turncoat who ran away to Europe rather than support our glorious Southern cause, and now comes here, bringing her whorish Paris fashions and ways. No proper southern woman would be caught dead wearing rouge to church."

CHAPTER 3

Sunday, December 31, 1865

Reverend Williams climbed the three steps up to the pulpit slowly. He was dying, and he knew it even if no one else did, but before he went, he wanted to deliver this one last message to his congregation–the children of his soul.

He scanned over the faces looking up towards his, waiting for his words. Some were polite, some were clearly bored, most were just waiting. He had one last hope to reach their souls, to guide their steps. He prayed silently, as he always had before he started his sermons, that he could find the words to reach one soul, touch one heart.

"Today we take our text from Proverbs, Chapter Three, verses thirteen through eighteen.

Happy is the man that findeth wisdom, and the man that getteth understanding.

For the merchandise of it is better than the merchandise of silver, and the gain thereof than fine gold.

She is more precious than rubies; and all the things thou canst desire are not to be compared unto her.

Length of days is in her right hand, and in her left hand riches and honor.

Her ways are the ways of pleasantness, and all her paths are peace.

She is a tree of life to them that lay hold upon her; and happy is every one that retaineth her."

He paused for a moment to catch his breath, then began his homily.

"And all her paths are peace. What a wondrous statement. Paths of peace. When this year began, we trod the path of war, a war that pitted brother against brother, father against son. A war that sundered our families, our lives, and the very land beneath our feet. But in this year, this year, we have seen the end to that war. For some of us, God has seen fit to return our brothers, our sons, our husbands to us. I look out and see faces that I have not seen for four long years and I rejoice that we have seen the wisdom to step away from the path of war and place our feet upon the path of peace.

Yet still I mourn, for I know that there are faces that will never return to these hallowed walls, faces of men and boys who will live on only in our memories. As I look out, I also see new faces, of men and women who have come to our community to begin anew, to find that tree of life, and to seek happiness after a time of great grief and sorrow.

For those of you who have returned, President Johnson has seen fit to offer you that most precious of gifts, amnesty–peace, in exchange for a simple pledge of loyalty to our country.

As this year begins, and the days become longer, we set our feet on that path of peace with each other. I pray for each of you that you may find wisdom and God's understanding.

I know that many of you think you have come back to what you see as ashes and husks, yet I tell you that God, in his Infinite Wisdom, has reserved for you wealth and riches beyond your imagining, if only you can see them. For in Matthew, Chapter Six,

Verses nineteen through twenty-one, He has told us where to find our wealth, our treasure.

Lay not up for yourselves treasures upon earth, where moth and rust doth corrupt, and where thieves break through and steal:

But lay up for yourselves treasures in heaven, where neither moth nor rust doth corrupt, and where thieves do not break through nor steal:

For where your treasure is, there will your heart be also.

Look around you, my friends. Here, in this room, on this day, we see the splendid fruit of that tree of life, the wealth and treasure of the soul. Before you are the greatest treasures that God can give–the treasures that are home, family, friends, community. In our hearts we can see that most precious gem, more valuable than rubies–the love of little children, and the forgiveness of pure hearts.

For here, my friends, lies your treasure, your hope, your heart, your home. Look around you. Here are the faces of your brothers and sisters, who, as you place your feet upon the paths of peace, will join with you to pull together and rebuild our lives, not just for the benefit of a few, but for the peace, and joy of all.

I pray that you will all find the wisdom to lay your feet upon this new path, to step away from the anger and strife of war and to welcome, in full fellowship, those who walk in the ways of pleasantness and the paths of peace."

For a few wonderful moments, the old priest's face had been lit with a luminescence that seemed to shimmer and shine from within. But as he came to a close with his short, loving homily, the disease that was stealing his breath again gripped his frail body. Reverend Williams coughed, holding a crumpled handkerchief to his lips. It came away spotted with tiny droplets of his lifeblood.

After church, the attendees hurried out to collect their wagons and carriages and get home as quickly as possible, given the frigid air. The congregation divided into two distinct groups–those who were going out to the Redmond's for the New Year's Eve party and those who looked on them as traitors to the confederate cause.

Several of the confederate veterans and proponents who had already returned were very demanding of the young boy, Darby, to bring their horses around first, forcing the Redmonds and their friends to wait in the cold. It was a small thing, but one that reflected the animosity that many of the southerners held for the Yankee interlopers and those from the community that befriended and apparently supported them.

The New Year's Party had become a tradition at Redmond Stables. Everyone who was anyone socially in Culpepper trooped out to the house to enjoy Sarah's wonderful cooking and to bask in the elegance that was rapidly returning to the great house. Of course, it helped that Charlie and Rebecca were gracious hosts. After dinner, the gentlemen and many of the ladies often wandered out to the paddocks to discuss the charms of the various horses that had been added to the herd. Today, with the cold, blustery weather, the ladies had opted to stay indoors. Dancing would begin later in the evening and be followed by an elegant supper.

The Redmonds rushed home to settle last minute issues before the guests began to arrive.

"Reg, did you bring up the good whiskey? If General Grant comes, I want to have it available."

Charlie stood in the middle of the ballroom, looking at the bustle going on around him. Great fires had been built in both fireplaces to take the chill off the big room, as well as in the formal dining room. For the week between Christmas and New Year's, Beulah had taken command, cleaning, waxing, and polishing. The women in his life were all absorbed in furbishing their ball dresses. Except for the now traditional Redmond Stables Sunday dinner, meals for the last few days had been sparse. Sarah and her staff had been focused on preparing for the formal dinner and late-night supper that would be served today.

Rebecca, her hair wrapped in a bandana and her dress covered with a large white apron, came bustling into the room. "Beulah, where in the name of Jezebel is that spruce rope for the band's alcove?"

"Miz 'Becca, I have no idea. I told that no-good Reg to bring it in this morning and he--"

Reg, who had been standing behind the General, stepped out and pointed to the most shadowed corner of the alcove. "Beulah Jones, it's right in front of your nose, and has been since before Gen'l Charlie had his second cup of coffee this morning. Don' you go putting yo' messin' 'round on me."

"All right, it does not matter now; just get everything in place. Charlie, what are you doing to help?" She smiled at her husband, knowing full well she was calling him out on the fact that he simply seemed to be standing around, watching.

"Why, darling wife, I am organizing the libations for our guests. It would be entirely de trop to not be able to offer them anything and everything they might like to warm themselves after a cold ride in this weather–or to cool themselves after a brisk dance or two."

He smiled virtuously. "Reg and I have also set up the card tables in the back parlor for any gentlemen who wish to retire for a hand of cards, a cigar and a brandy. We have also set up the front parlor as the lady's retiring room." After last year's party, he knew where to go to get out of the way of this mayhem. The New Year's party was quickly becoming the peak of Culpeper's social schedule and his wife was a pure shrew if things were not absolutely perfect.

Lizbet came running into the room just then, in tears. She ran directly to Beulah and threw herself on the woman's substantial breast. "Beulah, I swear, I don' know how you put up with that woman. I have tried, I swear I have, but I jus' cain't get her hair right to save my soul."

Rebecca sighed. Actually, it was more of a growl, which he knew well. She was becoming irritated. He absolutely did not want her irritated. "Lizbet, if you cannot seem to satisfy Miss Charlotte, then perhaps she should simply be left to her own devices. You are a superb lady's maid, as is evidenced by the way you tend to Miss Rebecca. Leave Miss Charlotte to stew in her own juices."

Rebecca shot an appreciative look at her husband.

"Now, Lizbet, go and have yourself a nice cup of tea. Then, if you would be so kind, please touch up my cravat for the evening and lay out Miss Rebecca's clothes. After that, I think that Ginny and Tess might like a hand with the children."

He knew that he would need to beard his 'cousin' in her den and have a word about disrupting his household. "Mrs. Redmond, perhaps you would join me in the back parlor for a cup of tea?" Calming his wife down was next on his agenda.

He limped up the stairs, thinking that he would need to take a nap–or at least get the weight off his leg for a while–if he were to survive the demands of the evening. He approached the door to Charlotte's room with a bit of trepidation. As much as he disliked having his staff reduced to tears, he also preferred to avoid confrontations. She was not ingratiating herself with his household. Somehow he suspected this was not going to be a pleasant conversation.

Taking a deep breath, he tapped on her door.

The answer was soft, but unmistakable. "Come in."

He stepped into the room, stopping as soon as he could get the door closed. He leaned against it, and commented on her state of dishabille, "Charming, Cousin Charlotte, but I fear the effect is lost on both me and my staff. And I have sent Albert off on an errand."

"Really, Charlie, must you always think the worst of me? There was a time when you gave me the benefit of," the pause was purposeful as she shrugged into a robe, "the doubt. I am not sure that Rebecca has been a good influence on you in every way."

"Charlotte, I do not think that Rebecca is the issue at all. In the seven days you have been here, you have managed to insult my household, put my servants into tears, intimidate my daughter, cause furor in my church, and place my family at risk. We both know that you are capable of doing things that do not reflect outstanding judgment or even plain common sense. If you want to make your place here, I am willing to help you. But you have to help yourself. You are no longer Washington's premiere hostess.

You are plain Charlotte Redmond, a young woman from the south, without pretensions and dependent on the good will of your cousin's family. I suggest you start acting that way or this whole arrangement will fail–quickly and miserably."

"Do you have any idea how difficult all this is for me? Is there no room in your heart for a bit of sympathy and compassion?"

He raised his eyebrows, almost to his hairline. "Humm. Difficult? Yes, I do understand how difficult it must be. For example, you had to throw yourself on my wife's sympathy and generosity because of a series of stupid decisions you made. Sympathy and compassion? Well, I seem to recall telling you how much I wanted to put Charlotte behind me, yet I have enough sympathy and compassion to allow you to use that identity. And I have enough trust in you that you will not use that against me. However, for this whole subterfuge to work, for you to create the new life that your indiscretion now requires of you, I suggest that you need to take a look at your behavior and at least make an effort to play the role and not disrupt my household. Because I warn you now, Lizzie, if you try and force me to choose between you and my wife, you will lose."

Lizzie Armstrong looked at the shuttered expression on his face. This was the general who had led troops into battle, who had faced death and beat it. "Yes, Charlie. I realize that I did not understand the situation clearly. I promise I will do better."

"Be sure you do. I expect to see you as you should be this evening. A proper, demure, single woman, dressed appropriately and acting as you should. And no more harassing my servants. If you must, get your own lady's maid and train her as you wish." With that, he turned on his heel and slammed the door.

～

Close family friends started arriving around one. The rest of the party attendees would join them around four. Richard and Elizabeth, the Coopers, Samantha Carter and Duncan Nailer, and Jocko Jackson and Esther White were all in early attendance.

Elizabeth stood, warming her hands at the crackling fire that heated the back parlor, a room that was normally reserved for the family. Today, every room in the house was heated against the bitter cold. "Lord, I swear, I think I may be catching a touch of this grippe that has been plaguing us all."

Mrs. Cooper looked concerned; it was not normal for the reserved doctor to complain of even the slightest personal discomfort. "What makes you say that? Are you not feeling well?"

"For the last couple of days, I have just been feeling a bit off. My appetite is not what it usually is and I have been feeling a bit queasy now and then. Nothing serious. Perhaps I simply ate something that disagreed with me."

Mrs. White smiled and bit her bottom lip. "How long have you and Richard been married now, dear?"

"Oh, a bit over six months. Why do you ask?"

Every woman in the room chorused a soft 'uh-huh' at the very same time, most of them trying very hard to hide the smiles twitching on their lips.

Samantha Carter piped up. "You know, that is how I felt when I first realized that Jeremiah was on his way."

Elizabeth looked startled. *Pregnant? No, I cannot possibly be pregnant.* She just looked at the other ladies disbelievingly.

Charlotte sipped her tea and then asked the obvious question, "Are your courses regular?"

The doctor looked at her with a look of annoyance. "No, but then, with all of the strain of the war, they have not been regular for quite a long time. So I really do not think..." She trailed off, thinking intently as to just how regular her courses had been since she had settled down with Richard.

Again, every woman in the room murmured in unison, "Of course." Rebecca stood and joined Elizabeth at the fire, wrapping her arm around her dearest friend's shoulders. "You are pregnant," she said with just hint of a grin.

"I am no more pregnant than you are. I just ate something that disagreed with me, I am tired from dealing with all the folks with the grippe in town, and I have a touch of an upset stomach." She stood ramrod straight, all five feet of her, and declared, "I am perfectly all right."

"Of course you are, dear. You are only pregnant," Esther White finally chimed in from her seat near the window.

Elizabeth looked from face to face in the room, all of them smiling softly. Slowly, her expression changed from exasperation to a look of confused disbelief. In a tiny, choked voice, she said, "Pregnant?"

Rebecca hugged her and whispered in her ear. "Pregnant. Congratulations, dear. I do envy you."

She paled and was grateful for Rebecca's support, as she suspected her knees were going to give out very soon. "Pregnant? I cannot possibly be pregnant. I have far too much to do, what with the new clinic and the new house and all..."

Mrs. Cooper joined Rebecca and they helped settle the small woman on the davenport. "Think of it, Elizabeth... A baby. A wonderful and blessed event. Richard will be overjoyed," the older woman offered even as she placed a cup of tea in the doctor's hands.

"But... if I was going to get pregnant, why not sooner? I mean, it is not as if..." She blushed a deep, rich blush, thinking of the number of nights she had spent enjoying the carnal aspects of marriage with her always eager husband.

Rebecca chuckled, knowing exactly what Elizabeth was thinking and realizing that if it were in Charlie's power, she would have been pregnant months ago. "Elizabeth," she started softly, "the good Lord gives us children when it is our time for children. Apparently, it is your time."

Pregnant. I am pregnant. I am pregnant with Richard's child. Oh, my God. Her hand covered her mouth, and then she looked up at Rebecca and all the other women in the room. "Oh, dear. Whatever will Richard say?"

"Well," Mrs. Cooper smiled. "I would imagine, knowing Richard, he will shout it from the top of the church, and you will find yourself being very spoiled for the next few months."

She shook her head in continuing disbelief. "Richard? Children?

I just cannot quite see it. I mean, I know he is a good uncle to Emily, but a father?"

Rebecca sat next to the doctor and continued to offer her support to her friend, who was obviously having a difficult time with this pronouncement of the Culpeper Ladies Pregnancy Guild. "Richard is going to be a wonderful father. He loves and adores Emily and the boys. I do fear for him when your baby comes though; we know how possessive Emily can be of her uncle Richard. I am sure she will be quite jealous."

Samantha Carter added, "You know, he has been taking Jeremiah around with him, and has been teaching him to ride. Jeremiah is almost as fond of him as he is of Duncan."

Mrs. White glanced back from the window where she had been watching the men, and more precisely Jocko, work with two of the new horses. "Absolutely. Colonel Polk is a good, kind man, and when this baby comes, he will be the epitome of the beaming father."

Mrs. Cooper looked thoughtful. "You know, there is a lad who has been coming around looking for chores and such. Darby, I think his name is. Richard has been working to find things for him to do. The boy seems to be very devoted to him. If how he deals with Darby is any indication, he will be a splendid papa."

Rebecca slowly rubbed Elizabeth's arm. "You do not need to worry, dear. He is going to be absolutely beside himself and I think you should prepare to tell him as soon as possible. He is going to know by the startled look on your face something is amiss."

Elizabeth stared down into her lap, where she had been twisting her handkerchief into little knots as the ladies had been making their comments on Richard as a father figure. The handkerchief was now little more than a bunch of shredded linen and lace. "Yes, but will I make as good a mother?"

Rebecca hugged her dearest friend close to her. "You are going to be a wonderful mother. Buddy and Andy both adore you; every time you come into the room their faces light up. How can you doubt it?"

She shook her head. Slowly, the panic started to recede and be replaced with a sense of wonder. "A baby? Our baby? A son for Richard?" A small, wondrous smile slowly crept over her face. "You really think so?"

Rebecca nodded. "Yes, we are all in agreement on this one. You should find a way to prepare the father to be. Should I have Charlie and Jocko there to catch him when he faints?"

Rebecca's joke helped to restore her equilibrium. She smiled an evil little glint in her eye. "No, dear, I think I will spare him the embarrassment. Anyway, he is a big boy; he can pick himself up off the floor when he comes to."

More guests started arriving around four in the afternoon. Charlie and Rebecca stayed in the front hall for over an hour, greeting people as they came in. Charlie sat beside the libations table and offered them a cup of mulled wine to warm them as they divested themselves of their wraps and entered the great ballroom. Charlotte had appeared on time, dressed in a soft pastel blue dress with a lovely lace insert to keep from showing too much décolletage. Her hair was pulled back into a simple Phoebe knot.

They joined their guests in the ballroom, who were milling about, exchanging greetings, drinking Reg's milk punch and nibbling on the bits and pieces that Sarah had made to pass the time until dinner. The party would follow the southern tradition – first a fine, multi-course meal, then dancing, and later, a smaller supper, with lots of delicate little treats. If the party went well, the local guests would be there until midnight or later and those visiting from farther away would be spending the night.

While waiting for Reg to announce dinner, Charlie and Rebecca separated, making their way through the knots of guests, with a graceful word here and a joke there. Rebecca noticed that Esther White, leaning on Jocko's arm, was looking particularly pleased with herself.

"It is so good to see you, Esther, Jocko," she said automatically. She was too busy trying to figure out what was different in the woman's face from just the day before at Sunday dinner. She looked directly at the older woman. "You are looking particularly lovely tonight."

"Thank you, Rebecca. I am feeling particularly lovely tonight."

Rebecca stopped short. She looked closely at Esther's face, which had a light blush, giving the woman a very youthful look. She looked closely at Jocko's also slightly blushing features, then burst out laughing. "You two? You finally got this old reprobate to settle down?"

"I did, indeed." Esther grinned outright, while Jocko was finding the tips of his boots to be fascinating right then. "We want to keep it quiet, though. I would rather not steal Samantha and Duncan's thunder, you know."

"May I at least offer to host this event for you two?"

Jocko cleared his throat. "We would be honored, Miss Rebecca, but there is no need. We were married by Mayor Frazier, since he is also the Justice of the Peace, yesterday in his office. We will ask Reverend Williams for his blessing when he feels better."

She chuckled. "I see. Our wedding put the fear of God into you, Jocko?"

"Well, I never was much for fancy parties, you know. It was one of the things that Charlie and I agreed on."

Esther tapped Jocko lightly on the arm with her fan. "John Xavier Jackson, you are a fraud and a liar. You know perfectly well that you enjoyed putting General Charlie through his paces for his wedding."

She looked at the two of them with definite amusement. They already had the quality of an old married couple. "I can see we will have to continue this discussion at greater length, but now I fear I must see to the rest of my guests. Dinner should be ready soon, and I expect to see both of you out on the dance floor this evening."

Elizabeth and Richard, the Coopers, and Duncan and Samantha were deep in discussion with concerned looks on their faces, as Charlie walked up. "My dear friends, this is supposed to be a happy occasion, yet you all look like you are attending a funeral."

Elizabeth looked into her friend's eyes. "In a way, my friend, we are. I stopped in to see Reverend Williams today. I am afraid it is consumption, and with his age and constitution, I see very little hope."

He took a deep breath and let it out with a sigh. "I had hoped . . ."

Edward Cooper put his hand on Charlie's shoulder. "I know it is a bad time, but perhaps we can take a few minutes after dinner to talk about this, and what we will need to do for the community?"

"Certainly, Edward. Perhaps while we share our after-dinner cigars?"

"Perfect. I hate it that the parish has to depend on you so much, but . . ."

Just then Reg tapped a small gong and announced in his most stentorian tones, "Ladies and gentlemen, dinner is served." He threw open the doors to the main dining room, and the guests started moving en mass toward Sarah's loving efforts.

Dinner had been a true indulgence. Sarah had put her heart in the meal and the guests were deeply appreciative. The menu was wide and varied, and included traditional southern dishes such as chicken pirleau and hoppin' john, as well as a beautiful saddle of venison, a pit roasted steamship round, several smoked hams, baked trout garnished with candied walnuts and grilled grapes, yams, collard greens and a spectacular trifle for dessert made with Sarah's special strawberry preserves. After stuffing themselves to near somnolence, the guests moved on to the next traditional activity of the evening. Charlie led the gentlemen to the back parlor for brandy and cigars, while Rebecca escorted the ladies to the front parlor for tea and gossip.

As soon as he settled his guests with snifters of good French cognac and some elegant Cuban cigars, Edward Cooper cleared his throat and tapped on his glass with his wedding ring. "Gentlemen, I hate to bring up an issue like this during one of General and Mrs.

Redmond's wonderful parties, but we have an immediate problem and I need your advice."

Immediately, the various clusters of men moved closer to their senior deacon.

Mr. Cooper got straight to the point. "Dr. Walker visited Reverend Williams today, and I fear that our beloved minister is not going to be with us much longer. She says he has consumption, and there is little she can do for him but make him comfortable."

Shaking heads and murmurs of sympathy went around the room. Every man there had seen what consumption could do–and how quickly it could take someone.

Rafe Johnstone, the apothecary, spoke first. "I was afraid that was the problem, given what Dr. Walker has been prescribing for him. I suppose you should write the bishop, Edward, and ask them to send us a new priest."

"I shall but that is not the biggest problem I foresee. Normally, the church has sufficient funds to provide for our minister's widow, but what with the war and all, we just do not have the resources. What will we do with Mrs. Williams?"

A long silence ensued. Unlike her husband, Mrs. Williams was not well loved by the men in the room. Finally, Richard spoke up. "You mean other than shoot her and let her join her husband?"

Charlie and several other men snickered at that decidedly snide remark, then Charlie added dryly, "I am sure that Rebecca and some of the other ladies would have some ideas to contribute."

A few more snickers went around the room. Finally, Mayor Horace Frazier took a deep sigh and spoke up. "I suppose I can find a cottage that has been taken for taxes after the family fled from the war that we can put back into livable condition. We could give that to her and perhaps have a special subscription to raise some money for a stipend."

Henry Armistead, who ran the new lumber mill, offered to provide whatever wood was needed to fix up a small house, and other men pledged their support as well, but not a word was forthcoming about the most essential thing that Mrs. Williams would need–money.

Charlie decided to end this uncomfortable impasse. "Thank you, gentlemen. Mr. Cooper will write the bishop and I am sure we will discuss this further at the deacon's meeting next week. But until then, it is New Year's, we are at a party, and we should rejoin the ladies shortly. Please, enjoy your brandy and cigars, and gird your loins for the dancing to come."

The gentlemen in the room wandered back to their previous clusters, with the few younger men who had joined the party, all of them southern veterans, clustering around Albert. They were all horsemen, and all involved in the growing horse breeding and trading community that was emerging in Culpeper. Conversation was lively, with heated comments on the attributes of various sires they were breeding.

Albert led the conversation away from what was rapidly becoming an outright argument to a more general discussion of the thing that concerned all of them–the availability of feed. The winter was hard and had come early that year. As a result, all of them were worrying about having enough fodder for their horses–all of them except Albert, who had worked hard with Rebecca and Charlie to make the hay barn sound and put up extra stocks.

"Excuse me, gentlemen. I will be right back with you."

He sidled up to the general and whispered in his ear. "Cousin Charlie? Some of these boys are worried about being able to feed their horses this winter. Do you think I could offer to help them out for reasonable fees?"

He looked at him closely. "Do we have enough?"

"Yes, sir. I made sure we did."

"Will they take assistance from me?"

"I think if you do help them out, it would go a long way toward making friends. They love their horses more than they love holding grudges. At least, these boys do."

"Go ahead. Be sure to let them know that we will do what we can, no promises, but that we love horses more than grudges, too."

Albert grinned at him. "I think you ought to be the one to tell them, sir."

Charlie looked at the man he had once been so jealous of and grinned. "You are a sly one. Let us go and be generous."

The front parlor was filled with the ladies, most of who had gathered around Samantha, Esther, and Elizabeth to talk about weddings and babies. Discretely, various women excused themselves to wander upstairs and find Lizbet, Beulah, and Tess, who had been commandeered from the nursery to help care for the ladies that night. Corsets that had become too tight after Sarah's outstanding meal were loosened just enough to be bearable, though not exactly comfortable.

Charlotte had seated herself in a quiet corner of the parlor, at the far edge of the gaggle of women, listening to the conversation that she personally found abysmally boring, and trying to look demurely interested. Two of the younger women approached her shyly and introduced themselves.

"Miss Redmond? I know we have not been formally introduced, but I hope you will not hold that against us. I am Mary Simms, and this is my friend, Katherine Reynolds."

"Good evening, Miss Simms, Miss Reynolds. It is a pleasure to meet you."

"Oh, please, Miss Redmond, we are not that formal here in Culpeper. Please call me Mary.

"And I am Katherine, or Kate."

"Well, then, please do call me Charlotte. It is so pleasant to be welcomed by my new neighbors. Cousin Rebecca did not tell me that there were so many charming young ladies here in Culpeper." *Cousin Rebecca probably wanted to keep these two as far away from Charlie as possible, possessive minx that she is.*

Katherine Reynolds got straight to the chase. She wanted news and wanted it badly. "We heard that you have just returned from Paris, Miss . . . Charlotte. We were wondering if you could tell us of the latest fashions. I mean, what with all the men returned from the war and all, we were thinking . . . well, we are hoping that our little town will become more social again. And we are so far behind the fashions."

She laughed. *Ah, yes, the little girls are hunting for husbands now that there is a supply of fresh meat.* "Why, I would love to share with you. I brought some pattern books with me that I am sure you would enjoy. Perhaps Cousin Rebecca would let me invite you to tea some afternoon and we could regale ourselves with women's talk."

"Oh, yes, please. That would be lovely."

"Why then, I will be sure to ask my cousin as to what would be convenient for her and will send around a note." *And unless I miss my guess, Cousin Rebecca will want to be as far away from the house as possible when these two and their friends over there in the corner twittering show up for tea.* "So, Kate and Mary, would you introduce me to your friends?"

Charlotte rose from the stiff-backed side chair she had occupied. *Well, I never worried about making women like me before, but there is a time for everything. And some allies outside of the Redmond house would probably be good.* She sailed across the room like a diaphanous vision of modern, though modest fashion, to regale the eager local girls with tales of Paris, fashion, and European style – all of which was totally fictitious, gleaned from reading magazines, newspapers, and pattern books.

The party had lasted until the early hours of the morning. Though Charlie could no longer dance, the other gentlemen at the party had ensured that Rebecca was not a wallflower. A constant supply of milk punch, planter's punch and champagne had kept the guest well lubricated. Sarah's collation provided a wonderful supper around ten o'clock, and with the dancing and flirting that had been the dominant activities of the evening, it was a welcome break.

The clock was striking two when Charlie and Rebecca escorted the last of the guests to either the front door and their carriages home, or to their bedroom doors.

He turned to his wife, who was slightly flushed. "Wonderful party, darling."

She cleared her throat, with hopeful expectations that it might clear her slightly fuzzy head. "Yes, we seem to have done very well, darling. I am, however, exhausted. I think we should retire."

He offered his arm to his wife and turned to escort her to the stairs. To his surprise, she stumbled, then leaned against him rather heavily. "Are you all right, darling?"

"I am fine. I think perhaps I chose to try a little of all the libations available. The milk punch was exceptionally good."

He laughed and shook his head. "Oh, Lord. You are going to be sorry in the morning, I fear. I have always found that mixing liquors usually results in a seriously painful hangover."

"Ah, yes, well, a warning that would have been welcome several hours ago." She chuckled as she used the banister with her other hand to steady herself even further and to put less strain on Charlie's recovering body. "I suppose I will be having a large glass of "The Cure" with breakfast."

He chuckled. "I think that Sarah gets a certain level of pleasure from administering "The Cure," you know." He helped her up a couple more steps, thinking ruefully to himself that between her inebriation and his incapacitation, stairs were becoming their greatest challenge. "Seems to me you have become more accustomed to "The Cure" lately. Does it get better with practice?"

"I think it kills the taste buds. It is not nearly as repulsive as it used to be."

"Perhaps, dear, you might want to try to avoid it more often."

As Richard and Elizabeth were preparing for bed after a long, pleasant day with their friends, she considered how to break her news to him. "Um, Richard. How was your evening, dear?"

"Oh, it was tremendous!" He pulled off his jacket and hung it on the wooden rack by the fireplace. "Charlie has this horse out at the stables that he and Rebecca are getting ready to put on the market.

The first horse from Redmond Stables and he is the finest beast in all of Virginia. Charlie said he was going to ask two hundred for him, but I think if I offered him one seventy-five he would take it." He winked at his wife. "As a favor to an old friend."

"That is a great deal of money, dear. Um, are you sure we can afford it? I am afraid we may have some additional expenses coming soon that might put a strain on our finances." *Wonderful, Dr. Walker. You want to tell your husband that his first-born child is on the way and you are talking about finances? Where is your spine, woman?*

"Oh, I think so. Things are going well and some of my investments are turning a nice profit dear. If it will make you more comfortable, I will ask him if he is willing to extend me terms for the horse." He stripped off his shirt, leaving him bare-chested, in his trousers and socks. He rummaged around in his cabinet looking for his sleeping shirt. "You should see this horse, darling. He is the most exceptional animal I have ever seen. I would never say this to Charlie, but I think he is twice the horse Jack is."

She sat at her dressing table, absentmindedly brushing her hair as she did every evening before bed. "That is nice, dear. I am sure you are an excellent judge of horseflesh, but I am still concerned. You see, er, I know there will be other things that we will need more, um, urgently."

He stopped rummaging and looked to his wife. Slowly, he crossed the room and knelt by her. "Is there something wrong, Elizabeth?"

She smiled at her husband and gently stroked his face. This was the time to tell him, now that she actually had his full attention. "No, dear, there is nothing wrong, exactly."

"Exactly? What do you mean by exactly?" His brows came together in the very center of his forehead and the look of worry on his face grew greater with each passing second. "Have I done something?"

She could not help but chuckle at that. "Yes, dear, you could very well say that. In fact, you have done something–something very good."

He felt like he was about to combust. Normally he did not mind the fact that his wife liked to beat the bushes rather than getting straight to the point, but in this instance it was about to drive him insane. "Then tell me, darling, what is this good thing I have done. Please, do not leave me on pins and needles."

She blushed. *How strange. Here I am, a doctor who deals with the raw facts of people's bodies all the time and I am having the very devil of a time telling my husband he is about to be a father.* "Well, dear, it seems that our conjugal evenings together have served their biblical purpose."

He blinked, trying to decipher this rather muted message from his wife. He ran the words over again in his head and then smiled. "Elizabeth? Are you...?" The words trailed off as his heart started pounding in his chest and he sent a silent prayer to God hoping he was guessing right.

She took his face in her hands and looked straight into his eyes. "Yes, Richard. I am. We are going to be parents."

He could not speak. He could only smile as he felt tears well in his eyes. He had seen so much death, this news was the greatest that he had ever been given. The woman he loved most in the world was going to give him a child. "Thank you. I love you, Elizabeth. So very much." He wrapped her up in his arms and pressed his lips to her forehead.

"Me too, Richard."

Rebecca had gone up to get ready for bed before Charlie, who had taken a few minutes to finish his cigar. It also gave him a moment to steel himself for what he suspected would be a less than joyous chat with his beloved wife.

He threw his cigar in the fireplace, drained the last drops of brandy from his snifter, and banked the fire for the night. He turned down the wick in the gas lamps and quietly left the small parlor, making his way carefully up the stairs. Going up was always easier than coming down, he thought to himself.

As he reached the top of the stairs, he noticed Albert hovering outside Charlotte's door. "Good night, Cousin," he called.

The young man jerked; startled that he had been caught. "Good night, Cousin Charlie," he stammered as he scuttled down the hall toward his own room, trying to look innocent.

He looked to the ceiling. *Oh, God, not this. I will have to speak to Rebecca about keeping him on the road looking for new stock as much as possible.* He heaved a heavy sigh as he opened the door to her sitting room.

"There you are. I was beginning to think I was going to have to come and find you." *And if I found you with her, there would be hell to pay, Charles Huger Redmond.*

He looked at his wife carefully, trying to gauge her mood. She was sitting in her robe, vigorously brushing her hair. Not a good sign. He spoke very softly. "No, darling. I finished my cigar, banked the fire, and came up. I did, however, have to run Albert off to bed. I really do not think that lurking in the hall outside her door is quite the thing, you know."

She nodded and continued brushing her hair. "There is an auction in Richmond next week; we will send him there."

"Yes, dear."

"Then I suppose we will have to find every auction and show in three states to send him to. I intend to get her out of here as soon as possible, but not with my cousin."

He stood there, looking at his wife, and thinking about the changes that Charlotte's presence had created in just a few days. Lizzie was a charming hostess; Charlotte was a spoiled houseguest. The number of trunks and boxes that had been carried into his house on Thursday was terrifying.

"I assume you and Elizabeth are planning to introduce her to eligible gentlemen as quickly as possible. Shall I ask Beulah to have the ball room cleaned up?"

She turned to him and tried not to look as mad as she felt. Having Lizzie as a semi-permanent resident of the house was wreaking havoc on her nerves and good sense. "Yes, we do intend to find a suitable gentleman for her and hopefully marry her off."

He breathed a deep sigh. What he was about to say went deeply against the grain for him. But it was do this or suffer even more than he was already. "How can I help?"

"Charlie." She left her dresser and moved to the settee, patting it with her hand. "I am going to tell you something that pains me a great deal. I thought I could tolerate you remaining friends with Lizzie, and if it were not a situation like this one, I am sure I could have at least tried. But the truth is I am," she looked to the ceiling and sighed, "God, forgive me, jealous. I do not like having her here. I do not like having her under the same roof. I do not like having her so close to you. I am going to do everything I can to not take this out on you; it is not your fault that she came here."

He sat down beside her and listened very carefully to what she was saying. A small smile slithered across his lips. Ah, that jealousy thing again. He spoke just as carefully as she had. "For starters, darling, I am not particularly joyous about having her here either. But I gave her my word, and I do owe her—we both do in a way. She helped me become, well, me. I am particularly not happy about the circumstances that brought her here. I feel like I am walking on eggshells between the two of you—you because you are clearly not happy and her because of, well, because of what brought her to our doorstep in the first place. Payne was a very dangerous man." He took a deep breath. "And to be perfectly honest, from what little I have seen in the past few days, I am not looking forward to living with her any more than you are."

"I am very concerned about the circumstance that brought her to our doorstep. I swear to you on everything I hold dear and holy, that if anything or anyone threatens our home and our children, I will not be held responsible for what may happen to Lizzie. There is nothing more important to me than you and the children and I am quite prepared to defend you if I must."

He smiled at his very feisty wife. "I believe you. I thought you were going to kill Montgomery and every other rude Yankee if given half a chance on the day we met." He shifted a bit and wrapped his arm around his wife. "Darling, we will get through this. It is annoying, irritating, a major inconvenience, and a downright nuisance. And just so you feel a bit better about the politics of the situation, I sent messages to both General Grant and General McClellan on Thursday to let them know that she is here and that I am keeping an eye on things."

"Charlie! You sent a telegram? So the telegram operator knows?" She looked a bit panicked at the thought.

"Love, I am still an old army man. I used code. Our secret is safe." He shifted to get more comfortable and to draw her closer, hoping that would help relax the small woman. "This is just one more example of McClellan's political gaming, I fear. We just happen to be on the receiving end this time."

"I am very sure I do not like this game. The war is over. Why must we continue to fight these battles?" She relaxed into him, feeling his heart beating under her hand as she rested it on his chest. The sound and the feel of it gave her comfort that she could not explain. "In the meantime, Elizabeth and I will make sure that Miss Charlotte is kept quite busy and out of trouble."

He chuckled. "I am sure you will. And this is not a game about the war, dear. It is McClellan trying to figure out how to become President and making sure he has as many cards tucked up his sleeves as possible."

"It is all the same to me, Charlie. A snake is a snake, no matter how many times it sheds its skin."

"That about describes McClellan. I can only pray that Johnson manages to survive the maelstrom and carry out Mr. Lincoln's plans."

He shifted again, trying to get comfortable while he held her, but it was past time for his evening dose of laudanum and he was feeling it. He was just plain twitchy.

"Time for your medicine, dear?"

"Yes, please."

CHAPTER 4

Saturday, January 6, 1866

Elizabeth drove up to Redmond Stables in the small pony trap she used to make house calls. But this was not a house call. It was her regular Saturday Afternoon Tea Party with Rebecca–the Anti-Biddy Brigade, as Elizabeth thought of it to herself. Reg was waiting for her on the front steps, expecting her arrival, to take her little pony around to the warm barn and feed it a small bucket of oats, molasses and hot water, which the pony loved.

Beulah was also waiting for the doctor. She met her in the front hall, and divested her of her heavy coat, muffler, gloves and galoshes, then hustled her into the back parlor, which was warm, filled with light from the windows, and where Rebecca and a tempting lunch Sarah had assembled were waiting for her.

The rest of Charlotte's wardrobe and other personal possessions had arrived from Washington two days earlier. Her room now looked like a small tornado had come through, but she was dressed demurely.

Restlessly pacing her sitting room, she heard the trap jingling up the driveway, and looked out of the window to see who was coming. "Ah. Dr. Walker at last. I was hoping she would show up sooner or later and I really want her to hear this, too. Gird up your loins, girl. Get down there to make your apologies," she thought.

Rebecca was sitting in front of the fire with a large basket in her lap. There were multiple skeins of yarn in various pastel colors, and a number of sticks jammed in and around the yarn. "Ah! There you are! Do you want to eat first or would you like to start your lessons?"

"Lessons," said Elizabeth warily, eyebrows crawling upward. "Lessons? What lessons?"

"Well, dear. Unless you intend to dress your child in Richard's old uniforms, you need to learn to knit. I thought we could start today, so that you would have a good six or seven months to get ahead of the need. You do know you need to fill your baby chest."

"Baby chest? What baby chest?" She continued to look bewildered.

"Elizabeth, dear, every woman who has a baby gets some kind of baby chest. Usually from their own mother, but given the circumstances, I think I can fill that role. It has baby clothes, flats, safety pins, rattles, blankets... all of the things that a newborn needs. Filling it is your job while you are waiting for the child to arrive."

Elizabeth stood there, staring at Rebecca, blinking her eyes and feeling rather overwhelmed. She knew how to deliver babies–for other women. She had not a clue as to how to be a mother herself. Finally, she stuttered, "F-f-flats?"

"Yes, dear. You need something for diapering the baby's bottom. Good muslin, cotton, flannel...anything soft and absorbent. With both babies, we go through about twenty flats a day. I use the muslin in summer, and flannel in fall and winter."

"Oh," she said rather flatly.

"Now sit down. You need to learn how to knit booties, caps, mittens, blankets, oh, all sorts of things. You do know how to knit?"

"Um.... I never found a lot of time for that while I was studying for my medical degree."

"Well, you can learn."

"Ah, can we eat first, please?" She was trying to buy a bit of time to wrap her mind around these new aspects of her life.

As Rebecca moved to the table to serve up plates for them, a quiet tapping at the parlor door caused her to pause and look up. "Come in," she called.

Charlotte slipped into the room, softly closing the door behind herself. She continued to hold onto the doorknob.

"Why, Cousin Charlotte. You look as if you were ready to bolt and I did not think I was that much of a harridan," Rebecca softened her words with a welcoming smile. "We were just about to have lunch. Would you care to join us?"

Elizabeth sat back, watching the interaction with interest. How was Rebecca going to deal with her so-called cousin today? And it was a great distraction from the basket of yarn and knitting needles that had been set aside and she regarded as if it were a basket of snakes and worms. *Then again, if they go at it, knitting needles could be pretty ferocious weapons.*

"Ah, um, yes, thank you. Some lunch would be lovely," murmured Charlotte. Lunch was another delay before she would have to abase herself. *Thank God.*

The three ladies ate their lunch fairly quietly, chatting intermittently about the current weather, the conditions in the town, and other non-consequential subjects. As they finished the last pieces of roasted chicken, biscuits, and stewed pears that Sarah had put up that fall, Rebecca served coffee to the ladies, and poured a dram of the brandy sitting on the side table for herself into her coffee.

Charlotte cleared her throat. "Ah, Rebecca. And you as well, Elizabeth, if I may call you that."

Elizabeth nodded but did not say anything.

After a pause, she went on. "I fear I made a poor start of things over the last week. I came to you frightened, threatened and in need of creating an entirely new life. But to be honest, I was not ready to give up my old life." She paused and took a deep breath. "Rebecca, I know you and I talked of my becoming a retired widow in a small town and doing charitable work with the church, but that was for some day. And I truly resented having my 'some day' becoming this day. I truly had no idea that I was supporting the southern cause by holding a few letters for a friend. I was forced out by Seward and McClellan. They threatened to take all of my possessions; they threatened to charge me of spying. They even threatened to hang me, as they did that poor Mrs. Mary Surratt." With that, a tear ran down Charlotte's face.

"I swear to you both, I never thought I was doing anything wrong. I was just being stupid." Another heavy sigh broke her lips. "But whatever the cause, I am here now, and it is time for me to make a new life. I apologize profusely to you, Rebecca, for being, well, not to put too fine a point on it, a bitch to you and your family. I was angry and frightened, and I took it out on you all. I will not do that again. I am turning to both of you to ask you to help me build a new life for myself."

Rebecca and Elizabeth looked at one another. Slow smiles crept over both of their faces. Rebecca turned to Charlotte, and spoke with compelling honesty, "Of course, Cousin Charlotte. It is entirely understandable; you have been under huge stress. But we are family, and this is what family does for one another. In fact, I have asked Lizbet to ask around and see if we can find a ladies' maid for you. With yesterday's delivery, I suspect you could use some help."

The relief that flowed over Charlotte's face was transformational. "Thank you so much, Cousin." She moved to the third chair by the fire and looked down at the basket of yarn and needles. "So what have we here?" she asked.

"Oh, yes. Today Dr. Elizabeth, who can sew with the finest, needs to learn how to knit so she can prepare for the baby."

"Yes, the baby. I love babies. I always hoped to have some of my own one day." Absent-mindedly, she reached into the basket of yarn and extracted a ball of fine wool and two very narrow needles.

The ladies began to chat about how to best go about helping Charlotte create her new persona as a proper southern gentlewoman. Various interests were discussed and discarded, until they agreed that a school for the children of the community was needed, and that the church could use new hymnals. The clicking of the knitting needles in Charlotte's hands punctuated the dialogue. Talk turned to the problems of dealing with Mrs. Williams when her husband passed away, and Rebecca and Elizabeth regaled Charlotte with tales of Mrs. Williams' less than charitable or even Christian attitudes.

The clicking continued. At least until Rebecca realized that her objective of teaching Elizabeth how to knit had been completely subverted by Charlotte's touching apology and declaration of her intention to take on a new life. "Ladies!" Her voice had the pitch of command as she interrupted the ongoing tales of the biddy brigade. "We have completely lost sight of the purpose of this afternoon. We still need to teach Elizabeth how to knit, or her baby will not have any clothes when it comes into the world."

Elizabeth looked miserable. Fortunately, Charlotte piped up immediately. "Oh, I love to knit. I used to occupy myself with knitting in the carriage whenever I had to travel any distance." She smiled and held up the item she had been clicking away on for the past two hours. "And I am very fast at it." A perfect little pair of baby booties hung from her needles, ready to be cast off and deposited in the baby chest, as soon as a chest could be found.

Charlie and Richard had spent the afternoon in town. Tomas had come into town and collected both men, taking them out to Redmond Stables so that Richard could drive his wife home. As the two men entered the hall, they could hear uproarious laughter coming from the back parlor in waves of sound. Charlie heard Rebecca's laugh, which turned into a guffaw until she lost her breath. Richard recognized Elizabeth's roaring laughter. The third laugh was one the general had not heard in a long time, but he recognized it. The only time the men had heard laughter like this was when someone had told an outrageously dirty joke in camp. The two men looked at each other, then crept up to the door and opened it just a crack to peek in.

There sat the three women, with Charlotte waving something on a pair of sticks. Tears were running down Rebecca's face. As soon as the women noticed the men at the door, they stopped laughing, though they could not wipe the grins off their faces. Quietly, Charlie and Richard backed out, closing the door. "There is brandy in my office. I think we both need some," he said as he led the way up the stairs. The laughter in the parlor broke out again as they trod the first step.

When she regained her breath from the last round of laughter, Elizabeth said to Charlotte, "Well, then. Is it settled? Will you knit the baby clothes for me? I would be happy to pay you."

"Oh," scoffed Charlotte. "Just tell me what colors you prefer. Consider it my baby gift to you. It is my first act of neighborly concern as the newest member of the Culpeper community."

A short time later, Richard and Charlie, fortified with a good dose of brandy, returned to the parlor, where they were properly greeted by the ladies.

"My dear, it is time for us to go home. I am sure there is a lovely dinner waiting for us, since we managed to retain Sarah's sister as our cook." Richard held his hand out to Elizabeth as he spoke.

The ladies rose as one and walked out into the hall. Beulah appeared, holding Elizabeth's outdoor ware. Once Richard and Elizabeth were bundled up, Rebecca escorted them to the front porch, where Reg was waiting with Elizabeth's pony and trap. As they were getting ready to get into the trap, Rebecca said, "Oh. Richard. A moment." She pointed at a lovely cedar chest sitting behind one of the pillars. "Please. Take this with you. Elizabeth is going to need it."

~

Wednesday, January 10, 1866

Charlie and Richard walked into Jocko's bar, taking a seat at a large table in the corner. In the fading light of late afternoon, it was hard to see who else came into the bar, but slowly, the rest of the church's deacons filtered in. They had agreed to meet here so that they could be sure they were nowhere near Mrs. Williams or her band of biddies. Being overheard right now was not an agreeable option.

Mr. Cooper cleared his throat, and with a sigh, started the conversation. "I have written to the bishop in Richmond and got his response today. He says that he already has someone in mind for our church–an Englishman who has been transferred from the Church of England to our Episcopalian Diocese after having served as a missionary abroad for several years. He should be arriving by the beginning of next month."

"Excellent," said Richard. "I do not feel that this community will fare well without an active minister. The church is truly the center of the community. We can only hope that this Brit is not a stuffed shirt."

Charlie spoke up, "The real question is what to do with the new minister if Reverend Williams is still resident at the Manse. We had talked about finding a cottage for Mrs. Williams after the reverend passes, but there is nothing ready yet. I suppose he could stay with Rebecca and me while he finds his feet in the community."

Rafe Johnstone tapped his fingers in nervous frustration. "Well, that is settled, then. So what are we going to do with Mrs. Williams?"

Mayor Frazier offered. "Well, we have found a lovely little cottage around the corner from the church, and just down the street from the Reynolds' house that the town can contribute to the cause."

Henry Armistead asked, "What kind of condition is it in?"

Frazier hesitated, then said, "Well, it does need some work, but since you offered to provide lumber, I was hoping…"

"Ah, yes, I suspected you would say that," responded Armistead. "Well, I do have some decent lumber–mostly oak and pine–at the lumber yard, but I have no laborers to do the work."

There was a long silence around the table. Finally, Charlie spoke up. "I have a fellow named Big Ben who can do carpentry. And I think, if we ask nicely, Duncan Nailer will probably help out."

Mr. Cooper sighed and added to the solution. "And I think that we have some used furnishings that we could contribute to make the place habitable if need be."

Mayor Frazier looked around the table. "So, who will we ask to actually move Mrs. Williams out when her husband passes?"

No one volunteered.

Frazier finally said, "What about Dr. Walker? She is a physician, she is well regarded, and she has the patience of a saint."

"She has to, to be married to Richard," Charlie murmured.

Richard blanched. "Well, one of you has to ask her. If I ask her to tangle with the head hen of the biddy brigade, I assure you, I will end up sleeping over here at Jocko's for a few days. Perhaps you can ask her, Charlie. She loves you."

Charlie just grunted.

As the men walked out of the bar to go back to their respective places of work, a non-descript young man sidled up to Charlie. "Excuse me, Mr. Redmond. My name is Robert Brooks. I understand you are making hay available to those of us who do not have enough to feed our horses and cows this winter. I was wondering if I could buy some."

"Good to meet you, Mr. Brooks. Yes, of course. Our cousin, Albert Randolph, handles this for us. I will let him know you will be out tomorrow, so please, tell him how much you need. And if you are short on funds, tell him I said to just open an account."

Brooks hated being indebted to this Yankee, but he needed to feed his horse and milk cow more than he hated the man. It was going to be easier dealing with Albert Randolph, who was at least his kind of people. "Thank you. I will see Albert."

Charlie could see how torn the man was by the look in his eyes. Albert had been inspired when he suggested this plan. He made a mental note to have Albert give him the best price he could and to let him run a tab. Money was a problem for most of the returning soldiers.

~

Friday, January 19, 1866

The boy swallowed hard before approaching the back steps of the fine house. His mama had always wanted to live in a place like this, but that just would not be possible now. Darby shook his head to keep from crying and clenched his fists determinedly and took the steps one by one. Knocking on the door, he waited, shivering against the cold air and wishing he was home to make sure the fire was still burning.

Sarah had finished cleaning up from luncheon for the children and Miss Rebecca. Gen'l Charlie had eaten in town today–probably better for him, as it meant he did not have to ride home and then return to town in this bitter cold.

She heard a timid tapping at her back door. Opening it, she saw a slender boy, perhaps just a bit younger than Master Jeremiah, dressed in rags. "Lawsy, lad, come in from the cold." She bustled the little boy into the warm kitchen, settled him on a bench in front of the fire, and fetched a mug of the broth she had simmering on the hob by the fire. "Now, lad, what can we do for you?"

He looked at the woman and sighed. "Would you have any milk? Mr. Cooper said I might be able to buy some here. I have money." He reached into his pocket and pulled out a few pennies.

Sarah looked at the boy. His clothes were rags, but they were clean. He had no shoes and no coat though the weather was bitterly cold. Miss Rebecca would want to see him. "Well, lad, we do have some milk, but you would have to ask Mrs. Redmond about it. She is the mistress of this house. If you would sit here and warm yourself, I will see if she can see you."

He took the mug and nodded. "Yes'm. I will be right here and I promise not to touch nothin'."

Sarah hurried up the stairs to the back parlor, where Rebecca was going through her breeding records. She tapped on the door and entered without waiting for a response. Rebecca looked up questioningly at the slightly breathless cook. "Miss Rebecca, there is a boy downstairs askin' to buy some milk. But there is just something 'bout him. I am thinking you want to see him yourself."

She looked at her intently. Usually if one of their neighbors asked to borrow some small food item, Sarah just gave it to them without bothering her. She found out about those little variances in her stocks when the two of them met each morning to discuss menus. There was something different about this boy, or Sarah would not have come charging upstairs. "Why is he different?"

"I am not sure, ma'am. I just think this one needs your attention."

"Well, then, you know I trust your instincts. Bring him up."

"Yes, ma'am. Right away." She turned toward the door, then looked back. "Oh, and ma'am?"

"Yes, Sarah?"

"I think I should bring up some tea and maybe some cookies or something."

"Hungry looking, is he?"

Sarah just grinned and scooted out the door.

She returned to her own domain and bustled about as she explained to the boy, "Miss Rebecca wants to see you, and asked that I make tea for the two of you. So we will take it up to her together."

The boy looked at the door, wondering if he should just excuse himself and leave. Then he thought of Suzanne. "All right," he said quietly.

In just a few minutes, Sarah had piled a tray with little sandwiches, biscuits, and cakes, had a pot of hot tea steeping and was leading Darby up the stairs to the main floor of the house. "Miss Rebecca is a lady, so you watch your manners, but she is a generous one, so you just tell her what you need, lad."

He remained quiet but again nodded as he brushed his hand through his unruly hair.

Rebecca looked up from her notes as the door opened and Sarah entered, followed by the boy. He was certainly a handsome fellow, slender and whippy, dressed in ragged but clean clothes. He was barefoot, and had no coat, just an old sweater that was too big for him. The sweater had a couple of holes in critical places. An old, gray muffler was wrapped around his neck like a necktie. "Good afternoon. Welcome to Redmond Stables. I am Rebecca Redmond. Will you have a seat, young master…?"

"Darby, ma'am. Darby Sweet."

"Well, Master Darby Sweet, come in and sit down. Would you like some tea?"

He looked around the room and smiled. It was full of books. He loved books; he just did not have any. He managed to pay attention again as he unwrapped his scarf; with the fire going it was quite warm in the room. "Yes, ma'am. Thank you, ma'am."

She immediately noticed the shine in his eyes as he looked around the room. If the books in this room got this boy's attention, he would think Charlie's library upstairs to be truly a piece of heaven. "So, Master Darby, how do you take your tea?"

"Um, just regular, ma'am." He took a step forward, eyeing the small sandwiches. The broth he had taken in the kitchen started his stomach rumbling.

"Well, I like mine with a little honey and some milk, so will that do for you?" She proceeded to prepare his cup as he nodded. "Help yourself to the sandwiches. I like the ham and biscuit ones, myself."

He took yet another step toward her and picked up a sandwich from the plate. His first bite was fast and the way he chewed made it clear that he was a hungry young man. He realized what he was doing and slowed his eating. After swallowing, he offered, "It is very good, ma'am."

"Sit down, please. You are reminding me of a half-trained colt who wants the carrot but is afraid of the halter."

He quickly took a seat and began twitching. He needed to ask for the milk and get home, but it would be rude to try and rush with this lady who was being so kind. His mama taught him never to be rude, no matter how much of a rush you might be in. "Yes, ma'am."

"You look to be a young man on a mission. What is it that we here at Redmond Stables can do for you?"

"Yes, ma'am. I was wondering if you might have some milk you can spare? I have money, ma'am. I can pay."

She looked at this earnest young fellow and knew there was more to his story. "Darby–may I call you Darby? You look like you need more than just some milk. Are your parents ill? I know that many folks around here have had the grippe this winter."

"Yes, ma'am, Darby is fine. My pa was killed in the war." He resisted telling the rest of the story, hoping she would let it go. Ma had warned him that if anyone found out, he and Suzanne would be taken away from each other and probably sent off to some home somewhere, never to see each other again.

"So it is just you and your mama? I think there is probably at least one brother or sister, as well."

"Yes, ma'am, Suzanne. She is four now." He carefully picked two sandwiches up from the plate, and when he thought Rebecca was not looking, slipped one of them into his pocket.

She did notice. Only one sandwich, not two. *Something is very wrong here. No mother would let her son out in this weather without shoes or a coat, either.* "So the milk is for her, I think. And what about you and your mother? Do you have enough food for the three of you?"

"Umm." He looked down, not wanting to lie to the nice woman, but knowing he had to. He certainly would not look her in the eye and do it. "Yes, ma'am. Ma and I are fine, but Suzanne could use some fresh milk if you have it."

"I will have Sarah pack up a basket for you with milk and a little treat for your little sister, then. While she is doing that, would you like to come upstairs and let me see if I have a coat that might fit you? I have a number of things of my brother's in the old cedar chest and my own sons are still infants."

"Oh, no, ma'am. I cannot pay and that would be wrong, to take something if I cannot pay for it. Thank you though, ma'am."

"It is not something I would take money for, Darby. If you do not take it, I fear I will have to simply throw it away, as we need the storage space for the babies' things."

His cold and tired body was warring with his manners and upbringing. He fidgeted and swallowed hard. "If you are sure, ma'am, I could take it off your hands. I mean if you are only going to throw it away."

"I am quite sure. Let me ring for Sarah to get your milk, then we can go upstairs." She suited her action to words. Sarah appeared at the door almost instantly; obviously she had been waiting in the hall for Miss Rebecca's instructions. "Ah, Sarah. Could you get a large flask of fresh milk for our friend Master Darby?" She rose and moved toward her cook, adding in a whisper, "and put up some cornpone and a bit of ham as well as whatever else you think a boy his age could manage? I think you were right."

While Rebecca was busy with the cook, Darby placed something on the corner of her desk, and then took a moment to look at the books again, slowly walking over to the shelves and trying to see if he had ever heard of any of these titles. His pa had owned lots of books before the war, but his ma had either sold them or used them for tender in the fire. He missed his pa's books. He missed reading and being read to. He missed his ma and pa. He had to do everything he could to keep Suzanne with him.

In a gentle voice, Rebecca called his name. "Darby?" He seemed enthralled by the books, but the sad slump of his shoulders said there was more to his story than he had told, if she could only discover it. "Darby? If you are ready?"

"Oh yes, ma'am. I am sorry, ma'am." He turned dutifully and waited for her to lead him upstairs.

As they walked up the broad staircase, she looked at the boy beside her. He was a neat little fellow, obviously tried to keep himself clean and tidy, but the condition of his clothing told her that if he did have a mother, she was not keeping up the basics like mending. "So, Darby, what is your mother's name? I think I know most of the families here about. There are several Sweet families; I was wondering if I knew your parents."

"Charity, ma'am." He really wanted to be on his way before she asked too many more questions.

"No, I do not think I have met her. You do not attend the Episcopalian church, do you?"

"No, ma'am. We have not been to any services since my pa was called away. And we are Baptist, not Episcopalian."

"Ah." She continued up the stairs and into the storage room. "Well, here we are. Now, my brother's old things are in this chest." She opened it, rummaged around and pulled out a wool jacket, two pair of well-worn but good quality woolen trousers and a couple of heavy shirts. Further rummaging found two pair of boots, one pair a little larger than the other. "Here you go. I hope these fit you. And I know we will never use the boots again, so if either pair of them fits, please take them."

He nearly licked his lips at the sight of the warm clothes. It had been a very long time since he had anything new. He sat down in the middle of the floor and took the smaller pair of boots into his hands. They were very soft; he quickly put them on, and they were just a little big, but he knew he could grow into them. "These fit, ma'am." He smiled at her. "Thank you."

"You are welcome, Darby. Now, I think that Sarah probably has your basket ready. Shall we go?"

He gulped. "We?"

"Well, I am a lady, and I always show my guests out," she teased gently. *Ah, another hint. He seems terrified that I would take him home.*

"Of course, ma'am." He quickly gathered the things she had rolled for him and hoped he could get out of the house very quickly before she got more inquisitive.

The two walked downstairs quietly, with Darby wishing he could get away before she got any more suspicious and Rebecca thinking of how she could follow this boy without him knowing it. They arrived at the kitchen to see Sarah just putting the cover on a fairly substantial basket of goods–not so large he could not carry it, but big enough to give him some decent food for a day or two.

Rebecca looked into her fellow conspirator's eyes and got a slight nod toward the corner where Reg usually sat when he had a free moment. *Ah, good girl, Sarah.* Reg was already positioned to follow the lad and find out where he was going.

She turned to the boy and extended her hand. "Well, Master Darby Sweet, it has been a pleasure to meet you. I enjoyed your company. In fact, if you are interested, I think there are several tasks that I could use the assistance of a bright young man on."

"Really?" He brightened considerably. "I am a very hard worker, ma'am. Never afraid to put in a hard day's work. My pa always said it was what a good man did."

"Well, I noticed you seem to like books. Do you read well? And is your handwriting clear? My husband has an extensive library, and it needs to be indexed."

"Yes, ma'am. I have read just about every book my pa owned before the war, and my ma taught me writing. I can do both. I know some ciphering...um...mathematics, too."

"Well, then, Darby, you can come back here Monday and meet General Redmond. I am sure we can put your skills to good use, and for a fair wage." She smiled at the boy, treating him like the responsible adult he wished he could be. "Until then, if you need anything more, please do not hesitate to call on me. Good day to you." With that, she turned and left him at the back door.

Darby nodded and looked to Sarah. "Thank you. Very much." He gathered everything and walked out the back door, intent on getting home to check on Suzanne. She would certainly be hungry by now and the fire would need tending so they would not freeze through the night.

Rebecca ran up the stairs to watch the boy leave the property. She wanted to see what direction he took and make sure Reg followed him. After a moment of watching, she saw him emerge onto the back lawn, loaded down with his roll of new clothes and the basket of staples. He turned toward the path to the north bridge over Gaines Run, heading towards the area west of town. A moment later, Reg slouched along the same path. She went down to her office to wait. She noticed on the corner of her desk the four pennies he must have had in his pocket. "Oh, you poor, gallant boy," she sighed.

The afternoon progressed uneventfully. Charlie returned around teatime, and the two of them had no time to talk privately, as the children occupied their entire attention. Teatime was rapidly becoming a family tradition. Papa usually returned from town around then. Em finished her lessons and the boys woke from their afternoon nap. It was very much a family event.

Just as they were finishing up and sending Em and the boys off with Tess and Ginny, Reg finally returned. He knocked softly at the door, as this was time that Gen'l Charlie and Miss Rebecca did not like to be disturbed.

"Miz 'Becca? Is it all right to come in? I have that information you wanted."

She opened the door and ushered him in. "Yes, Reg, please come tell us what you found."

"Well, Miz 'Becca, I followed the boy out to a small cabin about an hour's walk west of town. It looked pretty run down. He went in, but I swear, I did not see anyone else there. In fact, ma'am, I do not think that there is anyone else there. I am sure he did not see me; he was just hurrying along like he needed to get somewhere fast."

Charlie looked at his wife and his major domo with an expression of startled confusion. "So what is going on that you are following boys around, and evidently being sneaky about it?"

"Well, love," She took her seat next to him. "A young man came here looking for milk today." She sighed, "There was something just not right about him. A bright boy, but he was in rags and extremely careful about everything he said."

He raised his right eyebrow, "So you told Reg to follow him and find out if he was all right?"

"I did not tell Reg to follow him." She smiled, feigning a defensive voice. "Reg is a smart man; he knew to follow him."

"Um, ma'am? Gen'l Charlie? It was Sarah tol' me to follow him."

She snorted, which then became a chuckle. "Yes, Reg, I know. You did fine. Thank you."

Charlie looked at his wife, knowing full well that she was like a lioness with her cubs whenever she saw a child that needed help. It did not matter whose child it was; all children were hers. "So shall I assume we need to go and rescue this lad?"

"Well, I am not sure he needs rescuing, darling, but I think he certainly needs help and is far too proud to ask for it. He kept trying to impress me with how hard he could work, and I had a devil of a time getting him to take some of Andrew's old clothes. The boy had no shoes, no coat and he was obviously hungry." She lifted a brow. "Does this story sound familiar to you, dear?"

He smiled a grim little smile. A moment of kindness to a boy in similar circumstances twenty years earlier had landed him on the path that eventually led him to Rebecca's arms.

He thought for a moment, and then sighed. "Reg, please have Tarent bring the four-man coach around as soon as possible. You will be driving." He warmed his hands before the fire for a moment, and then looked at his wife. "Why, dear, are you not upstairs getting ready to go out into the cold?"

She laughed richly and kissed him on the cheek. "I do not have a good answer for that, my dear husband, but I will be down shortly." With that, she did indeed leave him there staring into the fire as she went to change.

Within a few minutes, they were standing together at the front door, bundled against the bitter cold, with a couple of hot bricks wrapped in flannel to keep their hands and feet warm, a pair of heavy woolen lap rugs and a flask of hot tea.

Reg drove the coach up to the door and started to jump down and assist them, but Charlie waved him off. He handed Rebecca up inside, tossed the other items in, and hauled himself up, thumping on the roof of the coach with his cane to signal Reg to move out. A whistle to the horses, a slap of the reins, and they set off at a brisk trot. What had taken an hour by foot would take no more than twenty minutes at this pace.

"So tell me about this boy and your suspicions, dear."

"His name is Darby. He came here asking to buy milk. He said his father was killed in the war; he let it out that he has a four-year-old sister named Suzanne, but he would not talk of his mother. Something is not right here."

"Are you thinking his mother is ill?"

"I am concerned, Charlie, that his mother may be more than ill. He slipped a little food into his pocket when he thought I was not watching. It was not enough to feed two children and an adult."

"If you are right, are we about to acquire two more children?"

She just made a sound that sounded like 'hummphh' and placed her hand in the pocket of his coat. "Hush."

"Rebecca, I am quite serious. If Darby and his sister are alone in the world, I know you will want to take them in. I am not opposed to the idea, you know that. I just wanted to know what was going on in your ferociously motherly mind."

"We cannot leave them if they are alone, and if they are not alone, then they must still need help."

"Well, let us see what the lad needs, then we will go forward." He pulled her closer to him. This was one of the things about her he loved—her passionate, generous soul that reached out to anyone in need and opened her heart to those most in need—like him.

In the faint light of dusk, they looked at the little cabin set back in the rolling hill country west of town. The yard had an untended look, there was a startling lack of the animal population that was common in small farmsteads like this, and though the little house had two chimneys, only one had smoke rising from it.

The sound of the horses' hooves had warned Darby of the arrival of unexpected visitors. As they pulled to the front door, he emerged, holding a rifle in his hands that was almost as long as he was tall.

Charlie cautioned Rebecca to stay in the coach until he got control of the situation and then he carefully stepped down. "Relax, young Master," he paused and she whispered his last name, "Sweet. We mean you no harm. My wife is concerned for you, so we came to check on you."

"Who are you? How did you find me?" The boy was confused and very scared. This looked like an official kind of person. Maybe one of the ladies in town had recognized him and sent them out to take him and Suzanne away.

"My name is Charles Redmond. You were in my home today, young sir. You spoke with my wife."

"Gen...General Redmond? Well, sir, thank your wife. She was

very kind to me. But we are fine, sir." He dropped the butt of his gun to the ground but made no move to invite Charlie into the house.

"Well now, Darby." He took a step forward. "Would you mind too terribly much if we spoke with your mother, just to make sure?"

He looked up into the kind eyes of the tall man with the cane and knew that it was all over. He was going to come into the house and find the things he had done to take care of Suzanne after ma and Judah had died; he was going to know that they were alone; he was going to take them away and he would never see the last member of his family again. He hung his head, trying manfully to stop the tears, but failing. Without a word, he stepped aside to let Charlie pass.

He signaled for Reg to help Rebecca from the coach, and once she was at his side they entered the house together. They looked around at the little farmhouse. Like so many others, it was just two rooms and a loft. The room they entered had been the main room, where the family gathered for meals, cooked, washed, and lived.

The other room was probably the parents' bedroom, while the children would have slept in the loft. But instead of the orderly farm living room they expected, what looked like all of the furniture the family owned was crowded into the room, in various states of disassembly. The kitchen table was turned on its side and shoved to one side of the door into the bedroom. They looked at one another, then went to the bedroom door.

Every piece of furniture had been removed, and all the bedding had been laid on the floor. A carefully tended fire was burning to keep the little room warm, and a spider was set to one side with a small pot hanging from it. Clearly, the boy had been warming the soup that Sarah had included in his basket at the fire. Sitting in the middle of the room was a little girl, happily playing with her rag doll. She looked up and smiled. "Hello. Are you Darby's friends?"

Rebecca gripped Charlie's arm as she managed to force a smile to her face. "Yes, we are Darby's friends. Are you Suzanne?"

"Yes, ma'am." The little girl stood up. "Where is Darby?"

Her brother was standing behind them and he rushed around to speak to her. "I am right here, Suzanne. Everything will be all right. I promise." He looked to Charlie. "Please, do not take her away. I am taking good care of her."

Charlie looked at Darby, then at Suzanne and finally at Rebecca before returning his attention to the boy. "How long have you been taking care of her by yourself, lad?"

His head dropped. "Since ma and Judah passed a month ago."

Rebecca pulled away from her husband and moved the table so she could enter the room. She knelt down next to the little girl and brushed her red hair from her face. "Suzanne, how would you and Darby like to come back to our house? We have plenty of room, lots of good food, clean clothes and soft beds, and there is another little girl there you could play with."

Suzanne perked up at the mention of another little girl to play with.

All Darby heard was Rebecca talking to Suzanne about taking her away from his home, from their home. He did not hear that he was invited as well. He turned away, sobs shaking his thin shoulders. He was about to lose the only person in the world he loved and who loved him.

Charlie's hand settled on his thin shoulder. "Hush, lad. You are both welcome. It has been a hard month for you, has it not? And I need a good lad to come and help me. Getting around is not real easy for me." He gave his cane a couple gentle taps on the old wood floor.

The boy looked up and wiped his nose on the sleeve of his sweater. "I can come, too? You mean you do not just want her because she is a girl?"

"You can come too, lad. But you have to tell me what happened here over the last couple of months–what happened to your mother?"

"She and Judah got sick. It got worse." He looked over at the cradle where the small child must have slept. "Judah went first, then ma just closed her eyes one night and never woke up."

"So why did you keep it secret? You could have come to town, gone to the church and gotten help. And what did you do with their bodies, Darby?"

"I, I, I buried them, sir. And I read from the bible. It was as proper a burial as I could make it. I swear it was. I just did not want to lose Suzanne too. She is all that is left of my family. My sister is all there is, sir."

He looked at this boy, young man, really, with compassion and deep respect. He could not be more than ten years old, but he had shouldered a burden that had broken many men before him and survived.

Very gently, he answered, "No, Darby, Suzanne is not all there is. Mrs. Redmond and I are here now, and I promise, we will not break you and Suzanne apart. So, what is it to be? Will you come with us?"

Darby nodded. He knew that even if they decided not to keep them together, they would probably keep Suzanne because she was a sweet little girl and she would have a good life. "Yes, sir. We will go with you."

He put his hand on the boy's shoulder again, giving him gentle reassurance. "You know if you come with us tonight, it will change your life. You will be raised as one of our children, sent to school, expected to study and learn. I do not do things like this lightly. I was cast out of my own home as a lad and had to make my own way. I know how hard it is. I also know how hard it is to trust someone you just met, but I think we can make a go of things, if you are willing."

The boy nodded. "I promise, sir. I will do whatever you like. I told Missus Redmond I am a hard worker. I promise not to disappoint you, sir."

He smiled at the boy. "I think the real issue is whether Mrs. Redmond and I can manage to not disappoint you and Suzanne. Come along, get your things together and we will go get a good, hot dinner and a warm bed for you."

Quickly, he went around the room, gathering up what few rags of clothing they had and throwing them into the center of a patchwork quilt. The last thing he retrieved was an old bible that he had kept in a place of honor on the mantel. Sadly, he looked at the empty bookshelf, then shook himself, bundled up the sad little bunch of cloth and said, "Shall we go, sir?" He took Suzanne's hand, the one that was not holding her rag doll tightly to her chest, and, with his head up, walked out the front door.

Rebecca kissed Suzanne on the forehead, smoothing back her curly red hair. She realized as she looked into the girl's sleepy brown eyes that her brother Andrew's hair had been about the same color. "Sleep well. Everything is all right now."

"Where is Darby?"

"He is downstairs talking with General Redmond."

"Are we really going to live here now?"

"If you like. We have plenty of room, and two more children are just what this house needs."

"I hope he decides we can stay."

"Do you always do what your brother says?"

"Yes, ma'am. He says I could get hurt if I do not listen to him."

She tucked the blankets around the girl and smoothed them over. "Darby is a very bright young man. He loves you a great deal."

"Ma told him to take care of me."

"And he has done a wonderful job, but he is just a boy himself and should be allowed to be a boy, so we hope that the two of you will choose to live with us."

Suzanne nodded and her eyes fell shut. Rebecca kissed her again and stood to check on Emily, who was sleeping across the room. On her way out, she lowered the wick on the lamp leaving the room bathed in moonlight from the widows.

Downstairs she entered the back parlor to find Charlie, smoking a cigar and playing checkers with Darby. The boy had been bathed and looked much better than he had several hours ago. He was dressed in a nightshirt they had found for him in more of Andrew's old clothes. She was very glad that she still had some of her brother's clothes and that they were being put to good use again. They both looked to her, Charlie winked and Darby put the glass of milk he had been drinking on the table.

"And how are you two doing? Suzanne is safely tucked in."

"Master Darby and I have come to an agreement. The lad is going to be my assistant, and with his sister Suzanne, will be staying on with us."

"I am delighted to hear that." She settled on the sofa and tended to her tea and removed some sewing from her basket. "I hope you and Suzanne will be happy here, Darby."

"Yes, ma'am. I want to thank you for helping us. I did not know how much longer I could keep taking care of her. I was taking odd jobs in town when I could, but I hated leaving her alone so much."

"Well, now you do not need be concerned any longer." She lifted the shirt she was mending and checked the stitching. "Do you have any relatives we should try and contact?"

"We have an Aunt Victoria, but she lives in Kentucky and I am not sure where."

"We will do everything we can to find your family, Darby, and let them know what has happened." Charlie looked at the game board and knew this match was at an end. "Now lad, go on up to bed. Miss Rebecca and I will be up in a few minutes."

"Yes, sir."

They watched him leave the room and then they both sighed at the same time. He looked over the rim of his brandy snifter. "Are you happy now?"

"What?"

"Two more children for the Redmond clan?"

She smiled, "Well, Charlie, what could we do?"

"Exactly what we did. Just tell me now, should we look at adding onto the house?" he teased, pushing himself up on his cane.

"Very funny."

He extended his hand. "Come on, darling. Let us tuck the newest member of the Redmond family into his bed."

~

Taking the steps slowly, Rebecca watched Charlie struggle to climb them as he often did after a long day or when it was particularly cold. She considered the situation and knew that they would have to find a way to fix this. She could not stand to see him in pain and walking these stairs every night caused him a great deal of it.

They walked silently into the room they had given Darby. Being an older boy, they had decided he would have a room of his own, since the boys still woke through the night and sharing a room with the girls was not an option with a boy of his age.

Entering the room, they found him climbing into the big bed. It looked as if the bed was going to swallow him. Rebecca sat on the edge of it. "Sleep well, Darby. You are safe here."

"Thank you, ma'am." He smiled at her and sighed as he sank into the fluffy pillows. "The bed is very soft and warm." He yawned, no doubt relaxing for the first time in months.

"Enjoy it. It is yours."

Charlie made sure the fire was properly tended as she took care of the boy; a slight smile twitched at his lips when he saw her lean over and kiss him on the forehead. There was no doubt that Rebecca Redmond was meant to be a mother. After the fire was cared for, he moved to the bed and gave Darby's foot a tug. "Rest well, lad. You will forgive me for not bending over; it is very difficult for me to get back up."

"Of course, sir."

Once they were sure he was tucked away for the night they went to their own room where he took his medicine and she rubbed the lotion over her partner as had become their final evening custom.

CHAPTER 5

Wednesday January 24, 1866

He sat, his chin resting on the back of his hand that rested at the top of his cane. He was happy to have accepted Rebecca's suggestion of converting two bedrooms at the end of the house and combining his office and library into the larger new room on the second floor. But the mayhem of actually building the office was playing out before his eyes as workmen bustled around while trying to avoid the men moving furniture in and out. Everyone dancing around the three women who were busy trying to get a handle on the dust and dirt kicked up by all the traffic. He was tired just watching them.

It was true; it would be much easier for visitors to climb the stairs to see him here than for him to trudge down to the ground level every day. Being a few steps from his bedroom was a blessing he had not considered until the project had actually begun and his wife told him it was his responsibility to make sure that the rooms were done to his liking.

As he watched the bustle going on around him, his mind turned to the two new additions to their family. Suzanne and Em had bonded immediately. He suspected that both little girls had been hungering for a playmate and certainly Suzanne's life had not been much fun in the past few months, no matter how hard Darby had tried to take care of her.

Suzanne had been a bit reticent for the first hour or so, but she and Em had quickly fallen into a partnership that looked like it had been there for all of their respective three and four years of life. Within three days of mutual discovery, they had become little terrors in taffeta, and were driving Rebecca and Tess to distraction at times with their creative mischief.

Darby was a whole different issue. The boy was so grateful to them that he was driving both Charlie and Rebecca crazy. He wanted to work, to help in any way he could. As a result, he wanted to learn everything.

He peppered Rebecca with questions about how the house ran and the barns and how she knew when to buy new horses. Charlie got questions about the library, and the work he was doing to start a bank. It was making the process of getting Cooke's already complicated paperwork done even more difficult when you had a ten-year-old popping up over your shoulder asking what this or that means.

He knew that things would get better, if for no other reason than the office shelves would soon be finished and he could put the boy to work cataloging and shelving their books. On the other hand, he dreaded the number of questions that he could probably generate about each of the books he was to shelve.

The experience gave him a much greater appreciation of what Rebecca had to deal with, as he had not even begun to consider the two boys, Buddy and Andy, who were only a little over a month apart in age and nearly a year old. Neither of them had considered the pandemonium that having five children, four of them close in age, would cause in their household. It had been easy to image it would always be quiet and manageable when the boys were infants in cradles and Em and Suzanne were content to play with dolls all day.

They were wrong. They were terribly wrong. Now when

Rebecca was not chasing down the girls, trying her best to make them into proper young ladies, she was soothing a toddler who had just been beat about the head and ears with a hard wooden block by his manically laughing brother. She told him she was absolutely sure those boys knew what they were doing when they began their little tussles on the blankets in the nursery. She said they were jockeying for their position in the family. Having them so close to the same age was going to present some interesting challenges.

"General Charlie?" Duncan brought him back to the present and he smiled at his friend.

"Yes?"

"S-sir, if you could s-step over to t-the library I w-would like to s-show you the b-bookcases that we have j-just f-finished."

"My pleasure."

He followed Duncan a few steps into the next room, which had been partitioned off by a heavy canvas to try and control the sawdust. His eyes grew large when he looked at the beautiful oak bookshelves that had been built into three of the four walls. These shelves would hold hundreds and hundreds of volumes. He was really glad to have Darby willing and ready to help him get them all cataloged.

"This is beautiful work. You have really outdone yourself."

"I could not have done it all without the assistance of my man, Eddie Rainey. I hired him a couple of months ago to help with some rough work, but found he is a very skilled carpenter."

"I would like to meet him and thank him for his hard work, then."

"J-just one more t-thing." Duncan grinned in a way Charlie knew well. The man had done something damn clever and he was dying to tell him.

"Yes?" The general played along. Like training a young colt, he gave Duncan his head.

"W-w-ell, sir, the men and I t-thought that r-reaching high up could be a p-problem f-for you and getting up a l-ladder would not b-b-be an option at all?" Duncan nodded slightly, looking for Charlie's agreement.

"Absolutely."

"So, w-w-we did this." He moved to the first set of cases. "You w-w-will notice the c-crank here." He pointed to a small brass and wooden crank at the bottom of the shelves, where they stopped and cabinets with doors continued to the floor. "If you g-give it a t-turn..."

He demonstrated by slowly cranking the handle. The shelves began moving forward, and as he continued turning the handle, the shelves slowly parted left and right, revealing yet another set of shelves. "T-this way, you get the s-same amount of s-space as t-tall cases, but you d-don't have to reach or c-climb."

"That is brilliant!"

He plucked the crank out of its socket. "If you t-t- take this and put it h-here," he placed the crank in a small hole at the base of the cases that had been revealed. "And c-crank it again."

The second set of shelves began rising, revealing three more shelves that had been built, tucked in behind the under cabinets.

"Damn clever, Duncan! Damn clever!" He nodded his approval and appreciation of the master carpentry job the young man had done.

Duncan beamed with the praise. Even now that they were no longer commander and commanded, he was glad they were friends and it gave him great pleasure to see his friend so happy with something he had done. "Thank you, C-c-charlie. I did this last s-s-s-set by myself. I thought the c-concealed s-shelves could be useful if you n-n-needed to h-hide s-s-something away."

"I will tell you now. You are the official carpenter for the Redmond family. Which reminds me; I have a project for March I will need you to work on. A surprise for Miss Rebecca's birthday in April."

"It will b-b-be my p-p-pleasure."

Before he could launch his idea at the carpenter there was a knock on the wall, and a tall, well dressed young Negro man pulled back the canvas and said quietly, "General Redmond, sir?"

He turned, not recognizing him, but motioning him into the room.

"I do apologize, sir. I did knock but…" He gestured to the other side and all the noise.

"It is quite all right. How may I help you, Mr.?" He extended his gloved hand.

The young man hesitated for only a second, before carefully taking the man's extended hand. "Coleman. Tomas Coleman." He shook his hand with a firm grip. The general was already impressed with this young man.

"What can I do for you, Mr. Coleman?"

"Well, sir, your cook, Sarah, is my aunt. She said that you were looking for a manservant, sir. I would very much like to apply for the job."

"Then please, let us go talk about it, Mr. Coleman. You are the first soul brave enough to inquire."

"Tomas please, General Redmond."

"Then you should call me Charlie." He grinned and led the man out of the noisy construction space, back toward the sitting room attached to his bedroom. "Give me just a moment, please."

The young man nodded and allowed Charlie to enter the room first. Very quickly he peered back and motioned him in.

"I just wanted to make sure Mrs. Redmond was not using the room. Come in, please."

Both men entered the room. Charlie immediately took his favorite spot in a well-padded chair near the fireplace. Tomas followed, but stood stock still in front of him.

The general gestured to a chair, "Please, sit down. Let us talk."

"Thank you, sir."

The young man unbuttoned his suit jacket and took a seat in a chair across from him.

"Tell me, Tomas. Where is it you hail from? Please, excuse the briskness of the statement, but you are clearly a well-educated Negro. You have not been raised around here."

He nodded. "You are right, General Redmond. My father, Sarah's brother, was a slave named Luke. He was the blacksmith for the Raeburn family. As you well know, sir, a man with my father's skills had certain liberties when it came to earning a bit of extra income. When my father found out I was going to arrive, he began saving."

Charlie nodded. He completely understood the motivations of a father when it came to his children. He was grateful he would never have to make such a horrible decision for his own brood. He plucked two glasses from the tray next to him and poured brandies. He extended his hand offering one of the snifters to his guest. "Please, continue."

He accepted the glass with a smile and a nod. "Thank you. My father bought my freedom before I was a year old. I was sent north to a live in a Quaker community. They raised me. They educated me and they taught me a trade. I remained in the north until after the war. I thought it would be very different than it is."

The general nodded again, understanding completely without the man having to elaborate. Many free Negroes thought the north would be a welcoming oasis after the war. They had been very, very wrong. In some ways, the victorious free north was far worse than the defeated former slave holding south.

"So, I came home, sir. Sarah and her kin are my family and I would rather be here trying to help make something good happen than sitting up north waiting for the other shoe to drop."

"I am afraid, Tomas, that footwear is still dangling here as well." He lifted his glass before knocking it back.

"Yes, sir. I understand, but I would rather be here with family. If I am to make my way, I need a job. I think that I would suit your needs very well, sir." He put his own drink down quickly before clearing his throat. "I even have," he paused, "military experience."

"Really? Under whose command?"

He sat straight in his chair and looked the general in the eye. "Colonel Robert Gould Shaw."

"You are hired," he stated, refilling both their glasses.

"So," Rebecca carefully tugged Charlie's boots until they both came off, landing with a thud as she tossed them away. "Tell me about this new man you hired today."

"Mmmm..." He groaned, wiggling his toes, finally free from the daily confines of boot leather. He reached out and took her by the wrist, pulling her to the couch next to him. "Only if you sit and rest with me."

She truly loved him and everything about him. This was one of those moments when she was reminded exactly why. He never asked more of her than he asked of himself.

Gratefully, she settled on the sofa next to him and unbuttoned the cuffs of her dress. He whistled slow and low as he reached out and undid the first few buttons on the back of her dress. "I wish, wife, I had the vigor to lay you down tonight." He chuckled giving her neck a gentle massage with his good hand.

"And please trust me when I say I wish I was awake enough to let you do it. This family life is tough, General."

"Yes." He nodded, completely amused as she sat there, allowing him to rub her neck. "Yes, it is, my darling. Had Lincoln had you commanding troops like you do the stables, children and the household, we could have ended the war a year earlier."

"Flattery will get you everywhere." She laughed, allowing her head to drop further under his practiced touch.

"I will have to owe this one. Perhaps after Buddy and Andy are off to college..."

They both dissolved into laughter. Rebecca fell back into his good shoulder and relaxed as his arms wrapped around her. She felt his lips on the top of her head and though she fought valiantly, it was not long before she was sound asleep in his loving embrace.

Though he knew they would be more comfortable in bed, he rested his head there, on top of hers, content to just sit there on the sofa, holding her and letting her rest. There would be plenty of time to tell her about Tomas tomorrow. It was not long before his eyes dropped closed and they both spent the night sleeping curled against each other on the davenport.

Thursday January 25, 1866

As the early morning sun penetrated through his eyelids, he immediately regretted his choice of sleeping places and positions. Though his body had been carefully numbed with laudanum and brandy by the time she had relaxed in his embrace, now the medication had worn off and the weight of her was excruciating.

Quietly, slowly and gently he began trying to rouse his slumbering partner. "Rebecca. Darling. It is time to get up." He kissed her brow and she gripped the front of his shirt. "Please my love. My hip…"

Immediately she was awake and up. "I am so--"

"Shh." He placed a finger over her lips. "It is all right. This just might not have been our best option for sleeping." He groaned and sat forward, trying to will both good and damaged muscles to relax.

She rose and immediately called for someone to bring a pot of tea and something to eat. She felt guilty that she had fallen asleep on him like that, knowing he would suffer through the night, never daring to make her move. "Charles Redmond…" She grumbled as she moved to his medicine cabinet and poured the morning dose of pain killer.

～

Shortly after lunch, Lizbet knocked on the door to Rebecca's office, and led another young woman in after her when Rebecca called "Enter."

"Miss 'Becca, this is my sister, Priscilla. We call her Sissy. I think she is as good a lady's maid as I am, and we both have learned our lessons from Aunt Beulah. I was thinking Sissy would be a good maid for Miss Charlotte."

She looked at the young woman standing beside Lizbet. The girl looked back, meeting her gaze calmly and straight on. Sissy said, "And I know how to keep my mouth shut. If I do not, Aunt Beulah will tan my hide."

Rebecca smiled. She had come to rely on Beulah and her family as if they were her own blood. "Well, Sissy, if Miss Charlotte likes you, I would be happy to welcome you to our household."

∼

Sunday January 28, 1866

It was the first Sunday in weeks that had dawned clear and at least not bone chillingly cold, just finger, toe, nose and ear numbing cold. Charlie ordered the largest rig to be brought around in time to convey the entire family to church. The two infant boys were well bundled and carried by Tess and Lizbet, the two little girls were in their Sunday best, and Darby was proudly wearing his first suit with long pants that was not a hand me down. Charlotte brought up the rear.

Rebecca had taken Darby and Suzanne into town the morning after they had first arrived at Redmond Stables and had ordered clothes for both of them. The suit and Suzanne's lovely Sunday dress and coat had been delivered the day before. Both children were thrilled and a little overawed.

As Tomas climbed into the driver's seat, Charlie and Rebecca settled their brood. He commented, "I do believe we will see a big turnout this morning. In the past month, the men who were in some of the farther flung Virginia divisions have started returning. I believe we even have a couple who were out on the western front back in town now."

"Yes, it is good to hear how many men from the old families have returned. I doubt we will get back to the bustling town we had before the war, but it is nice to see some familiar old faces."

"Oh, I think Culpeper may be able to return to economic health faster than you think. Several new businesses have moved into town – a blacksmith, a tailor, a chemist... why, we may even have a mantua maker opening a shop soon."

"Not even a new hat maker will help some of these women, Charlie. Sows' ears and silk purses and all that..."

"Oh, so you think that the biddy brigade will not benefit from her efforts?"

She chuckled and took Buddy from Tess. The boy was being particularly fussy and it was clear from his cries that is was the comfort of his mama he desired. "There is very little that could help them."

"Oh, dear, you are being a bit hard. Just think about all those poor, war weary men and boys that are coming home and looking for a welcoming smile. I suspect that the ladies will look good to them, regardless." He grinned at his wife. He generally enjoyed her little attacks of cattiness.

She only smiled and continued to cuddle the baby. "Perhaps they will stop fawning all over you as the other gentlemen come home."

He laughed at that. "I think that Richard, Jocko, and Duncan have all had their share of attention as well. What say you, cousin?" He looked at Charlotte, who was playing cat's cradle with the two little girls.

"I think that your wife is correct. The young ladies still find their heads turning when you drive by in your carriage. I do believe they are very jealous of Mrs. Redmond. To have caught the only man in several hundred miles with means and station. Things they very much desire themselves."

"Perhaps you will meet someone who touches your heart in these returning heroes."

"I am sure there will not be anyone who will pique my interest," Charlotte said quietly.

"I will be happy to introduce you to some of the gentlemen in town." Rebecca looked to the woman with a sincere smile. "If you decide otherwise."

"Thank you. I will keep that in mind. And thank you as well. Sissy seems to be working out just fine as a lady's maid."

Charlie looked at the two women, relieved beyond belief that they had settled the irritations between them and rekindled their burgeoning friendship. He much preferred this over Charlotte sniping and Rebecca angry.

~

The churchyard was filled with buggies, horses and farm carts when the Redmond contingent arrived. Richard and Elizabeth were standing in the portico of the church, waiting for the family to join them.

As they approached the church, Charlie heard some whispering around him, but paid it little attention. He was more concerned by the serious look on Elizabeth's face.

The doctor just shook her head as he and his family approached. "I do not think Reverend Williams will be with us much longer."

Charlotte looked toward Mrs. Williams, standing beside the choir inside the church. "I wonder how she will handle her change in circumstance when he is gone."

Edward and Grace Cooper joined the group by the door. They all exchanged greetings and asked Elizabeth about Reverend Williams' condition. Finally, Rebecca looked up, a strange expression on her face. "What will happen to Mrs. Williams when we lose Reverend Williams?"

The adults looked at one another sadly. Em tugged at Rebecca's skirt just then. "Mama? May I have my church cookie now?"

"Not yet, Emily, you must wait until we go inside. Be patient. Patience is a virtue." She caressed her daughter's face. "You are a big girl and can wait a few more minutes."

Charlie stated, rather gently but as matter of fact, "When Reverend Williams passes, we will find a new minister and he will take over the rectory."

Grace Cooper spoke up. "Well, I for one, hope that Margaret Williams has family somewhere that she can go to when he passes. Preferably family far from here."

"I suppose," Rebecca sighed, looking to her husband, "Someone should inquire, gently."

He raised his eyebrow. "Are you suggesting that I should? What about Richard here – as Provost, he is the official government representative here."

"Oh, no, Charlie. This is a community issue, not something the government should get involved in. Remember the whole separation of church and state thing in the constitution?"

Mr. Cooper stepped in. "Gentlemen, gentlemen, as much as I regret saying this, I am the one who must handle this issue. After all, I am the senior elder of this church. Speaking of which, if you will excuse me, I have to don my robes. Since the reverend is unwell, I have to conduct the service in his stead today."

"Of course, Mr. Cooper," Rebecca offered, taking Emily and Suzanne's hands. "Come, children, let us be seated." She entered the church with all the Redmond clan in tow except for her husband, who was still on the front steps talking to Richard.

She was pleased to see more faces this Sunday. New faces mixed with the old and some of the men she recognized as some who had gone to fight. She settled the children and continued to be the proper lady as several people spoke quietly with her as they waited for the service to begin.

Several men looked closely at Charlie and Richard as they entered, thinking that they recognized the tall dark-haired man with the cane, but unable to place the face. One in particular mumbled something about carpetbaggers invading Culpeper as he went to take his place in his family's pew for the first time after four years of absence.

Alexander Raeburn looked over to the Gaines' pew. He had heard of Mr. Gaines death and hoped that his widow would be open to his advances after her mourning was over. Instead, he was surprised to see Rebecca surrounded by a small troop of children of various ages and accompanied by a woman who Raeburn had gotten to know during the war. Yes, her hair was darker, her clothes were more subdued, but he was certain that the woman sitting with Rebecca Gaines was Lizzie Armstrong. He had met her several times when running courier service for General Lee's command.

The two gentlemen who had been chatting on the front steps entered. The heavier set one took his seat right behind the Gaines pew with a small, austere looking woman dressed in demure black and white. The taller one took his place in the pew beside Rebecca and took her hand in his own possessively.

Raeburn looked more closely at the man. No uniform, and a cane, one hand encased in a black leather glove, but the clean-shaven features were unmistakable. This had to be Redmond. Raeburn's men had faced him in skirmishes just before Vicksburg, and he had heard of the encounters between Redmond and Early's troops in the last months of the war from the handful of men who had made it south down the Shenandoah Valley after Custer had surprised Early at Warrenton. Alexander Raeburn sat in his pew and seethed, never hearing the gentle service, filled with hope for peace and reconciliation delivered by Mr. Cooper but clearly from the pen of Reverend Williams.

The service ended and the folks filed out. A slow buzz worked around the people chatting in the churchyard. They were subdued in respect for the reverend's illness, but after the hard winter when no one could make it into church, they were eager to greet old friends and welcome back those who had been far from home during the war.

Charlotte gracefully greeted Misses Simms and Reynolds, and with Rebecca's concurrence, invited them to tea on the following Thursday. A few people came up to introduce themselves to Charlie and several were surprised that Rebecca had remarried. Finally, Raeburn presented himself to her.

"Miss Rebecca. I was saddened to hear of the death of your brother and husband. I trust you are doing well?"

"Thank you for your condolences, Mr. Raeburn. I am very well. It is good to see you home." She turned towards Charlie. "Mr. Raeburn, I would like you to meet my husband, General Charles Redmond."

Alex turned and looked at the tall man at her side. Yes, indeed he was, and the man had the audacity to offer him his gloved hand. Raeburn ignored it. With a sneer, he responded, "Redmond. I swore outside of Vicksburg to deliver this to you if I ever met you face to face." With that, he balled his fist and delivered a fast, hard uppercut directly to Charlie's chin.

Rebecca watched in horror as his head jerked backwards and he fell hard to the ground. "Charlie!" She looked to Raeburn before turning to her husband. "Have you lost your mind, Alex?" She knelt on the ground next to him. "Darling?"

Richard stepped up and grabbed Raeburn's arm, clearly cocked to deliver another blow, before the man could strike out again. "What the hell do you think you are doing?"

Jocko charged over from where he had been standing with Mrs. White, Duncan and Samantha Carter and several other local people discussing the upcoming nuptials.

Several of the newly returned southern soldiers stepped to Raeburn's side. The situation looked like it was going to get ugly quickly, when Charlie spoke from the ground. "Good shot, Mr. Raeburn. If that was all the retribution I have been promised as a result of the war, I consider myself a lucky fellow."

Emily broke free of Tess and ran to where her parents were still on the ground. "Papa!" She flung her little body over his and then turned to Raeburn. "Bad man!"

Somehow the image of the little black-haired girl protecting the tall general, even if he was on the ground, was a little too absurd for even the angriest of the returned southern soldiers. Raeburn looked to his colleagues, then stepped back from Richard's grip. "Miss Rebecca. Gentlemen. Good day." With that, he extracted himself from the situation with as much grace as possible.

Richard's shoulders dropped with relief. He helped Charlie get up from the ground and handed Rebecca up as well. "Papa is fine, little one. Shall we go home?"

Rebecca looked at his face. Papa was obviously not fine. His left jaw was red and swollen and his eye was starting to darken noticeably. She needed to get him home and put some raw beef on that eye as quickly as possible.

No one noticed that Charlotte was pale and shaken. She had recognized Raeburn; now she could only pray that he had not recognized her.

～

Late that afternoon, Charlie came and collected Rebecca from the back parlor, where she and Charlotte had been knitting baby things for Elizabeth. His cousin looked up and winked at him as he took Rebecca's hand. He led her up the stairs to his new office.

There was a fire burning brightly, and the divan had been drawn in front of the fire. A small table sat before it, draped in a white cloth, while a bottle of champagne was resting in a bucket on the side table with two shining cut glass flutes waiting beside it. It was the last bottle left from their wedding. Leaning against the champagne bottle was a large white envelope. He whipped the white cloth from the table. There was a lovely meal of delicate finger foods, cheeses, rolls, fruits, and sweets waiting for them.

Wrapping his arms around her from behind, he whispered in her ear, "Happy anniversary, darling."

Leading her to the divan, he seated her, then opened the bottle of champagne and poured each of them a glass. "To the first year of what I anticipate will be a wonderful life together, my love. You have given me a home, a family, and most importantly, the love of my life."

She smiled at him and placed her hand gently on his abused face. "And to you, my rather battered knight in shining armor. Can we please stop having you be bruised and bleeding for the rest of our life together?"

He laughed and tossed back his first glass of champagne. "Darling, I truly cannot promise to avoid every fist that comes my way, but I will do my best and I promise to keep you out of it at all costs if our being together causes problems."

"And I will try to keep you out of situations where random fists are flying." She sipped her champagne. "But you know, Charlie, we may never get to go to town together again, with all the southern soldiers returning home.

He laughed and nodded. "So, darling, Sarah has made us this lovely supper. Can I get you something?"

For the next few minutes, they picked through the goodies that Sarah had assembled and reminisced about all the happenings of the previous year – both good and bad. That they had both survived the year seemed a bit of a miracle, and the degree to which their lives had changed, both because of one another, and because of the overwhelming number of displaced people and especially children.

He reached to get them more champagne and was reminded of the white envelope he had set aside. "Oh, by the way. Since it is our first anniversary, and the tradition is to give a paper-related gift, I got you this." He opened the envelope and pulled out a whole sheaf of documents.

"Why, Charlie! A whole pile of papers just for me?"

"Smart aleck. Please, read them."

She turned up the wick on the oil lamp on the table beside her and scanned the documents. It was the deed to forty more acres adjacent to their property. It was forty acres of prime farm and grazing land with a small grove of fruit trees at one corner and a lovely little vineyard in the other. It was enough to make Redmond Stables a full hundred sixty acres in the heart of Virginia horse country.

Her jaw dropped open. "How can we possibly afford this much land?"

"How can we not afford to add this much pasturage to our little horse farm? Anyway, I know how much you like the apples and grapes from that little grove."

She threw her arms around his neck enthusiastically.

He flinched, "Ouch," as he returned her embrace.

She looked a little embarrassed; both at having added to his discomfort with the bruise from Raeburn's fist and at the fact that his gift, in her opinion, completely out-shown her own. Rather hastily, she let go of the death grip she had on his neck.

"I did get you a little something. I had Beulah bring it in earlier so that you could find it when you came in here next." She took his hand and pulled him up, then led him to his desk. There on his desk was a beautifully detailed desk set, with a large leather blotter trimmed in silver and a matching pen and ink set with a delicate ormolu trimmed clock in the middle of the stand. On the pad lay a silver card case, opened to show new calling cards with Brigadier General Chas. H. Redmond (Ret.) and the notation 'of Redmond Stables, Culpeper, Virginia' on them.

~

Wednesday, January 31, 1866

Charlotte left the Cooper's store with her packages bundled in her arms. She knew Tomas would be nearby to assist her soon. She walked slowly down the street, waiting for the carriage Charlie had loaned her. She was slightly startled when a low voice burred in her ear. "So tell me, how is it Redmond has his wife and his whore living under the same roof?"

She looked around, startled, and frightened by this low, threatening voice with its southern drawl masking the venom in the question.

"Charlotte Redmond? Really, Lizzie, do you honestly think you can pull this off?"

She looked into Alex's malevolent eyes. "Mr. Raeburn, really, this is unseemly. And my name is Charlotte, not Lizzie." Her eyes scanned the street, hoping that Tomas would show up with the trap, or that Mr. Cooper or Colonel Polk would come around the corner.

"You are Lizzie Armstrong, whore and Confederate spy. You might not remember me, but I certainly remember you. Now if you would like me to keep your little secret, I am sure we could reach some kind of an arrangement."

"Sir, I am Charlotte Redmond, of Charleston, South Carolina, and I am General Redmond's cousin, regardless of whomever else you may believe me to be. Now, as the gentleman that I believe you to be, I ask that you leave me alone." She saw Tomas and the trap round the corner just then, much to her relief. "Now, my carriage has arrived and I will leave you."

Tomas noticed them as he drove up and could see that Miss Charlotte seemed to be very distressed. He stopped the buggy and jumped down, immediately placing himself between her and the man he knew was trouble. "Miss Charlotte, are you ready to return to the farm, ma'am?"

"Yes, Tomas, thank you. Here are my bags; just put them in the carriage and we can be on our way." She turned to Raeburn. "Good day, sir."

The ride home was tense. She had to tell Charlie and Rebecca what had happened. What would she do if he spread this ugly, and unfortunately true, rumor?

∾

Thursday, February 1, 1866

After the encounter with Raeburn the previous day, Charlotte was more determined to make friends with the ladies of the town, if for no other reason than to help dispel the rumors that he could start if he chose. She needed to convince these women that she was indeed General Redmond's cousin who had spent the war years in France. The Misses Simms and Reynolds were due that afternoon for tea. Rebecca had been very kind, asking Sarah to prepare an especially nice tea for the ladies, but had found an excuse to absent herself.

The afternoon came, and the two ladies showed up at the front door. Reg let them in and escorted them to the formal parlor, a room which was not used much by the family but held Rebecca's best furnishings and decorations.

She had brought down her latest pattern books and a couple of French magazines she had gotten last year when trade opened up between Baltimore and Europe. She had every edition of Godey's Lady's Book published in the past five years, and several lovely pattern books with full color prints.

The ladies oohed and aahhed over the new dress lines, with the slimmer skirts and the more flowing lines. They enjoyed the lovely little delicacies provided by Sarah, while Charlotte regaled them with tales of French dinners that were entirely drawn from novels and magazines. She told them of making sketches of lovely gardens and fountains, and the charming manners of French gentlemen. All in all, she did a fairly decent job of manufacturing a life in France that was believable and not overstated, but vastly appealing to the fashion-starved, provincial ladies of Culpeper.

When they left, she retreated to the back parlor. Rebecca, in her normal farm clothes, was sitting there scanning some papers, when she walked in. "My God, they can do nothing but simper, whine, and wrangle. Is this the level of all social interactions in Culpeper?" She flopped into a chair, shaking her head. "If this is who and what I have to deal with in my new life, I swear, I shall go insane."

Rebecca laughed. "No, they are not the indicator of social sophistication here. I think you will like Grace Cooper, and Missy Frazier is incredibly funny and charming. You have met the younger representatives of the biddy brigade, led by Mrs. Williams. Doomed to be forever trying hard and failing miserably."

~

Wednesday, February 7, 1866

The children were just waking up from their afternoon naps when Tess and Mama gathered them all up and took them into the nursery playroom. A large square of canvas had been laid out in the middle of the floor, and Papa was sitting in the middle of the canvas with a pile of pillows under him, waiting for them. Sarah had come up from kitchen personally, bringing a large tray covered in a huge white cloth. She sat the tray down on the floor beside Charlie and pulled the cloth off to reveal a veritable cornucopia of goodies surrounding a large pot of tea.

There were butterscotch cookies, bowls of bread pudding and cream, another bowl of stewed apples with raisins popping through the rings in the center, and lovely little cakes with lemon curd filling. There were dried apricots stuffed with cream, and a small bowl of Turkish delights covered in a fine coating of powdered sugar.

Em burst through the door, took in the feast that surrounded her father and immediately dove to his side, grabbing for a butterscotch cookie as she went. Tess and Rebecca put the two boys down on the canvas and joined them. Darby took Suzanne's hand and the two of them took seats on a small bench to one side of the room.

Charlie looked up at the two children. "You two. Come on down here. It is Buddy's birthday, and in this house, we celebrate birthdays. Not only can you have as much as you like, but there are no table manners here, because, well, there is no table."

"Yes, sir, General Redmond." Slowly, Darby and Suzanne eased over to the canvas and sat themselves down on the edge of it.

Charlie shook his head. They were still adjusting to life in what was now a noisy, boisterous family. He knew it would take time, but it would be worth it.

Em piped up just then. "Suzanne, try these cookies. They are the best!" She was already leaving a trail of crumbs as she reached across the canvas to give the older girl a cookie.

Rebecca grabbed a small bowl of bread pudding and a spoon and started stuffing the sweet treat into Buddy's gaping mouth. Tess did the same for Andy.

Very tentatively, Darby reached out for some of the stewed apples, taking a spoonful. The expression on his face was priceless. It was as if he had just put a spoon full of the ambrosia of the gods into his mouth. Suzanne found the Turkish Delight.

Over the course of the next half hour, every child on the canvas had managed to taste all the delectable goodies. Taste them. Smear their faces with them. Smear their parents with them. Smear their hair with them. In fact, the occupants of the room looked like they were the survivors of a vicious food fight. Or perhaps viscous food fights. Sarah stood to one side, enjoying the sight of these children wallowing in the product of her culinary efforts.

As the feeding frenzy subsided, Sarah stepped aside and pulled the bell down to the kitchen. Reg and Tomas were waiting for the signal from Sarah to bring up buckets of hot water. Everyone in the room needed a good scrub.

CHAPTER 6

Friday, February 9, 1866

Charlie sat reading the paper and drinking his morning coffee. Whatever he was reading caused him to shake his head repeatedly. Rebecca watched this for a few minutes, then said, "Darling, what has you so annoyed?"

"Oh, the idiots in Washington are about to create a bloody mess. Some of them want to punish the south for the war, some of them want to leave the Negros in limbo, neither truly citizens nor slaves, which some say is as good as leaving them as economic slaves, and some just want to pretend that none of it ever happened and go back to things as they were before the war except that the Negros are no longer property."

She looked at him, a concerned frown line between her brows. "Well, you and I both know that conditions are pretty harsh. You have been down to Slabtown. Conditions there are terrible and there is no one to speak up for them."

"Frederick Douglass went and called on Mr. Johnson last week, asking him to support giving Negro men the vote. That was not well received. According to the paper, Mr. Johnson told Douglas that "if the poor whites and the poor blacks were thrown together in the ballot box, a race war would ensue."

He looked up from the paper. "I fear that if the black man does not get the vote, eventually a race war will ensue. Someone has to defend the rights of these people, and if the old powers that be – the rich white men – continue to control government, especially in the south, then the role of the black man will continue to be servitude in one form or another." The general shook his head again. "Johnson is a fool. In some states, there are more blacks than whites. What will happen when the black man gets fed up with being kicked like a dog? I fear they will turn, just as a cornered dog would attack."

Tuesday February 13, 1866

Charlie was very comfortable in his new second floor office. On cold, damp mornings like this, he could dress in the warmth of their bedroom, limp a few feet down the hall, have his breakfast brought to him at this desk, and work there with his back to the fire, and the view of the lake and paddocks in front of him. The entire back wall of his office was windows and French doors, opening onto the veranda that surrounded the back of the house.

While Tomas worked on the library side of the room with Darby, carefully cataloging and ordering the books, his morning had been spent going over the significant amount of paperwork that Cooke, Fisk, and their friends had forwarded about implementing a sound long-term investment program for the proposed Farmers and Merchants Bank of Culpeper.

After several hours of trying to make sense of the complex numbers through the blur of an additional dose of laudanum to deaden the pain that last night's snowfall had brought, he had finally given up. He just sat there, looking out over the pond, the willow tree, and the rolling fields all clothed in a thin blanket of white.

He stood up and limped over to the window in the far corner of the room, meaning to adjust the window sock, the roll of fabric filled with sand that blocked any drafts around the window sash. As he approached the window, he noticed a small, gray something crouched on the outside of the window ledge.

The gray thing moved, seemingly sensing him at the window. It was a cat. Apparently a barn cat had found its way out of the snow and to the windowsill. The cat uncurled and stood to stretch, having been disturbed from its nap. As his back arched, Charlie noticed that this relatively young cat looked almost as battle worn as he was. There was a significant chunk missing from its left ear, a large scar on the back of its head, and there appeared to be a permanent crook in its tail.

Instead of sealing the window more soundly, he pulled up the sash. The cat walked in and jumped to the floor with a slightly awkward twist followed by a definite thud. It seemed as if he had been waiting for Charlie to open the window. "Not light on your feet today, are you, fella?" He shook his head. If Rebecca knew he had let a barn cat into the house, she would have a hissy, mostly about fleas. He sighed, smiled to himself and closed and sealed the window.

Charlie and the cat limped back over toward the fireplace. The man headed back toward his desk, and the cat made a beeline to the hearth.

The cat looked at the fire, turned his head slowly to Charlie then back to the fire. He made small circles for a few seconds and then folded himself up in a neat compact pile on the hearthrug.

All was quiet in the room for several minutes; the only sounds were the slow ticking of the clock over the mantle and the low hum of the cat's purring. Promptly at twelve o'clock, several things happened at once. The clock on the mantle began ringing the hour. On the third stroke of the chime, the door burst open and in bounced Em and Papa Puppy, followed by Sarah carrying a tray with Gen'l Charlie's lunch. The Jack Russell terrier immediately noticed the interloper on the hearthrug.

Even before the dog could get a proper sniff, the cat rose in a classic feline arch with claws bared and swiping at the puppy. A direct hit sent to dog squealing to little Em. The cat sat down, staring directly at the dog, daring it to come back near the hearth. Before Em could react to what was happening to her precious Papa

Puppy, the dog scampered out the door. With a sniff and a quick lick to his claw, the cat resumed his position on the rug.

"Papa, what is that? And what did it do to my dog?" She was torn between chasing after her dog and examining the new feature of her father's office.

"Easy, Em." He was quick to scoop up his little girl. "This is a kitty that has come in to get warm, but I do not think he wants to be disturbed. He let Papa Puppy know that. Your pup will be fine."

"Papa got a kitty! Papa got a kitty!" She bounced up and down on her father's lap, a behavior that he tolerated most of the time.

When she had started this practice of bouncing back and forth on his knees, he had been completely healthy and she had been an underfed, skinny two-year-old. But now, the little girl was not as light as she used to be, her body solid with good food, plenty of exercise, and the natural growth that time inevitable brought all healthy children.

She finally noticed her father's set jaw. "Papa hurting again?" She immediately settled into his lap and looked up at him with concern in her young eyes.

"Just a bit, little one. Now, will you join me for lunch? And," he plucked a cookie from the tray, "you may have Papa's cookie if you promise not to mention kitty to Mama."

She looked at her father with a sly glint in her eye. She had come to recognize bribery when she saw it. "Mama thinks cats should stay in the barn," she declared while eyeing the cookie.

A short silence ensued while he waited to see what his daughter's devious little mind would do with this information. Her next declaration was based on personal experience. "Mama would make kitty go back there."

A few more minutes passed, as both father and daughter picked at the slices of baked chicken that was the main part of their lunch. A bowl of succotash, put up the previous summer, a couple of biscuits and butter, and some collard greens completed the lunch, with butterscotch cookies for dessert. She eyed the cookies again, chewing on another slice of chicken. "I have cookie now?"

"Do you promise? Not a single word to Mama. I think it is perfectly fine for the kitty to be in my office."

"Two cookies? And no succotash?"

He sat back in his chair and stared at his daughter. "One cookie and half your succotash."

She screwed her little face up. Succotash was not her favorite vegetable by any means. But half was better than all, so she grinned at her father and nodded. Still, it was worth one more try. "One cookie, no succotash, and extra greens?" She liked collards the way Sarah fixed them.

"Oh, Heaven help me," he mumbled to himself. "She has been taking lessons from Rebecca." He cleared his throat and nodded. "Yes, that is acceptable, but if you mention kitty to Mama, no cookies for a week."

Em looked very serious as she held out her right hand to shake with her father. She knew that deals were always sealed with a handshake.

He took her hand, feeling as if he had just signed a deal with one of Lucifer's little demons. He knew he was in real trouble when the boys started walking and talking.

While this intense negotiation had been going on, the cat had quietly moved from his place by the fire. He now lurked under Charlie's chair, sniffing the air with intense interest. Chicken, biscuits, butter–they all smelled fascinating to the scrawny tomcat.

Charlie felt something patting him on the leg, at first gently, then insistently. He looked down to find the cat, now perched on his foot, gently patting his pant leg. Without looking away, he retrieved a piece of chicken skin with a bit of meat from his plate. "I see your stomach has warmed up too." He lowered his hand, half expecting the chicken to be snatched from his fingers. He was pleasantly surprised when the cat gingerly took the offering.

He alternated between feeding his daughter and his cat the rest of his chicken. *Well,* he thought to himself, *there's plenty of succotash and biscuits.*

Saturday, February 17, 1866

It was a rainy night, with a cold wind blowing from the

northeast, but from the light and warmth in the dining room, it may as well have been a tropical evening. The three older children, Darby, Suzanne and Emily, had been invited to join the adults for dinner that night. While Darby usually ate with the adults, having dinner with the grown-ups was a treat for the two girls. And tonight was a special event. It was Emily's third birthday.

For this momentous occasion, the adults had dressed for a formal dinner. Tess had put Emily in her best dress. She was seated to her father's right, the seat always reserved for the guest of honor.

As she did for all birthdays, Sarah emerged from the kitchen, escorting Reg and Tomas, who were bringing up trays of food covered with warmers. The first course, in fact the whole meal, was composed of Emily's favorite foods. There was a lovely green pea and cream soup, followed by baked trout with corn stuffing. The centerpiece of the dinner was a roasted haunch of venison with mushroom gravy, and roasted baby potatoes and carrots. Dessert was a very fancy presentation of floating island. In fact, the dinner was Emily's first real grown-up dinner.

Emily and Suzanne both did their best to emulate Charlotte, as the most elegant woman at the table, in their manners, use of cutlery, and napkins. They probably would have emulated Rebecca, but since Charlotte sat across from them and Mama was at the far end of the table, it was easier to watch the tall, dark-haired woman.

Charlie and Rebecca kept glancing at one another, both trying desperately to suppress giggles of amusement at their three and four year old daughters attempting to behave as ladies of the Washington social scene.

As the meal drew to a close with minimal destruction of clothing and table linens, Charlie suggested to the ladies and Albert that they go to the sitting room for coffee while he and the children adjourned upstairs for some after-dinner games.

He led the children out, with Darby bringing up the rear. As they ascended the stairs and turned down the hall, the children were all surprised when he led them past the door to the nursery and down to his office. He ushered them in, where there were a stack of new games and a lovely doll sitting on the floor in front of the fireplace.

"Happy birthday, Em. I hope your doll joins the family as well as Reb did."

"Oh, Papa. She is beautiful." Em grabbed up the dark-haired doll and hugged it to her. "I think I will call her Lotty."

Suzanne looked on, wistful that she could not have such a nice doll.

Charlie grinned at Em. "I am glad you like it." As Emily carefully inspected the new member of her doll family, Charlie turned to Suzanne. "Sweetheart, it occurred to me that Em and Lotty would need to have a playmate, so would you get the box on the bottom of the pile over there?"

She looked very confused, but dutifully went and retrieved the bottom box from the pile.

"Go ahead and open it."

She tugged at the ribbon securing the box and pulled off the lid. Inside was a beautiful doll, the red-headed mate to the doll he had given Emily. She lifted it out of the box with great reverence. "Oh, Papa Charlie. She is beautiful!"

He smiled at her. It was the first time she had called him Papa Charlie.

Darby looked on, relieved that his sister was being treated as a full equal within their new family.

Charlie looked up and caught the boy's eye. He winked. Darby smiled back and nodded.

An hour later, Rebecca realized that Charlie had not come down for his after dinner coffee and brandy, nor had the children come in to say good night. She went to the stairs and listened. It was far too quiet. She carefully walked up the stairs, intending to creep up on them and catch them in whatever it was they were doing that they were not supposed to be doing. She cracked the door to the nursery. No children. She tiptoed down to Charlie's office, noticing that the door was slightly ajar.

There on the floor in front of the fire she found them. All four of them. Lying in a pile, Em, still clutching her new doll, with her head on Charlie's good shoulder. Suzanne was wedged in under Em's arm, with her head lying on his stomach and her new doll tucked under her chin. Darby lay beside his sister, his arm draped over her waist, his head on the General's good thigh. Charlie's head rested on a small pillow, the new story book he had bought Darby lying splayed open across his chest.

She smiled down at her little brood, pulled a throw from the back of the davenport and spread it over the four of them.

And for the first time in her life, Rebecca Redmond willingly went to bed without her general.

Tuesday, February 20, 1866

Edouard Huger, attorney and financier, originally from Charleston, South Carolina rode up to the imposing portico of the house he had been told to go to in order to meet General Redmond. Mr. Cooke had sent him and the two young clerks accompanying him to finish the paperwork to establish the Bank of Culpeper and the exchange and service agreements between the new bank and the other banks in Cooke's financial empire. The general had sent a coach to collect them at the train station.

The name Redmond had interested him. Once, long ago, he had a younger cousin named Redmond – a girl whose father had been a tyrant in the home and whose mother had been his aunt, his father's younger sister. She had disappeared long ago. He wondered if this general was any relationship to his long lost cousin's family.

Huger and his staff were met at the door by a proper southern butler, well dressed, well mannered, and well spoken. He was expected, and after appropriate steps to take their hats and coats, Mr. Huger and the clerks were escorted upstairs to General Redmond's office.

The tall man who stood up from his desk chair to greet him startled Huger. Here, in a taller, leaner, younger version, was the spitting image of his own father, black hair streaked with gray, eyes that flashed from silver to ice blue, square shoulders and regular features. "Ah, General Redmond. Edouard Huger at your service, sir."

Charlie took a deep, calming breath and, making every effort to deliberately mask his own Charleston accent, he offered. "Welcome, Mr. Huger. Will you and your assistants have a seat?" The tall man indicated a table with several chairs set to one side of the room. "I have ordered tea and a light bite to eat, as I am sure you are tired from your travels."

"Thank you, General. Forgive me, but you bear a striking resemblance to someone in my family. Do you have any relations in Charleston?"

He cleared his throat gently and retook his seat. "I do believe I may still have some distant relatives in Charleston. My cousin, Charlotte, is a guest here, and she is originally from Charleston."

"Charlotte is here? My God! We all thought that she had disappeared for good. I would love to see her again after all these years. You know, her father was a true tyrant. We heard he beat her publicly and that is why she left."

The general was very careful to keep his face neutral. "Yes, Charlotte has spent a great deal of her life abroad. She returned home after the war. She said she had no family left in Charleston and that is why she has come here. I am sure she would be delighted to see you. Would you join my family for dinner this evening?"

"Sir, I would be honored. But I have to say this. You yourself are the walking image of my own father. Are you sure you are not also related to my family somehow?"

He smiled nonchalantly, "Anything is possible, sir. You know how family histories can become jumbled."

A discrete tap on the door announced Beulah and her tea tray. "Shall we have our tea while you catch me up on the latest news from the city?" Charlie turned to the housekeeper. "Beulah, would you please prepare a room for Mr. Huger and one for his assistants? They will be staying with us for a few days."

The men talked politely of the latest headlines and news from the financial world while they enjoyed the tea and sandwiches that had been prepared. When they were finished, Charlie rang for Beulah and asked her to escort Mr. Huger and the assistants to their rooms. "I will see you at supper, then, sirs, and you will be able to meet my cousin Charlotte. Until then, I trust you rest well."

He left the room right behind Beulah and Huger. He had to find Rebecca and Charlotte and let them know that his cousin was in the house. He found them both in the little parlor at the back of the house, tending to some mending.

He leaned against the door and shook his head, "Oh, God, we are in such trouble. The man that Cooke sent down with the paperwork – he is my cousin and has already questioned me about being family. What are we going to do? I do not think you can get past his grilling you, Charlotte – there are so many family members and connections and I am afraid…"

"Charlie," Rebecca was out of her chair and leading her babbling spouse to the chair nearest the fire where she handed him a cup of tea. "Relax, we have been preparing for this." She looked to Charlotte, "Have we not?"

"We have. I have memorized your entire family tree. And anything I miss, I can blame on twenty years in Europe and life with my father's cousin and his family first in Philadelphia and then in Edinburgh."

"But what about my looks. The Redmonds do not have black hair and blue eyes; they all have sandy or brown hair and brown eyes. And he knows about the beating I took. If he sees your back, without any scars, he will know you are not Charlotte."

"Why on earth, would he see her back?" His wife knelt before him and palmed his cheek. "Listen to me, you must calm down and let Charlotte and I handle this. You may very well give us away with your nervousness."

Charlotte added her reassurance. "Charlie, if I had not chosen the career I did, I would have made an outstanding actress, able to take the stage with the likes of Junius Booth. I am sure I will be able to handle this. And what if he does figure out what happened? He is your cousin, one who probably understands just how vicious your father was. Do you think he would chance giving you away and bringing scandal to his own family? I think not."

"She has a point, love," Rebecca added softly. "I do think we will be fine."

"If you both think so, then I will be the consummate gentleman. But I remember just how sharp cousin Edouard can be. He is smart, observant, clever, and very knowledgeable about all of our family's history. Please be careful, Charlotte. Please." He had never been this close to being uncloaked. He was clearly terrified.

Rebecca looked thoughtful for a moment. "Charlie, I would make one suggestion. When you have to sign documents, please, just use your middle initial."

~

Dinner that evening was very formal. None of the children joined them, and Reg and Sarah's staff went out of their way to present a very proper service. Sarah's cooking was a tour de force of her best recipes.

Charlotte came down for a sherry before dinner, being offered to their guests in the formal parlor. She was very moderately dressed, in a dark blue evening dress that showed absolutely nothing that was not appropriate. She was also doing an excellent job of being demure, and showing the symptoms of a headache but soldiering through it to greet their guests and her own supposed maternal cousin.

She entered the room quietly. Charlie reached out to her and escorted her over to the guest of honor. "Charlotte, I believe you and Edouard are related on your mother's side?"

She looked at the man standing before her. He had a close family resemblance to Charlie, and by extension, to her supposed identity. "Good evening, Edouard. It has been many years, I am afraid."

"Yes, Charlotte. We were afraid that we had lost you forever. After the confrontation with your father – and yes, we all heard about it – we were afraid you were gone, either run away or some suspected the old man had killed you and hidden the body."

"No, no. He did beat me, but I ran away. I went first to his estranged cousin in Philadelphia, who I had known as a young child, but had not seen for years. My father and he fought over the business, you see, and as a result, had not talked since. From there, I went to the family in Scotland, and then on to study art in France."

"Quite a journey for a girl from Charleston." Edouard smiled. "Perhaps I can catch you up on our side of the family."

Rebecca stepped in at that moment. "Oh, Mr. Huger. We are so glad you could join us. I know how important getting a bank started back up here in Culpeper is to my husband. I think it is a major step in helping the community recover from the war!"

Talk turned from the Hugers and Charleston Redmonds to the post-war problems and politics, the number of northern congressmen who wanted to punish the south, and those who held to Lincoln's philosophy of benign reconstruction, which Johnson was struggling to implement.

Dinner was announced just then. They adjourned to the formal dining room, and Sarah and Reg staged a brilliant show. But as dinner wound down, with the lovely dessert of Charlotte Russe, coffee and brandy to finish being placed before them, Edouard turned his attention to Charlotte and their family linkage again.

"So have you heard anything from your Charleston relatives?"

"No. When I left, I wanted to leave everything of that part of my life behind. Mother had been gone for a number of years, and my father was a cruel and domineering man. Fortunately for me, his cousin, and more importantly, his cousin's wife were much kinder. It was something of a coincidence that I not only inherited my mother's looks, but that my cousin was also of French descent and had the same coloring. So I fit into that side of the family very easily."

"If you were to return to Charleston, I assure you that the Hugers would be happy to welcome you back. And since your father died, there are no more Redmonds in Charleston. Some time after you left, your father became quite ill--a long, unpleasant disease. At any rate, by the time he died, there was nothing left of the estate."

"Thank you for your kind offer, but to be honest, I think I would rather not go back. I have far more unpleasant memories of my life there than I do happy ones, and I have created a satisfying place for myself here."

Rebecca finished her coffee and suggested the party adjourn to the parlor. Charlotte pled a headache and escaped the evening with both her and Charlie's identities intact.

~

Thursday February 22, 1866

Several days passed with Charlie and what he had come to think of as "The Cat" surviving in peaceful coexistence in his office. He would let the cat in each morning, feed him odds and ends of scraps from his breakfast and lunch, and let him out in the evening. Occasionally, The Cat would announce a desire to go out by wandering over to the French doors and making a soft mewling sound. Inevitably, he would be back within a few minutes, reaching up with both paws to scratch on the glass.

One this particularly cold, wet day, everyone was staying inside, and occasionally Charlie could hear them moving around downstairs. He knew that today would be the day that Rebecca would probably meet The Cat. She would no doubt come up to his office for lunch since she had no work in the barns to tend to.

That morning after Huger and his clerks had left for the train, he approached The Cat intentionally for the first time. Usually the two basically left one another alone, but he wanted the animal to look particularly good for his first meeting with the mistress of the house – the anti-cat mistress of the house.

He found an old hairbrush that had been discarded because the bristles were worn down, and he had it in his hand as he carefully approached The Cat, lying in his usual place before the fire. "Come here, fellow. We have to make you look as good as you can before you meet the lady of the house." The Cat looked at him with the ragtag ear cocked toward him. Charlie settled down in a chair near the little beast. First he gently petted The Cat, and then cautiously slipped his hand around the skinny body to lift the animal into his lap. "Good boy. We need to be on our best behavior today." Very gently, he began brushing the cat.

The cat seemed to melt into the human who held him so gently and as the brush passed over his body repeatedly, he began purring and drifted off to sleep, trusting that the man who had him would not hurt him.

As he groomed the little body, he could see just how much damage had been done. Aside from the obvious, the chunk missing out of his ear and the permanent bend in his tail, The Cat had a deep scar in the back of his head and another long ragged scar down one flank.

"Looks like you have been through your own battles, little guy." He continued to work on the animal sleeping trustfully in his lap, letting him turn and poke at him, both without seeming to notice. "And such a young fellah, you are. I'm not sure if you are even full grown. Guess you tangled with that big tabby tom that runs the barn and lost, huh?"

He did not hear the door open and only when he heard a tea tray rattle did he even look up to find Rebecca standing at the corner of his desk, her right brow slightly cocked.

"What do we have here?" she asked, somewhat amused at the sight of him sitting by the fire brushing a scruffy cat. "Where did that come from?"

He stood quickly, dumping The Cat to the floor rather unceremoniously. "Hello, dear. Tea for us? Thank you. I did not expect to see you until lunch." He tried to brush his trousers as he babbled, trying to rid himself of the telltale collection of short gray cat hairs that stood out on his blue wool trousers like fuzzy Scottish tweed. The Cat gave a miffed yowl as the clock chimed ten o'clock, walked in tight circles as the clock continued to ring the hour, then curled into his normal ball on the hearthrug as the clock finished its racket.

"Yes, Charlie, tea. Now tell me, dear husband, where did that – thing – come from?" she asked even as she began preparing their tea.

Her emphasis on the word "thing" made him a little nervous. "Thing, dear? Do you mean The Cat?"

She sighed, the same sigh he had come to associate with the children trying her patience. "Yes, the cat. Where did 'the cat' come from?" She placed his tea in front of him and took her normal seat in a high back leather chair at the side of his desk. "That gray cat. The one sleeping in front of the fire?"

He gave her his most endearing smile. "Oh, yes. The Cat. He came in a few days ago, and was so beat up and thin that I just could not bring myself to turn him out. He is really a very sweet young fellow, dear, and so badly in need of time to heal from his injuries and put a little meat on his bones."

She bit her tongue and did not say the first thing that came to mind about putting up with a semi-feral barn cat in the house. Looking into Charlie's eyes, she could see that he had his reasons for wanting this little beast. "Is he hurt badly?"

He suppressed a desire to sigh with relief. Somehow keeping this cat had become important to him, and he had expected her to object out of hand. "No, nothing that time and good food will not cure. He has lost a chunk of ear that will never grow back, and has a crimp in his tail. I suspect it got slammed in a door or stomped on by a horse. Otherwise, he has some scars that I suspect were the result of coming off on the short end of a battle with that big tabby that rules the roost in the hay barn."

"Then perhaps we should see to it that he has a little fresh cream every so often." She understood now. He wanted to help heal this battered creature as he had been helped when he had been brought home. "Does it have a name?"

He laughed. "I fear I am about as creative as Em in naming animals. I have been calling him The Cat." Secretly, he had taken to calling him Sheridan, because the feisty little fellow reminded him of his commanding officer in a strange sort of way, but thought that she would think him totally insane if he told her.

"The Cat? I think that sounds exactly like something that Em would have named him. So tell me, what did her silence cost you?"

She hid her smile behind her teacup. She knew that Charlie had to have bribed her to be quiet because Em had been up in the office every day and it was clear The Cat had been here for a while.

He had the grace to blush. "A butterscotch cookie and a reprieve from half a bowl of succotash. All in all, a cheap price for Em."

"Indeed." She reached out and took his hand. "You know this is your house, too. If you want a cat in here I certainly cannot stop you. You should not let her have the advantage like that. Now it is butterscotch cookies; in a few years it will be new dresses and trips to Paris."

He covered her hand with his injured one. "Yes, I know, but she has been able to wrap me around her little finger from the first day I met her – just like you have. And when the time comes for new dresses and trips to Paris, you know that I will cave in. I am just dreading the day when she brings home some young man or other and says, "Papa, this is the one." Someday, we will lose her, so until then, I think that a little indulgence is in order."

"I think you have a few years before you should worry about such things. Who says I will be letting her out of the house? Any young man who wants my daughter's hand will come here and ask. Besides, with the way you indulge her she will never leave home," she teased as she leaned over and kissed his cheek.

He smiled and turned the kiss to his cheek into a tender kiss on the lips. "She will if for no other reason than to find the same kind of happiness she sees us share." He kissed her again, leaning across the edge of the desk. "But until then, between us, I think we can balance discipline and spoiling."

"Yes, Charlie. I discipline and you spoil. Seems perfectly balanced to me." She reclined in the chair and eyed the cat again. "Keep The Cat out of my kitchens."

The Cat heard his name spoken by this new person and rose majestically – well, at least as majestically as he could manage – from his normal place by the fire, and trotted over to her side. Before she knew what had happened, Rebecca found herself with a lap full of scrawny tomcat, his back feet in her lap, his front paws on her shoulders, purring madly, and stropping his face against her neck.

"Listen, fellow." She gently moved him from her face. "The master of this house enjoys your company and because of that you are welcomed here, but I think cats should remain in the barn to clear it of rats and mice. So you really have no need to butter me up." She did give him a pat down his back, feeling his spine.

Flashes of Charlie's pale hand against an army blanket made her a bit teary as she made a mental note to have cream sent up for him with her husband's lunch.

"See? He is a good little fellow. And he does need to put some meat on his bones. I think he had gotten too thin to be comfortable in the cold anymore, so came here for the warmth."

"Well." Gently she moved the cat to the floor, where he found his way back to the hearth. "It has been bitter this year. If I did not need to trudge out there every morning I might just curl up by the fire all day, too."

Charlie stood up from his desk and moved toward a chesterfield on the other side of the fireplace. "We could rearrange the furniture and curl up together for a bit."

"What a perfectly lovely idea." She rose from her chair, taking their teacups with her. "Of course, Em will be here soon and she will want her papa's attention, but until then I think I will indulge myself."

~

Rebecca came into his office early that evening. "Charlie, the children are waiting for their dinner. Would you please join us?"

"Yes, dear. I will be right there. Would you put The Cat out for me?"

She looked out the window at the sleet that was falling, leaving the world outside glistening with ice. It was beautiful, but cold and miserable. "What do you do with him at night?"

"I put him out. What else should I do with him?"

"It is bitter cold out there tonight. Perhaps we should let him stay in if he wishes."

He looked up from one of his ledgers. "Really?"

She sighed. "Really." She had noticed that he had taken to leaving one of his windows open a bit, no matter how bitter the weather was, so the cat could go in and out. "We can leave this window open tonight. I will have the staff check the fire overnight to keep this room fairly warm." She made a mental note to herself to consult with Duncan the next time she saw him about coming over to make some sort of door for the cat so that the cold draft from the open window could be eliminated.

"I think that would be very nice, Rebecca. I thank you, and The Cat, I am sure, thanks you."

"You are both welcome. Now, please come to dinner."

"I will be right there, dear. Just give me one more minute."

He watched her leave, hearing her mumble something about him running late. Once he heard the door of their room close, he moved to the fireplace and leaned over to give the cat a pet. "You had better behave yourself, cat. You have just won over the lady of the house. Do not upset her. You do not want to see her upset." He smiled when the cat yawned, stretched and promptly fell back to sleep. "Welcome to the family, Sheridan."

CHAPTER 7

Monday, February 26, 1866

The tall man felt a tap to his leg and he looked up, moving his hat back to the top of his head from where it had been shading his eyes. "Yes," he questioned the Chinese man across from him.

"We're here, Edgar. You must wake up now."

"Yes, by all means. I must be presentable for the good people of Culpeper."

The Right Reverend Edgar Vile, third son of a lesser British nobleman, bon vivant, world traveler, and minister. There was a certain irony there that made the right corner of the good reverend's mouth twitch.

He was being banished to this tiny Virginia town because he had overstayed his welcome in Britain. While the Church of England was not ready to actually defrock him if he would quietly disappear, handing him off to the American Episcopalians was a good alternative. Pater was also happy to have him shipped off to the colonies; so much that his father had promised a quarterly cheque of not insignificant magnitude if he would stay in the States.

"I'll go get the bags." His companion nodded.

"By all means." He stood, ducking to look out the window at this particular acre of Hell.

He was bitter at having to leave his homeland, but the politics of being a potential embarrassment to the Crown, even if only by association, were too much for him to stay at home.

Besides, he had been promised the people of Culpeper would be most welcoming and agreeable to his arrival. "Do hope there is a card game to be had."

Reverend Vile pulled the collar of his coat tighter about his neck against the spring chill, when he realized the obvious. "I'm afraid, Rex, we've been forgotten."

"You think?" his Chinese companion retorted even as he began supervising the unloading of the reverend's worldly belongings from the freight car. He looked back at his tall companion one more time. "The usual?" he asked as he craned his neck to make sure the largest of the crates were not damaged during the unloading.

"Yes, Rex. I do believe so." He looked around hoping someone – anyone – would approach them at the platform.

"Very well." The smaller man scooted away and began yelling, "Careful you! No drop box!"

Edgar Vile surveyed his situation. It seemed dismal. He retrieved the cable from his pocket and reread it, just to make sure. Reverend Edgar Vile is requested and commanded...his eyes roamed over the rest of the words...take responsibility for the souls of Culpeper, Virginia beginning February 1866....report as soon as possible to Edward Cooper or Charles Redmond.

He folded the paper, tucking it back in his pocket. "Edward Cooper and Charles Redmond, you owe me."

"Rex!" He yelled over the releasing of the brakes and other noises common to a freight train yard. His companion turned to him. "I'll go find the local inn or pub. Join me when you can!"

The other man gestured his understanding and turned back to the men unloading the car. "Careful. Please!"

One of the men grumbled as he hefted a crate out of the boxcar to a waiting coworker, "First Yankees, now Coolies. Pretty soon we'll be takin' orders from women and niggers."

Edgar set off down the street from the train station, paying careful attention to the flow of carriages and the occasional local resident on foot, which led him to the front of Jocko's Tavern. Now this was more like it. He smiled as he pushed the door open.

As he walked inside, the smell was delectable. The residual aroma of a thoroughly satisfying lunch still filled the air. *Just one plate or bowl left is all I ask*, he prayed silently as he moved toward the ordinary where Jocko was busy cleaning tables. "Excuse me, good sir?"

For reasons he did not understand himself, Jocko stood straight up at the soft British accent. He turned to find the tall, cloaked man leaning against the jam. "Yes, sir?"

"Would there be any of the lovely food left, the aroma of which is creating the grumble in my stomach?"

Jocko nodded. It was not the first time some poor soul had missed lunch, but the aroma of Esther's venison stew would always lure a straggler or two. "Yes, sir. Would you like it here or at the bar?"

"I think the bar will be fine. Thank you."

As Jocko headed for the kitchen, the minister headed toward the bar. He removed his hat, gloves, and scarf, laying them over the back of a chair. Then he threw his cape over his shoulders before taking a seat. In just a few minutes, Jocko returned with a large bowl and a plate of freshly baked rolls. "Here you are. Would you like something to drink with that, sir?"

"A nice Irish whiskey if you please."

"Aye, that we can certainly manage, Your Lordship." For some reason, his mild Irish lilt was more obvious than usual.

"It is only Edgar; my father holds all the titles in the family."

Jocko went behind the bar and rummaged in a cabinet for a minute, pulling a dust covered bottle forward and pulling the cork with reverence that was normally reserved for a fine, old French claret. He picked a crystal glass from the back shelf and poured a good three fingers of the golden liquid. "There you are, sir. Jameson's best, straight from Dublin, and in a glass of fine Irish crystal. Welcome to Culpeper. We do have some of the more basic comforts of life here."

"I can see that." He lifted the glass in toast, took a moment to appreciate the color, and give it a swirl in the glass. "Sláinte chuig na fir, agus go mairfidh na mná go deo." With a wink and a grin he threw back the glass and drained it in one draught.

Jocko looked at this very dapper gentleman in front of him, who one could easily mistake for a gentleman dandy were it not for the minister's collar, with growing respect. Not only was his Gaelic perfectly pronounced, a difficult thing in good times, but his choice of toasts was the classic Irish one for any good, hard drinking womanizer – "Health to the men and may all the women live forever." There were only a couple of small potential problems. Keeping enough Jameson's in stock and maintaining his own reputation as the hardest drinking man in town. As he refilled Vile's glass, Jocko suspected the man could drink him under the table.

Edgar was very keen to find out why he had not been met at the station but the food before him was just too distracting. He savored the stew. It had been quite a while since he had something so lovely and filling. He nodded as Jocko set the whiskey down, his mouth too full to speak.

The Irishman laughed. "I have only seen men eat like that when they are home on leave or recently released from prison."

The minister nearly choked on his food from trying to fight laughter. He gestured for him to wait and swallowed. "I assure you, sir, I'm neither. Could you by chance tell me where I might find a Mr. Cooper or a Mr. Redmond?"

"Aye, you will find Mr. Cooper probably at his store this time of day. Three doors down on the right, across the street. Mr. Redmond I cannot possibly say. He is a gentleman who does most of his business from his home office. I would try Redmond Stables."

Before the last 's' had fully passed his lips, Charlie happened to walk through the door. "Damn cold day, Jocko! Please take pity on your old boss and bring me something hot and alcoholic."

"Or," the barkeep gestured, "he might walk through the door yelling at me like he still has stars on his shoulders."

The general limped to the bar as quickly as he could, as Jocko poured him a large mug of coffee topped with a respectable shot of very good brandy.

"Thank you," he said as he swigged down a huge gulp of the hot mixture.

"Gen'l Charlie, this gentleman is looking for you or Mr. Cooper," he said, extending his hand to Vile, then turning to face the gentleman, who was just finishing wiping the dregs of the venison stew out of his bowl, an act for which he had saved his last piece of roll. "Sir, may I present General Charles Redmond?"

He hastily wiped his hands and swallowed the last bite. "Good day, sir. I'm Edgar Vile, and I believe I am to be your new minister." His hand went out in greeting.

In that moment, Charlie looked the man up and down. *My God! He is a dandy!*

Edgar Vile was taller than the general. Slender, elegant, with tousled wavy locks of blue-black hair falling past his shoulders, and a finely sculpted mustache and short spade beard. An extraordinarily tall, flared black beaver top hat sat on the table behind him, along with gloves and a silken scarf.

A black cape that fell almost to the tops of his boots was thrown back over his shoulders, showing a beautifully cut dove gray morning coat with a delicately embroidered vest in pale blue and silver under it.

Suddenly, the normally elegant Charles Huger Redmond, in his well-cut gray suit, navy blue greatcoat, and felt slouch hat looked and felt very ordinary.

He watched closely as Vile looked at the black gloved, obviously maimed hand that he stretched out to him. *Ah, we shall see the cut of this dandy. If his character is like his clothes, he will either give me a woman's grip or avoid my hand completely.*

Much to his surprise, Edgar simply blinked once, and then

further extended his own hand and shook, with a firm grip, though not hard enough to hurt.

"It is a pleasure to meet you, General Redmond. I do hope that we will find many subjects of mutual interest."

Edward Cooper came bursting into the bar, in his shirt sleeves and wearing the apron he normally wore during the workday at the general store. Jocko had sent a boy to tell him that the new minister had arrived, and Edward had literally sprinted over to the bar.

"Reverend Vile?"

"I am and you are," the reverend sized up the man. "Mr. Cooper? I was told you would be meeting me." The minister's hand went out in greeting.

"I fear you have the advantage of me, sir. I had not received the notification of your arrival."

Just then, one of the boys the station master used as a courier, as he was also the telegraph operator, came running in. "Mr. Cooper! I am so, so sorry, sir. Mr. Randall gave me this to give you yesterday afternoon, and I forgot. He yelled at me right proper, sir." The boy handed him a rather crumpled, distinctive yellow envelope that was used for telegrams.

Reverend Vile started laughing as Mr. Cooper hastily opened the message and scanned the contents.

Cooper looked up at him and smiled apologetically. "Seems I was to meet you at the train station this afternoon at one o'clock."

"Well, that seems to be moot. Shall we sit? In this disgusting weather, I could use another dose of blood warmer, and I'm sure you could use one as well."

The three gentlemen sat at a table in the corner of the bar by the fireplace. Jocko served each of them with their drink of choice; more brandied coffee for Charlie, Jameson's Irish whiskey for Vile, and Kentucky whiskey for Cooper. Just then Rafe Johnstone, the town's apothecary, came hurrying in. The messenger boy had been busy. Richard Polk was on Rafe's heels. As the two additional men settled at the table, Mayer Frazier came in, huffing and puffing from both the cold and from the unusual speed at which he had scurried over.

Cooper made introductions around the table as Jocko brought each of the new men their drink of choice. They settled down with the normal small talk of a new meeting.

"Revolting weather."

"How was your trip?"

"Where were you before you were assigned here?"

Within a few minutes, a small man in ornate blue robes came into the bar, carrying three large cases.

Vile looked up. "Over here, Rex!" He waved to the little oriental. As he slowly made his way across the bar, still carrying the bulky cases, Vile turned back to the gentlemen at the table. "This is my man-servant. I cannot for the life of me pronounce his name so I call him Rex. If one of you gentlemen would be kind enough to show him where to take my things?"

Charlie cleared his throat. "Well, sir, since Reverend Williams is still with us, the manse is not yet available for you, so I have offered to have you stay with me and my family."

"How kind of you! But I would not want to intrude. Perhaps this lovely, proper inn has a guest room or two?" Edgar grinned at Jocko, who was standing beside the table, gawking at Rex and his extraordinary garb.

"Oh, no! You will not be intruding – at least not any more than any of the other folks who troop in and out of my house. Honestly, we have plenty of room and I am sure you and your man will be very comfortable."

He turned to his old batman. "Jocko? Jocko!" The barman was still gawking, but jerked his head up to look at Charlie. "Could you ask Tomas to come in? He is waiting out back with the carriage."

He nodded and hurried out the back of the bar.

"Well, that is settled," smiled Charlie.

A moment later, Tomas came hurrying in. He stopped at his boss's side, standing at near attention, befitting his standing. "Yes, General Redmond, sir?"

"Tomas, please go with Rex to the train station." He gestured to Culpeper's newest target of gossip. "And help him collect the rest of his things. Then come back and collect me and Reverend Vile."

The valet nodded, 'Yes, sir." He gestured to the Chinaman to come with him.

Vile stood up. "Rex, a moment, if you please." He stepped aside with his manservant and held a quick, whispered conversation.

While the minister was away from the table, Richard leaned over to Charlie. "I think we should lock up our wives. I was feeling fairly handsome until he showed up. Then of course there is that fancy accent that will have all the ladies swooning."

The general smiled. "You have no problem there, my friend. Elizabeth's accent is just as charming, and she is totally smitten with you. But what do you think about introducing him to Charlotte?"

Richard did a double take. "Charlotte? Your cousin Charlotte? Charlie, he has only been in town two minutes. We should give him time to unpack."

"Well, yes, but the sooner I get her married off, the happier Rebecca will be. And by extension, Elizabeth. He has the looks and style that I think will appeal to my rather continentally inclined cousin."

Edgar returned to the table. "Thank you all very much for your warm welcome, gentlemen. I will confess that I was concerned about my arrival in this little hamlet, but I can tell that we are well on our way to being friends. Tell me, would there by any chance be a card game in town that I might sit in on?"

Charlie grinned. *Yes, this was exactly the kind of man that would appeal to Charlotte.* "Well, if you like a hand of whist, we play after supper on Sunday." He thought for a moment. "Of course, you may not think that card playing is appropriate for the Sabbath."

Jocko smirked. If he read the man correctly, poker would be more to his taste than whist. "We often have a group of gentlemen who enjoy a hand or two of poker on Saturday evening."

"Ah, well, if it is on Saturday, then I would not be breaking any conventions, would I?"

With that, Jocko settled another round of drinks on the table, and fetched a whiskey and water for himself. He reverently set the bottle of Jameson's on the table for Edgar and the men settled into more of the normal "getting to know you" conversation, including detailed anecdotes about Reverend Williams and his harridan of a wife.

Some time later, Tomas and Rex returned to report that the carriage was loaded and they were ready to go whenever Charlie and Reverend Vile wanted. Both were damp, as it had started to rain again.

The gentlemen prepared to go their various ways. Edward Cooper made his apologies, as he had to get back to the store. Henry Armistead had a freight delivery due in at the rail station, and Jonathan Randall, brother of the station master, needed to get back to his blacksmith shop. Duncan needed to return to his shop as he was steaming some fine wood into a curve for chair backs, a delicate process.

Richard went home to check on Elizabeth, who continued to suffer from the effects of her pregnancy and got a bit cranky if he came in smelling of liquor. That left Charlie to escort the minister to his home. The two men climbed into the open carriage and arranged themselves around the piles of boxes and cases. Tomas, with Rex sitting on the box beside him, took the horses down the street at a gentle pace. As they approached the church and the manse just beyond it, Charlie asked the minister if he wanted to see his new church.

"No, no, old boy, there will be time enough for that. What I want now is to get home and dry. Mr. Jackson's libations were warming, but dry would certainly improve my humor."

Given that the minister had managed to work through about half a bottle of Jameson's in just under an hour, Charlie was particularly impressed that the man could still walk a straight line, not to mention that his speech showed no signs of slurring.

"Um, Reverend Vile…"

"Please, call me Edgar. I am far too young a man to be permanently stultified." The minister grinned through the small waterfall running off the brim of his now nearly ruined top hat.

So they went directly to Redmond Stables. Rebecca would

certainly be surprised. Beulah would probably be more annoyed than anything else with another unexpected guest to accommodate.

As Tomas turned into the driveway, Charlie turned to Edgar with a somewhat concerned expression on his face.

"I have to warn you, with the number of people, and especially the number of children, in our household... well, I have been in military camps the night before a battle that were less chaotic that my house can be on occasion. And I did not have a chance to send a boy out to let Rebecca know that you were coming, so it may not be as warm a welcome as you might expect."

The minster laughed. "Please, don't worry. I like children! And a little chaos will bring some excitement into what has been a pretty dull life, what with the voyage over here as the only passengers on a mail steamer, and then trains from New York to Baltimore to Washington to Richmond to here." He paused for a moment, then added, "And the company of a lady, even a somewhat put out one, will be pleasant."

"Ah, well, if you want feminine company, my cousin Charlotte is also staying at the house. But be careful, because Rebecca's cousin, young Albert, who is our horse buyer, has been lurking in the upstairs hall waiting for a moment alone with her and trying to be debonair and charming."

Edgar laughed as they drew up in front of the house. "Ah, youth. Bring in a beautiful woman and a young man's brains will turn to complete mush!"

Rebecca had heard the carriage coming up the driveway and hurried to the front hall. She knew Charlie had taken the open carriage, and in this unexpected, cold rain, she also knew he would be stiff and miserable. So when she flung the front door open, she was stunned to see the carriage loaded with boxes and bags, a strange man sitting wedged into the carriage with him and an even stranger figure in beautiful but soaked exotic blue silk robes sitting on the box beside Tomas. She reached for the bell cords to summon Reg and Beulah and yanked on them urgently. She was going to need them. Immediately.

She ran out onto the front steps. "Charlie, darling! Are you all right?"

He pried himself out of the carriage and slid down to the ground. The strange man followed him, and quietly and unobtrusively placed his hand under Charlie's elbow to steady him.

"Yes, dear. I am perfectly all right. Let me introduce Reverend Edgar Vile, who the church has sent to be our new minister."

Rebecca looked at her husband's face for a long minute. The lines of tension between his eyes told her that all right was an outright lie. Then she turned to the elegant gentleman standing beside him.

"Reverend Vile, I am pleased to meet you. We have been expecting you, but thought we would have some warning of your arrival." She extended her hand to him as she spoke. He took it, and bowed over it, lightly brushing her fingers with his lips.

"My pleasure, madam. I am so sorry, but the young man who was supposed to deliver the telegram announcing my imminent arrival seems to have stuffed the message in his pocket and then got distracted. I fear I was as much a surprise to your husband and Mr. Cooper and the other gentlemen in town as I am to you now. I would have stayed at that lovely inn in town, but your husband insisted…" He trailed off, amused at the look that this lady shot her husband.

"Well, sir. I am sure we can find an extra place at the table for you and your… exotic companion. Or is he your manservant? We have room for both of you. But first, let us get out of the weather."

Rex jumped down from the carriage box. "I unload luggage, sir."

"Oh, I have called for our major domo. He will help you and Tomas unload and we will find a place for your goods."

At that moment, Reg appeared at the door, having run up the back stairs as quickly as he could when Rebecca rang.

"Ah, Reg. Would you please help unload Reverend Vile's things and find places to store whatever he does not need immediately?"

Beulah appeared at the door right behind Reg, backing up to let Rebecca usher the men into the house. "Beulah, please prepare the suite we discussed for Reverend Vile, and help Reg get him settled. Also, could you find a room for his man upstairs? And ask Sarah to set an extra seat for dinner?"

Vile gently interrupted this string of orders. "Rex has been with me for many years. He will stay in my rooms with me."

"Ah, well, yes then. Beulah please set two seats at the table." Rebecca was still in control, though her jaw was a little stiff at the sudden appearance of more houseguests.

The housekeeper bustled off to set things in motion, while Rex quietly began directing Reg and Tomas to sort the boxes and cases into two piles on the porch and out of the rain. The smaller pile was obviously to go to Reverend Vile's suite of rooms, the rest to be stored until he could move into the manse.

Rebecca led the men into the hall, and waited as they divested themselves of their damp coats, hats, gloves and scarves. "Just leave them on the bench there. Reg will take care of them shortly." She then led them to the rear parlor, and went directly to the liquor table, while both men went to stand in front of the crackling fire.

She poured three glasses of brandy, carrying them over to the gentlemen. "I suspect you could use this after this drive. When you are sufficiently defrosted, please have a seat." She settled herself in her wing-backed chair and took a good swig of brandy herself. "Then you can tell me all about yourself, sir."

A little less than an hour later, Reg appeared at the parlor door. "Miss Rebecca, supper is ready."

"Oh, excellent, Reg." She turned to Edgar, who had been telling her of his life in London and his travels to the Far East, and said, "Sir, will you escort me in?" Charlie brought up the rear, stumping along with his cane hitting the floor just a little more solidly than necessary.

The three of them strolled to the dining room, entered and settled into their seats – Charlie at the head of the table, Rebecca in her place as hostess at the foot of the table, and Edgar, as he had asked her to call him, to her right. Charlotte breezed in wearing a lovely blue and ecru house dress, and took her place at Charlie's right. Darby led Em and Suzanne in right behind Charlotte, and Albert skulked in behind the children, racing to take the seat to Charlotte's right while the children dutifully went to give each of their parents a peck on the cheek before taking their seats. Em settled herself to the left of her father, with Darby and Suzanne beside her, so that young Suzanne was next to Edgar. That left the seat next to Albert for Rex, who came in last.

As the people were settling themselves at the table, Charlie quietly took his small brown bottle out of his pocket and poured a bit into his water glass. A slight frown flickered over Rebecca's features. Rex, ever observant, noticed both actions.

Sarah and Reg came in with a steaming tureen of lovely pea soup topped with fresh cream for the first course. As they served the soup, Charlie introduced the people at the table to the two new members of the evening assembly. As Edgar and Charlotte looked at one another for the first time, Rebecca recognized the expressions on both of their faces – two people of summing one another up and liking what they saw. 'Hummm,' she thought. 'Perhaps I was wrong about Edgar and Rex.'

Charlie invited Edgar to say grace, and after the final "Amen," Rebecca slipped her spoon into the soup bowl and started dinner for all of them.

The dinner proceeded quite pleasantly, with Em being charmingly childlike, Suzanne and Darby quietly eating their meals like the half-starved children they were while attempting to maintain good table manners, and Charlotte and Edgar beginning an interesting verbal dance between them – at least as much as occupying separate ends of the fourteen seat dining room table would allow. Sarah had prepared a lovely roasted leg of lamb for the main course, with a compliment of early greens accenting turnips, carrots and sweet potatoes from the root cellar. Dessert was a trifle made with pound cake, whipped cream, and Sarah's lovely raspberry preserves.

Tess came to collect the children after dinner and take them off to prepare for bed, while the adults all adjourned to the parlor for coffee and brandy.

Rex gravitated to a chair set toward the back of the room, away from the fireplace and from where he could watch all of the others in the room. Rebecca went to pour the coffee, while Charlie served up snifters of brandy to anyone who wanted one.

Edgar took two snifters from Charlie, and carried one over to Charlotte, handing it to her gallantly, taking a seat on the loveseat beside her. The energy between the two of them was palpable.

Albert took his snifter, looked at Charlotte and the new, handsome, dapper and worldly man sitting together, threw his brandy back in one gulp and rather sullenly excused himself. Rebecca watched him leave the room. 'Going to go sulk, I expect,' she thought.

The talk turned to the recovery of the town of Culpeper after the war, and the stress of trying to mix migrating northerners with returning southerners in a town that had been swept through by both armies on multiple occasions. A short time later, Tess came to say that the children were ready for bed. Charlie and Rebecca excused themselves for a few moments to tell their children goodnight. That left Charlotte and Edgar chatting in front of the fire and Rex quietly watching from the corner.

They returned some time later, laughing together over something one of the children had said as they were tucked in, though Charlie was now moving very stiffly, his limp far more pronounced. Rex watched as he took another sip from the small brown bottle in his pocket. It was clear that everyone in the room was starting to feel the effects of a long day, and after another half hour of small talk, Rex quietly stood and motioned to Edgar to excuse himself.

Charlie and Rebecca escorted Edgar to his room, with Rex again quietly trailing behind. Charlotte went to her room and firmly shut the door. Albert peaked out of his door, watching the activities in the hall before firmly, and not as quietly as he could have, shutting his door.

~

Rex had sorted out their most urgently needed things from the piles of luggage, and had laid out Edgar's night shirt on the bed. He had also thrown a blanket over the day bed in the sitting room for himself – his normal sleeping arrangements when his company was not requested in the bed.

As the two men prepared for sleep, Rex remarked, "So, Edgar. Will you be pursuing this dark-haired beauty? You usually prefer the lighter haired women, but I noticed you seemed to be taken with her."

"I really don't know. She's a beauty for sure, but it might be inappropriate to abscond with the affections of my host's cousin just as I am settling into a new post."

"Since when did being inappropriate ever bother you before?"

Edgar laughed. "Yes, well, you certainly have a point there. We'll just have to wait and see, won't we?"

CHAPTER 8

Tuesday, February 27, 1866

Edgar and Rex joined the family for breakfast on their first day at the Redmond abode, both conducting themselves very quietly, and respectively paying a great deal of attention to the coffee and tea pots.

As the family was finishing their meal, Edgar addressed Charlie. "General Redmond, I do hate to impose on you this early in our stay, but I feel it imperative that I call on Reverend Williams as soon as possible. Would you lend me a trap and a horse so I may go into town?"

"Why, certainly. Or you can come with me, as I also need to go into town to see our friend Mr. Armistead about some wood and Mr. Nailer about some building I need to have done. Rebecca and I have decided to build a small collection of houses on the edge of our property for our staff. I am thoroughly disgusted by the conditions in those damn shanty towns they are trying to survive in. No human being should have to…" He stopped and shook his head. "I do apologize, I am afraid I get a bit frustrated with the situation. It will take me a couple of hours, at least, and if you are done before I am, I believe Jocko has something of interest to you at the tavern."

Edgar realized in that very moment that he and Rex had been welcomed into the home of two fine people who truly did care about all those around them regardless of rigorously imposed societal rank or station. "Thank you, General. I would be happy to accompany you. Rex and I can be ready as soon as you are."

A few minutes later and Edgar and Charlie were seated in the back of the trap, with Rex on the box beside Tomas. The day was bright and clear, the rain on the previous day had washed away any dust and there was a bright sparkle to the spring-time greenery.

Charlie casually pointed out the various points of interest on the way, although Edgar really could not tell the difference between one grove of trees and another. The fields and the many little streams that wove through them were equally pastoral and boring.

Tomas pulled up in front of the manse. As Edgar and Rex disembarked, Charlie offered, "Jocko's is one block up this street and three blocks that way." He pointed. "If I am not out front waiting for you when you are done, I will meet you there."

Edgar smiled up at his host. "Thank you, General. We will see you in a short while." Then he turned, squared his shoulders, arranged his bible in his left hand, straightened his collar and strode up the walkway to knock on the door. He had already heard plenty of tales of what he was about to encounter in the form of Mrs. Williams.

The door was opened almost immediately by a short, plump woman dressed in black with white lace collar and cuffs. "Mrs. Williams? I am Edgar Vile. I have come to call on your husband."

"Come in, Reverend Vile. We heard you arrived yesterday and have been expecting you." Her tone implied that she thought he should have presented himself immediately upon arrival.

"Thank you, madam. I would have come sooner, but given that I was soaked to the skin, and that your husband is so ill, I felt it advisable to get dry and make sure I had not contracted the grippe in the weather before I called."

"Oh, yes. Of course." She certainly had not expected the precise, upper class British accent. Nor had she expected someone so tall that he literally looked down his nose at her. "May I fetch you a cup of coffee? Or tea?"

"No, thank you, madam. I would like to meet your husband. Perhaps you could show my man, Rex, around the house, so he can get an idea of what will need to be done."

For the first time, Mrs. Williams looked directly at the little Chinaman who had been following Reverend Vile so quietly. He could be a definite fly in the ointment of her plans to stay on as the unmarried minister's housekeeper. But she smiled, a rather forced smile, and replied, "Yes, of course. Mr. Williams is right in here." She opened a door into a sunlit room with walls lined with bookshelves, a large desk, and a wan gentleman lying on a day bed where he could look out the windows. "James, dear. Reverend Vile is here to see you."

Edgar walked in and knelt beside the sick man, taking his hand into his own. "Reverend Williams, I am Edgar Vile. I am so sorry we have to meet under these circumstances."

"No, no, Reverend Vile. Every man has his time on this stage of life. Now it is my time to prepare to move on to be by the side of my God. So please, pull up a chair so we can have a proper conversation." The sick man's voice was barely a whisper, yet even so muted, Edgar could hear traces of the gentle power the man must have had when standing in the pulpit.

"Let me cut right to the chase, Reverend Vile. I am not much longer for this world, and will never be in a position to mount the pulpit steps again. So you must take on the responsibilities for these souls as quickly as you can. I fear that I can only give Mr. Cooper my best homilies for another Sunday or two until the congregation catches on that he is reading old sermons." The sick man smiled a gentle and slightly ironic smile." And Cooper never did have the presentation a good minister has to have to get through to his audience."

"Well, sir, shall we find out what a proper British accent will do to their listening skills? I believe I can handle this Sunday's service, if you wish."

"Oh, I more than wish. If I could, I would order you to, I would. I think perhaps the Good Samaritan? A fine introduction for you, sir, who are yourself one." He drew a labored breath, coughed, then murmured, "Would you pray with me?"

For a few minutes, the two men sat in silence together, then Edgar, very softly, began reciting a prayer for the sick from the Book of Common Prayer. When he was done, the old man was sleeping peacefully.

He looked around the bookshelves for a few minutes, noticing that there was a good, though conventional, collection of theological works that he suspected would stay with the house. He then let himself out into the hall, and sat down to await the return of Rex and Mrs. Williams.

∾

Mrs. Williams looked askance at the Chinaman, in his heathen robes of black silk trimmed in red and his obsequious manner, and brusquely said, "Come with me."

She led him through the formal front parlor, which was decorated in hideous pink and white flowered chintz, into the formal dining room with its walnut table and side board, and into the back parlor/breakfast room that was even more hideous with flower prints, flowered wall paper, and silk flowers in small vases on every flat surface.

"These are our formal rooms. Reverend Williams' office is on the other side of the hall, as you saw, and the pantry and winter kitchen are just over here." She crossed the hall into a cramped kitchen with a wash area and a large iron stove set into the old fireplace.

She then went back out into the hall and let him up the back stairs. "Our bedrooms and washing room are up here. There is one large washroom, and five bedrooms. If you look out the back window, you can see the summer kitchen, the outhouse, and the chicken coop. We keep a milk cow and Reverend William's pony in that little barn. All in all, it is not huge, but it is cozy and there is plenty of room for a family, should your master have one."

Rex said very little, just nodded and smiled, and thought to himself, *Dear God. Every room in the house would need to be stripped to bare plaster and redone. Did this woman only have taste in her mouth?*

Mrs. Williams looked at the little man with a calculating expression. "Your master does not have a wife, does he?"

He shook his head.

"Then he will need someone to look after the house and serve as hostess. Perhaps you might suggest to him that I could serve in that role until he meets the right woman for him?"

He shook his head again. "No, Missus. I look after house."

"Of course you do, Rex. But you cannot be the reverend's hostess."

"Reverend not need hostess. He good host. I good cook. We do fine."

She dropped the subject. This little heathen was definitely a fly in her ointment.

~

Thursday, March 01, 1866

Edgar and Rex could hear the gentle conversation, punctuated with the occasional laugh from one of the two occupants beyond the doors. He knocked soundly and waited for permission to enter. Once given, he opened the door and Rex dutifully followed him through.

"Ah, Edgar," Charlie gestured from his chair. "We did hope you would join us."

"Wouldn't miss it for the world, old boy. These evenings spent with such beautiful and charming company are balm for the soul."

Rebecca looked to Charlie and laid her hand on the man's forearm. "Do you want to be beautiful or charming?" she laughed.

"It is very clear that you are the beautiful one, dear." He winked at his wife, who just shook her head at the antics.

Edgar gave Rebecca a smile and continued, even as she handed him a drink. "I'm grateful that Rex and I have made such good friends so quickly. To that end, there is something we need to tell you."

Oh, here it comes. She sipped her brandy and waited for the revelation.

The minister unbuttoned his jacket and took a seat in a chair across from his host and hostess. Rex actually took a seat next to Edgar and not the one in the corner that was his usual.

"Rex and I have been friends for a very long time. We met at university when his father sent him abroad to study."

"It was when we became lovers the problems began," Rex added bluntly, causing two sets of eyebrows to go straight up. The man before them was now speaking clearly in concise, full sentences with a British accent and no trace of the clipped oriental accent they had known for the last few days, when he spoke at all.

He nodded, amused. He had seen this reaction before. "I was made to choose." He looked at the man next to him with great devotion. "I chose him."

"We have had to spend the vast majority of our life," Edgar continued, "moving from one place to the next to keep the rather annoyed monarchs in our lives from nipping at our heels."

"In our travels," Rex smiled, "we have discovered that the manservant act is most beneficial. You would not believe the things people will say in front of you when they do not think you understand them."

Rebecca nodded as she sipped her brandy, "Oh, yes, I would. I know what people will say when they know perfectly well that you understand them."

Both men smiled and they continued in that vein, each of them filling in a bit more of Rex's story, including the fact that 'Rex' was a bit of a joke between them about his royal titles.

When they were done with their story, they both sat forward in their chairs, looking a bit tense, waiting for Charlie's and Rebecca's reactions. It took a moment, as their audience blinked a few times, taking in all of the implications of their rather convoluted tale.

Finally, Charlie leaned back in his chair and broke into a hearty belly laugh. "Well, gentlemen, I have to say, you certainly have a much more worldly background than most ministers and their friends. I would say that the two of you are well-equipped to cope with the peculiarities of Culpeper's rather diverse little population!"

Rebecca did not say anything. She was too busy giggling.

～

She was still giggling when they finally retired to their room for the night. Charlie sat on the sofa, watching her brush her hair and trying not to laugh.

"What exactly is it you find so funny in all this?"

She set her brush down and turned to him. "Charlie, my darling, think about it. Between Charlotte and these two, if things keep going in this direction, you and I will be the last thing in this town worth talking about.

He shook his head as she finished at her mirror and joined him on the sofa. "I suppose there is some truth to that."

"To think there was a time when I did not think my life could get any more interesting than it was when there was an entire regiment of Union soldiers on my land."

"I promise to keep it interesting," he teased.

"I can see that." She entangled their fingers and tugged him toward their bed. "Come on. I can also see you are tired and I suspect it will be a long night."

He knew what she was talking about. "I would be happy to sleep here tonight."

"You most certainly will not. You know I do not sleep well without you, even if you do have a terror or two through the night. I would rather have you with me."

He stood and wrapped his arm around her waist, guiding her to their bed. "Yes, dear."

～

Sunday March 4, 1886

That morning, Edgar, accompanied by Rex, left the house before the rest of the family to prepare the church and himself for the Sunday service. He quietly let himself in the side door, and he and Rex set about lighting candles, arranging the flowers on the altar, making sure the hymnals were in the pockets in the backs of the pews, and generally ensuring all was in order. He laid the selection of music for the event, carefully and clearly written on a good sized piece of paper, on the organ bench, where it would be waiting for Mrs. Williams to arrive, along with the music book with each selection marked with a scrap of paper.

Edgar checked his watch. It would be time to ring the bells soon. He slipped into the entrance foyer and up the stairs to the bell tower. He watched out the window as people began pulling into the church yard. Apparently word had gotten out that the new minister was giving the sermon today and everybody in Culpeper who could get to church that day was going to come see the newest show in town.

Rex quietly took a seat in the far corner of the back pew, being as small and unobtrusive as he could be. He quietly watched as the bells rang out and people started to file into the church, chatting in the aisles and taking their seats.

Mrs. Williams had settled at the organ and was playing the processional piece that Edgar had laid out for her. When everyone was settled, and was looking around for the minister, many of them craning their necks to watch the door to the side of the altar, Edgar slipped in the back door, closed it and stood firmly in front of it.

Every man, woman and child jumped when the minister's voice boomed out from behind them. "Welcome! Grace, mercy and peace from God our Father and the Lord Jesus Christ be with you."

Startled he was speaking from the back of the room, still the congregation responded to the opening lines of the service automatically, though rather raggedly, "And also with you."

Edgar walked to one side of the church as he recited the next line, "O Lord, open our lips."

Again, the automatic response, though this time it was a little surer, "And our mouth shall proclaim your praise."

He was now standing underneath the raised bench where Mrs. Williams sat at the organ. "Give us the joy of your saving help."

As he walked across the front of the church, though not mounting to the pulpit yet, the parishioners answered. "And sustain us with your life-giving Spirit."

When he walked to the center of the room and stood in front of the pulpit, he spoke as if he were thinking out loud. "We have come together in the name of Christ to offer our praise and thanksgiving, to hear and receive God's holy word, to pray for the needs of the world, and to seek the forgiveness of our sins, that by the power of the Holy Spirit we may give ourselves to the service of God."

He paused and looked out at the audience, taking care to catch the eye of every person in the room, including those up in the balcony reserved for the colored members of the church. He then spoke with force. "Jesus says, 'Repent, for the kingdom of heaven is close at hand.' So let us turn away from our sin and turn to Christ, confessing our sins in penitence and faith."

As the congregation made their response, he climbed the steps to the pulpit and took his proper place as their minister, and continued with the service.

But this was not the only surprise of the morning. His choice for the first hymn of the service, As When in Far Samaria, foreshadowed what he was going to preach about.

The service proceeded as they expected, until he introduced the next hymn. Some of the people in the congregation, particularly Alex Raeburn and his associates, choked on In Christ There is No East or West, in him no South or North, but one great fellowship of love throughout the whole wide earth.

Edgar waited a long minute after the hymn was completed before the opened the bible to the day's scripture reading.

Even though he had given the congregation plenty of warning, there were a few gasps when Edgar started his reading. "Today's first reading is from Luke, Chapter 10, verses 68 through 79.

Blessed be the Lord God of Israel; for he hath visited and redeemed his people,

And hath raised up an horn of salvation for us in the house of his servant David;

As he spake by the mouth of his holy prophets, which have been since the world began:

That we should be saved from our enemies, and from the hand of all that hate us;

To perform the mercy promised to our fathers, and to remember his holy covenant;

The oath which he sware to our father Abraham, That he would grant unto us, that we being delivered out of the hand of our enemies might serve him without fear, In holiness and righteousness before him, all the days of our life. And thou, child, shalt be called the prophet of the Highest: for thou shalt go before the face of the Lord to prepare his ways; To give knowledge of salvation unto his people by the remission of their sins, Through the tender mercy of our God; whereby the dayspring from on high hath visited us, To give light to them that sit in darkness and in the shadow of death, to guide our feet into the way of peace."

He finished with the classic statement. "This is the word of the Lord."

He went on with the familiar service, with the 'Awake, O sleeper' exchange, followed by a traditional prayer. Then it came time for the second reading of the morning, this time from Luke Chapter 10, Verses 29 - 37. By now the entire congregation was pretty sure they were going to hear the story of the Good Samaritan. They were right.

"A lawyer said unto Jesus, And who is my neighbor?

And Jesus answering, said, A certain man went down from Jerusalem to Jericho, and fell among thieves, which stripped him of his raiment, and wounded him, and departed, leaving him half dead.

And by chance there came down a certain Priest that way, and when he saw him, he passed by on the other side.

And likewise a Levite, when he was at the place, came and looked on him, and passed by on the other side.

But a certain Samaritan as he journeyed, came where he was; and when he saw him, he had compassion on him,

And went to him, and bound up his wounds, pouring in oil and wine, and set him on his own beast, and brought him to an Inn, and took care of him.

And on the morrow when he departed, he took out two pence, and gave them to the host, and said unto him, Take care of him, and whatsoever thou spends more, when I come again I will repay thee.

Which now of these three, thinkest thou, was neighbor unto him that fell among the thieves?

And he said, He that showed mercy on him. Then said Jesus unto him, Go, and do thou likewise."

Edgar finished the reading forcefully. He made the last line of the reading a command, spoken in tones that would brook no opposition. He then paused.

When he spoke again, it was softly, but every person in the room could hear every word. This was his first sermon and it better be a good one.

"Today I come to you, as the Samaritan came to the man that thieves fell upon, and offer you the goodness of my heart, and the kindness of my soul, as the Lord Jesus has commanded. This is a time when people come and go, and as our Lord Jesus points out, the true measure of a man is in his acts. Look around you, and you will see those who are your neighbors, those who are becoming your neighbors. Think upon the love and devotion to the teachings of Jesus Christ, our Lord, and learn to accept that the past is indeed past. Now is a time for all of us, newcomers and old residents, to look at one another and see the neighbors that we have today, accept the gifts they bring, and to do as the Lord commanded. Show mercy to one another."

The sermon was so short and so to the point, it left the audience rather stunned.

Edgar finished his definitely obvious message for the day with his final hymn, The Ancient Law Departs, followed by the Credo. Mr. Cooper read the intercessions for the day, and ran the collection as Edgar stood back and watched the crowd, a look of intense curiosity mixed with a presence of stillness and peace. He returned to the pulpit to lead the Lord's Prayer and to pronounce the Benediction, "The peace of the Lord be always with you."

The response was again ragged. "And also with you."

He stepped down from the pulpit and walked deliberately to the back of the church, opening the doors to the outside. He stepped to the side, waiting for the congregation to begin filing out, so that he could greet and bless each of them as they left. It took rather a long time for the church to empty that morning. As much as Reverend Williams had been an integral part of the community, he was a mild and unassuming minister. This Brit was definitely going to be a different story.

~

Tuesday, March 6, 1866

Jerome Lord looked up and down the street of the little town, hoping to find something that resembled a hack or at least a livery stable. There was nothing that resembled such a service. So he threw his satchel over his shoulder and trudged diagonally across the street from the train station to the one place he knew he would be able to obtain some information and possibly a carriage – the inn.

As he walked down the street, he wondered how his friend had ended up in this one-horse burg. He had always assumed Charlie would end up in one of the big cities – Philadelphia, New York, or Boston. Not in a place like Culpeper. But then the war had changed people.

He walked into the bar, and was greeted by a small, trim man with a pronounced Irish accent. "Excuse me, good sir, but I was wondering if there was anyone who rented a carriage, or could drive me out to see General Redmond at Redmond Stables?"

"Well now, sir, Culpeper is a bit small to have a proper livery stable just yet, but if you have a seat I might be able to find someone who can take you." Jocko looked this fellow over carefully. He was about the same age as Charlie, maybe a little younger, but with the stuffy quality that Jocko had learned to associate with lawyers and bankers. What would one of them want with the general? Probably to do with the opening of the bank. "May I get you something while you wait?"

Lord looked around. It was too early for him to start drinking. He had learned that if he started drinking at lunch, by the end of the day his mouth would run before his brain engaged – a very bad trait for an estate and banking lawyer. "A cup of tea or coffee would be nice, please."

Humph. Teetotaler, too. Not Charlie's usual type of friend. "Certainly, sir. I have a fresh pot of coffee just brewing."

Jocko gave the man his cup of coffee, to which the fellow added cream and sugar, an act that reduced him yet another notch in Jocko's opinion, then went off to find someone to run this fop out to Redmond Stables. Within a few minutes, he had talked with Edward Cooper, found Cooper's delivery boy and wagon, and brought them around to the front of the inn.

"Well, sir, it may not be fancy, but young Jenkins will take you out in the mercantile wagon."

"Thank you, sir." Jerome dropped a couple of coins on the bar for the coffee.

He walked outside and pulled himself up on the box of a flatbed wagon. They drove out to Redmond Stables in total silence. He had no clue as to what to say to this country bumpkin and the bumpkin had no use for citified dandies.

They arrived at the house, and the bumpkin flicked the reins on his horse, starting back to town, as soon as Jerome's feet touched the gravel drive. He walked up the stairs to the front door and knocked. Shortly a stocky black man in black pants and vest with a crisp white shirt answered the door.

"Good day. My name is Jerome Lord. I am here to see General Charles Redmond." He offered his calling card.

The major domo opened the door more widely, taking the card in his fingers. "Come in, sir. I will see if General Redmond is available."

The attorney looked around the elegant wood-paneled hall as

the servant went bustling up the stairs, leaving him standing with his hat in one hand and his satchel in the other. Well, whatever else Charlie had done, this was a huge house and from the looks of the hall, well furnished.

A few minutes later, Charlie himself appeared at the top of the stairs. He was leaning heavily on a cane, but otherwise, still looked like the old Charlie Jerome had first met when they were both at West Point.

"Jerome! Come up! Come up! I would come down, but stairs are a bit of a challenge for me these days." He waved him up, and turned to the man who had let Lord in. "Reg, could you bring us some tea and cakes in my office, please?"

Ah, Charlie remembers that I do not drink while working.

"So Jerome, what brings you down here?" If his lawyer was at the door, it probably was not good news.

They walked down the hall toward the open door at the end, obviously leading into a large office.

"Well, Charlie, I have come because for the life of me I cannot get you to answer my letters. You have not answered any business questions by mail and things have gotten to the point where I absolutely have to have your opinion and direction on some key issues."

"What do you mean I do not answer your letters? I have written you back every single time you have written to me."

"Yes, you have. About the children, about the wife, about the weather, about the politics, about everything but the money. Now we have to talk about the money. Do you fall asleep before you get to that part, Charlie?"

"I have trusted you to handle my money since you and I both left West Point. You and your family have one of the finest banking and estate practices in the country. I trust you completely to take care of it."

"Oh, yes. And I have taken care of it. Very well, actually. I coat tailed on people like Vanderbilt and Cooke. You are a very wealthy man, you know."

"Very wealthy? Well, I know that my bank accounts at Riggs are doing nicely, but from the balance, I would not say I was very wealthy."

"Oh, no, Charlie." The attorney sighed. "What I put in Riggs for you is just spending money. You are actually worth…" He opened his case, pulled out a sheaf of papers, and flipped to one of the back pages. "As of the end of last quarter, you are worth approximately one point two million dollars."

He sat back and after a moment or two, managed to inhale. "One," he squeaked, cleared his throat and tried again. "One point two million dollars?"

"Yes. I told you, I coat tailed on the big investors, and you, and to be honest, I, have become very wealthy men. It is mostly from things like railroads, land investments, some trading in the materials and supplies during the war. We have done very, very well."

Charlie sat there, looking like he had been struck by lightning. "So the two hundred thousand I have in the Riggs accounts is just spending money?"

"Yes. If you need more, just let me know." He shuffled his papers for a few more minutes, letting his information soak in. Fortunately, Reg came in just then with a tray of Sarah's most delectable mid-afternoon treats and a pot of tea. Charlie used it as a good distraction to buy a little more time.

When they both had a plate of finger foods and a cup of tea beside them, Jerome started again. "We have to make some decisions about the direction of your investments. And about how to provide for your rapidly growing family. So we may want to consider trusts for the children. I know you have established a trust for Rebecca, but that is pin money compared to what you have."

Charlie nodded, saying nothing.

"And we need to decide if you are going to continue investing in railroads and real estate or if you wish to branch out. I recommend looking at steel and at natural resources, especially as the west is opening up and there are great tracts of timber, as well as various ores, such as copper to consider. There is also this new product that Rockefeller is touting, petroleum, that I think is going to be a world-changer."

'Ummm." Charlie was still in shock.

"So, what I have done is, documented where your investments stand today, and offered you a set of options for directions they could take. I have also documented a set of recommendations as to how to best set up trusts for your wife and children that recognizes your financial status." Jerome put a pile of papers on Charlie's desk.

"I am going to leave you with these papers. You need to look through them, you need to discuss the situation with Rebecca if you desire, and you need to get back to me with your instructions. I will give you until the end of April to send me answers. Otherwise, I will be back down, standing on your doorstep, demanding your time and attention."

The general looked up at Jerome, who had stood up to gather his papers. "Yes, sir."

"And remember, I bill by the hour, I charge for travel, and I am not cheap. Now, can one of your people take me back to the train station? I would like to catch the four o'clock to Washington."

Charlie rang for Reg, and exchanged rather strained small talk with Jerome, reminiscing about their time together at West Point. He inquired about Jerome's asthma, which had washed him out of the army and into the family law firm. His wife and eight children were the next topic of conversation. Jerome inquired about Charlie's progress of recovery from his injuries and how he was finding marriage and fatherhood in such a short time. Within a few minutes, Reg appeared to inform Mr. Lord that Tomas was waiting with the trap to take him to the train station.

As he slipped into his coat, he turned back to Charlie. "Remember. April 30th or I will be on your doorstep on May second."

"Yes, sir. Thank you, Jerome."

And the lawyer swept out of the house.

That evening, after the rest of the household had retired to their own rooms, Charlie escorted Rebecca to their private sitting room. He was holding a thick folder of papers, not his usual behavior before bed.

"I had a visitor today."

She smiled. "I know. I was wondering how long it would take you to tell me about it."

"It was my lawyer--Jerome Lord, the man who handles our finances."

She sat up straight. "Oh, Charlie. Is there a problem?"

"I would not call it a problem, exactly."

He poured himself a brandy, and offered her one as well.

"Well, it cannot be good if you are giving me a drink to fortify myself before you break the news."

"Oh, no. It really is not bad, dear."

He turned and stared into the fire for a moment. "So, Rebecca? Have you ever wanted to make love with a millionaire?"

"What do you mean?" She laughed. "Has a millionaire made you an offer for my company?"

"No." He grinned. "But when you go to bed with me tonight, you will go to sleep with a millionaire." He raised a slightly lascivious brow. "Eventually."

"Charles Huger Redmond, stop joking. I know we are comfortably well off. I have seen your statements from Riggs Bank. But a millionaire? Be honest."

"Turns out that the Riggs account is just the spending money. My lawyer has been investing and the results are astounding. Here. Look." He offered her the papers.

She flipped through them, scanning the information. Twice she held out her glass to be refilled. Finally she looked up at him. "My God! You are filthy rich!"

He smiled broadly. "Yes, dear. But it is we. We are filthy rich."

CHAPTER 9

Wednesday, March 14, 1866

The canvas had been laid down in the middle of the nursery floor again. Fortunately, with a lot of boiling water, Beulah and Reg had managed to get it clean from the last time the Redmonds had held a birthday party for one of the boys. Just five weeks later, the other baby was turning one and Rebecca planned another party.

So Sarah had again outdone herself, this time with little lady cakes stuffed with strawberry cream--a substance that formed a charming crust whenever it was smeared in hair or on clothing.

By the time the party was over, everyone was an amazing shade of pink. Emily and Suzanne thought that pink was a splendid color. Charlie and Rebecca did not agree. Charlie looked down at himself, and remembered the days of Em's oatmeal dried on his uniform buttons rather wistfully. Compared to what was dried on his shirt and suspenders now, the oatmeal had been a harbinger of things to come.

Last week, the freight men from the train yard had brought over the huge tub he had ordered. It was larger than the one that they had enjoyed at the Willard. Large enough for them to share very comfortably. Reg absolutely hated it. It took five trips, with two buckets each trip, up and down two flights of stairs from the boiler in the kitchen to the washroom off the bedroom to fill it.

The tub was large enough so they could either face one another or relax in one another's arms. With a little bit of padding, and with the comfort of the warm water, Charlie could hold Rebecca. Tonight, however, some scrubbing was in order. They both needed to be rid of the pinkness.

He looked at his wife and asked, rather plaintively, "Rebecca, how in the name of hell did we manage to get three children with birthdays within five weeks of one another?"

"Simply, darling, by taking in every lost child that came across our doorstep."

"Oh," he said flatly. He decided the gods of birthdays had it in for him. Rebecca's was next month.

She picked up a soapy washrag. "Sweetheart, turn your head. You have some strawberry cream in your ear."

As she managed to get the sticky substance out of his hair and ears he offered a suggestion. "We should raise the boys as twins."

"What?"

"They are only five weeks apart. We now have five children. I suggest we pick a day between their two birthdays and just raise them as twins, celebrating one birthday. This is going to wear me out before my time."

"That is a very good idea, my dear. I think it is perfectly reasonable, and at this age they will never know the difference."

~

Friday, March 16, 1866

Tarent rousted Rollins, the stable boy, out of his warm bed in the loft above the main stable. "Boy, get up. I need you to run up to the house and get Miss Rebecca. Tell her that Shannon is foaling."

The boy sat up and rubbed the sleep out of his eyes, peering out of the little window at the end of the loft. It was pitch dark and he could hear the rain pattering on the roof above him. "The big house?"

"Yes, boy. Up to the big house. Now! Miss Rebecca will have both our hides if her mare foals without her."

Rollins rolled out of bed and pulled on his boots and jacket. Although he normally took his meals with Tarent in the farrier's cottage, he had been up to the big house a few times, when old farrier was away, for a quick meal in the kitchen, but he had only been above the stairs once, when Tarent first hired him and the general had approved him. Going up there in the middle of the night to fetch the mistress was scary, especially on a nasty night like this. But he went.

Slogging through the rain and mud, he managed to stub his toe on one of the little steps cut into the side of the hill leading up to the house, and cursed under his breath in the dark. Cold rain was running down the back of his neck, too. As warm and comfortable as he had been a few minutes ago, he was now equally miserable. "Why do horses have to decide to foal in the middle of the nastiest night of the month?" He moaned.

Reaching the kitchen door, he banged on it, hoping to raise someone to let him in quickly. Through the window, he could see a single watch lamp burning on the kitchen table and the glow of the banked fire in the big hearth at the end of the room. He banged again.

Finally, Sarah came padding into the kitchen, wrapping a shawl around her shoulders and mumbling under her breath. She yanked the door open. "Whatch y'all want banging on the door in the middle of the night?" she grumbled.

"Mr. Tarent sent me up to get Miz 'Becca, ma'am. For Shannon, ma'am."

The cook smiled. She knew how much the mistress loved that horse. "All right, boy. Come in. You stay here while I fetch her."

Rollins came into the kitchen very carefully, mindful of the fact that his boots were covered with mud. He stood just inside of the door, being careful to keep his dripping to just that one spot.

Sarah climbed the back stairs and slipped into Miss Rebecca's sitting room. The door to the bedroom was closed, so she tapped gently. No answer. She tapped again, more firmly. Still no answer. Finally, she cracked the door and called, "Miz 'Becca? Miz 'Becca?"

Rebecca was burrowed into Charlie's left shoulder, with the covers pulled up around her ears. She was oblivious, warm, and happily asleep.

Charlie heard the cook calling them. "Yes, Sarah? What is it?"

"Mr. Tarent sent Rollins up for Miz 'Becca, sir. Shannon is foaling."

"All right. We will be down as quickly as we can. Have Rollins wait for us. Thank you for coming up this late."

"Yes, sir." Sarah pulled the door closed knowing General Charlie had it in hand.

He gently shook Rebecca from her slumber. "Darling?"

She murmured, giving him hope she might awaken quickly. "Wake up, honey. Your horse needs you." He shook her again, ever so gently.

Rebecca opened her eyes. Before she could focus, she could hear the wind and rain beating against the side of the house. "Of course she does. It is, after all, the middle of a dark and stormy night and I am so warm and happy here. Charlie?"

"Yes?"

"Horses have foaled for thousands of years without human intervention, correct?"

"Yes."

"So, theoretically, I could stay all curled up next to you and go back to sleep?"

"Theoretically? Yes." He tried hard to smother the chuckle he felt in his gut. "However, we know how our horses are. Shannon expects her mistress to be there."

"I knew you would say that." She grumbled.

Pushing the covers back, she lay there, for a moment, flexing her muscles and trying to wake up. Finally, she sat up on the edge of the bed with a groan, awake, but not yet completely functional. "It is going to be a long night."

He lit the candle on his nightstand and fumbled for his pocket watch. "Yes, dear, it is. It is just after midnight. Give me a moment and I shall join you."

"Oh, no, Charlie! You stay in bed. It is a horrible night. I can hear the rain and wind. I am sure it is cold and miserable out there. You stay here where it is warm and dry."

"Are you sure?" He really did not want to go slogging in the rain in the middle of the night, but for Rebecca and Shannon, he certainly would.

"I am quite positive, darling. I will make you a deal. When Jack has a foal, you can go tend to it. Even if it is in the middle of the night."

He laughed, rolling on his left side to watch her when she left their bed. "You, my dear, just got the short end of that bargain. But I will take you up on it. Just to be fair, I will tend to the children in the morning."

"Thank you. I do not expect Shannon to have a short delivery. I probably will not make it back by sun up."

"I know. First foals are always the most difficult. But between you and Tarent, I have full faith."

"Well–" She retrieved her work clothes from the wardrobe. "I will make sure that someone comes to the house once the foal arrives." Going back to the bed, she leaned over and kissed him gently on the lips. "Now go back to sleep."

"Yes, dear."

She shed her night gown, in one graceful movement. He watched appreciatively as she pulled on her work clothes and boots. He did so love this competent, capable woman. With one last kiss to his yawning face, she tromped out into the upstairs hall and promptly tripped over a small rolling horse that one of the children had left on the landing.

She caught herself on the banister post, just barely avoiding going down the stairs headfirst, again. The words out of her mouth were decidedly not ladylike. Down the stairs she clomped, and down again to the kitchen. There she found Rollins, still standing by the door in the middle of his personal puddle.

"Well, shall we go tend to my girl?"

The boy just nodded and followed her. He had never heard of any woman who got up in the middle of the night to tend to a foaling mare – and certainly not one who wore britches and boots to do so. The general and his wife were a very unusual couple.

She pulled her coat from the hook and threw it over her shoulders before grabbing Charlie's old military issue slouch hat. Her hair barely kept it from falling over her eyes. Heading out into the rain and wind, she made a mental note to pick up a hat that fit next time she went into town. Tightening the collar of her coat around her throat, she headed for the barn.

Once inside, she found Tarent, calming Shannon by giving her nose a rub with slow, gentle strokes.

"How is she?"

"She is fine, Miz 'Becca. Moving right along. And as far as I can tell, the little one is primed and ready to go as soon as Mama lets it through."

"Good girl." She dropped the coat and hat before going to her beloved mare. "You know, it would be fine if you would like to do this now so I can go back to bed. Jack's master makes a lovely warm nest I enjoy a great deal."

Shannon nuzzled into her mistress's chest and made a whiny little whickering sound, then backed up and shuffled around in the stall. She raised her tail and the next thing Rebecca knew, she was being sprayed with warm, salty water.

Tarent burst out laughing. "She got you good, Miz 'Becca!"

Rollins sat in his corner giggling hysterically.

Shannon majestically settled down, lying comfortably on her side on a thick pile of straw.

"Oh," Rebecca wiped as much of the liquid away as she could. "It is going to be that kind of night, is it?" Making her way into the stall, she settled in with her horse.

Shannon obligingly placed her head in Rebecca's lap. Tarent brought her a bale of hay and an old horse blanket to lean against as the night went on. With Rebecca gently stroking her horse's nose and neck, the contractions grew closer and closer. Shortly after dawn, Tarent checked on the mare's condition again.

"It will be soon now, Miz 'Becca."

The mare whinnied and shifted, kicking her legs out straight before her.

Tarent crouched down and felt for the feet. "Yup! Here it comes."

The next few minutes were a wonder. Shannon heaved hard, and small front feet, wrapped in the slippery caul, slid into the opening. Another heave and the little head popped out.

Another lurch of her muscled stomach and Tarent got a grip on the withers of the little horse, sliding the foal all the way out. Shannon perked her head up to look over her own shoulder at the activity down there, and then heaved again and the afterbirth slid to the floor and lay there, steaming.

Horse and human stood up almost immediately, both of them going to the little beast, lying there and struggling to breathe. Rebecca ripped the caul from its head with her fingers, and wiped out the little girl's nostrils on her breeches. Shannon started licking and nudging her firstborn, pulling the rest of the slimy membrane away and urging the little beauty to her feet.

"She is a sweetheart, Miz 'Becca. Her father's color, except for her mother's blaze."

A half hour later, the little darling was up on her feet for the first time – a little shaky, but up. Tarent and Rollins cleaned up the afterbirth and spread fresh straw, while Rebecca gently groomed the little girl and her mother, delighting in the stiff little brushes that would become her mane and tail. She was all legs, knobby and shaky. She was adorable.

By eight in the morning, the foal had managed to find her mother's teat, had enjoyed her first meal, and then settled down for a nap. Rebecca was more than ready to join her, but hunger won out. She trudged back up to the house, hoping that the coffee was still hot and that Sarah would make her a late breakfast.

She tromped into the mudroom and pulled her boots off. It did not help much; her socks were disgusting. She scraped off a layer or two of muck, but the only hope for the shirt and britches she was wearing were probably burning. "Sarah, I am tired. I am cold and I am starving. I know breakfast is over, but would you mind?"

"Not at all, Miz 'Becca! Miz Charlotte's up in the morning room having her breakfast late this morning, too. It is really no trouble. It will be ready jiffy quick. How is Shannon?"

"Thank you so much. Shannon is fine and the foal is the most beautiful little girl you have ever seen. Black, like her sire, but with a white blaze."

"A fine little girl, then. I hope she has her mother's temper. That Jack is a devil and now that Gener'l Charlie cain't ride him no more, the boys down at the stables say he is just got damn mean."

"I know." She felt bad for both Jack and Charlie. The stallion would tolerate very few riders that were not her husband, and with Albert, the second best rider in the Redmond extended family, away so much, the big black horse had not been given his head in a long while and it showed in his temperament. "So do I," she sighed over her shoulder as she climbed the back stairs to the morning room.

"Breakfast will be right up, ma'am."

Charlotte was sitting in the morning room, sipping her second cup of the wonderful coffee Redmond Stables had to offer. Reading the latest novel from Mr. Dickens, Our Mutual Friend, it was one of those moments when she could almost delude herself into feeling like things had not changed.

She was wearing her favorite morning dress, soft, flowing, and lacy. She was drinking exquisite coffee. She was reading a good book. The room was quiet and the servants had removed all traces of the little Redmonds. She had the room to herself, and could sit, relax and enjoy the lovely view out to the pond and the fields and forest beyond it.

When the door opened unexpectedly, it startled her. She dropped her book and almost spilled her coffee. The sight that greeted her eyes was even more startling. Her jaw dropped.

There was Rebecca, dressed in britches, a man's shirt and vest, a damp corduroy jacket and stocking feet. The woman was covered in mud and slime, and it looked like there were blotches of blood on her shirt. Her hair was hanging in greasy strings down to her shoulders, and there were bits of straw in it. There was a huge smear of mud and something else on one cheek, and deep shadows under her eyes. The smell that was emanating from her body was simply incredible.

She stumped into the room, bringing more of that horrific odor with her, pulled her jacket off, turned it inside out and spread it over her normal chair, then flopped down as gracefully as a half empty sack of potatoes.

"Good morning, Charlotte. Having a quiet morning, are we?" She asked as she rolled up the sleeves of her foul smelling shirt.

"What in the name of God happened to you? You look terrible."

"I had to tend to my Shannon this morning. She gave birth to her first foal."

She looked at her cousin with a bewildered expression. "What the hell is a Shannon? And a foal?"

"My mare? A gift that Charlie gave me last Christmas. This was her first foal. This is a horse farm. We have mares foaling regularly."

"But Rebecca, you have people to take care of the messy things, you know." She gestured in the woman's foul smelling direction. "For you. Surely you could have gone down first thing this morning to see the new horse."

"Excuse me?" Rebecca was duly insulted. "On this farm, I ask nothing of anyone else that I am not willing to do myself. Besides that, Shannon is my mare. It was only right I be with her. It takes everyone doing their share to make a farm successful. We are just getting started but we will have a successful program here."

"Does Charlie know you do things like this?"

"Of course he does. Charlotte, I run this farm. I take care of every aspect of it on daily basis. Charlie is busy with getting Culpeper back in order. We are partners in this. One of the things I love about him most is that he does not expect me to be a typical,

166

simpering, shrinking violet of a wife. He expects me to be as strong and capable as he is and I damn well intend to do it."

Charlotte just sat there and stared at her for a moment, until Sarah came bustling in with a plate full of food and a fresh pot of coffee. Her eyes bugged out when she saw what Rebecca was served for breakfast.

There were three eggs, four sausage patties, two biscuits, a thick slice of ham, a bowl of grits swimming in butter, and a pile of what looked like stewed apples. Rebecca tore into the food like a starving man. Neither woman spoke while she methodically worked her way through more food than Charlotte would eat in two or three days.

Eventually, she slowed down. The plate was empty and the woman was using her final biscuit to soak up the last of the egg yolks. Watching this woman eat, Charlotte thought to herself that Charlie had definitely found the perfect partner and companion. Rebecca wiped her mouth with the napkin, and asked for the coffee pot.

Finally, Charlotte found her voice again. "So, the ruckus in the middle of the night was because of the horse?" Based on the cursing that had awakened her, the woman before her not only ate like a field hand, she also swore like a sailor.

"Yes, I do apologize for that. I am afraid that someone left a toy at the top of the stairs. I nearly broke my neck on it."

She caught the look on Charlotte's face and she straightened in her chair before uttering, "You know, Charlotte, while you were living in Washington enjoying a very rich life, I was here, trying to keep my home together. The war took my brother and one other husband from me. It destroyed my way of life. While you were drinking champagne, eating fine food and enjoying the company of multiple suitors, I was hoping a handful of old seeds would bring me a few vegetables so I would not starve to death.

Before the war, I was a spoiled child of privilege. We had slaves to wait on me, to tend to me. I thought new horses came off a train. I had to learn to work hard. I had to learn to survive. My husband, in case you are wondering, supports me in my efforts. He is pleased with the things I do here. He wants for nothing. He knows he is valued, loved and his touch not only desired, but craved. I take care of him, the children, and this farm. They are my pride. This is my legacy. I have earned it. Tell me, what is your legacy?"

Charlotte looked at Rebecca Redmond, sitting there in all her filth, wearing the most inappropriate clothing possible for any lady of station, and realized in that moment something that would change her life. *For all my fineries and niceties and manners and the phantoms of old friends in high places, I will never be the lady that she is.* After a long pause, she swallowed. "I…Please, accept my apology. I was entirely out of line. Again."

Rebecca merely nodded her acceptance. "Now if you will excuse me, I am badly in need of a bath."

Charlie and Richard stood, looking over the wall of the big box stall at Shannon gently cleaning the little black foal. Rebecca had held Shannon's head while the little girl was born, and helped the proud mama clean her little offspring up. After that, she had gone up to the house to clean up. The two gentlemen had wandered down after breakfast to admire the gawky, lanky little horse.

"She is a pretty little thing. Her father's coloring. And already sweet and gentle, I think." Charlie looked at the mare gently nuzzling her hours-old offspring. His own lips perched in a bittersweet smile. "She looks like her papa."

Richard smiled at his friend, who seemed to have a touch of melancholy about him. "Charlie, something wrong?"

"Ah, nothing that anyone can do aught about." The general sighed. "I wonder what Rebecca will name her."

"Hey? This is me, remember? You can tell me what is bothering you. Are you two having problems?"

He barked a short, humorless laugh. "No! We are fine. It is just," he paused and shook his head," that I have been thinking. Well, you and Elizabeth are expecting. So are several other women around town, and now even Shannon is having babies. But I cannot give my wife children."

"I know she loves the little ones we have adopted, but I think she would like to have one of her own, one that was really hers. I see the way she looks at Elizabeth and the other ladies. There is certain wistfulness in her eyes. Something perhaps she thinks she is missing. There, I am sure, is a huge difference between taking in every waif that comes along and carrying your own child in your body. Feeling it grow and come to life."

Richard considered his friend and gestured a bit. "I am sure that you will find that she is expecting any time now." He gave Charlie a gentle cuff on the shoulder. "Come on, think about what you went through. It only takes time." He chewed the end of his cigar, and then pulled it from his mouth. "Of course, I do remember hearing that Rebecca could not..." He stopped and shook his head. "I am sorry. I know you probably want a son of your own."

Charlie reached in and gently scratched Shannon's ear. "No, Darby, Buddy and Andy are the only sons I will ever have. And it is not Rebecca's fault. She is perfectly capable of having lots and lots of babies." He rushed to get that information out.

If Richard had heard through the grapevine that it was Rebecca's fault, then he wanted to make damn sure that his friend could counter that kind of gossip and protect her reputation among the ladies. "The failing is all mine. I cannot..." He cleared his throat. "I cannot do the most basic thing one expects of a husband. Jack makes a marvelous stud; his master, unfortunately, does not."

"Your injuries?"

He flushed slightly. "Um, well yes, partly. My leg, arse and shoulder were not the only things that were injured."

Polk's eyes widened. He wanted to ask, but just could not bring himself to do it as he found a sudden need to adjust his own stance. "You would never know it by that simper that Rebecca wears on her face three or four days a week." He chuckled; trying to relieve some of the tension.

"I did not say I could not satisfy her, you idiot. I only said I cannot give her babies as other men could do." He had a partly amused, partly embarrassed look on his face.

"True." His friend sighed, wishing he could offer some real

comfort. "I am sorry for being such a dolt these last few weeks. I have been going on about Bess and the baby..." He shook his head regretfully. "I am sorry, my friend, I would never intentionally hurt you or Rebecca."

"No, Richard! You have not hurt us, in any way. I am very happy for you and Elizabeth. I am sure you will be a wonderful father. It is just that I wish I could give the same joy to my wife. You know, I have always thought that children were the physical manifestation of the love between two people. If I am right, then you and Elizabeth will have a beautiful baby indeed."

"Well, I hope the baby looks like Elizabeth, but has my charming personality." He smiled before tapping his finger in the wall of the stall and then finally looking to Charlie, leaning on his cane.

His attempt at humor had fallen flat with his preoccupied friend. "Perhaps you should think of happy children as the physical manifestation of the love between two people. Because you and Rebecca have the happiest children I have ever seen. And that is only because of the love you both lavish on them. She is a model mother and you are a wonderful father to them. Darby and Suzanne are starting to blossom under your loving care. The boys are healthy and growing into fine fellows and we all know what a terror Emily is when her papa is not around as much as she wants."

Charlie nodded, but his old second in command had known him long enough to know when he was agreeing to avoid a fight.

He tried one last time, "Listen, Old Friend, if you are really concerned about this, go talk to Elizabeth. She is your doctor. If there is anyone who might know a solution, it is our amazing Doctor Walker."

He nodded once again. He did need to speak with Elizabeth about his laudanum. And over the years he has consulted her on all sorts of outrageous things concerning his manly facade. She would no doubt be amused by this particular quandary. "You will be a wonderful father too, Richard. I have watched you with my little group of troopers. You adapted to gruel on your coat very nicely, I must say." He plucked a piece of straw from the bale beside him. "So, is it true? What they say about pregnant women?"

"That they are constantly changing their mind every two minutes and their emotions are like a heavy pendulum swung from a very high spot? And they crave the most disgusting things to eat at the worst possible times of the day and night? Yes, Charlie, it is all true. Perhaps you are blessed in ways you do not even realize by Rebecca not getting pregnant. I love you like a brother and your wife is a wonderful woman, but I have seen her puffed up and ready to fight. I do not suspect she would be a ton of fun if she were pregnant. Especially in the summer. So do make sure you try to avoid that."

Charlie laughed. "Yes, well, I am sure that after what you had to manage in the service, Elizabeth changing her mind every two minutes is easy to handle."

He had spent weeks envisioning Rebecca heavily pregnant and it was lovely in his mind's eye. Even if they came through this, there was always going to be some small part of him filled with the regret of being the one who could never make it possible to really see her like that. *She knows. She knows, we can never... I can never...*

"There is a huge difference between conflicting orders from the War Department and conflicting orders from one's cranky wife." Richard removed the cigar from his mouth and gestured wildly. "Do you know, I put my hat down in my regular spot the other night and she burst into tears?"

"So when you moved it, did that make her laugh hysterically?" Charlie was genuinely intrigued. The thought of Elizabeth Walker, field surgeon with nerves of steel, bursting into tears at the literal drop of a hat was decidedly anomalous.

"Joke if you will, General Redmond. It is not funny. No, actually she did not. She was not satisfied until we were in bed and I rubbed her shoulders. I have been doing a lot of that lately. I have taken to walking on egg shells around the house, especially in the morning."

Charlie's eyebrow rose. "Oh? Morning sickness still plaguing her?"

"No, she is just very irritable in the morning. I am not sure I understand. I am not sure I want to understand it. All I do know is that I hope it is over soon."

The general smiled at his friend's obvious distress. Richard had worried incessantly about being a good husband before Elizabeth had become pregnant. Now he fretted over being a good father as well. If she was grouchy, it probably made his friend even more anxious. However, there might be one redeeming quality, if the rumors were true. "Well, I have heard that pregnant women are often more amorous. If true, that must offer some compensation for being on the receiving end of her conniptions?"

Richard blushed. "W-well, y-yes," he stammered. "Well, there is that one benefit."

"My friend, take advantage of it, for when the summer comes and Elizabeth is as big as a barn and miserable with the heat, I doubt you will even be welcome in her house, let alone her bed."

"Has anyone ever told you that you are a mean man?"

"You have. Often."

~

Tuesday, March 20, 1866

Rebecca stood in the stall rubbing the nose of the little foal. She had not decided on a name for the little girl yet, but she knew if she spent enough time getting to know her, it would come naturally.

Shannon tossed her head and whinnied as the barn door opened. Rebecca looked up to find Charlie. She could not help but smile; he looked like a farmer, dressed in his boots, dark trousers, and white shirt with suspenders with a short tan jacket. She remembered the first time she had seen her mate like that--they had only known each other for a few hours and yet the second he had walked through the door of her parlor in civilian clothes her world started to right itself.

"And what does the gentleman of the manor require today?" she asked with a wink as she continued to let the foal nuzzle her hand.

He hemmed and hawed for a bit, kicking a bit of straw with the toe of his boot before he joined her in petting the little foal that would one day be a magnificent mare like her mother. "She is a beautiful little thing, is she not? The best of both of her parents. Yes?"

"Oh, yes!" She looked at the little beast which had already won her heart. "I am not sure I will be able to part with her."

"Perhaps we should keep her and use her as a--" he stopped short. "Our herd would not suffer with one of Jack and Shannon's foals also available for, um, yes…" He had never been shy when it came to discussing the breeding of horses, but now he felt like a young boy completely embarrassed by the subject.

"Perhaps," she commented thoughtfully. "We will have to make sure she retains her mother's temperament. If she grows up to be like Jack, well then…" She teased as she leaned over and gave her husband a kiss on the cheek. "And how has your day been, my dear?"

"It was some of this and some of that. I went into town to look at the building site for the bank. Stopped and talked to Mr. Frazier and Mr. Cooper. Looked over Jocko's plans for adding the Ladies Tea Room to the side of the inn. Saw Elizabeth."

"Sounds like a full day. How is Elizabeth? And the gentlemen are all well, I trust?"

"The gentlemen are all well. Busily planning ways to improve the local economy when they are not grousing about the stupidity coming from Richmond and Washington. I swear, they will elect Richard to the General Assembly just for spite. And Elizabeth is well. She sends her love, as always, to her dearest sister. It seems that her pregnancy is not affecting her at the moment, even though it has Richard in quite a muddle."

She chuckled. "Yes, well, I understand impending fatherhood has that effect on a man from time to time. I am sure Richard will be just fine."

He moved a bit more straw with the toe of his boot. He realized in that very moment that not only would he never see Rebecca as God had intended, but he would also never hear the magical words every husband who loves his wife longs to hear. He cleared his throat and hoped the emotion would be gone as well. "Have you heard that Samantha and Duncan are to be wed?"

"Yes, dear, I was there. Remember?" She ducked her head trying to get a better look at her partner's face.

"Um. Yes. Of course you were. Right. Well, then. How was your day?"

"It has been pleasant." She began. Clearly he was not ready to talk just yet. "I have been tending to this little one and checking on the other two mares that are in foal. Tarent is still having trouble with that blasted forge and we think we may have to have it repaired or even replaced. It simply will not draw right. It may be better to just build new. I have the financial and breeder books to catch up tonight and I am sure I will fall into bed exhausted, but very content."

He nodded absent mindedly, "I am very grateful that you have the skill to run the stables. I swear, this whole thing about the bank is just taking up all my time."

"Yes, but it will be worth it. You are doing a wonderful job. Everyone I have spoken with is exceedingly grateful that Culpeper will have a bank of its very own and so soon after the war."

He looked rather pleased. "Yes, well, I am also starting to research the new investments that Jerome asked us to look at. I am a bit uneasy with all the railroad companies and land schemes. I think I will look more closely at the raw materials for this boom. I suspect that will be more stable."

He stuck his hands in his coat pockets, where he found a new bottle of laudanum. "Oh, I got another bottle of medicine from Elizabeth. She warned me to be careful with it, for she will not get a new supply for a week or so."

"Then we will have to make sure it is properly put away." She gave the horse a final pat and left the stall. She gave her husband further consideration. "What is it that is bothering you?"

He turned away and stuffed the bottle back in his pocket. For this moment, in his world, he was ashamed to be her husband. "I was talking to Elizabeth today."

"Yes? About? Is something wrong? Are you ill?" She moved to stand in front of him, placing her hands gently on his arms. Her eyes were serious and concerned when she told him, "Talk to me, Charlie."

"No, I am not sick, at least not physically. I was thinking, with all the ladies in town expecting their own babies, I figured I would ask if there was any way..." he stopped, looking rather lost and hopeless, tears clearly forming in his eyes.

He cleared his throat and continued. "Any way for you and I to..."

She smiled gently and palmed his cheek, gently stroking the skin of his face with her thumb. "Charlie, you know that is not possible."

He hung his head, again feeling very insignificant. "I know."

He looked up at her, with an oddly determined expression. "But I also know, you would love a child. One of your own, a baby that you would carry and give birth to. I was trying to find out if there was a way to find us...to find...an umm, surrogate – who maybe, well maybe if he looked like me... who could, you know," he gestured aimlessly, feeling his heart breaking at the thought, but continued, softly, "with you..." He gulped and continued doggedly on, "provide the seed, if there was a way to..." He sighed, slightly defeated in his attempts to explain. "Anyway, Elizabeth said that the only way is the regular way."

Her brows rose. She was touched at the thought of him, giving this issue so much consideration, but very surprised he would go to Elizabeth to discuss it. "Yes, that is the only way and I have absolutely no interest in it."

"But," he stressed, "if you wanted," he gestured again, not knowing exactly what to do with his hands, "really wanted a child, of your very own, we could go to Washington, Boston–or even Philadelphia or New York, spend a couple of weeks and find a man..."

"No! Charlie, listen to me!" She stood up straight, setting her jaw and getting the footing that he instantly recognized as his wife about to go on a full blown conniption. "If I could have babies with you, in the natural way, then we would do it. But we cannot. I have no desire to have children with anyone but you, Charles Redmond. So you just get that nonsense right out of your mind, right now. I love you. You are the only one I ever want to raise children with."

"Oh." He looked startled and, to be honest, a bit relieved at her very vehement declaration. "But, dear, are you sure?"

"I am very sure." She gently wrapped her arms around him in a tender hug. "You are all I want and need. We have a family. Children who already love and need us. Let us not be concerned with things that are not meant for us and be concerned with those things that are. There is a reason we were brought together and given these children, Charlie. This is our family. Our destiny. Our legacy."

He dropped his cane into the corner, and wrapped her up in his arms. "If you are sure, darling. For I would give you anything you want – anything – if it were in my power."

"It is in your power. Give me a long and happy life at your side. Treat me as your partner and equal and I will be the happiest woman on the face of the earth."

"You know that I consider you my equal in every way," he whispered into her hair. "I just did not want you to miss out on something so personal."

"I am sure. Please, put this to rest, along with the remainder of your fears. It is only you I want. I did not tromp a hundred and fifty miles through mud, blood and death to sit at your bedside and beg you to live for something like this to get between us now."

With a gentle kiss to her forehead and a smile, he acceded. "Yes, dear."

CHAPTER 10

Friday, March 23, 1866

Duncan made sure to keep a slow, steady pace as he and Charlie walked toward the pond. He watched with anxiety as his friend struggled with certain places in the well-worn but bumpy foot path. He so admired the man next to him, but some part of him also felt very sorry for him.

He had been part of more than one conversation in town about Charlie and what a shame it was that this proud cavalry officer, who had spent his entire army career on horseback was now reduced to hobbling around aided by a cane. His leg was so badly damaged he would never ride again, and his hand was mangled, seemingly useless, and hidden in a glove.

And what about Rebecca, they had asked? To be saddled with a scarred and wounded man who obviously would never give her children of her own.

He hated all the gossip about his friends and he had been irritated more than once by people who said the gallant man should have been allowed to die of his wounds. Did they not understand the will Charlie Redmond had to live?

The general had been wounded in the very last days of the war. It was almost a cruel joke to all those who knew the officer and how he had always gone above and beyond as a commander for his troops.

Even though they were now separated from the army, Duncan had decided he would always stand by the man who had not only made sure he made it home alive and intact, but also gave him confidence he did not know he had.

General Charlie had never once judged him on his stutter and he would never let that kind of friendship falter. Because of this gentle man's constant reassurance, he had become a husband, stepfather and successful business owner. He owed the general more than he could ever repay.

"It is b-b-beautiful here, s-sir."

"Yes, it is." A gentle smile played on Charlie's lips as he thought of Rebecca on one of their excursions to the pond when he had simply been Colonel Redmond, trying to convince the Widow Gaines to allow his men to winter on her property. "Miss Rebecca and I have had some lovely times here and I would very much like to be able to continue doing so, however..." He lifted his cane aimlessly.

Duncan nodded knowingly. The simple walk out here had probably been exhausting.

"So, my friend, what I would like you to do is build us a lovely gazebo. Out here by the pond, where we can sit and maybe have a charming summer dinner together when we are old and gray."

"I c-can certainly m-manage that."

"And I would like it to be a surprise."

The carpenter's eyebrows crawled toward his forehead. "Umm, yes, s-s-sir, b-but w-we are a b-b-bit out in t-t-the open h-h-here."

Charlie noticed in that moment that the little stutter the carpenter always had, got worse when he was nervous, so he told him the same thing he had always told him through the years when he knew he was in such a state before an engagement. "I have faith in you, Duncan."

"Yes, General Redmond."

Duncan waved to the young man who had been following them at a discrete distance. "Sir, you r-remember me speaking of m-my c-carpenter? W-who helped w-with your office?"

"Why, yes. You spoke highly of him when you were working on my office."

"I w-would like to introduce h-him to you." The young man was now standing behind Duncan. "G-general Redmond, this is Eddie R-rainey. H-he has been w-working for me n-now for a while, and I think h-h-he is an outstanding c-carpenter. He came out t-today to h-help me t-take m-measurements. Eddie, G-general Redmond."

"Mr. Rainey." Charlie smiled as he extended his hand. "Our friend here has told me about your skill as a carpenter. I am very grateful for the service you have done for us. I hope you will be able to support him in this project. "

"I will do my best, Mr. Redmond."

The three men discussed Charlie's vision for a gazebo on the pond, and Duncan and Eddie took some initial measurements. Finally, Duncan said, "I will h-have some drawings and estimates f-for you in a c-couple of days."

"Please do. Thank you, gentlemen."

~

Monday, March 26, 1866

Rebecca stood in front of the window of the back parlor, sipping coffee and staring at the wall of canvas that had once again invaded the property.

She sighed.

The first time it had been tents that housed Charlie's men. Now it was something entirely different. The circular walls about ten feet high were obviously meant to hide something.

When the door opened and Charlie entered, she smiled ever so sweetly. "Ah, there you are!"

He looked around quickly, trying to figure out who might possibly be eliciting such a response from his wife. He had known her for two years and she had never been this excited to see him first thing in the morning. When he realized no one else was around, he pointed to himself.

"Yes!" She practically sailed across the room and took him by the arm leading him to the window. "You dear man, are the only person capable of answering the following question."

She stopped and gestured to the large whitish/grayish kite looking thing blocking her view. "What in the hell is that thing blocking my beautiful morning view of the pond?"

He bit the corner of his bottom lip as he tried not to grin at her. "You can still see the pond." He gestured as he poured himself a cup of coffee. "Right there, that little corner is sticking out past the tarps."

"So you admit this is your doing?"

"Oh, yes, absolutely." He nodded, sipping his coffee and watching her from behind his cup. "There is no one to blame but me."

"You have no intention of telling me, do you?"

"Not a one. And, madam, I formally request that you refrain from going down there until such a time as your presence is requested."

"Oh, is that so?" Now she was smiling too.

"Yes, that is so. And if I find you trying to sneak down there, or you send any of your well-trained spies from our little group of troopers, I will place a guard around it." He lifted a playful brow. "With orders to spank anyone caught breaching the perimeter."

"Would I do something like that?"

His brow rose as his head cocked slightly sideways, giving a knowing look to her question.

"I promise." She finally laughed, knowing full well she was well and truly caught. She reached out and played with a loose thread on the lapel of his jacket. "You need new suits."

He captured her hand in his and kissed her fingers. "My suits are fine. However, if you are looking for an excuse to go shopping,

I will happily take you to Washington or Philadelphia. Perhaps New York?"

"Charlie, there is too much to do here."

"Exactly, and it will all still be here waiting for us to do it when we get back." He caressed her face with his fingertips. "We deserve it, 'Becca."

She smiled at the nickname he only used when they were entirely alone and usually at their most intimate. "We have not been away since our honeymoon. No one will perish if we take a few days and go to New York."

She moved closer to him, and he wrapped his left arm around her and rested his chin on the top of her head. "Other than Em. She will be quite put out Papa is leaving." She relished feeling the deep chuckle rumbling under her hands as they caressed his chest. "Do you think you could stand the trip? I know train rides can be jarring on a good day. Are you up to it physically?"

"Yes, my dear. I will manage, especially for a chance to be alone with you for a few days and let the stress between us melt away."

That evening after dinner and the children were tucked into their beds, Charlie, Rebecca, Edgar and Charlotte gathered in the back parlor to play some whist. Rex sat to one side, observant as ever, quietly fingering a small, intricate wooden box.

Charlie went to the liquor cabinet and poured four glasses of brandy. He offered a glass to Rex, who declined. Rebecca poured coffee for all five occupants of the room. After a few minutes of arranging cups, chairs, and glasses, the four of them settled down as Edgar shuffled and dealt the cards.

As the minister went through these ritualized movements, Charlie slipped his laudanum bottle from his pocket and quickly took a sip. With attention focused on Edgar's quick hands and the cards, no one noticed but Rex, whose eyebrow twitched and eyes narrowed as he watched the general wash down the opiate with a swig of brandy.

Through the course of the evening, Charlie reached into his pocket between hands several more times, only now he did it when he got up to refresh the players' brandies.

Rex watched him very carefully, noting that as he continued to mix the opium-based medication with alcohol, his hands became shaky, and his speech began to slur ever so slightly. What concerned Rex most of all was that the impact of the combination of drugs and alcohol was not as pronounced as it should have been.

Eventually, Rebecca noticed her husband's shaking hands as he tried to hold and focus on his cards. "Darling, are you tired?"

"Well, yes, I think just a bit. It has been a long day."

Edgar looked into his host's seemingly exhausted eyes and said, "Why, yes, it has. Perhaps we should call it a night after this hand."

Charlie agreed with a nod. A look of relief flittered over his face. "Perhaps we can pick up the game tomorrow evening?"

"Yes, that sounds perfectly lovely," Charlotte chimed in.

Within a few minutes, they all stood, gathering their things to retire for the night. Rebecca placed the used glasses and cups on the tray, as she knew that Beulah would have them cleared first thing in the morning. They bid one another good night as they trudged up the stairs, going their various ways in the upstairs hall.

As Rex closed the door to the suite that he and Edgar shared, he leaned back against it and said, "You know, he's addicted."

Edgar turned and stared at his companion. "Addicted? To the laudanum?"

"Very much so. Every time he poured a brandy, he took a dose. And while washing the drugs down with brandy did affect him, it didn't have the impact it should have if he were not fully acclimated to it. Edgar, if he keeps doing this, he will be dead in a matter of months. Perhaps weeks."

"So can you help him like you helped me?

"I think so. But he will have to be willing to accept the risks and the consequences. You know that."

"I suggest you start by talking to Rebecca. If she sees the seriousness of the situation and is convinced that you can help him, it will make things much easier."

~

Wednesday, March 28, 1866

Rebecca stood in the dining room, wondering why Charlie had commanded, for the first time in his life, the entire staff to come together. The house staff milled around looking uncertain and worried about what could possibly have happened that the general was calling a meeting.

Everyone knew Miss Rebecca ran the farm.

The men and boys from the barns and stables looked more than a little uncomfortable to be summoned like this. They all stayed clustered together in a corner like spring foals, trying to hide behind Tarent, their boss, and doing their best not to track mud and manure across the highly polished floors. They failed at both.

Eventually, they all heard the rhythmic tapping that always announced Charlie's arrival. He opened the door, fumbling a bit with a few papers and ledgers he had tucked under his right arm. Tomas quickly stepped forward to relieve his boss of his burden.

"Thank you." He smiled and took his place at the head of the dining room table. All eyes were on him. Tomas placed the pile next to his left hand for easy access. He was pleased with how quickly the young man was adapting on his own to the little things that made his life easier.

He looked around the room at the faces of the people who worked for him and smiled. "Please. Relax. Everything is fine."

"We figured there had to be some sort of trouble, Gen'l. You don' usually call us all up here like this. Someone has to be getting fired," Tarent said from the back of the room. Some of the men and boys murmured their agreement.

"Better than gettin' whupped," a Negro boy about ten years old named Freddy, who Charlie knew was a new kitchen helper, said before getting cuffed on the ear by Beulah.

"You hush your disrespectful mouth!"

"No." Charlie put his hand up. "Beulah, it is all right. Everyone has a right to speak here. Freddy, I do not ever want you to worry. You will never be whipped or beaten here. Those days are over, son. You are a paid employee of Redmond Stables. Miss Rebecca and I will always try to do right by you and that is all we ask you do for us in return. I think if you will talk to some of the others," he gestured to the back of the room, "including some of the men who used to be under me in the army, you will find I have always been fair to everyone in my employ or care. No one is being fired." He smiled at the boy, who was still smarting from Beulah's correction. "And no one is getting whipped, ever."

Rebecca was pleased when every head in the room nodded and murmurs arose from everyone with something positive to say about Charlie. She was also happy to hear a few very nice things about herself, too.

"And as gentleman of this house, it is my first and foremost duty to take care of the lady of the house. I have been lax and derelict in that duty." His brows rose as he looked to his wife. "Forgive me?"

"Charlie?" She was now more confused than ever.

"What I have discovered is this." He tapped the pile of books under his hand. "In just a few months, the farm has grown. Our family has grown. The number of houseguests we have coming and going seems to be endless. Miss Rebecca has done a wonderful job of not only handling it, but making it possible in the first place. It is only because of her determination that we have had such good fortune in such a short time. However, it is now time for her to be exactly what she should be, Lady of this House and Redmond Stables."

He was pleased to see almost every head in the room nod in agreement. All of them, except the one that mattered.

"Charlie," she stated harshly, placing her hands flat on the table as she stared him down. "You know I am perfectly happy to do what I do."

"I know you are and I would never ask you to stop. I would never try to take any of this away from you. I just wish to lighten your load a bit. He turned back to the assembled staff. "We are going to start working a bit like the army, only more efficiently. When we had the refugees here last year, we hired on more staff, but as they left, so did the people we had hired. We are not housing exiles any longer, but we still need help."

He took a few sheets of paper out and laid them on the table. "I have decided that we will have departments and department heads from now on. Beulah, for example, will now be the Head Housekeeper. That is her title. She will oversee all the other housekeepers and maids. Sarah is now the Head Cook and will hire more kitchen staff."

"What other housekeepers?" Beulah laughed. "In case you ain't noticed, Gen'l, I already is the head housekeeper, cuz I is the only housekeeper with a head." She teased, making him and everyone else laugh.

"Not anymore. You are now responsible for hiring as many housekeepers and maids as you require to make this house run properly. It is no longer your job to scrub floors or make beds, Beulah. Your job is to hire, fire and supervise. And you will find the new title also comes with a raise in pay and the ability to move your family into the first house on the edge of the property. It was finished last week. Mr. Tarent will see to it you have all the wagons you need for the move."

"Well, Lawdy, Gen'l Charlie. Thank you, sir! You know I will do my best."

"I know you will." He smiled gently at the woman and gave her a wink.

"Now the rest of the departments and those chosen to run them are laid out here on these lists. I want everyone to take some time. You can all work together to make this happen. While you are at it, please try to find us a couple of gardeners too. I very much want to get the conservatory up and running again."

He smiled and moved to wrap his arm around Rebecca's waist. "I am taking Mrs. Redmond to New York for a week. That should be plenty of time for you to implement our new plan and get the system in place that will ease her workload. She is still running the farm. She is still the final voice of decisions here, but I expect that she will no longer have to wash windows or hang laundry. If I see her with a broom or a mop bucket in her hand there will be Hell to pay."

~

He was standing with his back to his office door pouring two brandies when he not only heard, but felt the door slam shut. He took a deep breath and straightened his shoulders preparing for the onslaught.

"Would you mind telling me what that was all about!?" She growled at him as she made her way across the room.

He turned to his wife, who was already in a full blown conniption fit. He would have to handle this delicately.

He offered her the drink. "Not at all, my darling wife. Would you mind taking a seat and just allowing me to get it out before you take my head off?"

She took the snifter from him and placed herself on one of the cushioned benches by the windows, nearest the decanter. She was trying, but her hands were still shaking with the urge to lash out at him for intruding on her domain. She sipped her brandy as he pulled a stool over and sat down directly in front of her.

"My darling? My love?" He spoke softly and gently, placing his fingers under her chin, requesting she look at him. When she did, he continued, looking directly into her eyes so she would understand every word was the truth. "The reason that I did these things is so that we may start enjoying the life we have fought so hard to have. 'Becca, we are partners and equals in every way. I sit here in this office, every day, for hours on end, sometimes bored out of my mind."

He smiled. She laughed softly. He continued.

"I do not think that you should be slopping mop buckets around and washing windows when you could be up here bored with me." He shrugged nonchalantly. She smiled and looked up at him again, this time he winked at her.

"'Becca, my love, we should be sitting up here trying to decide what colleges we can afford to send our children to. Talking about the future that we want. I should not be looking out this window to see you hauling a laundry basket to the line. We have more than enough money to hire people to get those things done. I did not do what I did to try and take anything away from you. I did what I did so that I could try and give you more."

He sat back from her and with a sigh and continued on, "You have spent the last two years telling me and everyone in ear shot I am the gentleman of the manor. When I act like it, you get angry. I am afraid, my dear, I am caught between the proverbial rock and a hard place. I did what I did strictly out of my love for you. I hope you can forgive me."

He stood and moved himself to the fire, swirling his brandy in his hand for a few seconds before draining it.

She stood slowly and placed her glass on the table before walking to him and wrapping her arms around him from behind, laying her cheek in the center of his back.

"Yes, dear," she murmured into his shoulder. She smiled and hugged him just a bit tighter when she felt him shake with silent laughter.

∽

Saturday March 30, 1866

Richard arrived at Jocko's well ahead of the seven o'clock start time of their regular poker game. He knew Charlie would be there very early on this particular Saturday.

Pushing the door open he grinned when his old, reliable friend, was indeed seated at the bar with a plate of steaming food before him.

He tormented in a sing song voice, "I am gonna tell..." as he took a seat next to the tall man. "You like Esther's pork chops and gravy better than Sarah's."

"I will never give you another meal again," the general threatened without even looking over at his friend, as he tore the tender meat from the bone with his fork.

"You win. I will be quiet." Richard gestured to Jocko for a drink.

"I suspected as much." Charlie nodded before taking a bite of the wonderful food before him.

It was true; this was one of the more terrifying secrets he kept. If Sarah discovered he had found another meal in town he liked better than one of hers, there would pain and misery in his house.

"I am very glad you are both here." Richard gestured for Jocko to stick around.

The three friends formed a tight circle, their heads together as they had done many times before in the fifteen years they had all known each other. "I am convinced we may have some trouble brewing."

"What kind?" Charlie asked absentmindedly as he pushed another forkful of pork into the mound of mashed potatoes and brown gravy.

The provost sighed as he fingered the rim of his glass. "That is just it, I am not entirely sure. I have had some reports of problems out in Slab Town, rumors of problems over in Sweetwater, but I cannot quite place my finger on who is causing them."

"What kind of problems?" Jocko poured Charlie another cup of coffee and topped it with brandy.

"Some thefts, breaking and entering, some fights. But it seems as if someone else might be starting those problems, then getting the hell out."

"What makes you say that?" Charlie sipped his coffee, giving his friend his full attention.

"When I go out there to talk to them, no one wants to say anything."

"That seems about right to me." The barkeep nodded. "You are still the Yankee Government representative, Mr. Provost Polk."

Richard shook his head, "No, this is something very different. They are afraid of someone or something."

"Well," Charlie nodded to Jocko, "You know our friend here is the eyes and ears of Culpeper."

The batman turned innkeeper raised his hands. "I have not heard word one about this kind of problem. Then again, seems to me that these are the kinds of issues that would not get discussed publicly."

"There is that." Charlie agreed as he broke part of a biscuit off and dropped it in the remaining gravy on his plate. "If you have someone going out there to stir the pot so to speak, they are going to be far more surreptitious than discussing their plans at the local tavern."

"And in that lies the problem. I cannot be everywhere," Richard said before sipping his drink.

"True." Charlie agreed with a nod. "You could ask General Sheridan for some more men to come in and form another patrol."

"I could." Richard finished his drink and pushed his glass out for a refill. "I am concerned that it might inflame the situation if we bring more Federal troops in. We already have over 100 men spread across the county, and I think that their presence may be contributing to the problem, not helping to solve it. I am not quite between a rock and a hard place yet, but I do feel the mushy bits firming up. Perhaps I could ask for a couple of deputy provost officers instead of more troops."

Charlie nodded. "I think that is the place to start. And Richard, you know you have my support and for what it is worth, my back up." He gave a rueful grin. "I am afraid I do not handle a pistol very well anymore."

"Old friend, I hope it does not come to that. Just keep your ears open. Between you and Jocko, you are going to hear everything one way or another. And given I am not sure who I can absolutely trust other than you two, let us keep it between us for the time being."

~

Monday April 2, 1866

Charlie stood on the porch watching as Tomas and Reg loaded the large rig with everything Rebecca required for a trip to New York. He looked down at his feet where his solitary leather satchel held everything he would need for a week in the city. Then back to the wagon where he saw three large trunks, two smaller cases, three satchels and bags of varying materials, and hat boxes he was fairly certain were mating like rabbits. They just seemed to keep coming out of the house in a never ending stream.

"How many heads does she have?" He mumbled as he jammed a cigar in the corner of his mouth and struck a match on the pillar.

"Just the one, my darling," she offered as she came up behind him. "But if you expect me to be a proper lady and present myself as the model wife of the distinguished general, then I need these things. I would be happy to go back up and pack my work clothes, but then I think we would have to change the venue of the trip to those Western forts Phil Sheridan is always going on about when he wants to torment you."

He just smiled and nodded, "Yes, dear."

"Put your battle face on, General," she warned in low tones as she took his hand. "The children will be out shortly to say good bye."

"How is Em?"

"Trying very hard to be brave, but I fear actually seeing you depart may send her into a fit. Luckily, I think Edgar is quite capable of handling her."

He took a draw from his cigar and let the smoke out slowly. This was a good cigar and it had been a while since he took a moment to really appreciate the essence of truly fine tobacco.

He closed his eyes and took one final appraisal of the smoke through is nostrils, drawing a slow, deep breath before the cloud around his head dissipated. "Mmmm." His growl was nothing less than sensual.

"Enjoying that, are you?" His wife snickered, giving him a nudge with her elbow to wake him from his tobacco induced reverie. "I have seen that look on your face before," she said coyly. "I am a little disturbed that a cigar can put it there too."

"Rebecca!" He choked on the smoke, completely startled by her comment. He could feel his face and ears going red.

She threw her head back and laughed so hard he thought she was going to fall backward, so he extended his hand to steady her at the small of her back. "I think this trip has already been good for us and we have not even left the stoop yet." He kissed her on top of her head as her laugh settled and she patted his chest.

"I think, as usual, dear husband, that you are right."

After securing Charlie's bag, Tomas climbed up to his spot on the rig, with Reg sitting next to him to help him unload Miss Rebecca's things and to bring the rig home after they departed for New York. The valet was actually a bit excited to be traveling with his generous employer and his wife. They were bringing Lizbet as well. It would not do for the good general and Mrs. Redmond to travel without his valet and her lady's maid.

Charlie's head turned when he heard his group of little troopers making their way out to the porch. Tess and Lizbet carefully helped the boys toddle along. They wanted nothing more than to be up and walking on their own. Suzanna and Darby stood holding hands, trying to smile and failing. Em sat down on the threshold of the door, her little face in her hands, tears streaming down her cheeks, but she was doing her best to control them.

Oh, Lord, help me. How are you ever supposed to go anywhere with a clean conscience? He looked to Rebecca, who just smiled and shrugged one shoulder. He stepped forward and looked at Darby. "You will help with your brothers and sisters? You are the oldest. Mama Rebecca and I expect you to set a good example."

"Of course, Papa Charlie." The boy nodded, "We are just going to miss you."

"And we will miss you too, son. However, we will be home in just a week and I can assure you that Mama Rebecca will probably need another trunk for the things she will bring home to her well behaved children." He leaned in and whispered so only Darby and Suzanne could hear. "It will be like she robbed Father Christmas."

Both children giggled, and Rebecca just made a 'tsking' sound behind him. He kissed both of them on the head, reassuring them that they would indeed return and they were much loved. The boys were lifted up so he could give them each a kiss. They were too young yet to really care what Mama and Papa were doing. Then came Em.

He limped over to the door where his first child sat desperately trying not to cry. She was drawing quick, rapid little breaths as she tried to not to let her tears drop on her father's boots. He looked down at her. She refused to look up.

Rebecca's heart burst with pride as she watched her husband, slowly get down on the porch to sit in front of their little girl. She felt silly, quickly wiping away a tear that had formed in her eye. She knew what he was doing had to be excruciating for him and yet, there he was, doing whatever was necessary to comfort their children.

"Emily Adams Redmond, look at me." Her papa's voice was soft but firm. She lifted her eyes and looked into the only face she wanted to see every day of her life. She loved her papa and she hated it when he went away. "You are a big girl of three now."

"Yes, Papa."

"You know that Mama and I will be back in just one week?"

"Yes, Papa." She nodded, wiping a tear away in the same fashion Charlie had seen Rebecca do on more than one occasion. So like her.

"So you are going to be my big girl and be good for Cousin Charlotte and Reverend Edgar? You are not going to cause them any problems?"

"Yes, Papa. I promise."

"That," he caressed the child's cheek and leaned in so their foreheads met, "is my girl. I love you, imp." He always made sure to look into Emily's eyes when he told her he loved her. He did that with all his children, but for her, it was extra special reassurance.

"Love you, too, Papa." She rose from the threshold and put her arms around his neck hugging him as tight as her little arms could manage. He returned the hug, looking up to find Edgar and Charlotte staring down at him.

"Oh, Em." Charlotte helped her little cousin off her papa so Edgar could offer him a hand up.

"It is time for you go, Charlie, or you will miss the train."

He nodded his thanks to Edgar for helping him get back to his feet. He pulled his pocket watch from his vest and popped it open. "Holy smoke! We are late!"

Edgar and Charlie quickly got Rebecca and Lizbet settled in the rig. Before Charlie joined them, he fished a small leather bag from his pocket. He pressed it into Edgar's hand, "Five children, and one penny a day per child if you need it."

The minister laughed and hefted the little bag. "May I keep anything I don't need to bribe your children? For the church?"

"You may." Charlie snorted with amusement as he sat down next to Rebecca. "And I will triple anything you have left. Spend it wisely, Reverend." With that he gave Tomas' seat a tap with his cane. The next sound was the slap of the reins and they were off.

He looked back to see Edgar was now holding a sobbing Emily very carefully. Rebecca took his hand, giving him a reassuring squeeze. "She will be fine."

"I know she will." He fished his flask from his pocket and took a rather long draught.

"You do not intend to share that?"

He took it from his lips, looking rather abashed. "I am sorry, darling, but this is my medicine."

"Oh, Charlie, do be careful with that, then. You would not want to leave that out on your desk to have one of your friends or business associates accidently drink from it. I thought you had a smaller, brown bottle."

"I dropped it. Broke it into a thousand little pieces." He told a little white lie. "I figured this was the best replacement."

"Well, just be careful."

"Yes, dear."

Tomas, ever the dutiful and well prepared valet, handed back a flask from his own jacket pocket. "Here you go, ma'am. Brandy for you."

"Thank you, Tomas." The flask was passed from Lizbet's hands to Rebecca's.

CHAPTER 11

Monday April 2, 1866

The train pulled out of Culpeper on time, bound for Washington and points north. They just barely managed to arrive at the station in time to board. The weather was beautiful, the rail bed was fairly smooth and they made good time to Washington's Union Station. A brief layover in the city gave them just enough time to stretch their legs before the train was ready to leave for Penn Station in Maryland.

The trip to Baltimore was quick, just a little more than two hours, but when they pulled in, the conductor came to their private sleeping car to let them know that there was a delay on the tracks between Baltimore and Philadelphia, so that they would have to stay in the city for the night. He told them that they were welcome to use the car as their accommodations, but that they would have to debark to obtain supper.

Obligingly, they strolled onto the train platform, looking for Tomas and Lizbet. When they found their staff, Charlie handed Tomas a ten dollar gold piece and his business card as a means of identification, and told them to go and have a pleasant evening, but be back by eight that evening to prepare their sleeping car for bed. The young man looked at the coin, grinned and bowed, appreciative of the kindness his employer had shown. He offered Lizbet his arm and they strolled off into the crowd discussing where they might find dinner.

The general then went to the telegraph office in the station and wired a message to the hotel in New York that their arrival would be delayed.

"Shall we go exploring?" He offered her his arm. "Baltimore is famous for its seafood, so shall we find a place by the harbor?"

She thought, *Oh, Lord, Charlie and the disgusting slimy seagoing things that he will eagerly put down his throat are not on my list of favorites, but it is his holiday.* "Of course, dear. Do you think we will be able to see Fort McHenry?"

A few minutes later and they were settled in a hansom cab, heading down Charles Street towards Baltimore's inner harbor. The cabbie kept up a stream of chatter about the sights of the city until suddenly Charlie rapped the driver's seat with his cane and called out, "Stop!"

Rebecca looked around, wondering what had caused him to call out.

He handed a couple of coins to the driver and said, "Wait here. We may be a while, but I will pay you for your time." Obligingly, the cabbie pulled over to the curb. He climbed out, and handed her down.

They had stopped in front of a gunsmith's shop. He strode in, with her trailing after, a puzzled look on her face. He walked up to the proprietor and asked, "Sir, do you have one of the new Remington double barreled Derringers?"

"Why, yes, sir. I just received several from Philadelphia. Would you like to look at them?"

He nodded and looked over the tray of small guns the gentleman quickly retrieved and placed on the counter. One was silver plated with beautiful filigree work along the stock and barrel along with mother of pearl grips. He selected that one and asked for two boxes of the .41 caliber short cartridges that the little pistol took. Pulling out his wallet, he asked the gentleman, "How much?"

With the exchange of money, the clerk slipped a new, boxed gun and boxes of ammunition into a small brown bag Charlie quickly tucked in his coat pocket. As they walked out of the shop, she asked, "What is this all about?"

"Just a whim, dear. I think you may need protection some day. And if you have a gun, I will worry less."

"As long as I do not use it on you, I assume." She laughed at him. She made a mental note to grill him further about the little pistol later.

As they looked up and down the street for their cabbie, they noticed another store. Two doors back was a store unlike any that they had ever seen before. The sign over the door read, "Toy Bazaar. H. Schwarz, Proprietor."

They walked in, looking around in amazement at the toys that were displayed artfully all over the store. Unlike most stores, with a myriad of goods and products, this store only had children's toys, rows and rows of the most exquisite toys available from all over Europe.

These toys were made by master craftsmen and were the best available. They were not simply racked on shelves--they displayed in charming dioramas that gave the shopper an idea of how their children could play with these delightful creations.

There were dolls in complex doll houses. Wooden trains on mats of green cloth with houses, animals, and trees dotted around to make a little landscape. Wooden hobby horses with real leather tack and horsehair manes and tails. Large dolls with perfect porcelain heads, real human hair, and extensive wardrobes.

But the display that most attracted his attention was of tiny lead soldiers complete with artillery, horses, and battlements, painted in the colors of the British, Russian, and French armies, all set out on a field in the formation that every educated soldier would recognize as Waterloo. The general was lost for the time being.

Rebecca continued to wander around the shop, until she came upon a display of baby carriages and strollers. There were a pair of beautiful, hand carved wooden and canvas strollers, complete with striped awnings to keep the sun off the babies' faces. And the real miracle was that they were collapsible. She was immediately taken with the possibilities they offered for corralling her two youngest boys when they went out and about.

She went looking for her husband to ask him to buy the strollers for the boys. She found him talking excitedly with a young man and accumulating a pile of items.

"Oh, darling, look at what I have found!" He was regressing. Currently he sounded about twelve years old. She scratched just above her brow, and she could almost swear, if she had not known it to be impossible, that her husband was bouncing just a little.

"Darby and I will have so much fun with these!" A large number of boxes sat on the counter, each labeled as lead soldiers of various types. "Mr. Schwarz says he can have them shipped to the house. And look what I got for the girls! Is it not the most beautiful doll house you have ever seen?"

He pointed to the display model of a beautiful, fully appointed doll house. It was approximately four feet wide and three feet deep, with the two long sides open, revealing each of the rooms and the delicate furnishings.

There was a central hall with a carefully crafted stair case leading to the upstairs. Each room had a beautifully fashioned fireplace. On the main floor, there was a dining room, an elegant parlor, a music room, and a winter kitchen.

On the upper floor were four perfectly furnished bedrooms, with four poster beds, desks and chairs, and wardrobes and cedar chests. There were rugs in every room, and draperies at the windows. The exterior of the house was carefully finished to look like brick, as were the four chimneys. The roof was made of tiny wood shingles.

The doll house was as realistic as anything either of them had ever seen. It was a work of art that looked somewhat like a tiny version of their house.

Oh, dear. One doll house for two girls. I wonder if they will end up fighting the war all over again. "Charlie, honey, my darling. We have two daughters." She held up two fingers as if he needed a visual clue as well.

"But they play so well together with their dolls and their little tea parties and all their other toys. Surely they can share this."

"Yes, darling." He would clearly have to learn the hard way. *From the moment I met him, I would take a bullet for him. But when it comes to the children...* she just sighed and shook her head.

"So, dear, did you see anything you wanted?"

"Actually, I did. There are these wonderful folding strollers that would be perfect for the boys."

"By all means, if you want them, get them. And can you please pick out furnishings and figures to go with the doll house for the girls?"

Oh, my God, she thought. What have I gotten into? "You did not have a lot of toys as a child, did you, Charlie?"

He shook his head, "No," he answered softly. "My father considered them a waste of money."

At that point, the young man who had been standing quietly to one side as Charlie enthused over the toys stepped closer. "Mrs. Redmond? I am Frederick Schwarz. May I help you make your selections?"

"Thank you, Mr. Schwarz." She turned to her husband, who was looking back at the lead soldiers with a stupid grin on his face, the rarely seen laugh lines showing around his eyes. "Yes, Charlie, you can go back to the toy soldiers now."

Just then, a second gentleman stepped up. "Good afternoon. I am Henry Schwarz, the proprietor here. May I help you?"

"I believe my husband wants to look at the toy soldiers again. But, Mr. Schwarz? He has a limit. He is not allowed to buy your entire stock."

The German man laughed politely and followed Charlie back to the table where he once again stood, entranced by the little lead figurines.

Half an hour later, and a rather large check made out to Mr. Schwarz at the Toy Bazaar, and Charlie's card so Schwarz could ship the goods to Culpeper, the two of them returned to the street.

Unfortunately, the hack driver had given up on waiting for the out of towners.

Henry Schwarz looked out of the store window and saw his two best customers for at least the month and possibly for the year standing on the sidewalk looking for a hack.

In the time they had been in his store he had figured out they had five children. Three boys, two girls. The man of the house was a retired, but high ranking military man and the lady was long suffering. He also knew General Redmond was a man who would spoil his children and Henry was in the business of spoiling the children of wealthy men.

He hurried out to them. "I am so sorry. I see your driver has left you stranded. Would you be willing to let me lend you the use of my coach? My driver is out back, and he knows the city very well."

Before Charlie could say a word, Rebecca stepped in. "Oh, Mr. Schwarz, that would be lovely. We need to find something to eat, and then get back to the train station this evening. Would you mind?"

"Not at all, Mrs. Redmond. I think you will find my coach far more comfortable than a standard hansom cab."

He hurried back into the store and a few minutes later, a beautiful gentleman's coach painted yellow with the large wheels trimmed in red pinstripes and drawn by a pair of big bay mares, came around the corner. Mr. Schwarz bustled back out to hand them into his conveyance. "I hope the rest of your stay in Baltimore is pleasant. And if you want good seafood and a nice view of the harbor, there is an excellent inn over on Thames Street called The Horse that serves spectacular crab and has a lovely view from the garden."

"Sounds wonderful. Thank you," said Charlie, his mouth already watering at the thought of delicious crab cakes and oysters.

Rebecca just smiled.

Mr. Schwarz looked up at his driver. "John, take them to The Horse and wait. They will need to go back to the train station. I will get a ride home this evening with my brother."

They settled into the coach as John tapped the horses with the reins and they moved forward over the cobblestoned road. Usually driving over cobblestones set a coach to bouncing and bumping around, but the ride in this ridiculously well-sprung coach was as smooth as gliding over glass.

Charlie, who habitually tensed himself to withstand the bouncing and swaying, slowly relaxed back into the comfortably upholstered seat and enjoyed the scenery as he draped his arm over his wife's shoulders. John drove them down Charles Street until they reached Pratt Street, turned left and drove past the Inner Harbor. They crossed over a bridge and continued on until John turned down Bond Street.

Looking out over the water through the large glass window in the front of the carriage, they could see the famous Fort McHenry across the water. A huge flag, though not the one that had inspired the song, flew over this bastion that had stood against the British invasion in their futile attempt to retake the American colonies.

"Oh, Charlie. It is absolutely beautiful." In the light of late afternoon, the sun lit the gentle waves, giving the harbor a glitter that set off the streamlined hulls of the steamers and the pair of tall ships anchored in the harbor, as well as all of the small boats that sculled across the water.

Shortly, they reached the inn that Mr. Schwarz had recommended. The building was old and charming. A plaque on the side of the building said it had been built in 1768. They chose to be seated on the side garden where they could watch the waves and boats while they ate. John pulled around back into the stable yard to wait for them.

The waiter came to their table promptly, and offered a menu on heavy paper and with hand-lettered calligraphy presenting the options available for supper. There were raw oysters, steamed clams, steamed shrimp, spiced mussels, and a seafood bisque as starters, along with the option of a simple garden salad. Charlie was almost drooling.

For the main course, The Horse offered their famous Maryland Blue Crab Cakes, along with roasted mackerel, a baked sea trout, lobster, an oyster and spinach casserole, several types of fried fish, shrimp, and oysters, and one grilled steak, offered, it seemed, as an afterthought for the non-seafood eating guest.

The general chose to start his meal with raw oysters, which he slurped down with great gusto, and a small order of spiced mussels. Rebecca opted for the salad. She carefully avoided watching him slurping the slimy grey things floating in their own juices like they were manna from heaven. *If he thinks he is going to kiss me tonight after sucking those disgusting things down without sterilizing his mouth first, he has another think coming.*

He followed this display of disgusting lack of taste with a plate full of fried oysters and crab cakes. She opted for the baked sea trout with a fresh tomato topping. "Oh, sweetheart, you should try these crab cakes. They are absolutely wonderful."

All she could think of was the ten legged little monsters that looked like aquatic spiders. The thought of eating something that looked like an insect repelled her. "No, no, Charlie. You enjoy your crab."

Dessert for both of them was a simple bowl of early strawberries, probably grown in someone's hot house, and topped with sweetened clotted cream. All in all, except for the rather limited choices for someone of Rebecca's tastes, it was a very pleasant meal.

As they were savoring their berries and the beautiful view as the beginnings of sunset lit the crests of the waves in the harbor, she looked at her husband, her eyes crinkled in curiosity. "Darling, please, why do you think I need a gun?"

He thought for a moment, then responded carefully. "Well, dear, Richard, Jocko and I have had a few conversations about the mood of the community, and while they have not specifically said that there is a risk, the suggestion has been made that there are some people who are less than happy with things as they stand. There is some unrest in Slab Town and up in Sweetwater, and you have seen for yourself how the people tend to split into two groups at Church – those who are willing to try to put things back together and those who are resentful as hell about having lost the war. I just wanted to make sure you had something for your own defense in case you need it. I cannot be with you every minute, no matter how much I wish it."

She looked thoughtful for a few moments. Carrying a gun was not something she was terribly comfortable with, but he did seem to have good reason to want her to do so. "I just hope I never need it, love."

"So do I, darling, so do I. When we get home I will teach you how to load and fire it. Even with my bad hand I can handle a Derringer."

As the sun was starting to set, John drove them back to the train station, where their sleeping car had been pulled onto a siding that offered convenient access without having to trudge through the train yard. Someone had thoughtfully put a set of steps on the platform to make getting up into the car less of a struggle than it would have been if they had had to climb the short metal ladder to the landing that led to the car's door.

As they entered the car, he wrapped his arms around her from behind, and kissed her neck. "You do know, darling, oysters are supposed to be an aphrodisiac? I know you enjoy our morning pairings, but I do have a bit of extra energy tonight."

Silently, she unwound his arms from her waist and pointed at the wash basin, and specifically at the tooth brush, can of brushing powder, and mouth wash sitting in the little case beside it. "Not until after you have scrubbed your mouth out, General Redmond."

Wednesday, April 4, 1866

Just after breakfast, Edgar took his best friend aside. "Um, Rex. Would you do me a favor? I'd like to give Charlotte a surprise – let us say a gift for all the effort she has been putting in to keep the children under something resembling control. Perhaps dinner on Saturday?"

Rex watched Edgar as he made his request. It was unusual for him to be reticent about asking for a favor. Usually he just stated what he wanted. This has to be something special. Perhaps a seduction? "So you would like me to make dinner for the two of you? Something exotic, such as a traditional Chinese dinner? Something to put the lady in a particularly good mood?" A smirk played around his eyes. From the look on Edgar's face, he had hit the bullseye on the first try.

"Yes, exactly." He looked a little relieved and a little excited. "Perhaps some of that fantastic duck you make?"

He smiled. "I will provide you with a dinner in the traditional style. Let me talk with Sarah about what ingredients we may have available, and to make arrangements with her to take over her kitchen."

Edgar wandered off to the children's nursery, a room that was rapidly being transformed into a school room as the two little girls needed to start learning the basics. Darby was already settled with a history book drawn from Charlie's library. Teaching that boy was less about actually teaching and more about keeping up with his facile mind and giving him direction. His father needed to get him a tutor – and soon.

Rex went to find Reg and recover one particular case that had been put into storage, as it held his cherished wok, a large, flattened cooking pan that had been tempered over the course of many years of cooking and careful cleaning with just salt and hot water. Nothing would ever stick to it. He also needed a pair of well-tempered clay pots that he used to make stocks and sauce bases. And most important was his collection of spices and soy sauces. Every time he got close to a city with an oriental community, he carefully restocked his supplies, as one never knew when he would be able to do so again.

Together, they hauled the case to the kitchen, setting it gently in one unused corner. Rex then sat down with Sarah to discuss the possibility of using her kitchen.

"Miss Sarah, Reverend Edgar requests I make traditional Chinese dinner. I would not want to intrude. May I have permission to use your kitchen?"

She looked at him, a bit puzzled. "So, you cook different from what I cook?"

He smiled. "Yes. Very different. But very good."

She thought for a minute. "I can always learn something new. Yes, you can use my kitchen, if you let me help."

"Thank you." He smiled, all the way to his eyes and nodded. "So good. We can start gathering ingredients."

The two of them spent a good bit of time in the pantry and in the cold room, as Rex looked for ingredients that would substitute for traditional Chinese products. Then they marched out to the winter garden where he cleaned out the crop of newly sprouted green onions. From there, they went to the medicine garden to collect some ginger root, which Sarah usually only used for treating upset stomachs and for her mysterious hangover cure.

Finally, they went out to the poultry yard, where he carefully selected a chicken and a duck, which they butchered, drained of blood, feathered, and eviscerated.

Once the birds were prepared, he took them into the kitchen. The duck, he rubbed with a collection of spices and sauces from his box, then hung near the stove to dry. He cut up the chicken, dropped it into one of his clay pots and added an assortment of vegetables and herbs, topped with water and set on the back of the range to come to a slow simmer.

Every day for the next two days, he would come to the kitchen to do something else to the duck, and to check the maturity of the broth he was making.

~

Charlotte ran from room to room, looking for Em. First she checked the nursery, where the boys were napping. Then she checked the girls' bedroom, where Suzanne was quietly playing with a doll. "Sue, do you know where you sister is? I cannot find her anywhere."

"She took Papa Puppy for a walk, I think."

"Thank you, dear." She thought Emily and that puppy outside was not a good sign.

She ran down the back stairs and into the kitchen, where Beulah and Sarah were having a mid-morning coffee and gossip break. Both women stood up, startled, when Charlotte came in the door, breathing a little hard from her run down the stairs.

"Excuse me, but have you seen Emily?"

"Not recently. She took that damned Jack Russell of hers out for a walk a while ago," the housekeeper offered with a gesture toward the back door.

"Thank you."

Going out the back door, she scanned the yard, and beyond, down to the pond. Her greatest fear was that she would find Em's drowned body floating in the water. But there was no sign of the pink and white dress that she had worn that morning at breakfast.

There was, however, a small white and brown dog, obviously digging at something, down near the pond. And where Papa Puppy was, Emily would be as well.

She trudged down the path to the pond. The ground around the pond had been cleared for some project of Charlie's and a section was partitioned off with a canvas wall. It was soft and made easy digging for the little dog – and for the little girl.

"Cousin Charlotte. Look what I found!" Emily was holding a piece of rock with the imprint of some kind of ancient bug in it. Beside her was a pile of shells, several more rocks with fossil imprints, and an ancient shark tooth. Her lovely pink and white dress was caked in mud, her shoes were missing entirely, and it was hard to tell, but it looked like one sock was absent as well.

~

Saturday, April 7, 1866

Early on Saturday morning, Tarent, Reg, Sarah, and Beulah headed into town to recruit new employees for the Redmond household and stables. They took the buggy, leaving it in the stable yard behind Jocko's tavern. The house staff headed down to the colored parts of town, where they were going to recruit more staff from their friends and relatives.

Tarent headed over to the newly reopened blacksmith's forge.

James Granville, the smith, was part of the group of men who had returned with Alex Raeburn, and often the space in front of his forge was a gathering place for his compatriots. Tarent felt this was as good a place as any to look for more skilled help than Reg would find in Slab Town or Sweetwater.

As he approached, he did not notice Raeburn standing at the back of the group of men, and even if he had, he might not have recognized him as the man who had struck Charlie at church that day.

He called to the men standing around. "I am looking for a few good men with excellent horse skills to help build Redmond Stables into the premier breeding stable in the state. I need a couple of trainers, an exercise rider, two stable hands, and a really good tack man. The pay is fair, and General Redmond takes good care of his people. So, are any of you interested and able?"

Most of the men milled around, torn between needing jobs and not wanting to work for the damned scallywag who had taken over the old Gaines place. Raeburn grabbed one of his cohorts by the arm and hissed into his ear, "Get a job! I want to know what that bastard is doing out there."

Tarent finished his invitation to the men by telling them that he would be over at Jocko's having some coffee, and anyone who wanted a job could come and talk with him. He also warned them that they would have a trial period as he saw what skills they brought to the program, as it was his intention to create the best stable, with the best skilled people, he possibly could.

"I cain't work for that Yankee." Robert Brooks had found it hard enough to buy hay from Redmond, but to work for him?

"You can and you will, or I will personally break your arm." Raeburn jerked his head over toward Rainey. "Eddie over there has already done work out at that place. If he can work for the bastard, you can."

"All right, all right." Brooks nodded and started after Tarent toward Jocko's. As he passed Eddie, he hit him in the shoulder. "Drop it. It ain't yours." Rainey had been fingering a snaffle bit and was obviously planning to slip it into his pocket.

Rex was in the kitchen bright and early to prepare dinner for Edgar and Charlotte. He hung the duck in the coolest corner of the fireplace, using the rack that Sarah roasted meat on to suspend the duck. He then set to work, making delicate wheat and egg noodles, rolling out paper thin squares of pastry, chopping, mincing, mashing, braising, roasting and using his strange flat pan and long sticks held in one hand to pan fry all sorts of things.

He rolled delicate balls of pork mixed with spices, sauces, onion, garlic, and ginger, then wrapped them in the little squares of pastry. He played with the chicken broth, straining it, then dropped egg whites in to clarify it, and carefully balanced the flavors, tasting and adjusting it. He had a strange looking knife that looked almost like a cleaver but with a narrower blade, which he used to reduce heavy vegetables like cabbage and carrots to delicate little sticks. When Sarah returned from her recruiting expedition to town, he looked like he was less cooking and more dancing with the food.

After the children were fed and settled for the night, he began serving their special meal. Starting with the delicate noodles he made and then carefully chilled, tossed with matchstick thin slices of various vegetables, and sauced with a combination of garlic, ginger, vinegar, some of the black sauce he had in his case, and peanuts that he had mashed to a fine paste. Sarah had never seen a pasta salad, let alone a cold one.

While they were eating the noodles, he was back at the stove. He took a beautiful trout he had brought in from the stream, dressed and scaled it, and using that strange pan, fried it whole, along with garlic, ginger, carrots, onions, and a different version of his black sauce. This he served on a bed of rice.

He also carved the roast duck, serving it on a platter with little, paper thin things he called pancakes, some with scallions, others plain, and with a bowl of plum sauce on the side. The duck skin was so crisp you could hear it crackle as he cut it. This he served, again with bowls of rice on the side, between them on the table, so they could take what they wished.

As soon as he returned from serving the duck and the fish, he set the pot of broth to boil, dropping in the little pillows he had made of spiced pork wrapped in paper thin pastry into the boiling broth. Stirring it frequently, he checked the pillows to make sure the pork balls had set up, then poured the soup into a large, open bowl instead of the tureen she would have used, and topped it with a sprinkle of finely chopped scallions.

When the soup was served, he prepared the berries for dessert very simply, lightly sprinkled with mint, sugar, chopped nuts and a sprinkle of a white wine with strange figures on the label. Again, he simply sat the bowl in the middle of the table, with small plates and a few almond-flavored cookies, so they could take what they wanted.

Sarah was amazed. The cooking was so intricate she was sure it would take years to learn how to cook all of these dishes. But the presentation was even more amazing. Each dish was assembled so that it looked like a piece of art, rather than something to eat. Her dishes, swimming in thick gravies, looked messy and thrown together compared to what this man did to food. What amazed her even more was that he used things she normally used as ingredients in medicines as part of his normal cooking.

In anticipation of Rex's Chinese feast, Charlotte had enlisted her lady's maid, Sissy, in taking special care with her clothes and hair that evening. She recognized this dinner for what it probably was – the introductory steps of a seduction. It was exciting for Charlotte to have a man interested in her who would take the time and effort to properly romance and woo her.

They ate their way through Rex's amazing Asian feast. Each new dish brought exclamations over the beauty of the presentation, and sighs and murmurs of appreciation as the food was consumed, accompanied by small sips of a clear white wine that Rex had provided.

"Edgar, what is this wine made from? I do not think I have ever tasted anything quite like it."

"It is something that Rex loves. It's made from rice. It's called Saki, and it's actually from Japan."

The meal continued, with Charlotte exclaiming over each dish as it was presented. Edgar laughed as he watched her consume probably four times as much food as she normally did at a sitting, and said, "You know, in China, it is considered rude if you do not belch, and loudly, after a meal like this."

"Oh, thank goodness. I think I can summon up quite a compliment for Rex's cooking then."

When he came to present the fruit for dessert, both of them paid the Chinaman a culturally correct tribute.

CHAPTER 12

Monday, April 9, 1866

The train ride from New York to Washington had been horrible. Rain washed the windows so heavily that one could not see out. The wind buffeted the train so that the car rocked back and forth. It was as bad as being on a boat in a rough sea.

When they pulled into Washington's B&O Station, they were over four hours late. Charlie trudged into the terminal to send a message to Edgar telling him of the delay, only to find that the telegraph lines were down. He limped back to the train car, picking up a copy of the Evening Star on the way. The headline had caught his eye. "Civil Rights Act Passes."

He scanned the article. Johnson had pocket vetoed previous versions of the act; now the number of votes made it impossible for Johnson to ignore it. Whether he vetoed it or not, there were enough votes to override any veto.

When he got back to their train car, he informed his wife what the situation was.

"Oh, Lord! Em will be giving Edgar and Charlotte the devil of a time, with us being so late."

"Indeed. And this weather is giving me the devil of a time. Could you get my medicine, dear?"

While she fetched his laudanum from the other end of the car, he poured himself a brandy and settled down to read his paper. When she returned, he took a double dose of the laudanum, then went back to the paper.

"So what does it say?"

"Congress passed the Civil Rights Act. It says here that it gives citizenship and the same rights enjoyed by white citizens to all male persons in the United States without distinction of race or color, or previous condition of slavery or involuntary servitude."

"Does that mean that black men can vote?"

"I assume it does." He read on for a few more lines, and then dropped the paper to look at her. "You realize what this means?"

"I am not sure I do."

"It means that every old-school southerner is going to do their damned best to keep the Negro down, to keep them from voting, and to keep them from having any power, even if that means guns, lynching, fire, whatever it takes. We are in for a mess, I am afraid."

"So who can stop them?"

"Well, certainly not Johnson. That man has the spine of a jellyfish. And I suspect that he personally thinks Negroes should be kept in 'their proper place.' He is one of those old school Southerners after all." He poured himself another brandy. "It means every real scallywag and carpet bagger will take advantage of the Negroes and every old school southerner will try to beat them into submission. I am damned glad I bought you that pistol. You may need it." He finished his brandy in one gulp, then poured yet another one.

The weather was abysmal and had been on and off for two days.

The wind howled, the rain came down in sheets and the thunder and lightning seemed to shake the very foundation of the house.

Charlotte sat in the parlor, trying and failing to read a romance novel Edgar had presented her with the previous day. Charlie and Rebecca were late. Given the weather, her rational brain could understand it, but the worrisome part of her soul, like the children, was very anxious about the missing patriarch and matriarch of the Redmond clan.

She was very grateful for Edgar and Rex. While she had absolutely come to love Charlie and Rebecca's 'group of little troopers,' as their father called them, she was not nearly as skilled as the handsome minister and his friend when it came to calming the children. They both had a natural way with them that actually made her smile.

The thunder rang out again, reminding her of the storm raging outside, causing havoc inside. Em had been told her mama and papa would be home in the afternoon. That had not been the case, and she had let her displeasure be known all through supper, then through playtime with her brothers and sister. The fit continued through bath time. Edgar had hoped, close to an hour and a half ago, to get the girl to sleep. Charlotte continued trying to read her book.

Another half hour passed before Edgar finally entered. He gave a rueful little smile and shook his head. "I have had many trials in my life..." He just continued shaking his head as he headed for the tantalus.

"You have apparently been successful." She smiled.

"Indeed. I'm not sure if it was me or just the inevitability of having to sleep sometime."

"Oh, my poor dear." She dropped her feet from the sofa and gave the spot next to her a pat. "You are brilliant with them. One day you are going to be a wonderful father."

He gratefully took the spot next to her, allowing his hand to gently rest on her inner thigh. "You flatter me. First, I would have to find a woman who would tolerate me and my affinity for the peculiar or unusual."

"I happen to rather enjoy the peculiar and unusual." She grinned.

She could not help herself. She was attracted to this man. Really, truly, honestly attracted to him in a way she really never thought possible for herself with any man, other than maybe Charlie. She also enjoyed flirting with him because she wanted to and not because she had been paid to do so.

He smiled at her. "Well, my dear, I suspect you and I will find a way to spend many hours discussing some very interesting subjects then."

A particularly close sounding clap of thunder and a bolt of lightning caused Charlotte to jump, her book dropping to the floor. He was quick to retrieve it and hand it back. "I am sorry. Storms like this have always bothered me. I am worried sick about Charlie and Rebecca."

"Oh, I would not worry too much. I'm sure they are safely tucked away in a room in Washington for the night. I spoke to Colonel Polk earlier today and he told me the storms have caused problems on the rail line and knocked out relays in the telegraph system. I know the delay is worrisome, but I doubt it is serious. I sent Reg to wait at Jocko's since we really have no idea when they will be in I didn't want them stranded without a way home."

"Thankfully, you are here to think of such things, because honestly it never would have occurred to me."

The mantle clock chimed nine and they looked at each other. Both of them were tired from containing General and Mrs. Redmond's little group of troopers but not quite willing to give up the evening just yet.

"Edgar, you may think this terribly forward of me, but..."

It was close to midnight when a loud bang roused most of the house. It was not thunder, nor was it the crash of a tree going over in the storm. It was the front door bursting open and slamming into the wall behind it.

As the wind continued to howl and the rain came down in thick sheets, Rebecca, Tomas and Lizbet, all soaked to the bone, managed to half carry, half drag a very unconscious Charlie into the house.

Tomas tried his best to hold the man up as Rebecca and Lizbet forced the front door closed against the wind. When Rebecca turned around to start issuing orders, she noticed the movement coming down the stairs and she was very relieved.

Charlotte was on her way, her long robe flowing behind her as she descended the stairs. Edgar, barefoot and bare-chested, quickly fastening his trousers, followed only a few feet behind.

Edgar immediately took the bulk of Charlie's burden from Tomas while Charlotte helped Rebecca and Lizbet shed wet coats and hats. "What in the world?"

Rebecca spoke quickly, her eyes training in on her husband's lifeless form. "The train just managed, after several hours of literally crawling along the track, to make it home about forty minutes ago. There was a slight lull in the storm and we decided we had to try and get him home. Unfortunately it did not last. Edgar, Tomas, could you please take him to our room? I will be right up to get him out of those wet things."

Rex appeared at the bottom of the steps as Beulah also arrived in the foyer.

"Rex, help me," Edgar ordered so that Tomas could be relieved of his burden.

Rebecca took her two dedicated servants' hands. "Please, go get dry and warm and if you need food, feel free to find what you can in the kitchen. We can handle the general from here. Thank you so much. Get some rest. Beulah, please see to it these two take care of themselves and that there is hot soup and tea for Reg when he comes back from the barn."

"Yes, ma'am." The housekeeper ushered the soaked valet and lady's maid out of the foyer and down the hall.

Rex and Edgar carefully and slowly took Charlie up the stairs. Rex looked at Edgar, a serious look of concern on his face. "Do you smell it?"

The minister nodded.

Rebecca grabbed Charlotte by the wrist. "You have to help me," she commanded as she began dragging her up the stairs behind the men.

Once Charlie was laid out on the bed, Edgar and Rex took off his greatcoat. The tugging and handling resulted in low groans erupting from the unconscious man with every movement. Rex laid his fingers on Charlie's throat for a moment, then started rifling through the prone man's pockets while Edgar pulled off his suit coat.

"Where's the damn bottle?" Rex growled as he felt through the jacket Edgar had just removed.

Rebecca began trying to usher them out. "Thank you gentlemen, but we can take it from here."

Rex refused to be pushed out the door. "Wait, Mrs. Redmond. How long has he been like this?"

"Why?" She shook her head, not wanting to argue with the little man. "Perhaps two hours. Maybe a little more."

"Thank you." He turned on his heel and scurried down the stairs. His case with his herbs, elixirs and drugs was still in the kitchen.

Rebecca closed the door, barely registering that the two men went in different directions down the hall. She turned to Charlotte and began unbuttoning the cuffs of her dress.

"You are the only one I can trust to help me get him in bed. But first, if you don't mind, I have to get out of this dress so I can breathe. It is so wet I feel like I am carrying around an extra person."

Once Rebecca was out of her water-logged clothing and wrapped in her robe, they turned their attention to Charlie, with Rebecca telling Charlotte what she wanted to do next.

"All right." She nodded as she considered him. "Start with the boots. I will take the right one."

They managed to remove his drenched boots and socks within seconds of each other. Within a few minutes, they had also managed with some effort to divest him of his vest and tie, leaving him in shirt and trousers.

"Now, for the hardest part. Charlotte, we have to be very careful of his scars. These wounds cause him a great deal of discomfort and I know he is already in a lot of pain."

Charlotte nodded, not sure she really wanted to proceed, but knowing Rebecca needed her help. "Tell me what to do."

∾

Rebecca was exhausted, but still very awake, after the adventure that had been getting Charlie home and into bed in one piece. She sat by the fire in their sitting room, toweling her hair dry as Charlotte sat across from her staring into the fire and shaking her head. They had ended up there by mutual consent for a brandy after getting him settled into bed.

Charlotte, for the very first time, had gotten a good look at his wounds. The scars were ugly and the groans that emanated from him while they were tending him spoke to the depth of pain he was constantly in.

"I had no idea," she murmured. A tear slipped down her cheek and she wiped it away quickly.

"Most people have no clue. He hides the pain well. It is relentless in his life, every day. Some days he can barely walk. I do not know how he does it."

Charlotte turned her head and looked at Charlie's wife. Not just his wife, his partner in all things and the other half of his true soul. "Rebecca?"

"Yes?" Tired green eyes turned to her.

"I am really glad you and Charlie found each other. You are the reason he does it." That was all she could say to the brave woman before her. She could not admit aloud that she would not be able to handle these scars and the pain caused by them. That she would have left him.

Rebecca gave a tired smile. "Thank you."

"I think," Charlotte stood and gestured to the bedroom, "you should try to join him."

The blonde nodded. "I will. Thank you for your help tonight."

Charlotte shook her head as she opened the door, pausing she looked at the woman once again, "No. Thank you. Good night, Cousin Rebecca. I am very glad you and Charlie are home safely."

She entered the hall, pulling the door closed behind her. She stood there for a moment, recollections of the young, energetic, gallant Charlie Redmond vying for space in her mind with what she had just seen. She made her way back to her room, slipping through the door, into her bed and back into Edgar's strong, waiting arms.

~

Charlotte had been gone for less than a minute when Rebecca heard a quick rap on the sitting room door. She opened it, expecting to see her cousin, and was surprised that it was Rex standing before her, holding a small vial of some substance.

"Miss Rebecca, we must get this medicine into General Charlie immediately or he may die."

"Die!" She was stunned. "Die?"

He pushed into the room. "Yes. Die. He has had too much laudanum and too much brandy. Individually, they are both dangerous for someone in his condition. Together, they are deadly. They both suppress pain, but they also suppress breathing and the beating of the heart. Together, they multiply the effect. So as he lies there, his heart and breathing could slow so much that they simply stop. I have a stimulant to try to prevent that from happening."

She looked shocked and frightened as she followed the little man into the bedroom.

"Oh, dear. Miss Rebecca." He shook his head. "He cannot be allowed to lie flat. We have to at least sit him up."

Together, they pulled him into a sitting position. While Rex held him up, Rebecca packed pillows in behind him. Rex pulled a small glass straw from his pocket and dipped it into the vial, capturing a small amount of brown fluid in the tube. He opened Charlie's mouth and slipped the straw in, releasing the fluid down the back of his throat. Charlie coughed a little but swallowed the substance.

"Good, good," Rex muttered to himself as he continued to feed the medicine down the unconscious man's throat a few drops at a time. Periodically, he stopped and checked Charlie's pulse, then went back to dripping the substance into his throat.

After almost an hour, Charlie groaned and opened his eyes, looking around groggily. "Oh, uh," he grunted. "Home. Good." His eyes closed again and a small snore escaped from him.

Rex shook Charlie's good shoulder softly. "General, you need to drink just a little more of this medicine."

His eyes slit open. "Medicine?"

"Yes. Just a sip now." He tipped the last of the little vial to his lips. The general cooperated, swallowing it, then sagged back against the pillows.

Rex stood up from the side of the bed, where he had been perched for the past hour. He turned to Rebecca, who had been sitting at the foot of the bed all of this time. "I think he will get through the night now. But Miss Rebecca, you have to recognize that he, and by extension you, have a major problem. He is addicted to laudanum. And he mixes it with alcohol. Alone, the laudanum will eventually kill him. It is made from opium and it slowly steals the body's vitality. But mixing it with alcohol could kill him any time he does it, as it almost did tonight. He needs my help – and you will need help as well in getting him through this." He could see the fear in her eyes. "But tonight you need to get some rest. You will need your strength. And you will need to trust me as we go through this."

He left, assuring her that all would be well for the rest of the night. She sat before the fire, trying to relax before climbing into bed. It dawned on her that it was a year ago to the day when Charlie had received the wounds that had led them to this state. Would the ravages of war ever heal and leave her family alone?

~

Tuesday, April 10, 1866

The next morning, Charlie and Rebecca remained in bed through breakfast. Em came pounding down to the breakfast table, demanding to know where her papa and mama were. Edgar caught the little girl in mid-conniption and said, "Enough! Emily, your mama and papa got in very late last night and are still sleeping. You certainly do not want to wake them up, now do you? That would be very rude and mean of you. They will be down for lunch. I promise."

"They are home, Uncle Edgar? Really home?"

"Yes. They are home. Now settle down and eat your breakfast, and when they wake up, I will take you in to see them."

Darby and Suzanne had followed their more volatile sister to the table and heard Uncle Edgar's little speech. There was a mood of quiet – very quiet – excitement around the table.

Around ten o'clock that morning, Edgar and Charlotte could not contain the children any longer. They knocked on the door to Rebecca and Charlie's sitting room very softly. Rebecca immediately answered, calling, "Come in."

Charlie was sitting in front of the empty fireplace, sipping on a cup of tea. A glass that, from the residue in the bottom, had probably contained Sarah's gastronomically appalling hangover cure sat on the table next to him. He smiled, but it was more forced than anyone had ever witnessed before. Rebecca was sitting on the davenport, looking tired, wan and drawn.

Em ran into the room and threw herself into her papa's lap. "Back! You back! I miss you so much." She kissed him on the cheek and then she jumped down, much to his relief, and ran over to her mother throwing her arms around her neck. "Love you, Mama."

Suzanne and Darby were much more reticent, but Rebecca reached out to them, hugging each in turn. "Well," she chuckled. "It appears that we were missed." She looked up at Charlotte and Edgar. "And were our troopers good while we were gone?"

Charlotte hemmed a bit, but Edgar grinned outright. "Most of them. These two," he indicated Suzanne and Darby, "were absolute angels. Emily, on the other hand, was doing a reasonable imitation of the imp of Lincoln Cathedral. Good thing you had a member of the Church of England to take control."

Charlotte started giggling at that. He had been brilliant at handling the headstrong child, able to distract her at the first sign of a tantrum so that the week had actually been rather pleasant for all of them. Suzanne, on the other hand, had haunted her cousin Charlotte's every step all week, and while she could not complain about her behavior, she was happy to return her to Rebecca's control.

The three children and three of the four adults chatted for a few minutes, until Edgar interrupted them by sending the children off to their lessons. It was clear they were still in no condition to deal with the children.

As they were leaving, Rebecca walked to the door with them. Charlotte went ahead, herding the children to their lessons. She spoke very quietly. "Um, Edgar? Rex told me some very frightening things last night about Charlie and his use of laudanum."

"And you want me to tell you that he is being an alarmist?"

A look of relief flitted over her features. The minister quashed it immediately. "He is not. If anything, he probably understated the danger you husband is in."

She put Charlie back to bed after making him take in a few pieces of toast and another cup of tea. He was asleep almost instantly. She brushed the hair back from his forehead before placing a kiss above his brow. As she stood, she ran her fingers over the hair at his temples, noticing it was getting a bit more silver.

She dressed in her work clothes, just too damn exhausted yet to wrestle herself into a day dress. She tucked her shirt into her trousers and rolled up the sleeves before slipping into her soft leather boots and heading downstairs to find Rex.

She found him sitting at the dining room table, looking through a stack of books, flipping pages from one book and then the next. She watched him as he checked something in the book and then looked to a small case holding various vials like the one he presented last night.

"Rex?" She called his name from the door and was relieved when he turned his head and motioned her in.

"I have been expecting you, Rebecca."

She sat down next to him, placing her hand on his forearm, not quite knowing what to say other than, "Thank you."

"Don't thank me yet. We've barely entered the forest; we are certainly not out of the woods."

"What do we have to do? I was so frightened last night after you left. I do not think I slept thirty minutes the whole night. I just lay there with my hand on his chest feeling his heart beat and watching him breathe."

"Your fear is well placed. We have to convince your husband to let me help him before he kills himself. It was very close last night. Had your trip taken another hour, or had you actually managed to lie down and go to sleep next to him, it probably would have been for the last time."

"I will do anything I can to assist you. I cannot lose him. Especially not like this."

He smiled and nodded. "I have to acquire some supplies and it will take a few days. I would advise you not say anything to the general about our talks and most certainly do not tell him what transpired last night if he has no memory of it."

"Why not?"

"Two reasons. The first is that once an addict is confronted with their problem, they tend to get hostile and withdraw. If Charlie thinks we suspect a problem then it may make it harder to help him. The second reason is that he needs to agree to let me help him because he wants it, not because he believes he owes me something."

She nodded, understanding her husband and that he would indeed feel a debt to Rex over the previous night.

"So, for the week or so that it will take for my supplies to arrive, it is critical that you keep him away from the brandy and laudanum as much as possible. It may not be easy. He really believes he needs it, but he does not need it as much as he thinks."

She took a deep breath and let it out slowly, chewing her bottom lip as she began to consider the problem. She leaned in, once again placing her hand on his forearm and whispered quietly. "If I can get him to forgo the brandy for the time being, can you help me keep his laudanum under control?"

He simply nodded.

Later that evening, Charlie sat at his desk, still dressed in his nightshirt, robe and slippers. It was extremely rare for him not to bother dressing; today had been one of those rare days. He sat, drumming his fingers as he looked at the little bag before him. Rebecca entered with her sewing basket tucked under her arm, stopping just short of her normal chair by his desk when she saw the look on his face. "What?"

"We have been fleeced, my darling."

"What?" She immediately took her seat next to his desk, pouring coffee from the pot on hand, the sewing all but forgotten. She could not, would not, believe that someone they trusted was stealing from them. "What do you mean?"

"Do you remember the bag I left Edgar?"

She glanced at his desk, relaxing considerably. "The pennies?" she nodded knowingly.

"Yes, the pennies. I told Edgar I would triple anything he had left. Do you remember?"

"Of course I do."

"Now, we have five children. We were gone seven days. For a total of?"

"Thirty-five cents," she agreed with a smile as she pulled her sewing basket back into her lap and retrieved one of his favorite, but very well worn shirts. "Did they leave you enough for a new shirt? Because I think this one is beyond further help." She examined what used to be the collar. "This is now officially a rag."

A dark brow lifted playfully. "Ah, were you in on this little heist, wife?"

"Absolutely not!" She countered with mock indignity before returning her attention to the mending in her lap. "Would you please explain to me how our minister and our children planned and pulled off this grand theft?"

"I have no idea how they did it, but would you like to explain to me how there is fifty-three cents in this bag?" He tapped his desk briskly with his index finger.

She chuckled and nodded, "All right then, I will just have to patch this shirt one more time, because you just lost the one on your back."

"Little scoundrels. Led by a big scoundrel." The general grumbled as he counted out the coins that made up the promised triple payment and placed them in the bag.

As he tied the top of the little bag off there were three light raps on his office door. "Come in."

Edgar stepped through the door, closing it gently behind him.

"Come to pick up your booty, did you?" Charlie quirked a brow at the minister.

He licked his lips in a failed attempt to look innocent. "General Redmond, I came to collect my rightful bounty for the church," he smirked.

Charlie gave him a grin and tossed him the bag as he leaned back in his chair. "There you go, Robin Hood. Would you care to tell me how that bag ended up with fifty three cents in it?"

"Simple really, old boy." He moved to the door and pulled it open, answering before he left. "Every time they misbehaved, I put a penny in."

Rebecca lost the coffee in her mouth in one huge gush. Edgar could hear her laughter ringing down the hall as he walked away.

When she could finally breathe again, she dabbed the coffee from her dress and Charlie's desk as she asked, "Are you sure it is wise to play poker with him?"

His eyes were wide as he shook his head before lifting his coffee cup to his lips. "Not anymore."

She poured herself another cup of coffee and looked to her partner, who had taken to glancing over a stack of letters on his desk. "Charlie?"

"Yes, my dear?" He put the letters aside and gave her his full attention.

"Sweetheart, I have been thinking lately and I, umm..." She paused, looking briefly into her cup before looking back at him. "Well, I think I have developed a problem with brandy."

"Rebecca..."

"No." She put her hand up and shook her head. "It is true, Charlie. I am drinking far too much and I have decided that I need to stop, at least for a while."

He reached out and took her hand giving it a gentle squeeze, "Then, my darling, I shall join you on that wagon. It is always easier with moral support."

She smiled and squeezed his hand in return. "Thank you, love. I knew I could count on you."

CHAPTER 13

Wednesday, April 11, 1866

He rubbed his eyes. He had been staring at ledgers long enough so that everything was starting to run together. With a frustrated sigh, he flipped the book shut and set it aside. He realized all too well that when he was this tired, trying to balance the books was a fruitless effort that would only result in errors that would send Rebecca into a proper conniption. Since relinquishing the brandy, he found sleeping the night through far more difficult.

Glancing at his open pocket watch lying on the desk, he realized it was lunchtime and probably time for him to start his slow wander down the stairs to the dining room. Taking his cane in hand, he slowly pushed up and started for the door. Just as his hand landed on the knob, there was a knock from the other side that actually caused the tired man to jump a bit. He chuckled, as he turned the knob, opening the door to reveal Rebecca, lunch tray in hand. Behind her, Rex stood holding a black leather bag in one hand and a rather ornate wooden box in the other.

"I thought you might be hungry," His wife said as she and Rex entered together.

He closed the door and turned to his other half and their guest. "Thank you. I was on my way down to join you and the children."

"Tess has the children." Rebecca poured from the tea pot for all three of them. "Rex and I have something we very much want to discuss with you."

"Alright then." He settled in his desk chair, swiveling it to face the sofa where Rex and Rebecca settled with their cups. "What is it? You two look like you are most definitely up to something."

Rebecca had that false smile on her face. The one that told him she was about to drop a bombshell of some sort. He watched and waited as they looked at each other trying to determine who would speak first.

Rex took a deep breath and nodded at Rebecca before turning his full attention to Charlie. "General Redmond," he began.

Charlie raised a brow and looked at his guest. He still was not quite used to the difference between the man before him now, the proper Oxford gentleman with a thick English accent, and the role he played in public of the bowing and scraping little Chinese manservant.

He cleared his throat. "What exactly is going on?"

Rex leaned forward to place his cup on the table and made direct eye contact with the dark-haired man. "I can help you, General Redmond."

"Help me? With what?"

"I can help you recover from your injuries and the pain they cause you."

He smiled and nodded in a dismissive manner, "I am sure you think you can, but I have had the best medical care possible. Between Doctor Walker and the doctors in Baltimore, Washington and Philadelphia I have been assured that I am probably as functional as I will ever be."

"They are wrong, General. If you can trust me, I promise I can help you."

"Charlie," Rebecca leaned forward, placing her hand on his

knee. "Rex is well versed in treatments from his homeland. Remedies that his people have used for thousands of years; what could it possibly hurt to let him try?"

Looking into their faces he could see both complete empathy and very real concern. "What kind of remedies?" he asked cautiously. He prided himself on being a decently educated and learned man. He did not like to fall victim to his own prejudices, but he was not sure he would handle it well if Rex produced a live snake from one of his containers.

"First, General, we must address a very real problem. You, sir, are a laudanum addict. We must get you past that first."

Now Charlie sat up straight, beginning to bristle. He did not care how much the man could help or how well educated he seemed to be, to come into his house and insult him in such a manner. "How dare you--"

Rex put his hand up to stop the flow of words from his mouth. "You must be willing to admit it before anyone can help you, sir."

"I am not a laudanum addict!" The tall man hissed. He glanced at Rebecca with flashing eyes.

"I have had much experience with drug addicts. I am all too familiar with the signs and symptoms. Your body is completely addicted and your mind is quickly following. You are dependent on opium, a plant that my people have cultivated for thousands of years. We must get you over that so we can return your physical body and mental health to a stable foundation. If you continue on the path that you are on now, you will probably be dead in less than a year. You nearly killed yourself on the return trip from New York. Had I not been here with the appropriate medication, you would have died that night."

Charlie looked flabbergasted. Rebecca tried hard to choke back a gasp. She was not necessarily prepared to listen to Rex confront him in this manner, but she remained quiet, tightening her grip on her husband's leg. She begged him silently to just continue listening.

"Let me prove to you that you are addicted. Where is your flask?" Rex cocked a knowing brow.

The general hesitated, but only for a moment before reaching into the top drawer of his desk. Removing the silver flask, he handed it to the other man.

He gave a gentle shake before removing the cap and giving it a sniff. "You filled it this morning?"

"Yes." Charlie nodded.

Rex looked at Rebecca and smiled gently. "Mrs. Redmond, I am afraid I am going to have to ask you to leave us for a little while."

"What?" She looked startled. She had expected to help him convince her husband.

"Please, I ask that you trust me. Your husband needs to understand the depth of his problem."

She looked to Charlie, who gave an unconvincing shrug. "Alright." She leaned over and kissed him on the forehead, scratching the back of his head gently with her nails. "I love you, Charlie. Do not ever doubt that."

Rex escorted her to the door and closed it behind her. Then he turned to the dark-haired man and looked at a small pocket watch pinned to the inside of his robe. "Now we wait."

"For what?" The general growled.

"For you to want another dose of laudanum. I will give it to you when you absolutely must have it and not until then. I intend to show you the horror that awaits you if you do not shake the grip of this drug now. You are becoming an opium eater. There is no doubt that you are addicted to this drug physically and that your mind is starting to go with it. Fortunately for you, I arrived when I did. It's going to be hard enough now; if you had managed another six months without killing yourself it would have been a miracle. You're a very bad addict, because you don't know or don't care that you are addicted."

Within the first hour Charlie started to twitch. He rubbed his forehead and his eyes as he sat at his desk. Rex sat patiently in a chair near the window, checking his watch every few minutes.

Then the pacing began, along with the scratching at his arms.

"Is there a problem, general?" A slender, knowing brow rose as the time was checked.

"No, damn it!"

"We shall see." The Asian man nodded.

Charlie stormed across the room and stood looking down at the man. His breathing was fast and hard. "This is the manner in which you treat your host? A man who has opened his home to you..." His rant was cut short by the need to swat at his shoulder; he was sure something was crawling on him.

"Spoken like a true addict, and it only took..." Rex glanced at his watch, "...forty-five minutes. In another hour, I doubt you will be able to stand up."

"You are enjoying this!" The tall man grumbled as he stormed back to his desk where he stood, impatiently tapping it with his knuckles.

"Quite the contrary, General Redmond. I never enjoy seeing someone go through withdrawal and that is exactly what you are starting to do."

"I cannot be! I am not addicted!"

"Of course not." He shook his head. "Is your skin crawling yet? Have your guts starting hurting?"

Charlie gave a disgusted grunt and threw himself into a chair with his back to his tormentor.

Rex looked at his watch.

When Charlie had not moved or said anything for a half hour, Rex rose and moved to the chair where the general sat, unmoving. As he approached, he could see the fine sheen of sweat that had broken across his forehead. He could see the man's hands trembling in his lap; his breathing was rough and ragged. When he reached out to check his pulse, he got his hand slapped away. He only smiled, shook his head, and checked his watch.

"How do you feel now, General?" He tried again to take the pulse, this time from the neck rather than the wrist.

"I..." He huffed as he tried to pull away from Rex one again, but failed to do so. "I am fine, damn it! I just need my medicine." He was shaking and he was cold and what was happening to him only seemed to be partly real. "Get Elizabeth, get my medicine." He swatted at his shoulder again, as he was absolutely sure there was something crawling on him.

"Dr. Walker will not be giving you any more laudanum."

Rex noticed his patient was now drenched in sweat; it had soaked through his shirt and left his coat damp to the touch. Rex started stripping the wet coat from his body. "Tell me what hurts."

Charlie looked to him as if he did not quite understand what he was saying. He blinked in rapid succession and then took a deep breath. "I am fine." The shaking in his body and the sweat covering his face completely betrayed his words. "I only need a drink."

He pushed up from his chair and stumbled around the office, wiping his brow with the palm of his hand and trying to get whatever was crawling on him well away from his body. He picked up the brandy decanter with a very shaky hand, and Rex placed a gentle hand on his wrist. "You do not understand how bad the pain is. I need it."

Rex just sighed and shook his head. "No. That will not solve your problem either."

"I do not have a problem that a dose of my medicine will not cure," Charlie hissed. "If you do not have anything more to offer me, then get out." He began rubbing both arms quickly, trying his best to warm himself and keep his skin from crawling.

"Ah, there we go." Rex guided him back to his chair and removed the man's flask from his pocket holding it out.

Charlie made a grab for the container, only to have it swiftly pulled away while the smaller man used his other hand to reseat him. He looked down directly into his eyes and held his gaze. "You may have it when you admit you have a problem."

He blinked. "No." He shook his head. "It is not possible…"

"Then we continue to wait. Apparently, you need to go under water a second time before you learn your lesson."

"Learn my lesson! What in the hell are you talking about? I was nearly blown in half! I am in pain. I think I have learned my lesson!" He shook his head and mumbled with a humorless laugh, "Never ride at full gallop toward a loaded Howitzer."

His breathing was becoming so ragged that he was beginning to sound like a snorting bull. He raised his eyes to Rex; the look in them was not a friendly one. Never breaking eye contact, he rose from the chair and with what energy he thought he had, he attempted a rather pitiful swing at the man before him.

The smaller man easily and deftly caught his left hand in mid-swing and placed his thumb hard, directly into the palm of it, using a pressure point to drop Charlie Redmond to his knees.

He crumpled in front of his desk and wrapped his arms around his body as he began crying and shaking. "I hurt everywhere, Rex. Everywhere. I do not know how to stop it, except with brandy and laudanum."

Rex knelt and took the man's head in both hands, making the general look him in the eyes. "I know how to stop it. You know what you need to do. The fear you feel is the interest paid on a debt you do not owe."

Charlie's guts began seizing and suddenly he felt himself trying to vomit. He wrapped his right hand across his stomach as he knelt there on his knees, his stomach roiling, his mouth watering.

As he stayed there, trying to decide if he was really going to throw up, he could hear noise in the hall.

The children.

Their children.

His children.

They were coming up for lessons. He could hear them laughing and playing in the hall, Rebecca's voice firmly trying to herd them to their schoolroom. He shook his head and looked at Rex.

His children.

His wife.

There should be no other reasons needed to fix this. He could not do this to Rebecca again. She had lived through his stubborn bullheadedness once and it nearly cost them everything.

They should be enough! The thought screamed at him as he listened to them laugh and giggle just outside his door. He gasped at the man standing above him, reaching out with a shaky hand, "Help me, please. I have a problem."

Rex smiled and handed him the flask.

~

Wednesday, April 11, 1866

Charlie, Rebecca, Charlotte, Edgar and Rex were having a rather subdued after-dinner coffee in the rear parlor when they heard a loud rapping at the front door.

A few moments later, Reg showed a rather disheveled Robert Jenkins into the parlor. "Reverend Vile? Mr. Cooper asked me to come get you. Reverend Williams is not doing well. Dr. Walker is already there and says it is only a matter of a few hours at best. I have the wagon."

Edgar rose immediately. "Let me get my things and I will be right with you." He hurried out of the room.

Rebecca had the strangest look on her face, an odd combination of sadness and disgust. With a huge sigh, she turned to Charlie. "I should go with him. Elizabeth will need to focus on Reverend Williams. Grace will want and need help dealing with Margaret. Dear Lord, I wish I was not such a conscientious member of the community."

Charlie stood up and embraced his wife. "Darling, I would offer to go with you, but with the new regime that Rex has put me on, I honestly think I would be more of a hindrance than a help."

"No, dear. You stay here and rest. At any rate, I would not subject you to Margaret's histrionics even if you were in the best of shape."

She bustled out of the room, as she asked Robert to wait for her, ran up the stairs to gather her own things, and met Edgar at the front door. The three of them clambered into the wagon and were off.

Charlotte, foreseeing a truly boring and somber evening as Rex and Charlie waited for Edgar and Rebecca to return, decided to excuse herself and went up to her room and the latest novel she was reading, Miss Austen's Northanger Abbey. Though it had been published almost 50 years earlier, Charlotte had not read it before. It was one of several books she had found in the library and she was fascinated by Miss Austen's works.

Charlie and Rex returned to the parlor after watching the wagon rattle down the drive. Charlie went directly to the tantalus, reaching for the brandy bottle.

His remaining companion cleared his throat. "General Redmond. Do you really want to do that?"

He dropped his hand. "Yes. Yes, I do. But I promised Rebecca."

"Would you have done it if I were not here?"

He thought for a moment, then nodded, "Yes, I probably would have. How much harm can one shot of brandy do?"

"You know very well it would not have been one shot, General. Between the brandy and the laudanum, you were well on your way to killing yourself." He poured two fresh cups of coffee, set one beside Charlie's chair, and motioned for him to take a seat.

"The problem is that laudanum is made from opium, as you well know. What you may not know is the effects of mixing it and alcohol can be cumulative. You can go on mixing them for days or weeks and survive, until your body has too much stress. Then, just one glass of brandy and one dose of laudanum together will cause your heart and lungs to simply stop working. Then, you die. It seems to me that your life is a bit stressful at times, General. It is truly a deadly mixture."

Charlie looked into Rex's eyes. No one had been so brutally honest with him since his days in the military. He took a sip of coffee, set the cup down, and stared at his hands. "But the pain..."

"General, I know exactly how much laudanum you have had. The dose is more than sufficient to kill the pain. In fact, it is more than you should have, but your body has become so accustomed to it that you feel more pain from lack of the drug than you do from the injuries. The first thing you will need to learn is how to relax." He lit a candle and set it on the table between them. "Watch the flame and try to put everything else from your mind."

~

Robert Jenkins pulled his team up in front of the manse. Richard and Edward were standing on the front steps, smoking cigars and pacing. Through the light streaming through the front parlor window, it looked like Culpeper's entire biddy brigade was assembled to offer their support to Mrs. Williams. Rebecca's chin fell on her chest. "Oh, Lord, give me strength," she muttered as she slipped down from the wagon.

Edgar gathered his bible and the small case he carried his vestments in and hurried into the house.

She followed more slowly, stopping to have a word with Richard. "How are things going?"

He looked strained. "If it were me, I would have gone and passed an hour ago, just to escape the weeping and wailing. But he still hangs on. He has been waiting for Edgar."

She steeled herself, put an appropriately somber expression on her face, and entered the house.

She slipped into the parlor as quietly as she could, looking around at the faces in the room. Poor Grace Cooper looked like she had spent the last few hours of her life in purgatory. The Misses Reynolds and Simms were quietly shedding appropriately mournful tears. Several other ladies of the town were sitting quietly on the sidelines, trying to stay out of the way of the tempest that was Margaret Williams, who was giving a spectacular imitation of a howling banshee. Rebecca wondered to herself if Margaret was mourning the passing of her husband or her loss of her position in the town's social structure, not to mention the loss of the manse.

It took a minute or two for Margaret to notice her arrival. When she did, she heaved herself up out of her chair, flew across the room and threw herself, sobbing, into Rebecca's unprepared body.

It took a moment for the blonde to register that she was supposed to embrace the woman she so heartily detested. "Oh, Rebecca, what am I to do without my darling James? How am I to go on without him?"

"I understand, Margaret. I truly do. I was so afraid that I was going to lose Charlie. But you have to be brave and go on." She thought, *What a terrible time to give up brandy.*

"Oh, Rebecca, how can you compare my James to that man?"

Her jaw clenched and her teeth ground together as she patted Mrs. Williams on the back and disengaged herself from the chief biddy's octopus-like embrace. Grace Cooper, having heard this last exchange, came swooping in to rescue the older woman, because the look on Rebecca's face told her that if she did not, the town might be facing a double funeral.

Missy Frazier stepped in and pulled Rebecca aside, buffering her from the rest of the room. "Just breathe, dear. You know she is a hateful harridan, and I think that James' death will just make her worse. You are the better woman."

Rebecca stepped aside, took a deep breath, and joined the women sitting death watch on the side.

Edgar slipped into the room where he had been visiting Reverend Williams regularly over the past weeks. Elizabeth was sitting beside him, her fingers resting on his wrist.

"Ah, Edgar. He has been waiting for you." She stood and moved away so the minister could take the seat beside the dying man.

He reached into his case and pulled his stole out. Draping it over his neck, he reached out and took James' hand, resting both of their hands on the bible. "I am here, James. Let us pray."

Reverend Williams whispered, "Edgar, I am so sorry. I meant to get Margaret into the new cottage before I passed." He gasped for air. "Take care of my flock."

"I will, James. I will do my best."

James' fingers twitched in Edgar's hand. The minister sat, quietly reciting the prayer for the dead, as Reverend Williams breathed his last. He finished the prayer and then gently covered James' face with the sheet. He rose, nodded to Elizabeth, straightened his stole, and went out to break the news to the Widow Williams.

Friday, April 13, 1866
Reverend Williams' funeral was attended by virtually every

resident of Culpeper and the surrounding area. James Williams had married half of the people in the town, had baptized a large number of them, and had been the calm central point in the town as it survived the turmoil of the war. He was much loved, and would be greatly missed.

Edgar, with help from Rex, Rebecca, Charlotte, Grace Cooper and others within the community, staged a solemn and elegant funeral service for the old minister. Charlotte served as the organist, as it was inappropriate for Mrs. Williams to play the dirge for her own husband. It occurred to Edgar that if Charlotte took over Mrs. Williams' role in the weekly services, it would give them a good excuse to spend time together.

After the service, there was a quiet reception at the manse, where Margaret held court as the mourning widow and Sarah, Reg and Beulah, along with several others from the Redmond household, served a cold luncheon for essentially the entire town.

Late that afternoon, as he was preparing to depart, Edgar took Mrs. Williams aside. "Madam, as you know, I will need to move into the manse eventually, but I believe General and Mrs. Redmond will be happy to let me stay for a while longer as you get your affairs in order."

"Thank you, Reverend Vile. You know, the manse has been my home for so long. I was wondering, since you have no wife, if you would like me to stay on as your housekeeper and hostess."

He paused for a moment. Rex had warned him this might happen. He smiled gently, and said, "No, Mrs. Williams. I would not want to impose on your good graces for such a service. You have been a mainstay in this community for many years. With your husband's passing, it is time for you to enjoy the peace of a quiet life of retirement."

He turned away, missing the expression of frustration and resentment that passed across her face. He turned back to her. "Oh, and I have asked Miss Redmond to handle the music for Sunday's services. I would not ask you to perform such a function so soon after your husband's passing." As he turned away once again, the look Mrs. Williams gave him could have killed a lesser man.

~

Tuesday April 17, 1866

Rex went into town to collect the box of herbs that he had asked a friend of his in Washington's China Town to send him. He stopped by the apothecary's shop and gave Rafe Johnstone a list of some very specific, though fairly common products to stock up on over the coming weeks, then stopped in to see Dr. Walker.

He sat quietly, waiting for her to finish with her last patient. She came out into the waiting room and was surprised to see him. "Why, Rex. What brings you here?"

"Dr. Walker, I would like to discuss General Redmond's condition."

She was stunned. He had always addressed her using his coolie persona. This gentleman spoke with a perfect British upper class accent. "Charlie's condition? What do you mean?"

"I know you are aware of his addiction. I am not so sure if you are aware of how much he has been mixing laudanum and brandy. He nearly killed himself the other day. If I had not been able to administer a cocaine tincture, he probably would have died, his system was so suppressed."

"My God! I thought he knew better." She shook her head as she sat down. It took a moment for all of it to soak into her mind. "Administered cocaine? You have cocaine?"

"Yes, I have a full complement of medicinal herbs and substances, including some I doubt you have ever encountered. My people have a long tradition of herbal medicine, as well as being the source of the opiates the general is addicted to. We have learned how to deal with pain and addiction in ways the western world has yet to discover."

She considered this. "I have been very torn in dealing with him. I hate the fact that he is an addict, but I also hate the thought of him being in pain. It is a very difficult position for a physician, let alone a friend, to be in."

"I believe I can help him with both issues. We have ways of dealing with pain that are not dependent on drugs, and are very

237

effective, not only in dealing with the discomfort, but in restoring as much functionality as possible. I would like your support, as I do not think he will fully trust me without your approval."

She looked at him for a long moment. She knew nothing of this man, or of the type of medicine he practiced, but the calm, sure look in his eyes, and the fact that nothing else had worked for Charlie made up her mind. "You have it. Shall we go to him together?"

"No, because I believe he has to come to deal with the addiction on his own volition, not because anyone else has told him to. Trust is key, and he must trust me explicitly, regardless of what others may say. I simply wanted to extend the courtesy of sharing my thoughts with you, as his primary physician, before I started him on his recovery."

"I thank you. If there is anything I can do to help you, please let me know."

"Well, there is one thing. Please, tell Rafe Johnstone not to give Charlie any laudanum, and that I will be the only one getting it for him in the coming weeks."

~

Later that afternoon, Rex tapped on Charlie's office door, then slipped into the room. He sat down across from the general, who was sitting at his desk. "The supplies I needed to properly start your recovery have arrived. I am ready to begin whenever you are, but I have to warn you--the first few days of this treatment are going to be very difficult. You will not be fit company for anyone other than me. You have had but a small sample of what you will be going through. However, when we are done, you will no longer be addicted to laudanum, and I think you will be able to manage what little pain may be left from your wounds much more effectively."

Charlie considered this. He had come to realize that Rex tended to understate, rather than dramatize, any situation, so when he said that quitting the laudanum would be difficult, combined with his own short journey into withdrawal, it made him think very carefully.

"My wife's birthday is next week. If we start today, would I be able to celebrate her birthday properly?"

"To be honest, sir, I do not think so. Would you like to continue as we have been the past few days, with controlled doses and no alcohol, and begin after the happy event?"

"Yes, I think that would be best."

~

Sunday April 22, 1866

Rebecca came into the dining room expecting to find her family gathered for breakfast. Instead she found only Charlie waiting for her, a small basket dangling from the fingers of his right hand.

"Where are the children?"

"Having breakfast in the nursery. I wanted you all to myself this morning."

She smiled as she moved to him, allowing his left arm to settle in that very familiar spot around her waist. "Is that so?"

"Indeed." He nodded and guided her through the house and out a back door. "Time for you to see what is behind curtain number one."

"Really?" A smile crossed her face and she gave a little excited clap that made him laugh. She had been good to her word, staying well back from what was obviously a construction site.

"Really." The general saw Duncan give the signal that everything was ready and they began their stroll down what he now noticed was a wide, flat path that allowed him to properly escort his wife without stumbling. He looked to Duncan, who just smiled and shrugged, walking away to leave his friend to show his gift to his wife.

"I am very excited." Rebecca's right hand was intertwined with his left, and her left hand gently tugged on his shirt sleeve.

He reminded himself to surprise his wife like this more often if this was going to be the reaction. They made their way down the path, Charlie trying to stroll, Rebecca trying not to run.

"You are doing this on purpose!" She gave his hand a tug.

"I am walking." He sniggered.

"Like a turtle." She tugged a bit more.

He dropped her hand and gestured. "Go," he called out as she practically skipped down the path, "And happy birthday!"

With a very girlish laugh she did indeed run just a bit ahead of him. She moved around to the front of the canvas walls, made into a horseshoe shaped privacy screen. At the opening, she stopped and saw the beautiful new gazebo built overlooking the pond. Charlie joined her. She immediately threw her arms around him bestowing him with a wonderful thank you kiss. He hummed with pleasure as their lips parted.

Opening his eyes, he saw her smiling face just an inch from his. "I take it you like it."

"It is wonderful, Charlie!" She pulled his hand and they climbed the little stairs onto their new space.

Once again Duncan and his crew had outdone themselves. The gazebo was eight sided, with benches on six of the faces of the octagon, with the eighth side being the entrance. It had pillars at each of the eight corners, with a carved railing around the sides. Instead of a seventh bench, there were two ornate seats directly opposite the entrance, with hand carved arm rests and soft cushions on each seat.

From these two seats, the occupants could look out over the pond to the rolling fields and to the stand of woods to the left. It was a lovely view, one that would be beautiful at any time of year. In the center, there was a carefully crafted fire pit, so that the gazebo would be usable even in the winter. He placed the basket holding their breakfast on one of the benches.

She leaned against the rail, looked at the pond and inhaled deeply. "I love it here, darling."

"So do I, my love. That is why I wanted this for us. I hope we have lots of suppers together and that we get to bounce grandbabies on our knees out here."

She turned her head and smiled. "Grandbabies? It is a little early to be thinking about grandchildren."

"Not when you spend as much time as I do thinking about our

future. Darby will of course be the first one in the family to get married and father babies."

Now she was amused. She turned to him and leaned against the rail, crossing her arms over her chest. "Have that all figured out, do you?"

"Yes. Darby is going to be a fine business man. A very good husband and father to lots and lots of babies. I want grandchildren. Lots of grandchildren." He chuckled, and then continued. "Em and Suzanne will probably want to go to college."

"No, darling. If they go to college at all, you want them to go to school close to home."

"What do you mean, if? Of course our daughters will go to college."

"Charlie, be realistic. Young women get married, have babies, and raise families. What do they need to go to college for?"

"The world is changing, Rebecca. Young women become doctors like Elizabeth, scientists, historians, authors." He grinned, "Horse breeders. As well as having husbands and babies. Our girls will be just like their parents. They will do what suits them."

She sighed and nodded. "Yes, darling. You are right. What was right for me may not be right for them."

"And dear, please remember your first marriage was not exactly a bowl of cherries. And now you are poised to be one of the premier horse breeders in the state. Very traditional, Mrs. Redmond. Very traditional." He teased.

They both laughed, Rebecca a bit ruefully.

He continued with his vision for the children. "I think little Andy is going to want adventure in his life. Perhaps we should find him his own version of Rex, as he will need one. Buddy could probably have a spot at The Point if he wants it."

She cocked her head and considered her mate. She could only smile and move to him, wrapping her arms around him and laying her head in its familiar spot on his chest. "I love you, Charlie."

He hugged her close and kissed the top of her head. "I love you too, 'Becca."

They stood there like that for a few long moments before he

gently cleared his throat. "There is one more thing. I am not sure most people would find it an appropriate birthday gift and it is not actually meant to be one. It is just that the two projects came together at the same time. May I show you the other?"

His sudden change in mood was a bit unexpected. "Of course you may. Is something wrong?"

"Nothing is wrong. Just come with me."

He led her from the gazebo and turned left to continue down the new path Duncan and his men had cut. She scanned the area looking for whatever it could be that he was so concerned over. Then she saw it.

A patch of ground had been cordoned off with heavy, intricately woven wrought iron fencing. Two imposing gateposts stood guarding the arched entryway that simply read, "Redmond."

She closed her eyes and swallowed hard. He certainly had given thought to their future together.

"I do not expect you to thank me for this one," he said gently.

"Good." She nodded in agreement.

"But," he undid the latch on the gate, "there is one last thing."

He led her inside and toward the back of the little patch. There in the corner was a beautiful dark granite grave marker. "I know we can never bring him home," he whispered in her ear. "But I hope this helps."

1st Lieutenant
Andrew Michael Randolph
Beloved son of
Jonas and Ruth Randolph
Much loved brother of
Rebecca Anne Randolph Redmond
Lost son of the Valiant Confederacy
35th Battalion, Virginia Cavalry
White's Cavalry, Company B
Heroically fallen at the battle of Antietam
March 27, 1840 - September 17, 1862

CHAPTER 14

Tuesday, April 24, 1866

Two days after Rebecca's birthday, and at her urging, Charlie knocked on Edgar and Rex's door right after breakfast. Rex was the one to answer his call.

"I am ready," the general said simply.

The first seventy-two hours of his detoxification from the laudanum were horrible for everyone in the house. Rex had temporarily dismissed Tomas as Charlie's valet and then he locked himself and his patient in the office. Even Sheridan was banished from the room. Rebecca found a place for him in her office until he could rejoin Charlie upstairs.

Edgar and Charlotte did their best to keep Rebecca and the children occupied, but the fits of screaming fury that could be heard at all times of the night and day were terrifying.

Quiet periods were broken without warning by Charlie screaming in pain, anger, frustration or he could be heard smashing something. The children were frightened and Rebecca was worried sick about her husband's health.

She, too, had been forbidden entrance into the office. The only person allowed near the door at Rex's request was Edgar, and even he only left food and supplies for cleaning up in front of the locked door, alerting his companion to their presence with a quick and very particular knock.

She was pacing the rear parlor like a caged tiger when Edgar returned from his latest delivery upstairs. She turned pleading eyes on him. "How much longer will this take?! I cannot stand it. I need to see him!"

"Dear lady, please." He moved to his distraught friend and put his arm around her shoulders. "Rex knows exactly what he is doing. I suspect it will only be another day or so before you will be allowed to see him." He paused a moment, then whispered, "At least, that is how long it took for him to clean the opium out of me when we were at university." He did not know if she heard him or not through her own anger and frustration.

"When he was wounded on the battlefield, I was allowed to go to him! And now, now I am being denied in my own house. In our house! Our home!" Her voice, temperature and hackles were all going up.

He knew he had to get her calmed as quickly as possible. "Rebecca, really, do not do this to yourself." He led her to the small sofa and guided her to sit. "I promise you, Charlie is fine. He is coming out of a very difficult situation. One that Rex has a lot of experience with. You see, I had a problem, many years ago. He did the same thing for me."

"You?" She was a bit shocked at the admission.

"Yes. I was a stupid, angry young man who thought I could find the answers with opium. If it wasn't for Rex's care and vast knowledge of these matters, I would have died. When he confided in me about seeing the signs in Charlie, I am the one who suggested he approach you."

"Thank you for that! I had not realized how bad his need for the laudanum had gotten."

"As Rex said, the general is a consummate actor. He hid it well."

"I helped him take the damn stuff." She shook her head and sighed, disgusted with the admission.

"Of course you did," the minister soothed. "He's your husband and he was in pain. You did nothing wrong. If he had not been secretly abusing the drug, the doses you gave him never would have been a problem."

"When can I see him?" She looked to him with tired, pleading eyes.

"I do not know, my dear. Rex does things this way so that Charlie will not lash out at those he loves most while he is coming off the drug. Though he would have no way of controlling it, he is capable of both saying and doing very hurtful and hateful things. It has no impact on Rex. He is Charlie's friend and he knows what is happening. You, on the other hand, could suffer from both physical and emotional abuse from him right now. Not that he would mean it or even understand that he had done it, but it would hurt you none the less."

She nodded. That she could at least understand. She wished it had been explained beforehand, but she also knew the ambush and fear methods they had used to get him started had been the only way. Sometimes he could just be too stubborn for his own good.

Edgar took her hands in his. "Perhaps the best thing we can do right now is pray for him. Will you join me?"

"Of course!" She grasped his hand so tightly he flinched. "I need him to be all right. For the love of God, he has to come through it."

~

Monday April 30, 1866

After breakfast on this particular morning, Rex knocked softly on the door. "Miss Rebecca, would you come with me, please?"

She looked at him questioningly, but he said nothing, only extending his hand. Silently, he led her upstairs to Charlie's office.

She stepped into the office, anxious to see him, but somewhat afraid of what she might find. He was sitting in front of the empty fireplace, looking tired and drawn, with dark shadows under his eyes.

"Oh, Charlie!" She was shocked at how he looked. So tired, so worn out.

He stretched his right hand out to her. "Come here, sweetheart. I am fine. In fact, I am much better than I have been in months."

With a rush, she threw herself onto the small sofa and wrapped her arms around his neck. "Thank God!"

Rex quietly let himself out of the room as Charlie embraced his wife.

Some time later, he tapped on the door. They were sitting together on the divan holding hands and talking quietly when he came in.

"How are you feeling, General?" He walked over and looked into the man's eyes, gently pulling the skin under his lower lash so he could inspect the inner eye more closely.

"Washed out, but not too bad. There is a little pain in the shoulder and leg, but otherwise, not bad at all."

"Oh, Rex! Thank you." She grabbed his hands and bowed her head over them. He carefully extracted them before she kissed them.

"The worst is over. We have healed your soul of the curse of addiction. Tomorrow we begin the process of healing your body."

Tuesday, May 1, 1866

Rex rubbed his hands together, carefully warming them before he said to Charlie, "Your hand, please?"

He swallowed hard as he gripped the fingers of the black leather glove that encased his mangled extremity. He knew it was ugly and repulsive, and that is why he was always careful to keep it covered. He had a very real feeling it would scare his children if they ever saw it. Slowly, he removed the covering and offered his scarred hand to the man before him.

Rex gently examined his hand, carefully looking at the scarring and the curl to his remaining fingers. "The second finger is stiff and difficult to move?"

"Yes. It stays straight as long as I keep the glove on. When I take it off, it seems to naturally curve under. I can straighten it to some extent, but not all the way out." He absentmindedly scratched his chin with his left hand, realizing that after six days of not shaving, he had a few whiskers on his chin and cheeks that needed to be scraped off.

"The Chi is disrupted," Rex said knowingly as he leaned over and flipped open the latches on his wooden box.

"Chi?"

"Yes. Chi. Think of it as the energy that drives the body." He removed a small black box from the larger one. Turning his chair and settling in, he placed Charlie's hand flat on the table between them. "Your body contains muscles, ligaments and tendons. Chi flows through these fibers and allows your body to move at will based on the commands of your brain. When you mount a horse, you don't think about it; you just do it. That is Chi commanding your muscles."

He opened another box and removed a small lamp that he quickly lit with a match seemingly produced in his hand by magic. He adjusted the flame, then began preparing the other items plucked from his box and black satchel.

Charlie gave an audible gulp that sounded like it could even have been a strangled "no" when he saw the black box contained a variety of small needles.

"Deep breath, General." He had seen this reaction to acupuncture needles before. "I promise, it will not hurt."

"I have had more than my fill of needles. I feel as if I have already been poked and prodded to the near end of my life."

"Again, General, trust me." He passed one of the needles through the flame. Holding the man's hand very still, with a firm tap to the top of the needle, it was sticking out of the back of Charlie's hand nearest his first missing knuckle.

Rex chuckled when he saw Charlie sitting there with his eyes screwed tightly shut. "Cannon fire is apparently not a problem for you, but let a man bring a needle near and you turn into a quivering mass?"

He opened one eye and peered at his hand. There was a needle sticking from it and he had not felt a thing. He opened his other eye and smiled sheepishly.

Rex chuckled again and inserted another needle. "See? No pain."

"It is amazing," he said, his entire body releasing tension he had not even realized had been coiled in his healthy muscles. He actually watched with amazement as one by one, Rex inserted the needles in and near the scar tissue on his hand. "Do you really think I will be able to move these fingers more freely?"

"Absolutely." Rex nodded carefully as he inserted the final needle. "Give me a month and you should be able to move your remaining fingers and thumb without pain. Then we will begin working on your shoulder. After that, your hip and knee."

He felt his tongue between his lips as he fought the urge to tell Rex that he would never be allowed to work on his leg. He simply dropped his head and gritted his teeth against his own doubts.

"You smoke cigars, don't you?"

The general sat up straight, eyeing him warily. There were a lot of things in his life he would let go of, but his cigars were not among them. "Yes, and I will not give them up."

Rex laughed and shook his head. "You do not have to give them up." He continued to gently manipulate the fingers on his patient's hand. "I think you are ready to rejoin your family tonight," he mentioned gently as he adjusted one of his needles.

Charlie nodded. "Thank you very much for your help, Rex. I do apologize for the last few days."

"It's quite alright. I knew what we were in for when I offered to help you."

"Why did you do that?"

"Because it is the Christian thing to do? Because I had knowledge that would help you? It would be wrong of me not to offer it to you." The Asian man removed the needles from Charlie's hand and began massaging very nice smelling oil into it. "In my country there was a great man named Guan Yu."

The general sat there listening to Rex's story, feeling his hand and arm completely relaxing under the man's expert ministrations. He did not remember his arm feeling like this since before being wounded.

"Guan Yu was forced to leave his boyhood home after being accused of a crime." Rex looked up into his friend's face before taking his hand and putting it in a bowl of very warm water. "He fled his home and ended up in the army. He was a very learned man who was a very fair commander. He fought in many battles and more than one time saved our country from both foreign invaders and civil war. We have a great respect for Guan Yu. He is greatly revered and it is my duty and responsibility to make sure any warrior who has managed to survive many of the same kind of things is as well cared for as I can accomplish."

"I don't know about all of that, but I am sure that you have helped me, Rex. Just being away from the laudanum is a grand step in the right direction. Thank you so much."

"It is my pleasure. I will still be giving you small maintenance doses for a few more days to wean you off of it completely, but you are now capable of functioning outside this room." He took Charlie's hand from the water and held it up between them. "See if you can move that finger."

"So soon? You have only just started."

"Try."

He watched, not quite believing it, as his second finger not only moved, but began to straighten with very little pain.

"It will take more time and treatments to get it completely straight. Does it hurt?" He asked even as he touched and moved Charlie's fingers again.

"It would be tolerable. More of a gentle stinging than real pain."

"Eventually that will go away as well. We will have to treat your hand like this every day. I prefer to do it in the evening before you retire for bed." He released the hand and began cleaning up his equipment. "I will also show you some exercises that you must do every day. Preferably in the morning."

He gave his hand a sniff--that lovely oil could still be smelt. He could definitely smell sandalwood and something that reminded him of saddle leather. "What is that?"

"A special blend all my own. It's an ancient Chinese secret."

"It is, huh?" He smiled. "I rather like the smell of it."

"You're supposed to; it is one of the things helping you get better. Would not be a pleasant experience if my oils, salves and elixirs smelled of dung and rotten eggs. Now General, let us get the rest of you cleaned up so you may join your family for supper tonight."

"Of course." He nodded and reached for his glove. Rex stopped him.

"No." He shook his head. "This is also part of the healing process. Leave the glove on your desk tonight."

"My children," he began a protest.

"Will become accustomed to the fact their father is missing two fingers. Do not hide it from them. If you hide this, they will wonder what else you are hiding. Children are resilient. Give them more opportunity to show you that."

"I just do not want to scare them."

"It may." He agreed realistically. "At first. But then, you will just be Papa and your hand will be your hand. I understand the need for your glove in public and while doing business. We all have our own methods of dealing with people who might not be receptive to our differences."

For just a moment he affected the man Charlie had first met and that many still thought his true persona. The little Chinese manservant. He brought his palms together in front of his chest and bowed deeply, offering in a quick, clipped accent that was completely put on, "Right. General, sir. I go get shave kit now." He shuffled away.

He laughed as Rex straightened, resuming a normal gait across the room to the razor, mug and mirror. "We all have a part to play. But here, in the safety of your home with your wife and family, you should be completely free to be you. Scars and all."

He nodded. It was, after all, everything he had ever wanted and the reason he was so desperate to survive the war and return to Rebecca. He had wanted a home and a safe haven. She had given that to him and the last year he had tried to hide from it. "You are right, Rex. Thank you again. I am grateful that you are here to teach a hardheaded old solider the lessons he still needs to learn."

~

Edgar and Darby were busy telling silly jokes back and forth across the table, causing Charlotte and Rebecca to groan and shake their heads with each puerile punch line.

The boys were already fed and off to the nursery. Suppers now consisted of all the adults and children over the age of three. Suzanne, always a sweet tempered child, sat next to her beautiful cousin Charlotte, of whom she was in awe, trying to prove what a proper young lady she could be at the table. Em sat next to Rebecca, picking through her food and pushing it around her plate.

Her mother knew exactly what was wrong and she was fairly certain that if Papa did not return quickly, their first child would starve to death. "Emily, honey, please eat a little something."

"Not hungry."

"Oh, my darling." She leaned over and kissed her forehead. Darby and Edgar took a break from their two-man comedy routine as they watched her comfort the child.

"It is all right, Em," Darby piped up. "Mr. Rex is helping Papa Charlie get over something that made him sick. He will back soon."

"Sooner than you think," their father said from the door.

All the children bolted from the table, running to him and nearly knocking him from his feet. He managed to catch himself on the doorframe and hold himself upright on his cane as they all hugged him around various parts of his body.

Rebecca brought both hands to her gaping mouth and began crying with relief the moment she saw him with the children. He gave each of his children a loving caress and a kind word before moving to her side at the table.

"Please do not cry, sweetheart. I do hate it when that happens." He offered her a handkerchief from his ungloved hand.

~

Thursday, May 3, 1866

He was already in his office waiting. Sheridan perched on the corner of his desk demanding a scratch, when Rex entered carrying a long, wide box. He leaned it against Charlie's desk and crossed his arms over his chest. "How does your hand feel?"

He moved and flexed his remaining fingers. "I cannot believe the change in just a few days."

"Good." Rex nodded. "I brought you something to continue helping you get the movement and dexterity back in that hand."

He carefully removed the top of the box and then opened an interior case and removed a beautiful little Spanish style guitar, handing to his friend.

"Umm, I have no idea how to play the guitar."

"There was a time when you did not know how to be a soldier either, but you learned. This is far simpler. I'm confident you can master it."

He considered the instrument and nodded. "I suppose I can. You really think it will help?"

"No, General. I regularly give my patients pointless exercises to keep them annoyed and frustrated."

He laughed and held his good hand up. "Yes, of course. I do apologize."

"There are three or four simple pieces of music for you to learn in the case." Rex gestured to the box. "If you spend a few minutes every day, you should be able to play all of them in a month or so."

~

Saturday, May 5, 1866

Elizabeth had driven Samantha Carter out to Redmond Stables in her trap. At six and a half months pregnant, getting into and out of the little trap was becoming a bit of a logistical challenge for her, so the young woman's company was most welcome. Duncan had ridden behind on his own horse, as he had to make a call at the lumber yard later in the morning, so he would be departing before them.

The ladies had assembled that morning in Rebecca's parlor, sipping tea and plotting and planning for the upcoming nuptials between Samantha and Duncan. Elizabeth sat beside Charlotte, who was knitting a complex little jumper. Samantha and Grace Cooper were leafing through pattern books. Missy Frazier had joined them and brought her grandmothers recipe book – the one that had the fabulous fruit cake recipe her grandmother had always made for family weddings. Esther Jackson had brought her recipe book as well. Rebecca had asked Sarah to join them. It was a right proper hen fest. No wonder Duncan had run to the barn in search of Charlie.

The women started on the pattern books first. Samantha had been leafing through them beforehand and had already picked a dress she wanted. It was not a traditional wedding dress, but since this was a second marriage for the young woman, she felt that traditional white and lace was inappropriate.

Instead, she had found a simple dress in ecru with the new slim lines and bustle that had replaced the ante-bellum hoops and crinolines. It was a beautiful dress, simple and with sweeping lines that complimented Samantha's slim, elegant figure.

The ladies all oohhh'd and aahh'd as they came to agreement. It was clear that sewing was going to be a frantic activity for the coming weeks, as no one could think of wearing one of the old-style dresses to the wedding if Samantha was going to wear this piece of fashionable elegance. Even the ability to use Rebecca's lovely new sewing machine would only cut the desperate activity down by a day or so.

She also offered the use of the ballroom as a staging area for the seamstresses if they needed it. Several of the women thought that would be a lovely idea, especially since it meant they would get to use her splendid new Singer sewing machine. So she called for Reg, asking him if he would fit the ballroom with several long tables for the ladies to use to lay out their patterns and cut the cloth. Grace Cooper offered to recruit her husband into the plan so that material and trims could be ordered quickly and the sewing could start almost immediately.

Having resolved the most pressing issue of the wedding - the clothing - the conversation then turned to the reception. Of course, Charlie and Rebecca had offered to host the party. In fact, Edgar had added to the event by suggesting the wedding be held in the gazebo, as it was by far the most elegant piece of construction Duncan had achieved so far. And the setting was truly beautiful. Having a wedding not in the church was a bit of a novel idea for these folks, but Samantha was thrilled and it certainly simplified things by having everyone gather at the Redmonds' for the entire day.

And then for the most controversial part of the planning – the food. June first was just four weeks away. Planning the food for a wedding where at least half of Culpepper would be in attendance was a real challenge, and each lady had their own idea of what should be served at a wedding. They poured through the various recipes that each of the ladies suggested, with Rebecca scribbling notes, scratching them out, starting new lists, and trying to keep up with the suggestions that were being put forth.

Finally, Sarah took the ladies in hand, knowing what she could and could not produce in the amount of time they had, with the resources that were available, and with the produce that would be coming ripe at the beginning of June. She considered asking Rex to help, and between them, they would be able to present some surprises for the guests. Sarah and Rex had spent quite a bit of time together after his tour de force, while Rebecca and Charlie were in New York, trading secrets and learning new skills from one another. This wedding offered them an opportunity to play in the kitchen together again.

Sarah had fed the ladies a traditional southern lunch of chicken salad, fruit and tea, which had been consumed as an aside to thumbing through books and recipes. Now, as the sun started sinking toward the west, she presented them with tea and individual lemon cakes. It had been a long and productive day. Fortunately, they were all headed home as soon as tea was finished and before darkness fell.

~

Charlie hobbled toward the barn. He could see Darby and Freddy running around the barn, apparently playing tag or some other game that boys their age managed. As he closed in on them, Freddy stopped and suddenly dashed around behind the barn, clearly trying to hide.

"Freddy!" Darby called to his suddenly shy playmate.

"What is wrong?" His father asked as he drew up to his son.

Darby sighed and shook his head. "He is afraid. He does not think you will be happy that we are playing together."

The tall man sighed and nodded. "Freddy! Freddy, bring your backside out here right now!"

Now the boy was really scared. General Charlie never yelled like that. He managed to find a bit of courage and slid around to the front of the barn, where he stood staring at his feet. "Yes, sir?"

The general approached slowly. "Were you and Darby playing?"

"Yes, sir."

"Were you having a good time?"

"Yes, sir."

"Then why should you stop?"

Freddy was not expecting that question. He slowly lifted his eyes. "Sir?"

"If you were having fun, why should you stop? You are not needed in the kitchens or are somehow shirking your duties to Reg and Beulah, are you?"

"No, sir. Today is my day off."

"Then I see no reason why you and Darby should not have all the fun you want. Darby?"

"Yes, Papa?"

"Perhaps you could show young Freddy here your fishing gear and try to bring home some catfish or bass for dinner. I am sure Miss Rebecca would be happy to have some fresh fish."

Darby nodded and threw his arm around his friend's neck. "My fishing stuff is out in the storage shed, come on!"

Charlie watched with a smile as the boys charged off toward the shed then down the path for a morning of fishing.

When he entered the barn, immediately Jack began to dance in his stall. He stepped back and forth, shaking his head and pawing at the floor. He was clearly happy to see his master.

"There we go, my old friend." He entered the stall, dropping his cane in the corner, and offered his faithful mount a small bunch of carrots. "Let us go out for a walk. What do you say?" He gave him a loving stroke to the neck, leaning his forehead against the beast, while he scratched him under the chin. "I miss you, fella."

Jack nodded as he munched the carrots, tossing his head in the direction of the halter hanging on the wall.

"I know where it is." Charlie moved to the hook.

"General Charlie?" A voice he instantly recognized called from the open barn doors.

"In here, Duncan," he called back as he slipped the leather halter over Jack's head, quickly fastening it into place with speed that surprised him. Even with missing fingers, he could tack up a horse.

Duncan moved to them and leaned on the wall looking in as Charlie clipped a lunge line to Jack's halter.

"What can I do for you?" He retrieved his cane and began leading the horse out of the stall, with Duncan quickly opening the door for him.

"W-well, General Charlie, I-I I think I n-need some h-help with the r-ring part of this w-wedding thing."

"What can I do? Do you need money?" He started to reach for his wallet.

The young man held up both hands. "Oh no, s-sir! I have p-plenty of m-money. I just d-do not have a c-clue where to s-spend it.

N-no store in Culpeper sells n-nice wedding r-rings and I j-just do not h-have time to go anywhere to g-get one. S-suspect I w-would have to go all the w-way to W-washington anyhow.

Charlie nodded as they walked, leading Jack toward the barn door. He was contemplating his friend's predicament when suddenly he was jerked to a stop. He turned to look and Jack had just stopped walking.

"Come on, boy." He gave a gentle tug but the horse refused.

Both men immediately moved to the horse and began inspecting every inch of him looking for anything that might be making him act up.

"L-l-looks good here, G-general," Duncan said after inspecting Jack's right side. He gave the horse a pat.

"I do not see a damn thing either." Charlie lifted Jack's feet and inspected his shoes, making sure they were tight and properly fitted. He stood and gave the horse a scratch between the ears. "Come on, Jack." He tugged again. The horse refused, lifting his head and pulling to the right.

He scratched his jaw as he considered his faithful mount. He handed the lunge line to Duncan. "See if he will go with you."

Duncan gave a gentle tug and, with a click of his tongue, Jack followed him right through the barn doors and out to the front. Duncan turned the horse and they returned to Charlie's side.

The general looked at the horse. The horse looked at the General. He took the lead back from Duncan and took two steps toward the door. Jack stood there.

The carpenter watched with some amusement as the big black stallion stood his ground and refused to go another step further. He tossed his head to the right once again.

Charlie blew out a frustrated breath and moved back to his horse. "All right, it is very clear you are angry with me. I am sorry. I apologize. Can we go now?"

Jack took a step back tossing his head again.

Robert Brooks happened to wander in while his boss was arguing with the horse. "Is there a problem, Mr. Redmond?" the man asked as he placed a bundle of rope he had been carrying on a peg near the door.

"That is a very good question," Charlie answered with a shake of his head. "Would you mind?" He held the lunge out. "See if you can get him outside."

The man took the lead and Jack dutifully followed. Just as Duncan had done, he carefully turned the horse and returned to Charlie. He handed the line back.

"There you go. Anything else," he paused, "sir?"

"No." Charlie shook his head in frustration. "Thank you very much, Mr. Brooks. It would appear my horse is a bit pissed at me."

"Um, General?" Duncan had been watching Jack for the last few minutes. "Sir, m-may I t-try something?"

"Of course."

Brooks wandered away to a corner of the barn where he could watch the men as Duncan moved and opened the tack room door which was to the right of the horse. He returned a moment later with his saddle pad, placing it over the big animal with a loving pat. He returned to the room and reemerged with the saddle the men of Charlie's regiment had given him as a wedding gift. After a minute or two, the saddle was strapped into place and Jack took a step forward, giving Charlie a nudge to his left shoulder as if to push him through the barn doors.

He walked out of the barn with the horse right behind him. Jack got as close to his back as he could and gave him another nudge. He stopped and turned to his animal, giving him a scratch to both sides of his face at once as he spoke. "Now you listen here, fellow, I do not like this any more than you do. I wish it were like old times for us, but it is not. I am now an old soldier who can no longer ride." He dropped his forehead to Jack's broad face and stood there with his eyes closed. "But I still love you, old man. Come on; show Duncan how much you remember."

He led the big horse to the exercise ring and began letting out the lunge, allowing the horse to begin moving at his own pace. Duncan joined him in the center as they stood there watching the horse move around the ring.

"Well," the general chortled as he put a cigar in his mouth. "You helped me with my problem. Let me help you with yours. I have a friend in Washington that I think I can call on to help out. If you give me some idea of what you want for Miss Samantha, I will do my best to get it for you."

"T-thank you, General C-charlie. I h-h-have it here." He passed the tall man a piece of paper that the general considered for a moment before tucking in his vest pocket.

"I will see to it."

"General?"

"Yes?" He gave a whistle and Jack transitioned from his steady walk to a slightly faster trot.

"I w-was w-wondering. You w-wear a ring."

He glanced down at the gold band on his left hand and smiled. "Yes, I do."

"Most f-fellas..."

"Yes, well, I am not like most fellas. I want the world to know that Miss Rebecca has claimed me and there is no other in my life. For me, it is a matter of personal pride and I made the choice to wear a ring. There are no rules for this. You are not required to wear a ring."

"I k-know, b-but I think I would like to."

He smiled. "I think we can see to that too."

Charlie continued to work with Jack for another half hour or so until the animal got so full of himself the general knew it was time to put him away. Jack snorted and stomped his displeasure the entire time he was being brushed down.

"Well, you cannot just have a tantrum and not expect to get sent to your room. I have learned a lot from this fatherhood thing," Charlie chided as he continued brushing the horse long after it was needed.

It was only when he heard the squeals of a little girl that he could finally be torn away from his faithful mount. He made his way toward the sound of the giggling. Just behind the barn, over a little rise on the next little hill, he could see Em and her pup.

"Oh, no," he groaned as he made his way past the fence and up the little incline. As he drew closer he could see the pup digging furiously, throwing dirt up behind her and right into Em's face and hair.

Her shoes were crusted in mud and dung so thick she had been raised a half inch off the ground. Her dress was beyond help, torn in several places and stained from the shoulders to the helm at her little feet.

"Emily Redmond!"

The dog even stopped digging as two heads turned in the direction of the very unhappy human Papa coming up the hill. The dog immediately hid behind her girl. Charlie stood there looking down at his daughter and wondering if there was any way to sneak her past her mama. He decided no, there probably was not, and they were both going to be in trouble. He was not sure how this was his fault, but he found her, so he would share the blame and the guilt.

"Your mama is going to have a fit. What have you been doing?"

"Digging." She pointed at the pile of rock treasures she had accumulated through the morning.

"I can see that," he nodded. "Now we have to take you and get you cleaned up before your mama sees you. How did you get away from Tess?"

She looked down at the ground and dug what should have been the toe of a little black shoe into the ground. "Supposed to be napping."

"You snuck out?"

She nodded.

He groaned. His only hope was that the ladies were still at the house working on the plans for the wedding. He never thought he would have a reason to be grateful for a wedding until he looked at the child before him.

~

After just barely managing to slip his daughter past his wife, the general made a hasty retreat to town in case there should be any further advance on this particular situation. He did not want to be in that house when Mama saw that dress.

He entered the telegraph office and quickly scribbled a dispatch to Jerome explaining the problem and what they needed to fix it. He gave the note to the operator and waited while it was sent and the confirmation was received. He paid for the cable, leaving a tip for the clerk and headed out to Mr. Cooper's to pick up a package for Rebecca.

As he came out of the store carrying a small box and walked down the street toward Jocko's, he could not shake the feeling he was being watched. He stopped to pull his watch from his vest pocket, giving it a look as he also took a chance to glance up and down the street. There was nothing obvious, but he just knew there was a pair of eyes on him. He put his watch away and crossed over toward Jocko's. A slight flash to the right caught his eye, and he managed a glimpse of Alex Raeburn leaning against the post of one of the newest buildings in town.

He stopped and turned to face the man, making sure to make eye contact. They stood there for a full minute, neither of them willing to budge. Charlie watched as two of Raeburn's associates came walking down the boardwalk, laughing and joking. They caught their friend by the arm and convinced him to join them elsewhere, seemingly unaware of the standoff. With a sneer, Alex turned and walked away.

Across the street, another man stood watching this exchange. Sean Cady, one of the two new Deputy Provosts that Richard had been assigned, was already very aware of the division among the residents of Culpeper. He spent a good bit of his time watching Alex Raeburn and his compatriots, because to him, they stank of trouble looking for a place to happen.

Charlie just shook his head and continued on to Jocko's. As he stepped inside, his old batman already had a coffee cup on the bar.

He was a little shocked when his friend covered the cup with his hand, declining his normal shot of brandy as he took a seat at the bar. He quirked his brow. "You feelin' alright there, Boy-o?"

He just nodded and smiled. "Yes, Jocko. I just still have several things to do in town today and having a fuzzy head will not be beneficial."

That he could understand. He knew when Charlie was in professional mode, whether as a professional soldier or businessman, he always kept his head about him. "But you do not normally drop in here in the middle of the day, either."

"What are the grumblings in town?" He put a bit of sugar in his coffee and stirred it around, waiting for the intelligence report.

The Irishman smiled and leaned on the bar across from his old boss. "They ain't real fond of you, Charlie boy. I have heard a few mutters about you takin' over the Gaines place. Some folks think you coerced Rebecca into marrying you. Of course now, I have not heard anything that led me to believe you or Rebecca was in danger. If I had, I would have told you already. These fellas just seem to be blowing off steam mostly."

"I know that, Jocko. You are my oldest friend. I know you always have an ear on my side."

"An ear, eye, fist, gun…" The barkeep chuckled. "Whatever it takes, Charlie boy. Whatever it takes. You cannot really blame them. Here they come back home and they got little or nothing left and you are out there building up that big, beautiful farm and house. Your lady and children are wearing fine clothes. You are almost single handedly building or rebuilding every business in Culpeper. You got a lot for them to dislike, my friend."

"You would think the opportunity for gainful employment and a chance to get back on their feet would be reason enough to refrain from being outright hostile when I walk down the street."

"It is still all too fresh for them. And you are far worse than a carpetbagger. You are a rich Yankee general. And you landed the one lady in town everyone wanted for themselves."

"Anyone ever tell you that you are terrible at pep talks? Is there no one in this town that remembers I am from Charleston, South Carolina?"

"You know me, Charlie." Jocko wiped down the already clean and pristine bar. "I just call 'em like I see 'em. I am not going to blow smoke up your arse and give you a false sense of security."

"I do appreciate that, my friend. Always have." He lifted his cup and drained it. "I am off to the bank site. I will see you later. Thank you."

"I have had your back for nearly twenty years. I do not intend to stop now."

As he stood and dropped a coin on the bar, a boy came charging through the door with a yellow piece of paper clutched in his hand. "General Redmond, sir," the boy gasped, bending at the waist to catch his breath. "Telegram from Washington, sir."

The boy thrust the paper out. Charlie traded him the telegram for a nickel. The boy smiled and ran out of the inn, calling as he went, "Thank you, sir!"

He unfolded the paper:

Will acquire rings. Stop.

Will see you Monday. Stop.

Will not be cheap. Stop

Jerome

CHAPTER 15

Saturday, May 5, 1866

Rebecca sat brushing her hair for bed while Charlie sat by the fire smoking a cigar and playing around with his guitar. She watched him for a minute as he gingerly plucked at the strings. It made her smile to see him trying something new with that injured hand. She sniffed the air. "Is that a new blend of tobacco?"

"I have no earthly idea." He drew deep before removing the small nearly black cigar from his mouth. "It is something Rex gave me. Told me I should have it before bed."

She joined him on the couch. He set the guitar aside so she could cuddle up to his side. She pulled her feet up and tucked them into the hem of her nightgown.

He put his arm around her and kissed the top of her head. "I love you, my darling 'Becca."

"I love you too, my dashing general."

He took another drag of his cigar and let the smoke escape slowly. "I am feeling a bit more dashing tonight that I was a few weeks ago, that is for certain." He chuckled. He cleared his throat and blinked, feeling a bit lightheaded.

"Darling?" She searched his face trying to decide what was happening.

"I am fine. I think Rex's special blend may be very special." He knew he was smiling, but he could not help it.

She kissed his jaw and laid her head on his shoulder. "I am so glad for you Charlie, but you know it did not make a bit of difference to me. I am thrilled for you and happy for us, but I do not love you anymore today than I did yesterday."

"So?" He paused and then tried to hide the grin behind his hand as he said, "What you are saying is that you have stopped loving me," before having another draw on his cigar.

She knew that tone in his voice and reacted appropriately by poking him in the ribs. "You know what I mean, you evil man. You really are rotten sometimes."

~

Sunday, May 6, 1866

The family packed up and went to church that morning, expecting another one of Edgar's gently admonishing sermons, but when they got to the church, they found the people in the church yard grouped together and buzzing over something. What made Charlie uncomfortable was how the people had clumped together. There was a large group of men surrounding Alex Raeburn and all of them looked highly satisfied – almost gloating.

There were smaller groups scattered about, some looking angry, others frightened, still others, not to put too fine a point on it, looked outright disgusted.

He handed his family out of the coach, and then went looking for Richard. "What in the name of hell happened?"

"There were riots this week in Memphis. The police and the local white boys killed forty-six blacks, burned down houses, schools and churches, and generally made a mess. The army was called in but the damage had already been done."

"And Alex and his boys are gleeful, I take it."

"Oh, yes. And our colored folks are scared witless."

Edgar's sermon that morning was far from his usual fare. He started with "an eye for an eye," and went on to deliver a fire and brimstone sermon on the evils of violence. From the look on the faces of Raeburn and his cohort, it fell on deaf ears.

~

Monday, May 7, 1866

Charlie left for town immediately after breakfast. He wanted to meet Jerome at the train and have an opportunity to explain the situation that had caused the delays in getting all of his attorney's questions answered before he got to the house.

He asked Tomas to wait at Jocko's for them, then walked into the station to wait for the train. Fortunately, it was on time, and he was there on the platform when Jerome disembarked.

"Hello, Charlie. I was beginning to wonder if you were still alive."

He grinned sheepishly. "Well, to be honest, it was touch and go for a while. I seem to have become dependent on a pain killer. It almost became a Charlie killer. I know you wanted answers, and I have gone through all of your reports and questions, but it seems that shaking the grip of opium took a little more time and energy than one might think."

"Laudanum?" Jerome asked with concern in his eyes. Charlie nodded. The determined look on Charlie's face told his old friend he was on the way to recovery. "I have seen a number of cases in war survivors returning home. It is not pretty. All right, I forgive you. This time. But we do need to make some serious decisions, and fairly quickly, especially since you will be getting the charter for your bank soon."

"I agree. And there are some things that I have questions about. But first, shall we go over to Jocko's tavern and have a cup of coffee? Have you met Jocko? We were in the service together."

"The tavern keeper? I met him the last time I was in town chasing after you, but you have never properly introduced us."

"I can remedy that. And you will stay for the night? Rebecca wants to meet you." He grinned, "She is beginning to think you are a figment of my imagination."

"I rather expected I would, since we need to look at the paperwork for the bank as well as for your personal finances. Oh, and I brought the rings you asked me to get. The receipt is in the bag. I already took it out of the Riggs account."

He handed him a small velvet bag. Inside were two ring boxes and a slip of paper from the most fashionable jeweler in Washington. He looked at the slip, groaned softly, and put it in his pocket.

"I told you it would be expensive. Wait until you get my bill for this little errand."

Charlie laughed, a rather forced laugh, but still a laugh. "We need to make a quick stop."

They walked a few more doors down to Duncan's wood working shop, and stepped in. Duncan was just getting organized for the day. "Good morning, gentlemen. What can I do for you?"

"Duncan Nailer, this is my old friend, Jerome Lord. You should thank him." Charlie grinned and held up the little bag. "He brought you something you will need next month."

Duncan took the bag and opened it, dropping the two ring boxes gently onto his work bench. He reverently opened each of the boxes, looking at the two beautiful, matched wedding rings within them. "Oh, General Charlie. Mr. Lord. They are beautiful. I cannot thank you enough. What do I owe you, sir?"

His old commander smiled. "Nothing, Duncan. Consider them my wedding present to you and Samantha."

The two men left the carpenter still examining the rings, and chatted casually about their respective wives and children as they walked slowly over to Jocko's. A cup of coffee and a couple of Esther's ridiculously good cinnamon rolls prepared them for the drive back to Redmond Stables.

As they drove through the country, Jerome admired the lushness of the rolling pastures, hay fields, and timber stands. The land around Culpeper was prime horse and cattle country, but many of the holdings had suffered during the war. Charlie explained to Jerome that his hope was to use the bank to help the farmers and merchants in the area rebuild what had been a sound and flourishing economy before the war.

As they arrived at the house, Reg met them at the door. "Gen'l Charlie, Miss Rebecca has the ladies over. They are in the ballroom, working on dresses for the wedding."

"Thank you for the warning, Reg. Perhaps you could bring some tea now, and lunch for Mr. Lord and me up later in the office? Mr. Lord will be spending the night, so please have a place set for him at dinner and a room prepared?" He turned to lead his friend upstairs, then stopped. "Oh, and let Miss Rebecca know we are here – quietly, please."

They walked upstairs and settled in for a morning of going over Charlie's finances. As they sorted through the investments and returns, Charlie had a long list of some very astute questions.

"Oh, so you have been paying attention!" Jerome leaned back in his chair with a satisfied grin, "Finally."

"Well, with the obligations of a growing family, and getting the bank started and all, I decided I needed to learn what I could." He smiled. "And dealing with Jim Fisk on this bank issue has certainly honed my strategic skills in a whole new way. My God, that man is a rabid wolf when it comes to money."

"He is," the attorney agreed with a nod. "I have done well for us by riding on his coat tails. But I am not going to lie to you, he worries me. I am terrified he will grow too cocky and over-extend himself."

At that moment, there was a knock at the door. Charlie called, "Come in."

Reg entered with a tray filled with Sarah's best efforts. "Gen'l Charlie, Sarah is giving the ladies a sampling of what she could prepare for the wedding, so you get the benefit of her hard work too."

"Well, good for us, then. And we have managed to avoid being drawn into the wedding planning--also good for us."

After lunch, the men settled in for a cup of coffee and a serious discussion of the future.

Charlie had a very strained look on his face as he pulled out the pile of papers Jerome had left on his last visit, now covered with notes in the margins of the pages. "Jerome, I am very grateful that you have managed to make so much money for me from your investments. Please understand that. But I am also very concerned that much of that money was made by investing in substandard supplies for the boys in the army."

"For example, I had to deal with absolutely lousy boots made out of rawhide. Do you know what happens when rawhide gets wet? It shrinks and turns rock hard. I had to cut boots off the boys and Elizabeth had to deal with horribly infected blisters from them. We also had terrible problems with barrels of improperly cured pork and beef, green with mold, and sacks of flour that were filled with bugs and worms. I hate it that some of our money, my money, came from this kind of poor quality goods sold by unconscionable opportunists."

"I am also very concerned that we are at risk of being overextended with some of our investments in railroads and ironworks. It worries me that we might see some of these areas that have grown so rapidly blow up on us. It is like sending troops in without backup. They might get cut off and..."

Jerome nodded. "You are first and foremost a soldier. I get your point. Things like the railroads have grown explosively. A case of what goes up?"

"Exactly. Since I want the bank to focus on the farmers and local merchants here, I think we may want to take the same approach for my investments. And Fisk and Gould especially, scare me. At this point, I would settle for smaller returns from less volatile sources."

The banker thought for a few minutes. "I think I agree with you. We have been through a period of enormous growth. I think that we might want to look at things that are always in demand – coal, beef, wheat, iron, corn, timber – things that people always need, regardless of the maneuvering of the financiers."

"Horses. Why do you think my wife is a horse breeder? She takes the same attitude here, and it is a good one. It is no secret that profits explode when there is a war, but it is over. Can we work out a long term plan to provide my family with a stable income, rather than the big profit ventures? You might want to think about the fellows who are making kerosene. It seems to be replacing whale oil, and people always need light."

"Yes, I can do that. And you will still have enough money to finance your bank and your personal needs." He poured himself another cup of coffee. "By the way, what was that check to a toy company in Baltimore all about? That was a major expenditure for a toy store. Or is this another one of your off the cuff investments?" Over the years, Charlie had made modest investments in a number of small businesses, most recently in Duncan's woodworking shop and Jeremiah's leather working efforts, helping them to buy the tools they needed to practice their crafts.

"Oh, no!" He protested. "That was an investment in my children. I have to show you the wonderful lead soldiers I got for them."

~

When Rebecca entered his office, she expected to find her husband and his guest crouched over financial documents. Instead, she found them crouched over the table in Charlie's library that held his own little reproduction of Waterloo.

"Oh, good Lord," she sighed as she pinched the bridge of her nose trying to fight off one of those headaches only Charlie and his lead soldiers could bring on.

"It is Jerome actually." The lawyer's head swiveled toward the door.

Her husband howled with laughter. When he could finally breathe he guided her into the room to make the proper introductions.

"My darling wife! Rebecca Redmond, may I present Jerome Lord, our attorney and one of my oldest friends." He was still trying to fight the giggles.

"Oh, you do exist!" She smiled and offered her hand to the man at her husband's side.

Jerome bent over her hand gently brushing his lips over her knuckles, never breaking eye contact as he murmured, "Indeed, madam, and I can see I have been remiss in not demanding Charlie introduce us sooner." He graced her with his most charming smile.

"All right there, lover boy." Charlie tapped Jerome's shoulder with his cane. "The lady is married."

"Yes, but just to you," the lawyer retorted. He was feeling truly smitten by the lovely Mrs. Redmond.

She giggled. She enjoyed watching Charlie's friends give him grief. It was a sign of affection in her book.

"All right," he nodded. "Might I remind you, you are married too. With eight children?"

"No," Jerome shook his head. "I remember perfectly. That is why I am flirting with your wife."

"She has five children too," Charlie offered dryly.

Jerome stepped back from Rebecca, retaining a gentle connection with the tips of her fingers as he made a show of surveying her figure. "You lie, Charles Redmond."

Now she was laughing and wrapping an arm around Jerome's waist, his arm instantaneously draped over her shoulder. "Oh, I like him, Charlie. Think we can convince him to move to Culpeper too?"

"Absolutely not." Charlie shook his head emphatically. "I can already tell I am going to regret the next twenty four hours. There is no way I want you two living anywhere near each other."

Charlie had decided years ago there was no sense in getting angry or upset when someone teased you. It was a pointless waste of energy in his mind because he knew there would always be someone in line to give you a bit of your own medicine when you got too big for your britches.

Tonight was his night. The three of them had decided on a casual dinner in the parlor after Edgar informed them that he and Charlotte, and by default Rex, would be out for the evening attending to church business. Rebecca sent the children to have dinner in the kitchen. He was beginning to regret that decision, thinking that Jerome would have held back some of the more tantalizing tales had there been children present.

He sat there, face and ears glowing bright red as he vacillated between shaking and nodding his head. Jerome was regaling Rebecca with tale of a youthful Charlie's indiscretions and high jinks at West Point.

"The superintendent never did figure out who put the donkey in his office!" He pounded the table as he finished the story. Rebecca continued to dab the laughter-induced tears from her eyes as she had been doing for the last twenty minutes.

When this particular round of laughter was over, Charlie, his chin resting in the palm of his left hand as he leaned on the table, looked at his attorney and sighed, "I hate you."

And with that, his friend and his wife were off for another ride on the laughter train. The general just poured another cup of coffee and let them laugh. He enjoyed the sound of his wife's laughter and it did not matter to him what caused it to happen.

Tuesday, May 8, 1866

The next morning, Charlie and Jerome went through all of the documents that Jay Cooke had sent about the creation of the bank. Jerome wanted to catch the noon train back to Washington, but the paperwork for a federally chartered bank was damned complicated.

"When you meet with Cooke, do you want me along? I think it would be a good idea to have your lawyer on hand – he is a pretty slick operator."

"Oh, my God, yes! Just his paperwork scares the hell out of me.

What does this mean? 'Describe any potential management interlocking relationships that could occur with the establishment or ownership of the institution.' What is an interlocking relationship?"

Jerome shook his head. "Why in God's name are you trying to open a bank? You know nothing about banking. Hell's bells, man. It would take me, with my law degree and years of experience in finance, at least six months of non-stop work to get this thing off the ground. And then you would need to find an experienced bank manager to run the thing, or you are going to be bankrupt in a matter of a year or so."

Charlie looked up at his old friend. "Why, Jerome! Are you offering to move down here and get this off the ground for us? I think that is a wonderful idea." He thought to himself, *and I would have to put a twenty four hour guard on my wife.*

"Even with your good-looking wife, you cannot afford me, but I will go through the paperwork for you and see if I can protect you from Cooke. And I will find you a bank manager. Will that do?"

"It will have to."

"I will also start moving your investments around as soon as I get back to Washington to put you into a less risky position with decent long-term growth potential."

"Thank you so much. You know, we should get together more often. What would you think about bringing the family down for a long weekend?"

"Perhaps later this summer. I believe your wife has a wedding to plan first."

"Absolutely."

He packed his papers up, picked up his overnight case and prepared to leave. "I know that you have Tomas waiting to take me to the station. Please, tell Rebecca I truly enjoyed raking you over the coals last night and would be happy to provide her with more fodder for torment the next time I come."

"Oh, thank you so much, old friend. I look forward to it. In fact, I think I will see what I can do to repay the favor."

The two men shook hands, and Charlie walked Jerome to the top of the stairs. "I would see you out, but…"

"No problem, and Charlie?" He gestured up and down his friend's tall frame, "Stay off the laudanum. I want to keep you around."

≈

Monday, May 14, 1866

Charlie sat at his desk, cursing softly under his breath. Rain was falling so heavily that he had already lit all the lamps in his office, though it was only two thirty in the afternoon. The rain made his wounds ache and Rex was not allowing him any extra laudanum to temper the pain.

In his hand was a telegram from Jay Cooke requesting his presence in Washington for a last minute meeting the following evening. That meant that he was going to have to pack right away and catch the early morning train to Washington. Rebecca was not going to be happy.

Painfully, he pulled himself out of his comfortably padded desk chair and stepped over to the bell pull to summon Tomas and get the whole process started.

It only took a minute or so for the valet to enter. It was clear from his demeanor and dress that he had expected the rest of the afternoon to be a quiet one.

"Yes, sir, General, what can I do for you?"

He responded mildly, "I fear that I must ask you to pack my case. I have to catch the morning train to Washington. I will need a couple of suits for daywear and my evening clothes." He started scribbling a message as he spoke, and handed it to Tomas. "Also, have one of the stable hands take this to the station master so he can telegraph ahead for me. And ask Miss Rebecca if she can come up when she has a moment." He hated having to ask her to come to him, but on a chilly, rainy day like this one, under Rex's new regime he literally could not manage the stairs by himself.

"Yes, sir, right away. I will take care of everything." Tomas took the note and left the office with his task clearly in his mind and grateful that he was not the one who would have to face Miss Rebecca with this news.

A few minutes later, she entered the office. He was leaning against his desk, waiting for her arrival. Before she could say a word, he handed the telegram to her.

Reading it slowly she nodded and took a seat in the chair in front of him. "How long will you be gone?"

"From what he says, I suspect three or four days. I hate having to leave you with the boys teething and three mares in foal at the same time, but I really do not see where I have much choice if we want to get the bank started."

"Darling, this is what women do. I can handle the boys, and with Tarent, the farm will be fine. You do what you need to do. Do not be concerned for us. What concerns me most is you taking care of yourself. You should take Tomas."

He limped over to stand beside her. He bent down and kissed her forehead, murmuring, "That is not necessary, dear. I sent a telegram to the Willard asking for a room. I am sure they will tend to me properly. You have enough on your hands right now and I do not need to take any of the staff. I also wired to Jerome to join me in this adventure. I will be fine, I promise."

He paused for a moment. "By the way, have you seen my pocket watch and knife – you know the ones you gave me for Christmas? I want to take them with me to Washington, but cannot find them to save my neck."

She sighed. "I am sure they are around the house somewhere – no doubt in one of your little piles. I will tell Beulah and Reg to keep an eye out for them."

~

Tuesday, May 15, 1866

From the darkness of the sky and the unrelenting rain, it was hard to tell that morning had actually broken. Charlie stood huddled over the pot-bellied stove in the train station trying to get warm. It was a fruitless effort. The stove had only been lit a few minutes before when the station master arrived to start his workday and the wood had barely had time to catch fire, let alone heat the iron stove.

The train was late, slowed by the heavy rain and poor visibility. It was not a propitious start. A telegram from Jerome had been waiting for him. Jerome would not be available until tomorrow, as he was in Philadelphia visiting with his wife's family.

After a wait of almost an hour, the train finally pulled into the station. He heaved his satchel onto the one passenger car and then hauled himself up the steps. Because of the rain, all of the windows were closed in the wooden car, and a small coal stove puffed and stuttered in the corner, spitting out more sparks than heat. He wrapped his rain coat around himself and hunkered down into a corner, resigning himself to a miserable trip. A couple of sips of the medication Rex sent with him were a necessity. He pulled his hat over his eyes and let the laudanum take effect.

After what seemed a small eternity, the train finally pulled into the B&O Station in Washington. This was, of course, after having stopped at every single little station between Culpeper and Washington, and having had a number of human and non-human travelers join him in the stuffy, rickety little passenger car. The worst, thought Charlie, was the wet chicken who not only smelled of damp feathers, but was clearly unhappy about being caged and let anyone and everyone in the car know about it.

He limped out of the train station, expecting to hail a hack, enjoy a quick trip to the Willard in an enclosed carriage, and order himself a nice hot bath in the suite he had requested in yesterday's telegraph. But as he stood under the arched entrance to the station, he looked out onto a street that was filled with rain, mud, and the occasional soggy errand boy but no cabs. Not one. Anywhere.

He sighed deeply, pulled up the collar of his rain coat, settled his hat more firmly on his head, checked his oil-cloth covered satchel to make sure it was securely fastened, gripped his cane a little more tightly, and set out to walk the fifteen blocks up E Street to the Willard.

By the time he reached the hotel he was soaked. His coat was dripping, and the clothes under it were damp all the way down to his small clothes and the toes of his socks. His hands, feet, and ears were stinging with a chill, while the rest of him was slightly sweaty from the long, painful walk. His hip felt like it was on fire.

"Simpkins, please tell me you got my telegram and have a suite ready for me," he hailed the clerk at the desk, who after many years of staying at this establishment, was like an old friend.

The clerk sucked air through his teeth; he had sent a telegram only to have a response that the general had already left for the city. He was going to box the ears of the night clerk when the man came on duty. He truly hated to tell one of the hotel's best customers the bad news.

"General Redmond, sir, I am sorry to say that we do not have a suite. But I do have a small room on six. Unfortunately, it does not have a private bath but the freight elevator could take you to the third. I am afraid you would have to walk..."

He bowed his head and closed his eyes. The idea of walking up three flights of stairs was daunting, especially since he had just trudged almost two miles through the rain. On the other hand, getting out of his wet clothes and getting warm and dry was urgently important to him right then. "I will take anything you have, as long as I can get dry and warm soon. Perhaps you can find a better room for me tomorrow."

"You know I will certainly try, sir, but to be honest, the hotel is booked up for the next several days. I will see to it that your bag is taken up and that your room is prepared. Could I interest you in taking a meal in the Tap Room while you wait? On the management, General Redmond, for the inconvenience?"

He groaned. "I assume you are telling me the room is not ready and I need to wait?"

"I am afraid it is not, sir. I did not know if you would even want it. I am terribly sorry, sir. After so many years of your faithful business, I am sorry to have . . ." The man was nearly groveling now.

He heaved his satchel up on the counter. "Do what you have to. I need a room, I need to get warm, and I really have no other options right now. I will be in the Tap Room. Have someone come get me when the room is ready – and make sure to send a good, strong man. I will need help on the stairs." He shed his sopping coat and hat, piled them beside the case, and stumped off to the bar.

The bartender saw him heading into the room and immediately poured his preferred liquor, which was set on the bar before he was even seated.

"Good afternoon, General Redmond. Always a pleasure. Is there anything else I can get you, sir?"

"Afternoon, Galloway." He belted down the shot of brandy and nodded toward the glass for a refill, then changed his mind and asked for a cup of coffee. "No, this will do for now. I am too cold and wet to eat anything yet, but the coffee and the fire here should warm me up. I fear I will put a little cloud of steam into your room here, though."

The man chuckled as he poured the coffee for his customer. "No need to worry about it, sir. Seems to me that you need to be warm, and, with some luck, dry. If you need anything, sir, just give me a yell."

"Let me know when they have my room ready. Though, to be honest, climbing up to the sixth floor with this game leg does not fill my heart with joy, even though the thought of being dry and warm is a powerful motivator."

The bartender drummed his fingers on the bar as he carefully considered his next words. "Sir, might I make a suggestion?"

"I will take any recommendation under consideration as long as I end up with a bath and a warm bed."

"Yes, sir, I understand. You see…" he leaned in on the bar to be closer to Charlie. He was sure his employer would not appreciate this. "My mother, she has a large home. Since my father was lost during the war, she has had trouble making ends meet. She was speaking just the other day of taking on a boarder or two. I could assure you a large room, probably with a private bath and home cooked meals."

"A large home? Your father, was he the Galloway who had the stables out near Foggy Bottom?" The bartender nodded. "I am sorry you lost him." Charlie thought for a minute. "Are you sure your mother would welcome a guest, even a paying one, on such short notice? I am not a regular boarder."

"Trust me, sir; she will certainly welcome a distinguished gentleman such as yourself. She has been hesitant about taking in boarders since she is a lonely widow, but with you, sir, she will have no hesitation at all. I will be done here in about a half hour. I have one of my father's old carriages; I do a bit of cabbing on the side. I would be happy to take you there."

"Well, if you are sure? And promise me that I do not have to walk up to the sixth floor?"

"No, sir. I will explain the situation to my mother, and I am sure that she would be most willing to give you the rooms that my grandmother used." He smiled knowingly. "On the ground floor."

"Then let me go reclaim my bag and I will await your convenience." He hesitated, and then added, "And perhaps we can discuss your business conditions on the way. Your father ran a fine livery stable; it would be a shame to have the war destroy your heritage."

"You sit here, sir, and dry out and rest. I will send word to the desk to hold your things. Then after my shift, we will make our way to the house. It seems to me that getting you settled is crucial."

◁∾▷

Martha Galloway was not what Charlie expected. He remembered her husband as a big, robust man who could manhandle any horse God made. Young Galloway had taken after his father. But the Widow Galloway was tiny, thin, and intense. She reminded him of a cross between a wren and a hummingbird, always moving, but with the drab grays of the wren, not the stunning ones of the hummingbird. Her dress was gray, her hair was gray; even her eyes were gray. He looked around the house and saw the comfortable and gentile furnishings, shabby now with the loss of the senior Galloway and the profitable livery business. He stood quietly while Galloway and his mother talked intensely for a moment or two.

The elder woman turned to him and appeared to be sizing him

up. "General Redmond, is it? How long will you require a place to rest your head, sir? I will tell you now that in my home there is no smoking, drinking, or cursing. I would expect you to be in at a reasonable hour since I lock the door at seven sharp and of course there are to be no women. I prepare breakfast and dinner, which you are welcome to if I am told to expect you, and lastly I assume you are a good Christian man."

He took a deep breath. He was accustomed to Rebecca laying down the rules of the house, but not this bluntly. The Widow Galloway was clearly a woman to be reckoned with. "Madam, I want to thank you for your hospitality. I expect to be in town for three or four days, and I have at least one evening event with Mr. Cooke and General Grant that will probably put me in later than seven. As for smoking, drinking, or cursing, I smoke occasionally, but always outdoors; I drink moderately, as your son can attest. I curse rarely and only when profoundly provoked; and the only woman who ever shares my bed is my wife. As for my Christianity, I was raised a Presbyterian, but am now a member of the Episcopalian congregation in Culpeper and attend church regularly. If you will have me, I would be happy to pay you what room and board in a suite at the Willard would cost me, plus something for the inconvenience of my evening appointment."

He watched as the woman's shoulders squared and she considered his rapid fire response to her own barrage. She liked this man and assumed he would be a perfect addition to her home. "General Redmond, those terms are agreeable to me. My son tells me that you have special needs." She glanced at his cane. "That you have trouble climbing stairs. I have a pair of rooms in the back, used by my own mother, may she rest in peace. You are welcome to those. I am afraid they are decorated in a manner pleasing to an elderly woman, but if you find them suitable and think you will be returning, I would be willing to redecorate them in something more suitable to a gentleman of your status."

He smiled. A room decorated in a manner pleasing to an elderly woman. He had visions of lace and violet knickknacks. But a warm bed and no stairs were enticing. He was in Washington often and would probably be coming up more frequently between Grant's political ambitions and Cooke's financial ones. Even more attractive was the fact that the house was at 24th and I, just three blocks from Cooke's offices on K Street, an easy walk even for him. "Madam, if you would maintain rooms for me here, I would be more than happy to pay for any changes to the décor that I might want. It would give me a place in town that I could rely on."

She seemed to be considering it as a gentle smile lit her lips. "I am certain that between us, we can find an equitable compromise, General. Now please, let my son get you settled. It is just past dinner, but I may be able to find you something if you have not eaten yet."

"That would be lovely, Mrs. Galloway. Oh, by the way, on occasion, my wife may accompany me to Washington. Would it be a problem for you?"

"Your wife, sir? She will always be welcome. Any other woman will never be permitted."

"You have nothing to worry about, then, as I will have no other." He grinned. "Between my wife and my two daughters, I have all the women in my life that I, or to be honest, any man, would ever need."

CHAPTER 16

Tuesday, May 15, 1866

Rebecca awoke to a small voice whining in her ear and tugging at the comforter. "Mama 'Becca. I don' feel so good."

She opened one eye and gazed out. The fire was banked and provided only the softest glimmer of light. It was still dark outside. All she could see was the vague outline of a small child, but linked to the voice, it was obvious that it was Suzanne.

There was nothing that would pull her from a sound sleep faster than one of her children needing her. She lifted up on her elbow to find the little girl standing near the edge of the bed dragging her favorite doll and blanket behind her.

"Oh, my little darling." She flipped her own covers back. "Come up into bed with Mama." She lifted the child into the bed, immediately checking for fever and finding a small one. Suzanne was not burning up but she was definitely not normal either.

"I got hot. And my head hurts, Mama 'Becca. Make it better, please."

"Oh, little one, the best thing we can do is rest. You lay down here and Mama will get you a cool cloth." After tucking the child into her bed, she rose to fetch a cloth from the stand where she kept a pitcher of water. She had learned as she nursed Charlie always to have cloths handy. She poured the water into the basin and returned to the bed to try and make her daughter more comfortable. She lit the lamp so she could have a better view of Suzanne and saw the child was looking worn and sick.

It seemed that the Redmond household was about to have another round of sick children. "Thank God Charlie is in Washington."

As she laid the cool cloth over Suzanne's forehead, the child remembered her manners. "Thank you, Mama. That feels good. Makes my eyes less burny."

"You just rest, sweetheart. Sleep if you can. I need to go check your brothers and sister. I promise to be right back."

"Yes, Mama 'Becca. I will be here."

She found her dressing gown and tied it tightly around herself as she found another lamp and made her way out into the hall. She stopped before a door and rapped lightly. "Tess, it is Rebecca. I am sorry to disturb you but Suzanne is ill and we need to check the other children."

The nanny immediately roused from her trundle bed outside of the girls' bedroom. "Miz 'Becca? Little Suzanne? I am right there."

"I will go check the boys. Would you go to my room and sit with her until I return?"

"Yes'm. Little Suzanne is such a sweet thing. I hope it is just a little upset."

Rebecca sent Tess off to her room and then she headed down to the room the boys shared. Entering the room, she found the two sleeping fitfully, but sleeping.

She found Darby, on the other hand, in his room sitting up at the desk Charlie had given him shortly after their arrival. He was sweating buckets, even as he sipped water while trying to read a book.

"Oh, son, you are sick." She passed her hand over his face. "You should have come and gotten me."

He looked up at her, his eyes red rimmed and watery. A slight flush covered his forehead and cheeks. "It is alright, Mama 'Becca. Just a little cold or something. You were sleeping and I did not want to bother anyone."

"It is not alright. You are my son and you are ill. Come down to my room with me. We will get you fixed up." She held her hand out to him. "Come on. You can bring your book. I am sure that none of us will be getting much sleep."

Darby carefully placed his bookmark in the book and stood up, clearly shaky on his legs. "Whooo. I should not have stood up so quickly," he said as he grabbed the back of the chair to keep his balance.

"Easy, son." She wrapped her arm around his shoulders and guided him to the door. "Just lean on me."

As they made their way to the hall she found Tess exiting her room. "Miss Suzanne asked me to fetch a toy."

"Very well, Tess. After you do that I think you should probably wake Reg or Tomas and send one of them after Dr. Walker. It seems the whole of the house is trying to take ill."

As Tess nodded her agreement and started down the hall to the back stairs, a door at the other end of the hall opened and Em poked her head out.

"Oh, Lord," Rebecca muttered as she guided Darby to her door and sent him in to her bed before she turned to Em. "Why are you awake, little one? It is late. You should be asleep."

"I am hot." A harsh cough shook her frame. "And my throat hurts."

She realized that now was the time to wake the entire house and as she picked Em up in her arms, she called Tess back and gave her that order. She had nursed many ill people before but she had a feeling that her five children were going to make those experiences seem like a garden party. It was going to be a long day, and if her suspicions were right, an even longer week.

Friday, May 18, 1866

The move to the Widow Galloway's, complete with hot bath, warm bed and a thick chicken stew for dinner had not been enough to keep Charlie from catching a truly miserable cold.

The dinner meeting with Cooke and Grant had been highly successful; they had assured him that he would get the license for a National Bank and the political support needed to ensure a good start. All he needed now was a completed building and sufficient investment to guarantee cash flow. If his head had not been so filled with what felt like wet cotton batting, he would have been ecstatic.

Profound apologies were extended to both men for his inability to celebrate more vigorously with them over achieving this significant milestone. Three more days spent at Cooke's Washington offices, working with Jerome to fill out paper work and meeting with potential investors had taxed Charlie's reserves severely. He was looking forward to being home, warm and comfortable, in his own bed.

He arrived on the afternoon train, expecting to see Tomas, or at least one of the stable boys, at the station to meet him. After all, he had sent a telegram the day before announcing his return. No one was there. The stationmaster had put a sign on his door, saying he was at home today, feeling unwell.

He looked around, sighed, and picked up his bag. It seemed that walking from train stations to his destination this week was simply his fate. He limped down the street and around the corner to Stevens Street, where he turned left and marched down toward Richard's house.

He approached the house and then stopped at the gate. Richard and Elizabeth were standing on the porch, obviously arguing, and the doctor's one-horse trap was waiting at the gate.

"Elizabeth, be reasonable. They have a normal childhood illness. If you catch it, you could put our child at risk."

"Richard, you be reasonable, please. Everything we know says that if you have measles as a child, you will not get it as an adult. Jenner and Pasteur have done outstanding work to prove that. I had them when I was about Darby's age. So I am safe."

"What about our child? What if he or she gets them in the womb?"

"You are being absolutely ridiculous. Now, let me get on with it so I can be home for supper."

She turned away from her husband, who was standing there obviously fuming, and hailed Charlie. "Well, well you are just in time. I am on my way out. Would you like a ride?"

He blinked. "Out to my place? Are my children sick?"

"Oh, nothing to be worried about. Darby, Suzanne and Em have come down with the measles. They will be well in a few days, but right now I am afraid they are miserable."

"What about the boys? And how is Rebecca holding up?"

"Well, your youngest sons have decided this week is the perfect time to really start cutting another round of teeth. Your wife is an amazing woman, though I would suspect a holiday would be most welcomed when this is over."

He took that moment to try to sneeze his head off, coming up from behind his handkerchief with a rueful grin and watery eyes. "Um, I think I am going to add to her problems, rather than help, then."

"Well, at least you will have the good sense to rest and be quiet when she tells you. She has nursed you before; I am sure you will pose no further burden. Let us get you home. And try not to sneeze on me or Richard will pummel you."

He sat quietly and sniffled behind his handkerchief as she clucked the little Morgan she used for a cart horse to a brisk trot. Twenty minutes later, the two of them entered the house.

At first, Charlie did not notice anything was amiss. Then suddenly women seemed to appear from everywhere and they were carrying everything from food trays to dirty linens and chamber pots. He sneezed again and suddenly as if the sneeze was a bell, Tomas was at his side taking his coat.

"Oh, sir, let me help you and get you up to your office. I will tell Miss Rebecca you are home, but you do not want her to hear you sneeze. That will put her right over the edge. Why just this morning I heard her tell Tess and Lizbet that if one more person got sick, she was going to burn the house down to keep it from spreading. We think she might just do it, too."

The general handed Tomas his coat, hat and satchel. "I take it that things are a bit, um, stressful around here?" He cleared his throat. "And all I have is a cold, which should be better in a few days."

"Yes, sir, I imagine you will, but in the meantime let us get you and your cold up to your office."

Elizabeth chuckled and pointed with her chin. "You go on up, and I will send Rebecca to you while I check the children."

He moved dutifully behind Tomas, headed for the stairs and the safety of his office. What he really wanted was his own bed and a pot of hot tea, followed by a dose of laudanum and some sleep. That did not seem to be his fate.

With the help of his valet, he made it up the stairs. Tomas helped him pull out of his suit coat and boots, found a pair of carpet slippers, built up the fire, and went downstairs to ask Sarah to fix the general some chicken broth and a pot of tea.

He sat in his most comfortable chair, just staring out the window. "God. What a hell of a week. At this point, I would not be surprised to hear Gabriel's horn and the dead start to rise for final judgment."

Tomas, returning with the tea and soup, heard him talking to himself and just shook his head. He did not know the half of it yet.

Charlie had time to have one sip of tea before the door to his office opened. He expected his vibrant wife to come sweeping into the room like she always did. It was not to be. She looked horrible. Her hair was down about her shoulders. She looked pale and the dark circles under her eyes would have done a raccoon proud. She did muster a smile at him; it was sweet until he sneezed. Then she looked as if she might burst into tears.

"Darling, it is just a cold. I am home now. I can help." He opened his arms, expecting her to fall into them.

She did not fall into his arms, but set about finding him a lap rug, a shawl and making sure there was water in the basin. "You, my dear, will help me by staying in here and not spreading your illness around the house. I have three children with measles, two cutting teeth, and several household staff that will quit at their first opportunity, I imagine. None of us have had more than an hour's sleep since Suzanne woke us in the middle of the night three nights ago. There is no sense in trying to eat because the children throw up anything we give them, making it rather unappetizing for us. Please, Charlie, if you love me, if you truly love me, stay in your office."

He blinked at her, stunned. This was not the homecoming he had expected, even with Elizabeth's warnings. "But . . ."

"Really, I promise to tend to you as best I can, but the children need me. Tomas will make sure you have anything you might need and I will come in to make sure you get your supper. Please? I really do not need to worry about you too, and if you give the children your cold it will delay their recovery. The poor darlings are having a hard enough time between the fever and the itching and the . . ." She finally collapsed into a chair next to him. "I am so tired."

He started to rise and go to her, but she waved him away, and he sank back onto the couch. "I am truly sorry, darling. If there is anything I can do, please, let me know. Otherwise, you do not need to worry about me. I will be here; I will take care of my cold, and in a few days I will be right as rain and ready to take up the slack. You need to take care of yourself, love. Remember what happened the last time you forgot to sleep and eat. If you do that again, you will not be able to take care of the children. And what good will that do?"

"I know. I do eat as much as I can. I just need six solid hours of uninterrupted sleep to be right again. I promise you, darling, I am better than last time, but the children are being very demanding right now. It is not their fault; they are just so pitiful at the moment. It seems that one of the boys in their Sunday school class decided to share his measles. A perfectly Christian thing to do, I think."

"Well, darling, if you do not get some sleep tonight, I will ask Elizabeth to send one of the midwives that she has been using as nurses over to watch the children tomorrow. You really need to rest."

"We have already thought of that, but the entire town is sick right now. Elizabeth and Samantha Carter are very nearly the only two women standing and they are up to their ears as well. Elizabeth only comes out here because we may as well be family. She has not even been able to visit some of the outlying homes yet."

He bowed his head. "At least promise me to try and rest. I will stay out of the way until I am well, but when I am well, you will take a solid eight hours to sleep. Promise?"

"Oh, I promise, dear husband. When I have my first chance, Satan himself would not keep me from sleeping. I am looking forward to it."

As Rebecca marched out of the room to return to her sick children, Rex slipped in. He was carrying his case of tools and medicines.

"Rex! The very man I desperately need to see."

"Tomas came by and told me you have a cold. I think I can help with that."

Forty-five minutes later, Charlie was a lot more comfortable. Rex was a miracle worker.

~

Wednesday, May 23, 1866

Rebecca, Charlotte, Charlie and Rex had gathered in the back parlor for a casual dinner. They were all exhausted from dealing with fussy, itchy children for days. Today was the first day that the spots were gone, the coughs were stilled, and no one was running a fever. Now the children were just cranky from being confined to their beds for a week.

Edgar had escaped the worst of the day, as he had a meeting with the church deacons to go over the budget that afternoon, followed by the usual Wednesday evening prayer meeting. Even though Reverend Williams had been dead and buried for over a month, the little cottage they had found for Mrs. Williams was not quite ready, so she still held court in the manse and Rex and Edgar were still staying with Charlie and Rebecca.

Charlie smiled wanly at his wife. "At least we can get some rest now, darling."

"Rest? You think we can get some rest? Charles Huger Redmond, we have a wedding here in nine days. We have food, flowers, guests, seating, and dresses... all of the things we have to do for a wedding yet to accomplish. And have you gotten the wine and champagne for it yet?" Her voice rose with each word, so that by the time she drilled him on the beverages, she was almost shrieking.

He patted her arm. "Yes, dear. The wine shipment is due in on Friday. Duncan has the rings, and Missy Frazier is doing the flowers, and the musicians are coming up from Charlottesville. I think we can get some sleep tonight, love."

Charlotte, who had been watching this exchange with a smirk lurking around her lips, added, "And the dresses are almost done. The ladies have been taking advantage of the sewing machine and the room to spread out."

Rex smiled outright. "Sarah and I have already started preparing the food."

He grinned. "See, love? The world has continued to turn while you were busy with the children. So I think you can get that much needed eight hours tonight."

She looked around at the people in the room. "You have been doing this for me?"

Charlotte and Charlie and Rex grinned at one another. Finally, Charlie offered, "Yes, dear. For you, and the bride and groom of the event."

That evening, Rebecca was barely out of her dress before she was asleep. Charlie found her lying on the bed in her chemise and pantaloons. He sighed and carefully tucked her under the covers and headed down the hall to his office for his treatment with Rex. Rebecca's exhaustion had been given priority in the bedroom.

He sat at his desk, with a heavy sheet draped toga style over his torso, leaving his right shoulder and arm bare for Rex's ministrations. He was a bit nervous about the whole thing; it had been under very similar circumstances that Rebecca had discovered his secret.

"Relax, General. You should know by now these needles do not hurt."

He nodded and rubbed his eyes with his left hand, trying to concentrate on anything else. Rex placed the lit candle in front of him. After a month of treatments, physical therapy in the mornings and acupuncture in the evening, he knew what the candle meant. He was not relaxing the way his caretaker wanted. He began looking into the flame and in a matter of minutes he was in a light trance.

～

Friday, May 25, 1866

While Sarah bustled around the kitchen tending to the day's meals around the ongoing furor that was the preparation for the wedding, Rebecca sat at the table, drinking coffee and peeling apples.

She had decided to bake a pie for the family's dinner desert, and asking Sarah to do more than the bare necessities was too much with all the other activities going on. She had a few hours of peace while others carried out her orders. Plus, the opportunity to sit quietly in the kitchen and gossip with Sarah was too good to pass up. She enjoyed her cook's company. She was a smart woman with an outlook all her own.

They would trade stories of husbands and children and it did not take Rebecca Redmond long to understand the woman before her had the same dreams, hopes and fears she did. She knew people would be absolutely scandalized if they really knew what went on in her house and she decided, every time she looked at Charlie or one of their beautiful children, she did not care. Sarah, Beulah, Lizbet and Tess had become good and trusted friends with whom she shared at least a few minutes every day chatting when they all had time.

"So," Sarah shook her head, laughing at the story in progress. "My man is standing there covered in..."

Before the woman could finish, the clear, ringing voice of a former military commander could be heard coming through the open kitchen windows and screen door. "God damn it, Custer! Leave me the hell alone, you little bastard!"

Charlie had been down to the barn, discussing the plan for handling the horses of the guests that were expected for the wedding. He had also been to the ice house to ensure they had enough ice to chill the drinks and to meet Sarah's needs in the kitchen. Now he was trudging back to the house to chat with Reg about the wine selection.

"What in the name of Heaven?" Rebecca stood and moved to the backdoor, looking out the screen. There, before her eyes, was her husband, fending off a rooster attack with his cane.

The large reddish orange bird was furious. His feathers were all puffed out starting with his neck and going all the way down his body. His wings were spread wide as he tried to make himself look much bigger than he actually was. He was running, jumping, kicking and pecking at Charlie's boots as he tried to make his way up from the barn through a small flock of hens. When the bird would get in a good hit, his claws and the thick spurs on the back of his legs could be heard bashing into the leather of the high boots.

"I mean it, bird!" Charlie stopped on the path and held the rooster at bay once again. The bird pecked furiously at the end of the cane as the tall man looked heavenward, "God, I hate this fucking rooster." On the rare times Charlie Redmond released his soldier's vocabulary he did so in vociferous fashion.

The foul fowl, named Custer by Charlie, had become the man's mortal enemy in the early spring when he took his rightful place as the dominant rooster in Rebecca's new flock of chickens. Charlie liked the chickens and their eggs were delicious. The rooster he could most definitely live without.

She was laughing so hard she could barely breathe when she pushed the door open and called, "General Redmond? Sir, you do realize your combatant is an eight pound bird?"

"No, ma'am," he said, backing up toward the porch slowly, keeping his cane extended out and his eye on the beast, which was just looking for an opening to bash his foe's boots again. "I am in combat with an eight pound asshole!" He growled as he took the last two steps up onto the porch in one long stride, still watching the bird.

"Charles Redmond, your language is atrocious! What would you do if Edgar overheard you?"

"I would ask Edgar to ask God to have the damned rooster fall over dead." He lowered his cane as the rooster decided that following his hens back into the yard was more appealing than the pursuit of his nemesis onto the porch.

He watched for a few seconds longer to make sure the bird did not plan to double back. He had already been taken in by that little trick and the bird had managed to jump him in an attack that had left an actual puncture from his spur and a bruise on his good leg, on the shin just below the knee. "Then I would serve him a fresh chicken dinner."

"Charlie, please! Please, watch your language. I know you do not do that often, but I assure you, you do not want Em or Suzanne repeating any of that in church."

He nodded and held the door so they could go back in, still staring at the bird in case he went for a surprise attack. "Yes, dear."

Inside, she poured him a cup of coffee and Sarah put a piece of lemon cake down in front of him as he sat down at the table. He looked at both of them and the food before him. "If this is my punishment, I am going to get in trouble more often."

"Consider it the going rate of compensation for one rooster attack." Rebecca smiled as she retook her seat and once again began peeling apples.

"It is going to rain." He tried to get out around a badly swallowed piece of cake. He took a drink of coffee to clear his mouth and tried again. "It is going to rain. Hard, I suspect."

"What makes you think that?" she asked without ever looking up from her peeling. "Sky is perfectly clear."

"My ass knows." He chuckled as he managed to duck just fast enough to avoid her attempt to cuff his ear.

Sarah managed to keep her coffee in her mouth, just barely. She smiled as they sat at the table teasing each other gently. If there were two people under God's blue sky that deserved to be happy it was the general and Miss Rebecca. It was especially good to see the general on the road to recovery. Reverend Edgar's little Chinaman friend might be unusual to look at and talk to, but he had certainly done wonders for General Redmond. And it showed in the smiles on both their faces.

~

Wednesday, May 30, 1866

Activity at the Redmond house had become frantic. The wedding was only two days away and Rebecca was flitting from room to room, checking to make sure everything was in order. The guest rooms had been refreshed, one of the retiring rooms on the first floor had been set aside as the bride's preparation room, and the other was being used as the staging room for other activities such as the flowers. If one individual could mill around all by herself, she was doing just that.

She had a small wooden box in her hand that was carefully labeled "Charlie's Things," and as she went from room to room, she collected up the various bits and pieces that he had emptied out of his pockets and dropped onto the nearest flat surface over the past few days. She found a small pile of change on one table, a pocket knife and a piece of a broken halter buckle on one of the mantle pieces, a group of folded papers with notes on them in yet another place. There was a hoof pick on the tantalus in the back parlor and a box of Lucifer matches beside a half-smoked cigar on a side table in the hall. His money clip with twenty-two dollars in script and a silver pocket watch were on the side board in the breakfast room. All of it went into the little box.

She stomped upstairs, irritated as usual with her spouse's ability to create small, messy piles all over the house. She went into his office, intending to place the box of his clutter in the middle of his desk as usual, when she stopped, looking closely at Darby, who was standing in front of a display of Charlie's war mementos.

Darby stood in his father's library and for the first time, he took the time to actually look at something besides the books. He had looked at the maps framed on the walls. Most of them appeared to be campaign maps of some sort.

On the mantle, a pair of Colt 1860 .44 caliber revolvers sat in wooden cradles. Epaulettes with one star were framed, sitting between the pistols. A square brass and silver belt buckle with an eagle, its wings spread wide, and a golden pocket watch lay next to the frame.

Darby could just make out the inscription on the inside cover, "To Jonas. All my love, Ruth." He was not sure who those people were, but he was fascinated by the things on the mantle. He was a bit startled when his mother entered carrying a small box.

"Darby, sweetheart? What are you doing in here?"

"Oh, I was actually just returning a book," he said. "But then I started looking at Papa Charlie's things."

She nodded and put the box on Charlie's desk, tapping it with her finger. "A few more of those things, collected from various table tops around the house."

The boy laughed and nodded. He knew that his father's tendency to leave his possessions lying around drove his mama to distraction. "Mama Rebecca? Papa Charlie was in the cavalry, right?"

"He was." She nodded.

"Where is his sword? I thought all cavalry officers had a sword."

She swallowed hard, trying to fight the urge to cry. "It was lost," another deep breath was needed. "At Appomattox. When he was wounded, it was in his hand."

"I see," he answered quietly, nodding as they headed for the door of the office. "Can we replace it?"

She thought about it for a moment. "I have no idea. I would not even know where to begin. It is a lovely thought though. Very sweet of you." She caressed his face, cupping his chin in her hand so she could look in his eyes. "You make me very proud. I am very glad you are a part of our family."

"Me, too, Mama Rebecca." He gave her a hug around her waist, closing his eyes and savoring the feeling of her returning his embrace.

～

Darby was a boy on a mission. He had hitched a ride into town with Tarent, jumping from the back of the wagon in front of Richard and Elizabeth's house. He was just about to knock when Richard charged out the front door, nearly knocking him over.

"Whoa there, Darby!" The big man managed to catch them both before they tumbled off the small porch. When they had their feet back under them, Richard settled his hat on his head and slipped a cigar in his mouth. "What can I do for you, son?"

"Uncle Richard, I have a problem and I am sure you are the only one who can help me."

His brows rose to the crest of his hair. "What about your mother and father?"

"Well, Mama Rebecca already said she would not know where to begin to help me and I cannot ask Papa Charlie, because well, the problem concerns him."

"I see." He sat down on the stoop and gestured for Darby to join him. "Tell me about it."

He sighed. "Papa Charlie and I share a birthday, you know?"

Richard nodded and lit his cigar.

"I really would like to do something very special for him. To thank him for everything he has done for me and Suzanne."

"That is very nice, but where is the problem?"

"I want to replace his sword. The one he lost in the last battle."

Richard's heart jumped. He had done his best not to think of those days and weeks in a very long time. "All right. How can I help?"

"I thought maybe you might know how to do that. I mean, you were in the army too." He turned hopeful eyes to the man it was easy to call uncle.

Richard nodded and scratched his chin. "Yes, I think I might know who to call upon for this." He looked down to the young man and said honestly. "It will not be cheap."

The boy nodded. "I understand. It is end of May now. Our birthday is not until the end of September. That gives me all of summer to earn the money I need."

"It does indeed." Richard nodded, his brain quickly making important connections. "Darby, lad. I think I may have an arrangement that will be mutually beneficial."

Darby sat at dinner that night waiting for the time when his parents would call upon him to discuss his day. It was quickly becoming the routine at the Redmond family dinner table. Each child would be asked what new thing they had learned or done that day. The girls always went first because their tales generally resulted in giggling over some silly game they had played with Tess. He just ate and tried to be patient. Finally, Papa Charlie called on him.

"So Darby…"

"I went into town today and Uncle Richard offered me a job." It all rushed out of his mouth so quickly Charlie and Rebecca could only try not to laugh and grin at their eldest child.

"Is that so?" His father sat back, regarding the boy seriously. "And what job would that be?"

"Helping Aunt Elizabeth. Uncle Richard says that I would be perfect because she will not torment me like she torments him."

They howled with laughter. It took several minutes before Charlie could regain enough composure to continue the query of his son. He wiped a laughter-induced tear from his cheek. "When does he want you to start?"

"Yesterday," Darby answered seriously to another round of laughter from his parents.

Thursday, May 31, 1866

297

Rex and Sarah were up and cooking at the crack of dawn. Tomorrow was the wedding and it was time for the serious preparation to begin. Sarah had her staff put a whole side of beef in the smoker, where it would slowly cook to smoky deliciousness over the next twenty four hours. A pit had been dug in the back yard, into which a whole pig would be placed later that day.

In the kitchen, Rex took the largest cauldron Sarah had and filled it with whole chickens, carrots, onions, garlic, ginger, parsley, celery, and various substances from his case of magic herbs and elixirs. He was making his own special broth that would be the basis for a soup, as well as broth for various sauces.

There were piles of vegetables being peeled by Sarah's assistants. Potatoes for potato salad, cabbage, carrots and raisins for slaw, sweet potatoes, acorn squash, green beans, onions, broccoli, and other vegetables for something Rex would be making, fresh greens and fat back for Sarah's famous greens, a huge pile of green beans and a full side of bacon being chopped to make greasy beans. On the other side of the kitchen, Sarah was supervising the assembly of a huge cake, filled with alternating layers of strawberry and raspberry coulee, and iced with sheets of marzipan decorated with sugar flowers that were hard to distinguish from the real flowers she would use to finish the decorations.

It was a scene from Bedlam.

The family's meals that day were afterthoughts. Cold ham and cheese, crackers and bread, and a bowl of strawberries was all there was for lunch. They were on their own for tea that afternoon. Fortunately, Charlie had horded some of Sarah's ginger cookies. Dinner that night was even sparser. A salad of tossed together greens and tomatoes with plain oil and vinegar, some cold roast beef, a bowl of cold pickled beets pulled directly from the pantry, and nothing for dessert.

He sat in his office smoking an after dinner cigar with Edgar. He had no idea where Rebecca had disappeared to, and Tess and Ginny had herded the children off to their rooms after dinner, such as it was.

"Dear God, I wish this wedding were over! My household has

been in turmoil for a week, and damn, the food has been nothing but an afterthought. If I get plain oatmeal for breakfast for more than one more day, I swear…"

Edgar laughed uproariously. "Charlie, Duncan is one of your best friends and one of the most reliable men I have ever met. You can suffer this for one more day, if for no other reason than he deserves it."

He started to say something, but then thought better of it. Grudgingly, he responded, "You are right. If it were not for him, I would not be here today. Yes, he deserves it." He paused. "But, damn, I deserve a decent meal in my own house."

The minister laughed at him again, and shook his head. "From the smells emanating from the kitchen, I think you will be getting one tomorrow. I know that Rex is making a couple of his very special oriental dishes for this event. You would think that a man whose income make both of us look like paupers would not be able to play in the kitchen like he does, but he thinks cooking is one of the classic fine arts to be practiced with the greatest of loving care. And I thank God he does, as it means I have always eaten very, very well."

CHAPTER 17

Friday, June 1, 1866

The day of the wedding dawned clear and bright, but with a little crispness to the air that promised it would not be too hot.

Missy Frazier and a number of what Charlie thought of as 'Rebecca's Renegades' descended on the house early, and started hauling armloads of flowers and greenery out to the gazebo. Rex, Sarah and a troop of assistants were in the kitchen at the crack of dawn.

The smells coming from the kitchen were fantastic. It just served to make the morning bowls of oatmeal that much less appealing. He was delighted when Rex brought him a small bowl of raisins and dried apricots as a special treat to add to his bowl of gruel.

Reg, Tomas, Tarent and several of the stable hands were setting up tables and chairs all over the lawn. Right behind them came some of the ladies, spreading white table cloths and setting vases of flowers on the tables.

It was rather like watching a swarm of very large butterflies flitting from point to point.

Around ten o'clock, more people started arriving, so that the stable hands were busy running coaches, carriages, buggies, wagons, and traps and their respective horses back to the stable yards. Reg and his helpers had scrubbed out several horse troughs and filled them with ice. Two large punch bowls were filled and emptied multiple times as people started availing themselves of the refreshments. Trays of little finger foods were laid on the tables beside the punch bowls, and were replaced as soon as they were emptied with more tempting goodies.

The musicians set up on the veranda above everyone's heads, so they could be heard. By eleven thirty in the morning, the crowd had arrived and was starting to find places down by the pond where they could watch the service in the gazebo. Had it not been for the very different dress styles being displayed today, with the slim lines and sweeping trains, instead of the bell-shaped crinolines and hoops that had been popular before the war, it could have been a lawn party from the days of pre-war southern splendor.

Promptly at noon, Edgar moved to the center of the gazebo and motioned for Charlie to escort Duncan to his place of honor, which he did, after hastily checking his vest pockets for the rings. The minister signaled to the musicians, who began to play the processional that Jeremiah knew meant he needed to escort his mother and Rebecca, as Matron of Honor, to the gazebo.

The music began, and Jeremiah stepped out of the retiring room onto the lower veranda with his mother on his arm. Samantha was dressed in one of the new style dresses, made of a beautiful cream silk and ecru lace with a long train flowing behind her. Rebecca brought up the rear, in a dress of dove grey and the softest shade of lavender. Solemnly, Jeremiah led the ladies down the stairs and along the path to the gazebo.

When everyone was settled into their appropriate place, as they had rehearsed the evening before, Edgar cleared his throat, smiled at Samantha and Duncan and began the service.

"The grace of our Lord Jesus Christ, the love of God, and the fellowship of the Holy Spirit be with you."

The guests responded as one, "And also with you."

"A wedding is one of life's great moments, a time of solemn commitment as well as good wishes, feasting and joy. St. John tells us how Jesus shared in such an occasion at Cana, and gave there a sign of new beginnings as he turned water into wine."

"Marriage is intended by God to be a creative relationship, as his blessing enables husband and wife to love and support each other in good times and in bad, and to share in the care and upbringing of children. For Christians, marriage is also an invitation to share life together in the spirit of Jesus Christ. It is based upon a solemn, public and life-long covenant between a man and a woman, declared and celebrated in the presence of God and before witnesses."

"On this their wedding day, Samantha and Duncan face each other, make their promises and receive God's blessing. You are witnesses of the marriage, and express your support by your presence and your prayers. Your support does not end today: the couple will value continued support and encouragement in the days and years ahead of them."

"Love is patient; love is kind; love is not envious or boastful or arrogant or rude. It does not insist on its own way; it is not irritable or resentful; it does not rejoice in wrongdoing, but rejoices in the truth. It bears all things, believes all things, hopes all things, endures all things."

Edgar addressed the congregation. "First, I am required to ask anyone present who knows a reason why these persons may not lawfully marry, to declare it now."

No one spoke, though there were a number of grins.

He turned to Duncan and Samantha. "If either of you knows a reason why you may not lawfully marry, you must declare it now."

They both shook their heads, but said nothing.

The minister smiled at Jeremiah. "Who gives this woman to the rite of holy matrimony?"

In a clear, though slightly higher voice than normal, Jeremiah responded, "I do." He placed his mother's hand in Duncan's, and then stepped back.

Edgar turned to the groom. "Duncan, will you take Samantha to be your wife? Will you love her, comfort her, honor and protect her, and, forsaking all others, be faithful to her as long as you both shall live?"

It took Duncan three tries to get this answer out, the stutter being very pronounced. "I-I-I w-w-will."

Samantha was very clear, responding to her question in ringing tones.

Edgar turned to the congregation. "Will you, the families and friends of Duncan and Samantha support and uphold them in their marriage now and in the years to come?"

"We will," they responded.

The rest of the service progressed according to tradition, except that instead of the normal long sermon that Reverend Williams had usually done, Edgar smiled at his friends, and said, very simply. "Love one another. Be kind. Be generous. Be forgiving. And have a good time."

With the exchange of rings and a final benediction, Edgar asked Duncan and Samantha to turn to the congregation. "Ladies and gentlemen, let me present Mr. and Mrs. Duncan Nailer."

They walked into the crowd, all of whom had to shake Duncan's hand and slap him on the back, or embrace Samantha. Jeremiah slipped through the crowd to find Darby. The two boys went and quickly raided some of the food that had already been set out on the long tables, then they corralled Freddy from his spot by a table and the three of them slipped off towards the stable yards.

Reg and his team started popping bottles of champagne open and handing out glasses of the sparkling elixir. Sarah and Beulah supervised the transport of food from the kitchen to the long tables. Rex had set up a hot fire in a brazier and was using one of his weird flat pans to quickly fry a mountain of batter-dipped vegetables, which went onto trays on the table. Once they had been cautiously tasted by the guests, they started disappearing as quickly as they came out of the pan. It was hard to tell if the vegetables were disappearing more quickly than the beautiful clear broth with tiny pieces of vegetables and pork meat balls no larger than a penny floating in it. Sarah's traditional foods started being plated up, and the crowd ate heartily.

Charlie and Edgar were sitting together at a table. "Oh, thank God. Real food!"

"I told you that you would get a good meal today," laughed Edgar, sipping his champagne and nibbling on one of Rex's lightly battered, fried sweet potato rings.

It took a while for everyone to serve themselves and find a table to settle down. The yard sounded rather like a horde of buzzing bees, as multiple conversations were carried on at once, with the musicians playing softly in the background. Finally, the meal was consumed and Reg and Beulah's staff cleared the tables.

Sarah led the procession bringing out the wedding cake, which was set in a place of honor in the middle of one of the tables.

Charlie rose. As best man, as well as the host of the party, it was his obligation to propose a toast to the bride and groom.

"Duncan Nailer is one of the most reliable men I know. He may be slow to speak, but when it counts, he is quick to act. Samantha, I advise you to trust him when he does. As I know from experience, his ability to act quickly and wisely can be a life saver. Duncan, I have watched Samantha now for almost a year. She is steady, knowledgeable, and has a wide variety of skills. Trust in her, listen to what she has to say, and remember that the best answer is always "Yes, Dear." Ladies, and gentlemen, to Duncan and Samantha."

The yard resounded with the response, "Duncan and Samantha."

"Now, let the cake be cut and the music play!"

Late that afternoon, after much dancing, laughing and carousing with friends and neighbors, Duncan and Samantha were getting ready to head home.

Duncan walked down toward the stable yard, yelling, "Jeremiah! Time to go!"

But Jeremiah did not appear.

Charlie caught Duncan by the arm. "Give up. I saw him, Darby and Freddy; I suspect they are up to whatever ten-year-old boys get up to. They will be back by dinner time, and Rebecca and I will take care of him. You two go have a weekend to yourselves. While we cannot give you a honeymoon, we can at least give you a weekend. Enjoy it. We will give him back on Monday."

With a laugh and an appreciative "Thank you" to Charlie and Rebecca, Mr. and Mrs. Nailer rode home in a pony trap that had been artfully decorated with flowers and ribbons.

They saw the remaining guests to the door and on their way. Finally, the five regular residents of the house dropped bonelessly into chairs in the back parlor. None of them were up for food, as they had stuffed themselves on the amazing spread that Sarah and Rex had provided. It was time to relax after days of preparing for this wedding.

"It is done," Edgar spoke pontifically.

"Thank God. If I had to do one more day of this, I would have gone insane."

"Charlie Redmond, you love being able to throw big parties. So do NOT try to convince us of anything else," Rebecca chided him.

"Speaking of parties, what would you say to holding a big Fourth of July party in town?" Charlotte had been talking to Edgar and the ladies in town about ways to support the community of Culpeper.

Rebecca looked excited. "Oh, yes. I think that is an excellent idea."

Edgar simply smiled.

Charlie dropped his head into his hands.

∽

Wednesday, June 6, 1866

Rebecca met with Tarent and Albert every Wednesday morning immediately after breakfast to discuss the status of the breeding program. This morning, she invited Charlie to join them as she wanted his opinion on the direction of their activities for the coming months. This meeting was particularly important as more mares were coming into season and the best of the summer horse sales were coming up.

Rebecca started the meeting by looking directly at Albert. "Tell me, Cousin, what kinds of horses were being shown at the sales this spring?"

"It is quite a mix, I have to confess. As usual, here in Virginia, there are plenty of riding horses, mostly hunters with thoroughbred or thoroughbred warm blood crosses. But the big pulling horses, both for carriages and drays and for farm equipment are also coming along. General use farm horses are going for more than they did before the war, I think because there are so few of them and so many people trying to get started again. And then there is the usual small trade in ponies and such."

Tarent spoke up. "Many of the local men are looking for smaller multi-use horses that are cheaper to keep but can be used for both plowing and for pulling a buckboard."

Rebecca looked thoughtful. "So the thoroughbreds and thoroughbred/warm blood crosses have a market with the hunters, riders and carriage owners, but we are completely missing the farmers and merchants?"

Albert offered around a sip of his coffee, "That about sums it up." Tarent just nodded.

Charlie listened, fascinated at how these committed horse people thought and worked together. He knew how to manage horses and herds, military style. When he sat in on these meetings he understood there was a world of difference and Rebecca Redmond was conquering the world. He smiled and nodded his approval when she looked to him.

She looked thoughtful. "So, what about drafts and warm bloods? I think I would prefer Percherons over any other draft horse, if for no other reason that they have less hair – those tufts around the hoofs are a mess to clean up. But it seems to me that something as big as a Percheron would be more appropriate in a larger market, where the customers have heavier loads to pull." She tapped her desk, clearly thinking.

Tarent spoke up. "Actually, I would recommend we pull in more warm bloods. They have the strength and brains to do a number of things, from pulling a coach, wagon or dray to riding to the hunt. Very versatile horses, they are. And there are some smaller warm bloods that could also be bred for some of the farmers with smaller places. Versatile and less expensive to keep – sort of general use horses."

Rebecca nodded, a thoughtful look on her face.

Albert spoke up. "I am seeing more Morgans and Standardbreds coming into the auction – small to mid-sized horses, lots of smarts, lots of uses."

"Well, shall we start breeding Morgans and Standardbreds?"

Tarent cleared his throat. "I would say we start with Morgans. If we want something larger, we have the thoroughbred stock to crossbreed to a Standardbred type horse. After all, the standardbreds are just thoroughbred Morgan crosses."

She looked up at Charlie. He just smiled again. She and her staff had things well in hand. "So Albert, shall we get a small herd of Morgan breeding stock in here this summer? Say a couple of studs and half a dozen fairly young mares?"

He smiled. "Of course. I think this will work well for us. But I think I will go up to Pennsylvania for this one. There are some good breeders up there and I think I will find better stock for us."

"By all means, Cousin. We want the best breeding stock we can afford. Let me know."

Tarent offered, "Perhaps we should consider breeding some mules for the farmers. They are less expensive to maintain than horses, are good in harness either for wagons or for plowing, and far more cooperative than donkeys."

"So you think a couple of donkey studs would do to start with? We can breed them to the thoroughbred or standardbred mares."

"Yes, ma'am. That should give us a good start."

"Well, gentlemen, by all means, let us find a couple of decent donkeys."

She looked down at her desk, organizing her papers and obviously dismissing the meeting, but Tarent cleared his throat and made no motion to get up yet.

"Um, Miss Rebecca, there is one more thing. The other day, we found one of the fences down out by the apple orchard."

"Did we lose any horses?"

"No, ma'am. A couple of last year's foals had wandered into the grove, but we got them back."

"Good man. I suspect the last of the deadfall from last year got their attention."

"I do not think so, ma'am. The fence was clearly not broken; it was pulled down. I think someone intentionally brought it down."

She sighed. "The bane of every horse-breeder's life – rustlers and horse thieves. So have the men ride the fences on a regular basis and bring in as many of the horses as possible at night. That is all we can do."

"Already doing it, ma'am."

Charlie spoke up for the first time. "And make sure they are armed. At least with side arms, if not with rifles. Let me know if you need guns for them."

"Yes, sir, general." Old habits flared to life as Tarent threw his old commander a salute before bowing to Rebecca and leaving the office.

∾

Rebecca felt the thrashing before she heard a sound. She immediately sat up and looked to Charlie, who was lying stiff in the bed, his head twitching from side to side. His arms were jerking at his side.

"No," she whispered gently as she moved close to him and placed her hand on his chest, rubbing small soothing circles. Placing her lips to his ear, she whispered again, "No, Charlie. It is all right. You are safe. It is only a dream."

His breathing became rough as his head thrashed a bit more and his hand came up. She took his arm and put it back down "No… dying…" he mumbled in his sleep.

She began caressing his face. "Charlie, it is okay. You are home. You are safe. You are not dying. It is just a bad dream."

She continued this way as was her habit when he began having bad dreams. She soothed him, repeating words of love and calm until he finally settled into a quieter slumber.

She felt the tears pool in her eyes as she settled on his shoulder, wishing she could do more than stop them after they started. She could feel him relax against her as she continued to rub soothing circles on his stomach. "There you are, my darling, just relax."

～

Monday, June 11, 1866

Charlie and Tomas stood in front of his wardrobe. "I will take the blue and the dark gray day suits, and my evening clothes. You know the rest of the drill. And pack for yourself. Have you told Tess to pack for herself and the children?"

"I have not. I was waiting for you to talk with Miss Rebecca. Have to you told her yet?" The valet asked as he started folding shirts.

"Told her what?"

"That you intend to take the three eldest children to Richmond with you to get the bank charter?"

He gave his valet and friend a sheepish grin. "No."

Tomas laughed and dropped a shirt into the case. "I will help Tess get the children's things together. Assuming Miss Rebecca will let you take them."

"I would think she should relish the idea of only having to deal with the boys for a few days."

"You would think that, but I swear, General, I have never seen a woman so dedicated to her children. Not to mention that the women folk I know do not seem to think men can care for children for more than an hour or so. I am not so sure Miss Rebecca will be happy about this."

He nodded. "You may be right, but I am going to try."

～

The night was warm. A nice, soft breeze carried the fragrance of early summer blossoms and fresh cut grass as Charlie stood on the veranda smoking a cigar. The children were finally in bed. Edgar and Charlotte were off for an evening of who knew what. Rex had gone out on his own, in a little buggy he had loaned him, heading over to Sarah's little house at the edge of the property to share more cooking secrets and tricks.

The house was quiet and all was well. He had left Rebecca at her vanity, bushing her hair and getting ready for bed. He leaned on the railing, enjoying both the cigar and the weather. He smiled when he felt her arms go around his waist.

"Penny for your thoughts," she murmured, rubbing his back.

"Mmmm." He nodded, turning to embrace his wife. "I was thinking about the trip to Richmond."

"Oh, I know." She looked up to him. "I know it is important. Picking up the charter for the bank. You must be a ball of nerves."

"There is that," he agreed. "However, I also thought," he paused and gently kissed the top of her head, "that I would take Darby, Susanne and Em with me on this trip."

Instantly he felt her tense in his arms. She said nothing for a solid minute. Then she looked up at him. "Have you lost your mind?"

"Not at all, my dear." He slowly and gently rubbed her back with the palms of his hands, careful to avoid singeing her hair with his cigar. "I just think that you deserve a few days of relative quiet. Darby will love the trip. Suzanne will enjoy herself immensely, I think. And of course you will not have to deal with Emily's fits of conniption because Papa is gone again."

Rebecca patted his chest as she always did when trying to placate him. "I appreciate the thought, but I am not sure--"

He cut her off raising a dark brow. "That I can care for our children without you?"

"That is not what I said." She pulled back and looked him in the eye. "I know you are perfectly capable of tending the children. However, Charlie, three of them? One on three far from home?" She shook her head. "I am not sure that is a good idea."

310

"It would not be one on three. Tomas will be with me. The children like him as well and I will make them promise they must listen to him too."

She shook her head slowly. His brows came together. Was she really going to buck him on this? He drew a deep breath, letting it out slowly and waited.

"Take Tess with you at least," she finally said softly.

He smiled, pushing back just a bit so they could look at each other. "You are sure? You trust me with your children?"

She laughed and hugged him tight. "No, but we can always adopt more if you fail to bring this group home."

⁓

Wednesday June 13, 1866

Though Richmond was only twenty miles farther away than Washington, because the rail beds were so much more poorly maintained, the trip took over twice as long as the trip to Washington. Sarah had packed them a picnic lunch to eat in the train on the way. Tess had packed toys and games to entertain the girls, and Darby had his latest book tucked under his arm. So Charlie thought he was well prepared for the five-hour train trip.

He underestimated the challenge of handling two very excited little girls and one insatiably curious boy. Within the first hour, he had heard, "Ohhh, look, Papa Charlie" about a hundred times. Within the first two hours, he thought if he never heard the word "why" again in his life it would be too soon. "Are we there yet?" was asked at every stop the train made. By the time they arrived in Richmond five hours later, he was exhausted. How the hell did Rebecca deal with this every single day? he wondered.

They disembarked at the Main Street Station, which was just a block away from their hotel, the Ballard House, which in turn was just a block away from the Capitol building, where he needed to go to collect and sign the bank charter. With Tess assisting, he gathered his flock of children and herded them off to the hotel, leaving

Tomas to deal with collecting their luggage and retaining a porter with a hand cart to bring their bags along to the hotel.

The hotel manager noticed the tall man surrounded by three babbling children coming through the door. *Ah, yes. General Redmond, I would guess.* He scurried forward to greet the man. "Good afternoon, General Redmond. I am Robert Lancaster, the manager here at Ballard House. How was your trip, sir?"

"It was fine, thank you. Is my suite ready?" *The hell it was fine. The rail bed was bumpier than a logging road paved in untrimmed tree trunks. The average speed was twenty miles an hour. And crawling through the countryside with these three asking non-stop questions, the most common of which was 'Are we there yet?' not to mention the smoke and cinders coming in through the windows... oh yes, it was a fine trip.*

"Yes, sir. Please come with me. As you requested, we have assigned you rooms on the first floor." He led them up a single, very grand flight of stairs from the ground floor, turned right, and then left, and walked to the end of the hall. He opened a set of double doors into a sitting room with doors leading to several other rooms.

Charlie looked around. There was a room for the girls and a trundle bed for Tess, a room for Darby and a room for himself, with a valet's room that was part closet, part small bedroom for Tomas. But the best thing was the windows in the sitting room, which overlooked the Capitol building and the park-like grounds surrounding it.

"Thank you, Mr. Lancaster. This will do nicely. Could you send someone up with tea for my children and me? And my man Tomas should be along shortly with our luggage. Just send him up."

"Certainly, General. I hope your stay in Richmond is pleasant."

Tess took the girls into their room to clean them up, as both had ash on their hands and faces from the train's engine smoke. Darby retreated to his room to do the same, while Charlie collapsed into the most well-padded chair in the sitting room to await Tomas' arrival.

Tonight he would spend recovering from the trip. Tomorrow morning, he would walk over to the Capitol, sign the paperwork, and then show the children around the town that was just starting to rebuild from the ravages of the battles in the last weeks of the war. A quick trip to the Rocketts Landing ship yards, followed by a decent dinner at the hotel and then back home the next morning. He decided that with Tess and Tomas' help, he could do that.

~

Thursday, June 14, 1866

He was up early that morning. He had breakfast for himself, the children and his staff delivered to the sitting room. He gulped down coffee, eggs and bacon, and dressed for business. Leaving the children with Tess and Tomas, he set out for the Capitol building. It took him a few minutes to find the right office. A supercilious clerk took his sweet time gathering together the paperwork for him to sign, notarized the documents, and finally assembled the papers into a packet tied with a blue document ribbon. "Well, Mr. Redmond, you are now officially the owner of a bank. Good luck."

His business completed, he stumped back to the hotel. He stopped at the desk and asked Mr. Lancaster if he could get an open carriage so he could take his children on a tour of the city.

"Of course, General Redmond. In fact, I have an excellent driver who can give you a very good tour of the city and especially of the boat works down by the river."

"Oh, yes. I also wanted to take them by Rocketts Landing boat works and to the Tredegar Iron Works. My oldest son is fascinated with anything that involves design and building."

While Mr. Lancaster summoned the carriage, he went upstairs to gather his troops. By the time he had them organized and downstairs, the carriage had pulled around, and they were off.

They went around the Capitol building with the driver chatting away and pointing out places of interest, and then headed down toward Libby Prison, one of the most notorious prisons of the Civil War.

As they approached the site, Charlie leaned forward and hissed at the driver. "I have a young son and my two little daughters here. I

do not want them hearing about the things that happened at Libby."
They drove past the dilapidated building with the barred windows
and the old, weathered warehouse sign without comment.

They drove on to the Rocketts Landing ship works on the shore
of the James River, where they watched as great cranes continued to
rebuild the port while boats were loaded and unloaded at several of
the already repaired docks.

Their driver took them to a small inn near the river, where the
proprietor served an excellent lunch of butter bean soup, Virginia
smoked ham and hot biscuits with lots of butter and honey. Sitting
family style at long tables with the workers from around the area
was a new experience for the children.

Darby actually managed to strike up a conversation with one of
the local iron workers. The kind man sat patiently answering every
question the boy had, barely giving him enough time to eat his
lunch. Charlie cheerfully paid for his meal and bought him another
beer for being so kind to his inquisitive son.

The girls smiled and flirted with all the men and even the
roughest and toughest of the dock workers made sure to watch their
language around the two pretty, well-mannered little girls. All in all
it had been a wonderful experience for them.

After lunch, the driver took them around to the sprawling
Tredegar Iron Works, which had once made the cannons that
supported the Confederacy and now was creating the iron to rebuild
the city. Darby was fascinated watching the great cauldrons of red-
hot liquid iron being poured into molds to make all kinds of fittings,
from wrought iron fences to great brackets to hold girders in
buildings and bridges.

As the afternoon drew to a close, the driver took them by the
White House of the Confederacy, telling them of the activities
around this house, especially as the war drew to a close. Then he
delivered three tired children and three exhausted adults to the hotel
in time for an early dinner and bed.

CHAPTER 18

Friday, June 15, 1866

They were up early the next morning. Charlie grabbed a bag which had been delivered to the hotel the day before and took it to Tess. In it were britches, boots, and a shirt and a simple vest for each of the girls. He had concluded that simple clothing like their mother wore when working around the farm was much more appropriate for making the painful trip home than the girls' usual frilly garb. The nanny agreed wholeheartedly.

The bags were packed and Tomas had found a porter to haul them over to the train station. Charlie and Tess fed the children breakfast and trooped downstairs to settle the tab and thank Mr. Lancaster for his hospitality. Then they trudged over to the train station, boarded the train for Culpeper, and settled in for the five hour ride home.

Charlie had picked up a book on Richmond history. It kept Darby occupied for the entire trip. He had no such luck with the girls. They had to replay every single event in their exciting day. Three or four times. In excruciating detail.

Things got worse. There was some kind of problem on the tracks and the train slowed from its usual twenty mile an hour crawl to barely ten miles an hour. So the five hours became seven.

He just gritted his teeth and listened to the non-stop chatter, smiling and nodding at his daughters, and making non-committal grunts at appropriate points. Having heard each story four times before, he knew exactly when to nod and grunt without actually having to listen to them anymore.

They finally reached Culpeper, where one of the stable hands was waiting with a carriage to take them home. As they pulled up to the front door, Rebecca was waiting on the porch.

"I was worried sick, you were so late." She shook her head at Charlie, then looked at the girls in their britches and boots and their layer of soot from the train engine. She just looked at them, speechless, shaking her head again. She hugged each of the children in turn and then handed the girls off to Ginny to take them upstairs and clean them up. The girls tried to tell her all about the trip, but Mama cut them off. "You can tell me when you get cleaned up, dears. Now go with Ginny."

She turned to Darby, who was still reading his book. "Darby Sweet. Get your nose out of that book and say hello." He looked up, grinned and came over to give her a sooty hug. She looked at the handprints he had left on her dress, sighed, and sent him up to get cleaned up as well.

Charlie took her arm, leaving more soot marks on her dress. "See, they are home in one piece, no worse for wear." He walked her into the house and down the hall to the back parlor.

"So dear, how was your trip?" she asked sweetly. "And what inspired you to dress the girls in britches and boots?"

"Well, I am now officially the owner of a bank, along with the other investors. And the children got a lovely tour of Richmond. They were very well behaved. I thought the britches and boots would be easier on the train, what with the soot and all, rather than ruining their pretty little dresses." He tried to sound nonchalant, but was not as convincing as he could have been.

"And did you find that taking care of three children was as easy as you anticipated?"

"Ah, on one level, yes. Especially with Tess to deal with things like baths and dressing."

"And on the other levels?" She was waiting to back him into a corner.

"Well, they can certainly talk a lot," he said simply.

She stared at him, waiting for the rest of the truth to come out.

Finally he smiled ruefully. "In the future, if I take the children somewhere, I would very much like for you to please join us."

At that moment, the girls came bursting through the parlor door, with Darby right behind them. The girls started into their by now well-rehearsed blow by blow account of their trip to Richmond. Since Papa had heard it several times already on the trip home, he excused himself to go and get cleaned up, leaving a sooty kiss on Mama's forehead as he went.

~

Sunday, June 17, 1866

Darby had gone back to work at Elizabeth's on Saturday morning, running errands and fetching cool drinks for the extremely pregnant woman, planning to stay overnight and meet his parents at church the next morning.

Elizabeth was about eight months along--huge, hot, and miserable. She could feel the child doing chin ups on her rib cage when it became tired of doing summersaults over her kidneys.

This Sunday was Richard and Elizabeth's first anniversary. She was not sure she wanted to celebrate it. As a matter of fact, right now Richard was not her favorite person in the world for putting her in this miserable condition.

But she hauled herself off of the chaise lounge that she found to be the most comfortable place to semi-recline in the house. Lying flat in bed was hard on her back, while sitting upright was difficult because of the size of her stomach. She had developed a miserable case of hemorrhoids, which did not improve her mood. It would have been terribly inappropriate if she failed to go to church. She either needed to be in hard labor or at death's door to have a good excuse.

Edgar took pity on the congregation. While the week had been very pleasant, Sunday's weather had changed into the blaring, humid heat that marked the beginning of true summer in Virginia. He kept his sermon impressively short.

As usual, there was a caravan of buggies, wagons, and carriages wending their way out to Redmond Stables after church. Sarah and her cook crew scooted out of the church so they would be the first to get back to the house and more importantly, to the summer kitchen to prepare for the onslaught of the Polks, the Coopers, the Fraziers, the Nailers and whoever else happened to tag along for Sunday dinner.

Sarah had decided to create a true summer dinner. She had made a cold soup with cucumbers, onions, cream and sour cream that was smooth and cooling. She followed with cold roast chickens, several salads, and sweet dinner rolls. Dessert was strawberries and cream. It was the perfect cold collation for a miserably hot day. Served down at the gazebo, it made for as cool and relaxed a Sunday dinner as was possible given the weather.

As the meal drew to an end, Charlie had Reg brought out several bottles of champagne which he had chilled down in the spring house, so that they were deliciously cold and crisp. He offered a toast to his old friends. "To Richard and Elizabeth and to the additional member of the Polk family who will be joining us soon. May the years ahead go as well or better as the one that has just passed."

The assembled crowd joined in the toast. "To Richard and Elizabeth!"

Elizabeth mumbled to herself, "and no more summer pregnancies."

~

Thursday, June 21, 1866

Elizabeth had invited Charlie and Rebecca to join her and Richard to dinner for a change. To be honest, she wanted some adult company and did not feel up to making the buggy ride out to Redmond Stables.

That left Edgar and Charlotte to their own devices. Edgar saw it as an opportunity to enjoy more of Rex's oriental cooking and spend a pleasant evening with Charlotte without having to observe all of the proprieties of the Redmond dinner table. Rex smilingly agreed to prepare another treat for them and set about the process. It also gave him the opportunity to teach Sarah some more of his kitchen secrets.

Rex had grown tired of the southern style greasy beans and decided to show her how to prepare Szechuan style spicy beans instead. The dish was truly vegetarian, with green beans, garlic, ginger, red pepper flakes and sesame oil, cooked quickly in a very hot pan. To complement the spicy flavoring of the beans, he made a delicately sweet and spicy dish of pork, mixed with vegetables in a sweet and spicy plum sauce, and served with pancakes, so that the pork and vegetables were wrapped in the pancakes and eaten with one's fingers.

The two of them enjoyed the rustic meal, finishing with melon soaked in a light mint sauce and chilled glasses of coffee with heavy sweet cream. All in all, it was a lovely and very unusual meal.

As they ate, they discussed the upcoming Fourth of July party, which Charlotte had taken primary responsibility for organizing. Rex had contributed by contacting his friends up in Washington's Chinatown to arrange for a fireworks display. Mr. Cooper had contributed flour and other supplies to support a pie baking contest among the ladies, with various local farmers contributing peaches, apples, pears, strawberries, blackberries, and rhubarb for the bakers to create fillings.

The official reason for the supplies being provided by the church was so that all competitors would be on an even playing field. The reality was so that women who otherwise could not have afforded to compete, would be able to participate. Of course, Charlie and Rebecca had pitched in and there was a musical group coming up from Charlottesville to play a concert of patriotic songs in the afternoon.

As they exhausted the subject of the upcoming party, out of the blue, Edgar asked Charlotte, "So who are you really? I am perfectly certain that you are no more Charlie's cousin than I am Father Christmas."

Her face drained of blood, leaving her a pasty white. Her hands shook as she took a sip of her iced coffee, obviously delaying and attempting to form an answer.

Edgar, seeing her discomfort, offered a compromise. "I'll tell you my secret if you'll tell me yours." He grinned as he said it, taking more of the edge off the question. "I am sure you have wondered what a younger son of a lesser British nobleman did to get banished to a small church in Culpeper, Virginia."

She nodded, still not daring to speak.

He took a sip of coffee, settled himself and began. "Once upon a time there was a beautiful princess who was raised by two loving parents and educated by some of the most knowledgeable and astute people at the court. Her life was good, travelling around the country with her parents and siblings. But that lively, interesting and loving life suddenly came to an end when her father died of cholera and her mother went into a period of intense mourning that far exceeded what was considered normal or socially appropriate."

"This young woman missed her father, and could not reach her mother, who was lost in her own grief. Alone and desolate, the beautiful princess turned to the company of her father's librarian, a kind and intelligent young man with whom I was close friends. Whenever they could be together, they were. When circumstances separated them, they wrote letters to one another. I helped them in their relationship, by planning meetings and serving as a go-between, conveying their missives to one another."

"Alas, the queen found out about this unauthorized and, for a princess of the realm, inappropriate relationship. She sent the young librarian back to his home in Germany. I understand that the queen had betrothed the princess to a small-time German prince who will live in England where she can keep an eye on her daughter. She wanted the go-between, that is to say me, to remove myself from the country. Since the queen is also the head of the Church of England, it was very easy for her to see to it that I was traded to the American branch of the church, the Episcopalians. So here I am."

She nodded, grateful for the time to collect her thoughts. "Well, I can see where making the Queen of England angry with you would be a very reasonable cause for banishment. I have a rather different story."

She swallowed hard, and the next words came in a torrent. "I owned a social establishment in Washington, where I met Charlie. I also met a young man of southern sympathies who rather resembled Charlie." Edgar's eyebrows had risen somewhat when he realized that he was sitting across from a very skilled ex-madam, and rose even farther when it dawned on him that she had probably, even if not intentionally, helped a southern spy.

"I let Louis use my house as a way station for messages and packages he left for his friends. I truly did not know what was in them, but to be honest, in the midst of a war, I should have had better sense. Louis was hanged as one of the members of the conspiracy that killed President Lincoln. I was told to disappear or I would be tried for treason."

She sat there, her hands folded tightly in her lap, waiting for his revulsion, for her stupidity as well as for her former profession, to be voiced.

He thought about her story for a moment, then grinned and said, "Well, that explains some of your skills, and we have both managed to truly annoy the powers that be. Seems like a good match to me." A momentary twinge of jealousy toward Charlie flitted through Edgar's mind and was shoved to the back. It was obvious that there was nothing left of that aspect of their relationship, as Charlie was clearly besotted by Rebecca and she was secure enough in his fidelity to allow his ex-mistress in their home. He extended his hand to her with a lascivious grin. "Shall we retire upstairs and explore more of your skills?"

~

Monday, July 1, 1866

Charlie was just wandering past Duncan's shop headed to Jocko's for lunch before going back to the bank. Elizabeth had made him come in for an examination. She was curious to see how Rex's treatments were working.

She was delighted to see that his overall range of motion had greatly improved and that the pain was impressively reduced. And he had not touched any laudanum for several weeks. His drinking was sparse or nearly nonexistent. His weight was coming back up, and new muscle was starting to form all over his frame, including near the scars. They even took the time to discuss a very private and predictable problem for him.

"Any problem with courses resuming?" She tapped a pen against her notepad as Charlie pulled his shirt over his head and began buttoning it.

He shook his head. "I think your initial diagnosis was correct. These damn scars and wounds seemed to have served one reasonable purpose. There may be a bit of cramping for a day or two, but nothing else. I can certainly tolerate it."

She nodded and made a note. She had suspected this would be an additional, but much welcomed, result of his injuries. He had always done everything he could to stall or stop the natural cycles of a female. When he had been healthy, his physical regimen of running and vigorous exercise had done the job, and after his injuries, the medication and trauma had seem to perform at least one miracle as far as he was concerned.

"You feel good?" she asked gently.

"Better than I have in a long time, Elizabeth." He grinned.

She realized at some point she wanted to sit down and have a long talk with the little man who had done her dear friend so much good. She suspected there were things she could learn from him that would help her treat others like him. She released him from his exam with a smile and sent him on his way.

"General Charlie?"

The tall man swung his head toward Duncan's shop to see Jeremiah standing at the door of a small side shed his step father had built him after the wedding so he would have his own space for leather working. "Yes, sir, Mr. Carter. What can I do for you?"

The boy smiled. He liked the general because he treated him like an adult and had actual respect for the work he did. "Sir, I have something for you. Could you come here please?"

"Of course." He stepped inside the little shop, impressed with the level of order and tidiness. All the young man's tools and supplies were properly stored and hung. Projects sat neatly on workbenches in various stages of completion.

Jeremiah opened a drawer and removed a small object. All Charlie could tell was that it was light leather and had a few small straps. "I noticed, sir, that when you are out at the farm you have stopped wearing your glove."

Charlie flinched, afraid he had hurt the boy's feelings. Jeremiah had been making his special gloves since shortly after his arrival home. "Well, yes, out there…"

The boy shook his head. "Oh no, sir, I am not upset. However, it got me to thinking. So I made you this." He handed the item to him. "I thought they might be good for in town too."

It was a pair of prosthetic fingers. Made from very soft, light leather and crafted to look as much like real fingers as possible. Jeremiah had even taken time to etch fingernails and lines of knuckle joints into the top of them and give then a slight bend that made them look almost natural.

He removed his black glove and slipped them into place on the end of his hand. They were attached to something that looked like a quarter of a glove that fit over the outside palm of his hand and was held in place with a small strap around his wrist. Another small strap ran along the back on his hand, looping over his thumb, making the whole thing very stable. The device actually gave his hand a natural look he had not seen in a very long time.

"May I?" Jeremiah gestured. He held it out for him to check and slightly adjust the fit. "If it bothers you or rubs wrong in any way, let me know and I will be happy to make corrections."

The general smiled and offered his new hand to Jeremiah to shake. "Thank you, sir. Very much."

~

As Tomas drove him home, he took the time to inspect the new prosthetic. Jeremiah had done an outstanding job of making it look as natural as possible. He discovered as he continued his inspection that the fingers could be moved into different positions. He just shook his head marveling at the ingenuity. He was very glad Darby and Jeremiah had become such good friends. He suspected as they grew older they would make a formidable business team.

Tomas stopped at the front of the house, letting his boss get out and retrieve his leather notebook and cane before he took the carriage back to the barn. As Tomas drove away, Charlie made his way into the house, dropping his hat, cane and notebook on the bench by the door.

He made his way to down to the kitchen where he had hoped to find a cup of coffee, but instead found Rebecca trying to clean up two very dirty little boys. He moved into the room and scooped Andy up, holding him around the waist, tucked under his left arm, before he tried to make another get away while his mama wiped his brother down. Having Papa scoop him up like a bedroll made him laugh hysterically as they crossed to Mama and Buddy at the sink.

"Hello, darling." He kissed the top of her head and placed Andy on the counter next to his brother. He reached into the sink and took another cloth, gave it a squeeze and began wiping off his little dirt ball. "Where is everyone?"

"Well, dear husband, today is Tess's day off. Ginny has managed to turn her ankle and is in her room resting. Sarah is also off today, using the chance to finish moving into her new house. Beulah is trying to get two new maids trained. Reg is downstairs doing something in the wine cellar. Darby, Em and Suzanne are having lessons, and your sons," she gestured between the boys, "are trying to drive me to distraction. They have managed to get into no less than three messes today."

He chuckled as he considered the little fellow before him covered in what he hoped was dirt. "Are you and your brother making Mama insane today?" Andy nodded and giggled as Papa managed to get the wet cloth around his little throat and face.

Once the boys were cleaned up and settled at the little table in the corner with a glass of milk and cookies, Mama and Papa had a seat at the table for a well-earned cup of coffee. It was then she noticed.

Taking his right hand gingerly in hers she ran her thumb over the fingers. "Let me guess, Jeremiah?"

He nodded.

"That boy loves you almost as much as he loves Duncan. He is always coming up with something. They are very nice, Charlie."

~

Wednesday, July 4, 1866

Even though it was the middle of what so far had been a blistering hot summer, the day was beautiful. Not too hot, with a lovely breeze. Charlie was truly enjoying the day out with most of his family. Darby, Jeremiah and several other boys had disappeared shortly after their arrival, with a promise to Mama Rebecca that they would meet up for supper.

The citizens of Culpeper had managed to pull together a wonderful little festival for the Fourth of July.

The ladies of the community had baked pies and cakes for a contest later in the day with supplies provided by Edgar and Charlotte for the poorer families through the church. Some of the women were thrilled to be able to bake again with the goods. It appeared there was some semblance of normal returning to Culpeper.

There had been horseshoe throwing competitions and wood chopping contests for the title Bull of the Woods. Charlie was amused when Duncan took home that title by managing to get through a log a few seconds faster than his competition.

There was a three legged race for the younger children, along with an egg carry contest. The dunk tank built by Duncan and his crew of talented carpenters was the real success, especially when

Reverend Edgar had donned the latest in gentleman's swimwear and taken a seat over the tank of cold water. All proceeds were going to the church, of course.

The folding strollers they used for the rambunctious boys were the hit of the day, with every woman in town asking Rebecca where they had come from. Charlie made a note to suggest to Mr. Cooper he might want to stock one or two of them.

For him, it was a perfect day, everything he had hoped for during those last bleak days of the war. He was with the woman he loved. Their children were happy. The people around him were once again smiling, joking and having a good time. There was festive music playing throughout the afternoon. Day rolled into evening, with everyone gathering on porches and under tarps and tents to have a wonderful supper provided by all the families in town. Big Ben presided over a table full of smoked pork and beef, with his special sauce available in a five-gallon bucket.

As the final slivers of day gave way to the shadows of night, everyone tried to find the best spot in town to watch the fireworks display that had been promised to cap off the day.

Charlie's family settled on the boardwalk in front of Jocko's inn. It would give them a lovely view and keep them up off the ground at Rebecca's instance. They got the children settled in a pile around their mother on a blanket spread over the boards. Charlie leaned against the wall of the inn and lit a cigar.

His eyes were closed against the flame of the match when the first explosion happened. His eyes went wide. The cigar dropped from his lips as he looked up into the dark sky and saw the explosion of red, white and blue.

Suddenly, Culpeper was gone. Rebecca was gone. The children were gone.

It was all back in its horrific glory. The shouts of dying men. The screams of injured horses. The sounds... explosions... coming... one after...the other... the explosions, the never ending explosions.

He shook his head, but the visions remained. Men falling into the mire of mud and blood. He could not save them, no matter how hard he tried. The fire in his own side as the explosion ripped his horse out from underneath him. He remembered falling into the pits of Hell, sure he was dying.

He could not breathe as he tugged at his tie and ripped the top button of his shirt loose. The fireworks enthralling most of the crowd were causing a panic no one could have predicted.

He finally managed to push off the wall and stumbled toward the door of the inn. Jocko had closed for the evening, but he knew the door would be unlocked. He slipped inside and quickly closed the door behind him. Leaning on it and breathing heavily, he could feel the sweat breaking out on his forehead. He looked at his trembling hands.

He staggered to the bar and lifted the end that would allow him behind it. With very shaky hands he pulled down a bottle of brandy and poured a large glass, draining it in one try. Then he poured another. And another. And another.

He was half way through the bottle when the front door opened. He looked up and saw Alex Raeburn. The two men stood, staring at each other. His heart was already beating in his chest so hard he could hear it in his ears, feel it in his temples. His muscles twitched and flared uncontrollably. Every nerve in his body was alive. He was prepared for battle.

Raeburn walked to the bar and continued to stare at him. Without a word, the general simply sat a glass on the bar and poured the man a drink. He picked it up and gave Charlie a forced grin. "Truce," he said as he drained the glass, replacing it for a refill. He obliged and then poured himself another.

The fireworks only lasted thirty minutes at the most, but by the time they were over, a large contingent of the men of Culpeper, all former northern and southern soldiers, sat at Jocko's bar giving each other the strength to fight a battle they did not even know they were a part of. Some of them were talking quietly, some of them were drinking and some of them were even crying. They sat in small clusters, but all of them close enough together so they could interact with easy comfort.

When Rebecca finally tracked down her husband, she was

stopped by Elizabeth, who kept her from going into the inn. "My dear, just go home. Let them be." She pointed to a corner that held Richard, Jocko, Duncan, Charlie and several of the others. "They are fine. And apparently right where they need to be. I will make sure Charlie is taken care of tonight."

~

Monday, July 9, 1866

Today was the big day.

The bank building was finished, the paperwork was complete, there was cash in the vault that had been brought down from Washington by armed couriers, and the young bank manager that Jerome had promised had been settled into his new apartment above the bank and a housekeeper found for him the previous week.

According to Jerome, Frank Halliburton was one of the up and coming young bankers that had been working with Cooke's banks and would be a good match for Culpeper because he specialized in banking for farmers and small merchants.

Charlie had decided that opening the bank in Culpeper deserved the trappings of a major event. So that morning, the bank officers with the general in the lead were joined by Mayor Frazier and all of the businessmen and women of the city to cut the ribbon and open the bank. Rebecca, as Charlie's wife, had the honor of actually cutting the ribbon.

Mayor Frazier gave a speech, Edgar blessed the building, Charlie introduced Frank Halliburton to the crowd, and the sign was hung over the door. The bank was open for business. He had even hired Matthew Brady to come down from Washington to take pictures of the bank opening, and to take family portraits. He wanted a photograph of Rebecca to frame in his office, and one of her and the children to carry with him, especially since he was travelling so much.

All of the work, all of the hours spent slaving over papers and accounts, all of the meetings with Washington bankers... all of it paid off. Culpeper had one of the most important elements to its economic recovery. He stood at the door, greeting people as they came in to open accounts and begin using the resources of the bank. Mr. Cooper was the first businessman to open an account, with others following as quickly as Frank Halliburton and his assistants could process their paperwork.

As he stood watching the citizens of Culpeper come in the door to take advantage of the services of the new bank, an older woman came up to him. "Excuse me, General Redmond?"

"Yes, ma'am? You are Mrs. Allen from the house across the road?" He smiled, and thought to himself, *and the purveyor of the best moonshine in town.*

"Yes, sir." She was pleased he had recognized her. "During the war, I was a good unionist, sir. As you may know, I housed a number of union troops throughout the war, an activity that many of my neighbors were less than happy about. I was wondering if you might be able to help me."

"Of course. If I can help, I would be glad to."

"Well, sir, I never received compensation for the room and board I provided to the troops. I was wondering if you might be able to assist me."

"Certainly, Mrs. Allen. Come by the bank tomorrow, bring your records and I will do what I can to expedite an appropriate settlement for you."

"Thank you so much, sir. I could certainly use the money."

He smiled as he watched her walk away and melt back into the crowd. Jocko sidled up to him. "What the hell were you doing with her!" he asked, clearly annoyed.

"Just being polite. She asked if I could help her get paid for putting up union troops during the war."

"Humph. She is hurting my business. Do you know she has the best moonshine in town and refuses to sell me any? I lose customers to her every damned Friday night because I cannot get a single drop out of her for my place."

"Well now, you grumpy old bastard, perhaps if I am kind and helpful to her, I can negotiate something for you."

"Make sure you do." The Irishman growled before stomping off.

Charlie was happily watching people go into the bank when he noticed a small group of the black businessmen in town standing across the street watching the goings on. He immediately crossed the road and extended his hand to the obvious leader of the group. "Mr. Stewart, I believe? You own the dry good store over near Sweetwater."

"Y-yes, sir. General Redmond." The man took Charlie's hand and smiled at being recognized by the powerful man.

"Well, I would like you all to know that my bank is open to everyone in the community." He looked at each of them. "I do mean everyone. I would be honored to help you gentlemen in any way I can. My manager, Mr. Haliburton, will personally see to opening accounts if you wish."

"If we were to come to the bank, what times would we have to be there?" asked a bookish looking young man.

Charlie smiled and extended his hand. "You are?"

"Miles Tolliver. I am planning on opening a printing shop."

"That is grand to hear, sir. As to your question, the only restrictions for you would be the same for everyone else. The bank must be open. And it does not have an easily accessible back door so please do not look for one."

The men all smiled and in turn shook his hand taking the time to introduce themselves. Afterward, he walked them all across the street and introduced them to Frank. Before the end of the afternoon, four of the six had opened accounts with him and the other two promised to do so as soon as their businesses were properly stable.

～

The Redmonds had decided that it was a time to celebrate the success of Charlie's hard work. So they invited their close friends out to the stables for an evening barbeque. The previous day, Charlie had watched the pig being prepared for the event.

Big Ben was one of his best farm hands. The man was simply huge--close to seven feet tall, with muscles that seemed to go on for two weeks. If there was a horse that needed a firmer hand than usual, it was always Big Ben who got called to help. The general, who was no slouch, always felt miniscule standing next to the large black man. He usually found himself standing up a bit straighter, to be honest. Being near Ben was good for the posture.

The big man was about to place the pig that had been butchered into the roasting pit. He dropped the wagon gate and looked to the boss. "Now don' you be trying to mess with this here pig, Gen'l Charlie. I will take care of it."

"That is why you are here, Ben. I know you will handle everything and it will be delicious."

He nodded, chuckling as he hoisted the two hundred fifty pound pig onto his shoulders with ease. He dropped it with a thud into the pit and began the work of covering it with coals and sod. "By the time your guests arrive tomorrow night, sir, it should fall right off the bone."

"I am sure it will. Thank you for agreeing to help on such short notice."

"Aww, it ain't nothin,' Gen'l Charlie. You know all of us here would do anything for you an' Miz Rebecca. You are a good man, General. You treat us right, unlike some other "Christian" folks."

He could only nod as he leaned against the wagon, watching Ben work. It was true. There were more than a few people around who were still stinging over the outcome of the war and the Negroes were on the receiving end of much of that frustration. "I do wish it were different."

"You and Miz Rebecca make it different, Gen'l Charlie. That is why we do what we do. None of us want ever to leave here."

"As long as I am here, you will never have to."

"Thank ya, sir."

The group sat around the fire in the gazebo's fire pit. Dinner had been served and consumed. Spirits among the people were high and the ones being poured into cups and glasses certainly helped keep them that way. Sarah had made her special sweet mint tea for Charlie, who was still trying to avoid alcohol – at least most of the time.

Rebecca watched indulgently as he laughed at something Richard whispered to him as he refilled his mug with cold tea. It was so nice to see him smiling and laughing. As far as she was concerned, Rex had performed a miracle.

Elizabeth waddled over and took a seat on the bench next to Rebecca and offered her half a lap blanket. "They seem to be having fun."

She nodded, continuing to watch the men. Richard, Charlie, Duncan, and Jocko, brothers in arms. Men, who had come through Hell, defeated death together and lived to talk about it. The bond between them was almost palpable.

"So tell me, Charlie boy," Jocko said as he lifted his own cup toward his friend. "Why is it that you never sing anymore?"

Rebecca was suddenly very keen on this conversation. "What?"

Elizabeth smiled and gave her a nudge. "You mean to tell me he has never sung for you?"

"No!" She replied with a huge smile while looking directly at her sheepish husband. "Are you hiding talents from me?"

"Only the ones that do not matter, dear."

"Nonsense!" Richard gave him a gentle slap to his back. "He has a beautiful voice."

He just shook his head, bringing his cup to his lips and mumbling, "I do not believe this."

"Come on, General!" Duncan grinned as he sat on a log across from the embarrassed man. "J-j-just p-p-pretend we are in c-c-camp." The young man looked to Rebecca. "His songs always m-m-made us feel b-b-better."

"Come on, Charlie!" Richard joined in.

"I never sang unless I had had a bit too much to drink, and you know I have not had a drop tonight."

"To Hell!" Jocko interjected. "So lubricate your pipes, old man."

"I am not going to get out of this, am I?"

The entire group answered in unison, "No."

He nodded and took a deep breath before clearing his throat. Everyone looked on with anticipation as he began a familiar hymn.

"Shall we gather at the river,

Where bright angel feet have trod."

Rebecca looked at Charlie, amazed, then to Elizabeth, who was smiling. She had heard him sing this song many times. It was one of her favorites.

"With its crystal tide forever

Flowing by the throne of God.

Yes, we'll gather at the river,

The beautiful, the beautiful river;

Gather with the saints at the river

That flows by the throne of God."

He straightened as he continued this song, so clearly something that he held dear and important.

"On the margin of the river,

Washing up its silver spray,

We shall walk and worship ever,

All the happy golden day."

He smiled and gestured to Richard, who joined him in the refrain.

"Yes, we'll gather at the river,

The beautiful, the beautiful river;

Gather with the saints at the river

That flows by the throne of God."

For the next chorus, Duncan began quiet accompaniment on a mouth harp, as Jocko joined Richard and Charlie in the song.

"Ere we reach the shining river,

Lay we every burden down;

Grace our spirits will deliver,

And provide a robe and crown.

Yes, we'll gather at the river,

The beautiful, the beautiful river;

Gather with the saints at the river

That flows by the throne of God.

At the smiling of the river,
Mirror of the Savior's face,
Saints, whom death will never sever,
Lift their songs of saving grace.
Yes, we'll gather at the river,
The beautiful, the beautiful river;
Gather with the saints at the river
That flows by the throne of God.
Soon we'll reach the silver river,
Soon our pilgrimage will cease;
Soon our happy hearts will quiver
With the melody of peace.
Yes, we'll gather at the river,
The beautiful, the beautiful river;
Gather with the saints at the river
That flows by the throne of God."

Charlie smiled at the appreciative crowd and asked, "I have one song that always makes me think of Rebecca. Would you like to hear it?"

The assemblage nodded eagerly. A tribute to their hostess was appreciated, and it would be interesting to hear what made Charlie think of his wife. He smiled, taking her hands gently in his before softly singing…

"Amazing grace! How sweet the sound
That saved a wretch like me!
I once was lost, but now am found;
Was blind, but now I see."

CHAPTER 19

Tuesday, July 10, 1866

Charlie settled into his office at the bank that morning, looking at the pile of papers that Frank Halliburton had left on his desk after yesterday's opening. Fortunately, Frank actually handled the paperwork – he only left it for him to look at and keep an eye on him.

"Frank! We need to get someone in here to manage these files. I know we have to file them, and I also know neither you, nor I, nor any of the tellers have time."

The manager strolled in from the outer office. "Already anticipated you, boss. Please, meet Miss Eloise Langley, who will serve as our secretary and office manager."

Charlie stood. "Pleased to meet you, Miss Langley. I hope we do not manage to overwhelm you as we get started."

Miss Langley smiled as she took his proffered hand. "It is my pleasure, General Redmond. I kept all of my father's books – he was an attorney here before the war, though he has since passed –

and I believe I can give you the quality of support a good bank needs."

"Then welcome! I warn you, trying to keep me organized is a major challenge, as my wife will be happy to tell you about at great detail."

She laughed, then nodded at the pile of papers. "Are they ready to be filed?"

"Yes, please."

A few minutes later, Miss Langley knocked on his door. "General Redmond, Mrs. Allen is here to see you."

"Please, show her in. And do we have any tea or coffee we could offer her?"

"I will be right back with it, General Redmond."

He rose to greet Mrs. Allen and seated her across the desk from him before resuming his seat. "Good morning. You are certainly prompt."

"Yes, sir. But then, I need to be paid. Housing all of those men cost me a small fortune – at least a small fortune to me."

He nodded, understanding completely. A number of people had been hurt financially by the army's inability to manage their finances in the midst of war. "May I see your records?"

Silently, she handed him a bound account book. Listed in the book, by date and name, were the names of all the troops she had housed, and the expenses she incurred for feeding them. Every month, there was a tally of the expenses and of the rate that the army had offered her per man per day for room and board.

Quietly, Miss Langley entered and set a small tea tray down between them, pouring each of them a cup, then just as quietly, slipped out of the office.

He went through her careful accounting, then said, "You have been very thorough. I will be going up to Washington several times in the next couple of weeks. If you allow me, I will take this with me, along with a detailed invoice, and will do my best to have the Department of the Army expedite payment."

"Thank you so much, General. I cannot tell you how much I appreciate it. If there is anything I can do...?"

"Well, now Mrs. Allen, there is something you could do." He sat back in his chair and smiled at her. His eyes flashing with a bit of flirtatious mischief, Charlie understood how to charm older women. His accent was in full force. "I understand that you have a splendid source of a locally made beverage that is very popular with a number of the gentlemen here in town. I also understand that you have not been willing to provide my old friend Jocko Jackson with any stock. Would you be willing to reconsider if I manage to get you your due from the army?"

She thought for a moment. "Well, sir, I was trying to protect my primary income source and keep it from my competition, but with a decent payment, I suppose I could provide him with a limited supply."

"Thank you, madam. I will do my best to see to it that you get properly paid – and promptly."

He stood and escorted her out the door.

"Miss Langley? Thank you for the tea, and could you do me a favor? Go through this ledger and put together an invoice for the US Army? I think all the information you need is here. If you can, I would like to take it with me tomorrow."

∾

Wednesday, July 11, 1866

Charlie leaned down to kiss Rebecca as she sat at the table in the morning room, enjoying a second cup of coffee and reading the paper. Reg was waiting outside with the trap to take him to the train station. "I will be back on Saturday, dear. And if you need a message to reach me quickly, just send a telegram to Jerome's office. He knows what meetings I will be in."

"Have a good trip, darling. Be safe. Give my best to Jerome and General Grant." She smiled as she reached up to caress his cheek. "Bring me something pretty."

"Does that mean I have to venture into the haberdashery?" He laughed. His trips to the huge fabric store on G Street had been either intimidating in the extreme or outright disastrous on previous trips.

"Not unless my order arrives while you are in the city. If it does, I will send you a telegram. I am certain that you can find something pretty on your own. I have faith in you, Charles Redmond."

"Yes, dear." He smiled at his wife, entirely aware that those two words had become a staple of their relationship. And with that, he turned and went on his way, slated to spend the rest of the week in Washington meeting with Cooke and his banker friends to report on the bank opening, and with Grant and his political cronies.

When he arrived in Washington, the first thing he did was hail a cab to take him to the War Department offices at 17th and Pennsylvania. With his leather valise still in hand, he marched into General Grant's office, armed with Mrs. Allen's records and invoices. General Grant was coming out of his private office as he walked in.

"Charlie! What are you doing here? I was not expecting to see you until this evening."

"Good day, General, sir. I have an errand to perform for one of the residents of Culpeper before I can address other issues. It seems that one Mrs. Allen lodged and fed a number of Union troops, and has yet to receive compensation as promised by the Quartermaster's office."

Grant grinned at one of his most trusted comrades. "You always were one to jump in and take care of your people. Seems it extends to your civilian life."

The general looked around for an errand boy. "Ah, James. Please, go and ask General Meigs if he will please join me in my office as quickly as he can." The boy took off, running.

"Come in, Charlie. You look like you could use a cool drink. I have some nicely iced lemonade in my office."

Some polite conversation and a large glass of lemonade later, General Meigs arrived at the door. Grant let him in, and polite greetings were exchanged all around. Charlie masked his dislike of the man, given the terrible quality of supplies his men had experienced during the war. Then Grant asked, "So Meigs, how goes the reorganization?

"It goes, General, it goes. You cannot begin to imagine how complicated it is, with the various suppliers, the depots, the transport issues and the contracts that have to be sorted out, but it goes."

"Well, I think when you are done, it will simplify and streamline operations and logistics considerably."

"I am sure it will, sir. I am sure it will." Meigs paused and then asked, "With General Redmond here, I assume you had something specific you needed? I really do not have time for a social call today."

Charlie smiled at the Quartermaster General, a smile that did not extend to his eyes. "General Meigs, one of the residents of the town I live in has an outstanding invoice for the Army that it seems has been overlooked. She has been owed these funds for an extended period of time – well over a year – and I promised I would see what I could do to get her paid." He pulled the packet of papers that Eloise had prepared for him. "All of the documentation is here; as you can see, she is owed eighty five dollars, and I believe she should also receive interest for the delay in payment as well."

Wordlessly, Meigs took the papers offered. Eloise had done an excellent job of preparing them. He flipped through them quickly, scanning each page, and when he was done, looked at Grant, then Charlie. "Yes, these all seem to be in order, including the notation of the authorizing quartermaster. Let me see if I can get this handled immediately."

General Grant smiled. "Thank you, General Meigs. I think it is very important that the US Army not be seen by the people we are working so hard to bring back into the Union as an organization that reneges on its debts."

The generals exchange polite farewells, and Charlie set off for Mrs. Galloway's to drop off his bag before he met with Jerome and Cooke.

~

Saturday, July 14, 1866

He was a little surprised that one of the stable hands met him at the station that Saturday afternoon instead of Tomas, but he surmised that Rebecca was busy with plans for the church social, held on the third Sunday of every month.

He smiled at the young man who was loading the bundles and packages he had brought home with him. His darling wife's order had arrived at the haberdashery on G Street that week. She had sent him a very short telegram, "Pick up order – R," and he had dutifully done so.

"So, Bobby, are things a little busy at the house? I had expected Reg or Tomas to come for me."

"Don' know, Gen'l Charlie. They jus tolt me to come."

It was clear that Bobby was not going to be a useful source of information. The general sat back and enjoyed the sunshine, glad that it was a pleasant day for a change and that the sweltering heat of summer had abated for a few days.

He dropped down from the bench on the wagon, grabbing his satchel and a small bundle that held homecoming gifts for his not so little family. Bobby clucked at the horses, and pulled around to the back of the house to unload the assorted supplies.

No one was in the hall to greet him as he arrived, so he hung his hat on the rack and dropped his satchel in the hall. Reg or someone would get it eventually and take it up to the bedroom.

He looked first in the small parlor. No luck.

Then he hauled himself upstairs to Rebecca's sitting room. No one was there either.

Quick peeks into the nursery and the schoolroom provided no clues as to where his family was either.

He walked back downstairs to first the entrance hall and then down another flight to Rebecca's office and the winter kitchen. As expected, no one was in the kitchen, though a small fire burned to keep the teakettle simmering and hot water available for cleaning up. He looked out the window and saw all five children playing down by the pond, tended by Tess and Ginny. But there was no sign of his wife.

Finally, he opened the door to her office. She was sitting there in one of the wingback chairs by the empty fireplace, her hands folded in her lap, a perfectly blank expression on her face. The stillness that surrounded her frame was a sign that Charlie had come to know very well. His wife was angry – very angry. Given where she was sitting, obviously waiting for him, she was probably very angry with him, but for what, he had no clue.

"Hello, dear." He walked over to her, bent and tenderly kissed her forehead. He would have kissed her lips, but that would have required that she move her head, and she was definitely not cooperating. He stood up again, still holding his bag of gifts, and not quite knowing what to do with himself. "I got your order from the haberdashery. They are unloading it now."

"Thank you. I see you got my second cable."

He gawked at her. "Second cable?"

"Yes, the one I sent to Jerome's office after I received word that you were not at the Willard."

He looked even more confused. "Why would I be at the Willard?" He sat the bundle of bags down on the table near the window.

"Well, unless you have found other accommodations, you always stay there. So since the manager there has not seen you in three months, I have to assume that you have found other lodgings."

He looked a little baffled at her attitude. Surely he had told her about taking rooms with William's mother. "I took rooms with the Widow Galloway. Her husband had one of the best livery stables in Washington, but he was killed in the war and she is letting rooms to help make ends meet. The house is within a couple of blocks of Cooke's offices, and after the misery I endured on that trip in April, it seemed sensible."

"And you chose not to tell me? Why? There must be a reason that you did not want me to know where you were." She lifted her face and even in the shadows of the room it was clear she had been crying.

"Darling, I am so sorry." He knelt down next to her, trying to take her hand but settling for laying his own gently upon her knee when she refused to relinquish her handkerchief. "But when I came home, the girls and Darby had the measles, the boys were teething, you were running on short sleep, and I had a cold. We barely talked for four days, until I was over my cold, and then I took over from you with the children. It just slipped my mind . . ." He trailed off.

It was something he had done for pure convenience, and with the furor of the children's various illnesses and the two weeks of misery the whole house had endured while they were recuperating, it really had slipped his mind.

"Slipped your mind? Alright, Charlie, I understand. I really do." She looked at him with coldness he had never seen before and had not thought possible from his always loving wife. It pierced his heart. "All I ask is that you be discrete. Things are going very well here and I would prefer that people not start whispering among themselves."

"What do you mean, be discrete?" He stood up and looked down at her. "The Widow Galloway is sixty if she is a day, runs a boarding house near the financial district down on K Street, and would skin me alive if I showed up with a woman other than you." He sighed and looked up at the ceiling. *God, give me patience.*

"I do not know what to say to you right now. I know what I suspect. You seem to think I am thick or not aware of the things men do when they are away from their wives. You take up residence away from the Willard. You do not tell me about it. When I try to reach you, I get a polite response telling me that you have not had a room there for months. To me, the evidence suggests that there is another woman in Washington. If that is the case, then so be it. We will manage just fine."

He stared at her, his jaw dropping open. He closed it with a snap, turned and walked a couple of steps away from her, then turned back. "Rebecca, is that all you think of me? Is that all you think of yourself? Do you honestly think that if I am out of your sight for more than twenty minutes, I have to be looking for some other woman to play with?"

He stood there, the veins in his forehead popped out and pulsing. "If you think that I am going up to Washington to carry on some pointless dalliance behind your back, well, there is clearly nothing I can say to change your mind. I thought you and I had some level of trust, but clearly that is not the case." He paced up and down. "Jesus Christ, Rebecca. I gave you my word, I swore before man and God to take no other, to be faithful to you and you alone. I meant every single word of our marriage vows. Clearly, you did not."

He stood there, breathing hard. He could not believe she thought he was having an affair. He simply could not believe it. He thought they had a foundation of trust between them, but obviously that was false. "If you think I am having an affair, what do you think our marriage is about? Is this your way of telling me you have decided you want a real man instead of me? A convenient way of putting the blame on me? Has someone come home who has caught your attention?"

"Oh, no, you will not!" She came up out of the chair, furious now. Before she had been hurt, now she was angry. "You will not stand here and try to tell me what I want! What my marriage vows mean to me. If I did not want you, if I did not love you I would not have married you! I have been a wife before. I know what men do. It does not keep it from hurting. Especially when," she faltered in her anger and turned away to look out the window, "when I love you so much. I felt relief when he went to others. The thought of you doing it hurts very much." She drew her handkerchief to her cheeks and wiped away more tears. "If you say that you are not, then I apologize. I love you, Charlie. I do not want to lose you. No matter what."

He looked at her and shook his head. "Rebecca, I have exactly three women in my life. You are first and foremost. Em and Suzanne are the other two. I am the very model of propriety when in Washington, as a number of people can attest, including Jerome, his wife Amelia and General and Mrs. Grant. But the more important thing for me is that you would even think that I would or could cheat on you. I love you. Only you. I want only you." He held her silently for a few moments. "Tell you what. Let us finish the social on Sunday, and then run up to Washington for a couple of days of shopping. You can meet my Washington doyen and discover just how good a boy I am being."

"You do not need to prove anything to me." She relaxed into him, always feeling safe in his arms no matter what they were facing. "I am being unreasonable. I am sorry. I just want you to be completely happy here at home. Recently, because of Rex, you are feeling better and looking so handsome. I have always been afraid that in the end I would not be the kind of woman you wanted. Other women, like Lizzie, who are more versed in things I know nothing about, they must be appealing to you." She shook her head not knowing what else to say. All her fears and the wounds left by years of abuse and loneliness were out for the world to see and poor Charlie had gotten the brunt. "I am sorry."

"Rebecca," he whispered her name so reverently her stomach dropped. He slid a finger under her chin and tilted her head up. "Look at me. When you look at me, you see all of me. The good, the bad, the strong, the scared – all of me. No one else does. No one else ever has." A note of wonder entered his voice. "And you love me. The real me, not the image of me." He took a deep breath. "I am not a man like Gaines was. I am not like any other man in the world, yet you still love me. You have no idea how incredibly compelling that is for me. There is no woman on the face of the planet that holds a candle to you in my heart." He kissed her tenderly. "Is that absolutely clear? Can we move forward together?"

She nodded a slightly unsure motion that nearly sent her into further tears. "I can try, Charlie. I will try. I suppose some part of me will always expect the worst because that is what I know. I promise you to try harder. It is not fair to judge you by the failings of others."

"That is all I can ask, love." He held her quietly for a minute. "Anyway, if you saw Martha Galloway, you would know in a heartbeat that I have been a good boy. You would not even have to hear her voice – just look at her for a minute." He grinned, the image of his Washington landlady clear in his mind. She was the last woman on earth that Charlie could image himself – or anyone for that matter – having an affair with.

~

Monday, July 16, 1866

Charlie and Rebecca had packed their bags for a two-day shopping trip to Washington the night before, and broke the news to the children that Mama and Papa would be away for a couple of days, promising to be back on the Wednesday morning train. Charlotte and Edgar promised to chase after the children. Em was fairly good about it; she did not throw her usual conniption fit, but just sulked for the rest of the evening.

The train trip to Washington had been absolutely miserable. The weather was hot and muggy, so just to survive, the windows on the car had to be left open. That meant that the sparks, smoke and ashes from the big wood-burning engine would fly in the windows at the slightest cross breeze. Charlie's second best summer weight suit was ruined when a huge ember landed on his lapel. Rebecca's dress was not outright damaged, but it was smoky and dingy by the time they got to Union Station.

Galloway was waiting for them with his best carriage. In the past three months, he had managed to clean up all of the carriages, wagons and carts his father had collected, bought six new horses, and quit his position at the Willard to manage getting the livery and cab services up and running properly.

"Rebecca, this is William Galloway, the son of our landlady, and the proprietor of the livery service I told you I have invested in."

William doffed his cap and bowed to her.

"Mr. Galloway, it is a pleasure. My husband has told me about you and your mother in great detail. I look forward to meeting her."

"Thank you, Mrs. Redmond. My mother said something about maybe now General Redmond will let her re-do the décor of his rooms. I think you will be amused at where he has been staying when here – he is using my grandmother's old rooms and it shows."

She looked at her husband and grinned, then she returned her attention to the driver. "I cannot wait."

While Charlie handed Rebecca into the carriage, William loaded the bags into the boot, then hopped up and clucked his horses to a brisk walk.

Charlie looked at his wife and grinned sheepishly. "I actually did have an ulterior motive. I was hoping you would take the time during the day to shop for some fittings that would let me do something – anything – to get rid of the tatting, doilies, and violet-emblazoned knickknacks. I am sure that Galloway's grandmother was a delightful woman, but living in the midst of little old lady stuff has been a bit constraining."

Now she was outright laughing. His protests of "It really is not funny," certainly did nothing to help her as she tried to draw in air.

"I am sorry, Charlie." She paused only long enough to find another wave of laughter. "I will do my best. I must admit that the thought of you sleeping surrounded by the things that would be pleasing to an elderly woman is a bit," she paused for effect, "interesting."

"I told you this was for convenience, not pleasure. Now, be good so you can meet our landlady."

"I will be the picture of propriety, General Redmond."

"Please do or you will make my life up here even more miserable than it already is," he hissed as he handed her out of the carriage and escorted her up the walk to the front steps. Mrs. Galloway was waiting on the porch to meet them.

He bowed slightly and presented his wife. "Mrs. Galloway, allow me to introduce my wife, Rebecca Redmond. Rebecca, this is Mrs. Martha Galloway, our landlady and the mother of one of my business associates."

"It is a pleasure to meet you, Mrs. Galloway. I would like to extend my most sincere thanks to you for taking in my husband. It is nice to know that he is being well cared for when he is away from home."

Mrs. Galloway eyed her up and down.

Though they were of about the same size, the contrast between the two women was startling. Rebecca in her pastel colors, ribbons, hat and summer parasol, even smudged by the train's smoke, looked like the most frivolous of young things, especially when compared to Mrs. Galloway's unrelenting grayness and her hawk-like profile.

"Humph. Looks to me like you could use some taking care of yourself. And he needs to eat more. The man has no meat on his bones. What have you to say for yourself, missy, that your husband looks like a danged skeleton?"

"I . . . I . . ." she foundered as she looked at Charlie, who was obviously chewing on his cheeks to hide his smile. "I assure you, Mrs. Galloway, General Redmond eats as much as my finest stud when he is home. Unfortunately, his business associates here in Washington do not allow him as much time with his family as either he or I would like."

"Well, you will just have to come up more often. I have some recipes that I would be happy to show you that will put some meat on his bones. And if you are here, perhaps he will eat dinner at home, instead of going out with those men till all hours. Why, he often comes in as late as eight o'clock."

Rebecca coughed...hard. This of course was to mask the laughter that wanted to burst forth. She held her handkerchief in front of her lips as Charlie made their apologies and took her by the arm. He led her to his room and practically pushed her through to door. He shut it, standing in front of it with his arms crossed.

"You think this is funny?"

"Terribly," she admitted before giving into a full fledge guffaw. "You did not tell her of your Saturday night poker games at home, did you?" She removed her hat and gloves as she looked at the room still laughing out loud.

Mrs. Galloway had left a pitcher of lemonade in the room, as well as a freshly drawn pitcher of cool water from the well, both of which were welcome. As Rebecca continued to inspect their abode, he poured some water in the basin, washed his hands and face, and then poured them both a glass of lemonade.

As he went about the domestic chores, he commented, "Not only did I not tell her about the poker games, I do not smoke here, I do not drink here, I certainly do not curse here, and I try to remember to sit with my knees together. She is worse than my aunt Cornelia."

"Oh, Charlie, I think she is a perfectly charming older woman. Probably very much like I will be at her age," she teased. Then taking a deep breath, she moved to him and placed both her hands on his lapels, the index finger of her right hand finding the hole left by the hot ash. "We will need to buy you a new suit."

"Hmm." He agreed. He could tell she had more to say.

"I am sorry I doubted you, Charlie. Forgive me?"

"Already have, even before we left the house," he mumbled as he leaned down to kiss her. Once that was completed to his satisfaction, he looked deep into her eyes, a soulful pleading look on his face. "Now, sweetheart, could you please do something about this place for me? I may go insane from the abundance of tatting, lace and little things that have no purpose other than to display a terrible painting of a violet."

"Of course. I will make it properly masculine. Just like you."

He sat in one of the old wingback chairs near the window of their room reading the evening paper. It was, after all, the middle of summer and even at seven thirty in the evening there was more than enough light to read by coming through the window. He had pulled off his boots and socks because of the heat, as well as his coat, tie and vest.

Rebecca moved about the room, having stripped down a scandalous layer further to her underthings, collecting small ceramic knickknacks and other things he had called "the overabundance of little old lady things." He had not been overstating the situation. She cleared a small shelf, placing the items in a box provided by Mrs. Galloway, and turned to her husband, "You know, it just occurred to me, now I know how the children feel when we make them go to bed."

He looked up from the paper and laughed. Mrs. Galloway had

made a wonderful roast leg of lamb and fresh vegetables for her guests that evening and during supper had been very clear that they should retire and spend a quiet evening in because she was going to lock the door.

"Welcome to my Washington den of iniquity," he teased as he flicked the paper and made a show of going back to reading it.

She pushed his paper down from in front of his face. When he looked up at her she reached out and undid the top buttons of his shirt. "Could be tonight, General Redmond."

He groaned as he captured her hand. "Do you really want to risk her...?" He shook his head. "I am not sure." He growled when her nail traced ever so gently up and down his throat. That was a major spot for him and his wife knew it well. "Darling..." his voice was strained and about to crack under the pressure.

She backed away, slowly. She had stripped down to her chemise and drawers because of the heat. Now, standing before him, she slid her hands down her sides, outlining her breasts and ribcage under the thin cotton of her delicately embroidered v-necked chemise.

Her hands continued to trail down her own body, along the line of her hips, and flirting with her cotton and lace knickerbockers, reminding him that there was no stitching at the crotch, just enough cloth to overlap to provide protection. Her drawers reached down to just below her knees, and the rest of her shapely legs were as bare as the day she was born, as were her arms and shoulders except where the narrow straps of the chemise passed over them. She reached up and played with the straps, lowering one of them down her arm to show the soft curve of her breasts. She slipped the strap back into place, then slid the bottom of the chemise up, showing the smooth lines of her stomach and rib cage.

The torment continued, as she flirted with the open flap of her undergarment, turning her back to him and showing off the white skin of her ass through the open seam of her drawers. She reached up and loosened the tie at the back of her waist, letting the drawers slide down to ride on her hips. By now, he was sweating and shaking. He stood up, pulling off his shirt, but not taking his eyes off the show his wife was providing him. He pulled the shade, and stripped off his trousers.

Rebecca slipped her hands up his chest, removing the wrappings around his chest, and freeing his small breasts. Rebecca always marveled at the transformation of her very masculine husband into an athletic woman who reminded her of Greek statues of Diana, Goddess of the Hunt. She noticed that muscle tone had started to return to her partner's shoulders, arms and belly after the long period of recuperation from the injuries. She ran her nails down her belly, playing around her navel.

Charlie slid her hands up Rebecca's sides, lifting the chemise up over her head. Where Charlie's breasts were small and tight, Rebecca's were lush and voluptuous. It was one of the things Charlie truly appreciated about the blonde's body.

But then, there were a number of things Charlie appreciated about her body – the swell of her breasts, the roundness of her ass, the slight bulge of her belly below her belly button, the elegant curve from her waist to her hip when she lay on her side. There were just so many things that Charlie appreciated about Rebecca. He wanted to show her a wide variety of them right now.

He dipped his head, leaving a trail of kisses down a slender shoulder before ever so gently, catching a very erect nipple in between his teeth. He felt Rebecca's fingers tangle in his hair. "Oh, now is not the time to tease me."

Charlie rose up, looking down at his partner with an evil grin, "Was fine when you were teasing me."

Rebecca drew her fingernails over Charlie's back, enjoying the reaction she could not only see, but feel as she caused tremors all through the tall form before her. She smiled when she heard another throaty growl escape from her lover. "Like that?"

"Mmmhmm." Charlie nodded, slowly moving them back toward the bed.

It was an old four poster mahogany monstrosity with a canopy. On a previous visit, the general had knotted the old curtains at the top of the four posts so he was not worried about getting tangled in those as he moved Rebecca closer and closer to the edge of the bed.

Charlie wrapped his left arm around Rebecca's waist and pulled her very close, and then dropped his lips to a tender lobe and began a slow, very slow nibble. At the same time his right had dropped to exactly the place Rebecca wanted and needed it to be.

"Oh, God..," She gasped out, dropping her head onto Charlie's shoulder, her body already beginning to shake. If she did not get them onto the bed soon she was sure she was going to die.

Charlie knew he had her lover right where he wanted her. He could feel every muscle in Rebecca's body trying to pull them back to the bed. He actually felt a little laugh leave his lips as he drove Rebecca's passions higher and higher.

Rebecca had finally had enough; she did not want to hurt Charlie, but if he kept toying with her like this the possibility was on the table. Their eyes locked. The teasing and tormenting becoming too much for both of them, Rebecca moved back and Charlie went with her.

Their landing in the bed was not as soft as it could have been. There was a momentary pause on Charlie's part when he thought he heard a creaking, or perhaps a cracking.

"Charlie!" Rebecca was half begging, half demanding. "Oh yes…" she purred when they once again found that lovely rhythm.

Somewhere in the back of both of their minds they heard it at exactly the same moment. Somewhere on the edge of their consciousness they knew it was happening. The old bed was suddenly rattling from every joint. It was not just creaking; it seemed to be trying to walk across the room.

Charlie actually managed to pull herself out of the passion induced haze in time to mostly cover Rebecca's body to protect it from the falling canopy as the rest of the bed crashed to the floor.

The two of them lay in the ruins of the old bed in stunned silence for a moment. This was not the climax that Rebecca wanted or Charlie had expected. Quite the opposite. As they lay there trying to figure out what they were going to do next, there came a loud banging on their door. Mrs. Galloway was yelling "Are you all right? What happened?"

They struggled to their feet, disentangling themselves from the canopy, then leaping for their cases to pull out and don night shirts and gowns, robes and slippers. "Just a minute, Mrs. Galloway."

"What in Heaven's name was that loud crashing?"

Charlie, in his night shirt, robe and bare feet, opened the door as Rebecca finished tying her robe. "It seems the old bed was not strong enough to hold two people, ma'am. We were just getting into bed for the night when it just came down around us."

"Oh, dear me, General Redmond. I am so sorry." Mrs. Galloway was flustered and embarrassed at seeing both of them in their night clothes, let alone that her furnishings could not hold the two of them safely.

"It is all right, ma'am. We can make a camp bed tonight after we sort out the wreckage and tomorrow Mrs. Redmond and I were going to buy new furnishings for the room anyway."

"At least let me help you get things sorted out, General." Mrs. Galloway was clearly anxious about trying to make things right. She needed to keep the general as a boarder.

Rebecca spoke up. "No, Mrs. Galloway. General Redmond and I can take care of things for now. You go on back to whatever you were doing, while we pull the mattress and bedclothes out from under the debris. Tomorrow is soon enough to clean up the rest of the mess. And please, do not worry. These things happen sometimes."

They managed to shoo Mrs. Galloway away, then picked up their clothing, pulled the mattress out of the dilapidated frame, and set it on a clear space on the floor. After shaking the splinters and dust out of the sheets, they made up their makeshift bed. Dropping onto the mattress, they looked at one another and started giggling. Once they got started, they could not stop. It was just too funny an ending to what had started with Rebecca being jealous and suspicious.

CHAPTER 20

Thursday, July 19, 1866

Richard saw his friend walking out of the bank and was quick to run to catch up with him. "Charlie!"

He stopped and slowly turned to his friend, who looked a bit panicked. "Richard, what is wrong? Is Elizabeth all right?"

Polk pulled a large and rumpled handkerchief from his pocket, lifted his hat and mopped some of the sweat off his forehead. "Oh, yes, Elizabeth is just fine, if you consider that a woman who is nine months pregnant, about to deliver anytime, miserable from the heat, and able to find fault with everything I do, is fine."

He panted for a moment, a miserable, pitiful look on his face. "I just thought perhaps you would have time for a cool drink and I could enjoy some calm, male company and remember that I really am a competent, capable, mature adult."

Charlie's lips quirked but he managed to keep the smile off his face, "Of course, Richard. Where would you like to go?"

"Perhaps we could go over to Jocko's. I could use some of his nice, cool ale. Or perhaps one of those things he does with rum and ice?"

He chuckled and waved for his carriage. Tomas pulled the carriage up and jumped down, to open the door. "Gentlemen." He smiled and held the door as first Richard and then Charlie climbed in the carriage. "Where to, sir?"

"Jocko's, Tomas. Colonel Polk here needs a cool drink."

"Yes, sir."

Tomas jumped up on the box of the open carriage and whistled to the brown carriage horse. They set off at an easy pace; the weather was too hot to ask the horse to do more than a quiet walk.

Richard turned to Charlie, reached into his pocket, and pulled out a pair of cigars. "Join me? I cannot do this at home anymore."

"You know I never turn down a good cigar." He took one and sighed at his friend. "It is almost over. Very soon the baby will be here and Elizabeth will once again be her loving self."

"Yes, but right now, she is so sensitive to smells – all kinds of smells – that as soon as I get home, I have to strip and bathe and put on fresh clothes. Otherwise, the smells on me make her nauseous – not one of my favorite reactions from my wife."

Charlie laughed, even though it really was not funny. "So your presence makes her sick?" He leaned forward. "You know, I find this all so fascinating. I mean, early on you told me she cried when you put your hat down."

"For the first two months, she cried when I sneezed, she cried when I read her the morning news from the paper, she cried when Ruth dusted the parlor, she cried if the eggs were overdone, she cried if the sunset was beautiful. I was so thankful when that ended – little did I know what was in store for us next. And you, you just sit there with that smirk. You have a house full of children and have never had to go through this purgatory."

"I am sorry. Not for the house full of children or that I have apparently managed to avoid the female of the species when she is expecting, but for your difficulties. Elizabeth loves you, Richard. It will all be over very soon."

He nodded. "Esther Jackson is at the house now giving her a

thorough examination. Something my doctor wife does not really tolerate well when she is on the receiving end of the prod."

He chewed on his cigar for a moment, then, with a wistful look, added, "Well, it did have its advantages. In the spring, Elizabeth's, um, desires were, er, enhanced." A wicked grin lit his features. "In fact, it was rather draining, she was so demanding. Perhaps after this young'un joins us, she and I will be able to resume..." He trailed off, a flush over his features that was not entirely the result of the hot weather.

Charlie poked his friend's foot with his cane. "So I take it you have not been tossed to the couch yet?"

"Oh, yes, I have. Ever since this heat wave hit. I swear, Charlie, this is the hottest summer I have ever seen." He thought for a minute. "In fact, I think the heat has gotten to her more than anything else. Darby has been a blessing. He is never out of earshot and he runs and fetches anything she needs. The boy does not feel the heat like the rest of us do."

"No child does. Let me tell you Rebecca is happy that Darby is gainfully employed and assisting one of our friends. She's very happy to have one less under foot all day. The boys are starting to really walk now and the girls apparently think they are part heathen, as they run around chasing each other all day. I do not know how Rebecca handles the farm and the children."

"You got very lucky there."

"You have no idea, Richard."

"Well, I have been very grateful for the loan of your oldest boy. He is quite the young gentleman. You and Rebecca should be proud."

"We are, but Darby's personality was there before Rebecca and I took them in. He is simply a good, hardworking young man. But he has his moments of being the boy he should be. The other day Rebecca caught him trying to feed Em rabbit pellets, telling her they were sweets."

He chuckled when he remembered her meeting him at the door and telling him he needed to go talk to 'his' son. "Rebecca has never raised a hand to one of our brood in anger, but I think she was well on the way to caning Darby's hide that day."

"Oh, the boy has spunk in more than one way. I knew he had a spine from how he took care of his sister, but he seems to have blossomed in the past few months since he has been with you. And I swear that boy will be able to sit any horse you have. He seems fearless with the animals."

"Oh, he is going to be a fine horseman. We already have an eye out for a mount for him." The pride in a father's face was unmistakable. "So, Richard, it could be any time now. Are you hoping for a boy or a girl in the eleventh hour?"

"Boy or girl, I do not really care. I just want them both to be well and happy." Tomas pulled the horse up in front of Jocko's. "Here we are. I, for one, am ready for a cool drink."

The men entered the bar. Jocko was busy with a couple of men at a table near the rear of the room. Charlie gestured between the bar and the tables letting Richard pick were they would sit. Richard plopped himself down on a stool at the bar and let his head fall into his folded arms. Charlie sat down next to his friend and gave him a pat on the back. "It will be all right."

Richard turned his head, leaving it resting on his arms. "Sometimes I think the army was easier."

"I know there are times when the army was easier." Charlie nodded.

"Well now," Jocko boomed as he approached from the far end of the bar. "What did you go and do to him now, Charlie?"

"It is not me. It is the expectant wife."

"Aye." The barkeep nodded, pouring Richard the rum and ice concoction that had become his favorite in the heat. "Esther says she thinks it will be tonight or early tomorrow morning. She came and collected her overnight bag just a few minutes ago."

Richard shot straight up. Charlie just reached out and put and hand on his shoulder guiding him back to his stool. "Stay here."

"Charlie!"

"Richard!" He looked at his friend and smiled, again pushing on his shoulder to reseat him. "We will send word that you are here with me and that Darby can come get you when the women want you there. Trust me. They do not want you there right now."

"And you do not want to be there." Jocko chuckled, checking his ice supply. It was going to be a long day of keeping Colonel Polk sane while he waited for the baby to arrive. "It is a bit messy and if you think Elizabeth could yell before…" He just laughed and shook his head.

Richard, resigned, retook his seat and drained his drink. He gestured for another. "I am going to be a father."

It had not taken long for word to get around that the newest arrival to Culpeper was on its way, once Esther sent Darby on messenger rounds. Charlie smiled when he saw the Coopers walking along together. At the door of the inn, Mr. Cooper kissed his wife's cheek and sent her off in the direction of Elizabeth's house as he entered the bar. He clasped his hands together, "Well, this is perfect! Enough of us already here to start a card game to keep the expectant father occupied."

Charlie gave the bar a smack with his fist. "Grand idea, Edward! Jocko, break out the cards and the chips!" He grabbed Richard by the back of his collar and pulled him off the stool to a table. "Come on, Richard; let me lose some money to you. That will make you feel better."

Throughout the afternoon and into the early evening, the gentleman of town gathered to share good cheer, both the emotional and liquid types, with the expectant father and to try and keep his mind off the impending birth of his first child.

Charlie had indeed managed to lose close to fifty dollars to Richard. He chewed his lip wondering how good of a friend he was actually required to be until the baby arrived. He decided that his pitiful pair of threes with a jack high was just too much. He tossed his cards in the center of the table and stood up. "I need to stretch. Anyone like this seat? It is not the hottest one at the table, but I will not ask Richard to give that one up."

Edgar quickly took the seat. Charlie leaned over and whispered, "Be kind," and then stepped outside for a cigar. He had seen Rebecca drive by in her little trap about an hour before and he had to admit he was curious as hell about how things were going. He leaned against the post and lit a cigar. A few moments later he once again saw Rebecca in her buggy, headed straight for the inn. He stepped off the porch and met her even before she made it to the front door.

"Is everything all right?"

"Yes, Charlie." She smiled down at him. "Go get your best friend. There is someone waiting to meet him."

He whirled around and dashed as fast as he could to the door. "Richard! Come on! Rebecca is here to give you a…"

Richard very nearly knocked Charlie over as he ran from the inn. It was only because he managed to side step him that he was not knocked flat. Richard apparently did not realize Rebecca was there to give him a ride to his place and he just kept running down the street.

He raised his cane and started to call to his friend, but stopped when he realized it would do no good. He shook his head and let everyone inside the inn know that the newest little Polk had indeed arrived safe and sound.

He climbed up beside his wife, while several of the other men at the tavern accompanied them on foot. They strolled over to the Polk residence. Darby was sitting on the front porch, reading a book by the light streaming out of the front parlor window. He jumped up when he heard Rebecca's trap roll up and took the lead from her. The sound of women's voices could be heard through the open windows.

"So, can we meet the new little Polk? By the way, is it a boy or a girl?" Charlie asked Rebecca as she started to climb down from the trap.

"It would be more courteous for you to wait a few days. But if Elizabeth says so, of course."

She hurried into the house just as Richard emerged, wearing a huge, stupid grin. "I am the proud father of a fine, handsome and very smart son," he boasted, as he pulled out a celebratory cigar and lit it up. "His name is Richard – a good name, I have found." As an afterthought, he added, "but Elizabeth wants to call him Dickon."

He tapped Darby on the shoulder. "Lad, in my office behind my desk is a box of cigars. Could you please get it so I can share with my friends here?"

Darby ran into the house and returned in a moment, bearing a cigar box and a box of matches, which he handed to Richard. Soon the entire front yard of the Polk home looked like a dozen smudge pots had been lit, as the gentlemen of Culpeper celebrated the birth of another child.

~

Thursday, August 2, 1866

Charlie awoke late that night, the price he had paid for falling asleep much earlier than normal. It had been brutally hot, and after spending most of the day with Frank at the bank, starting to prepare the end of the month financial reports, he had developed a headache that would have made an artillery unit proud.

He had come home, eaten a cool salad with a lovely glass of mint tea, kissed all of his children, made his apologies to Rebecca and the other adults, and retired to bed. He had even declined Rex's offer to ease the headache; he only wanted to sleep. Now it was shortly past midnight and he was wide awake.

Rebecca slumbered peacefully in the middle of the bed, a position she had never actually given up in the entire time he had known her, even if she did think she slept on the left side. He slipped out from under her as she slept on his shoulder and replaced himself with his pillow. He smiled when she murmured softly and accepted the replacement. Grabbing his robe from the foot of the bed and pulling it on, he tied it closed, pulled one of Rex's special blend cigars from a humidor on the mantle and carefully, quietly, opened the doors to the veranda.

Stepping outside, he fished a match box from the pocket of the robe and lit his cigar. It was a beautiful night. Warm, calm and clear with a waning moon, but with enough light so he could see the expanse of the farm before him.

The pond glistened, the barns and new construction of the

enclosed winter exercise ring stood behind it in shadowed silence. He leaned against the rail, enjoying the slight lightheadedness that Rex's cigars caused. That and the feeling of being very relaxed and slightly out of his own body made the entire experience very enjoyable. Then there was that third benefit. Of course Rebecca was sound asleep and he was not sure she would welcome middle of the night advances from her randy husband. He would just have to shake that one off tonight and enjoy the peace and quiet.

It had been a long time since he had stood outside in the middle of the night. He actually missed doing it. The last time he could clearly recall doing it was the night before Appomattox Station. He had stood outside his tent after rereading the last letter from Rebecca. He had watched the stars and moon, knowing and understanding what the next day could bring. That night, all he could think to comfort himself was that they were under the same sky.

Now not only were they under the same sky, but the same roof. They were the couple he had hoped they could be. He knew with the spirited blonde at his side, there would be nothing they could not accomplish. It had been a long, hard road, but Charlie was feeling confident. They had actually triumphed and made it through.

As he stood there listening to the sounds of the night, the crickets, the cicadas and a couple of large bullfrogs living happily down by the pond, he realized there was something not quite normal in what he was hearing.

He cocked his head, first toward the pond and the barns, then toward the house. He began narrowing down the unusual sounds. Focusing in, he realized they were coming from Edgar and Rex's suite of rooms, the doors of which were open, no doubt due to the warmness of the night.

Giving it another moment's consideration, the realization of the situation playing out a few yards from him came into full mental visualization. He just shook his head and scrubbed his face as he normally did when he knew he was embarrassed.

It was perfectly clear that Edgar and Charlotte had formed some sort of relationship. By their own admission, he knew that Edgar and Rex had a long-standing relationship. Based on what Charlie was trying not to hear in the next room down, now Edgar, Rex and Charlotte were forming some sort of relationship.

He decided to finish his cigar inside.

～

On his way to the office that morning, he picked up a paper from the train station. He settled into his desk with a fresh cup of Eloise's excellent coffee, and opened the paper to scan the headlines before settling down to work.

The headlines made his stomach churn. New Orleans police had killed more than forty blacks and white Republicans and wounded over a hundred fifty people. This was bad or worse than the problems in Memphis two months earlier.

As he read the story, Richard walked into his office unannounced. "I see you have seen the paper. There is something you have not yet seen, though, that I fear is even worse. Sheridan sent me word that he heard Devil Forrest has started up a supposedly secret organization in Tennessee that is called the Ku Klux Klan. They now have their own little anti-black militia. I doubt it will take too long to spread here, especially since Raeburn served with that devil for a while."

"What are you going to do?"

"I am not rightly sure yet, but if I were you, I would be a damn sight more careful. And I would take care of your servants. They are prime targets for Raeburn at this point."

～

Friday, August 3, 1866

"So," Rebecca continued to gales of laughter from those gathered in the parlor. Even though the stories were about Charlie, he too sat there amused, chewing on a cigar and giving off his normal red glow about the ears. "It is truly the most amazing thing.

He is simply like a lump of wet straw. It is as if he has not a single bone in his body."

What she was describing was his state of being at bedtime after Rex had started working on the larger scars and wounds. She was curious because even though the treatments took place in their bedroom, so he could immediately go to bed and rest afterward, she had never been in the room while it was happening.

All she knew is that she would enter the room after Rex was done and he would be lying nude in their bed, a detail she spared the room in case he might actually die from embarrassment, completely boneless and sometimes incapable of communication for several minutes. She wanted to know what was being done to leave him in that state.

"I certainly have no objections to you being present if General Redmond doesn't," Rex offered lifting his teacup in her direction. "You would probably enjoy watching."

Charlotte choked on her coffee and Charlie felt the heat rising in his face and ears again.

"What?" Rebecca looked around the room at her friends. She thought Charlie was going to slide right out of his chair and allow the floor to swallow him up. Charlotte just sipped her coffee. Even Edgar was an interesting shade of pink with a grin biting at his lips. She looked at Rex, who simply looked pleased.

"Shut up, Edgar," Charlie admonished while trying to scrub the red from his own face.

"Did I say anything?" Edgard protested with a laugh.

"You think very loudly."

"What?" Rebecca demanded again. She looked to Charlie, and he mouthed, "I will tell you later."

Looking at all of them again, she nodded as she straightened her skirts with simulated indignity. "I see. Somehow I stumbled into the middle of one of your dirty little jokes. And to think one of you is a minister."

The entire room roared with laughter as Charlie leaned over and kissed his wife's cheek. "I love you so much."

~

At Rex's request, Rebecca had waited in Charlie's office for a half hour before entering the bedroom. She slipped in quietly as he had directed her to do before going to start the treatment.

The room was lit only by the glow from a small fire in the fireplace and two small lanterns Rex moved around as he needed to light his activities. She looked at her partner, who was lying on his left side.

His right arm and leg were draped over an ornately decorated silk bolster that was as long as he was tall. She could see a beautiful, delicate dragon sewn into the fabric, but what amazed her most was Charlie's state of undress. Apparently, he did start these sessions completely nude. She was stunned.

"He trusts you completely," she said softly.

"I am honored," Rex whispered as he gestured to a chair next to the bed, nearest Charlie's head. "He is sufficiently under. We can talk quietly."

"This," she gestured to her husband's sleeping form. "Does not bother you?"

Rex quirked a brow. "Why should it? It's perfectly clear to me that Charlie is simply a two spirited person."

"Two spirited person?"

"Mmmhmm." He nodded as he moved to the end of the bed. "A lovely way of looking at it, I think. It is a tradition among the Indians in your western frontier. Edgar and I were fortunate enough to do several months of missionary work a few years ago in our wide and varied travels. I learned many fascinating things from their medicine men and shamans. A two spirited person is simply one body containing the attributes of both genders. It is not uncommon for a two spirited person to be held in great reverence by their family and the tribe. Many of them become important leaders in the nation."

"I have never heard of such a thing. I mean I knew people like Charlie existed, but I had never given it any serious thought until…"

He smiled, "Until you met him?"

"You see him as completely male." It was not a question. She was enthralled.

"I do. He has always presented to me as male. It is clear he has a man's mind. His physical body holds no intrigue or attraction for me as it does for you. For me, he simply is Charlie."

She nodded looking at her husband's face, aided by one of Rex's small lamps. He looked completely asleep, but in an unusual way. There was no response of his facial features. His eyelids were still. His lips did not move as they normally did when he was asleep. His tendency to have difficult dreams was another thing she had become accustomed to. He sometimes talked or even cried out in his sleep. It bothered her that he looked almost dead.

"Is he truly well?"

"I promise." Rex began the process of inserting a long string of needles from Charlie's hand, up his arm, down his side, all the way to his knee. "He is in a self-induced trance. It is a method I taught him so that I may perform the healing without causing him stress or pain. All you need do to wake him up is snap your fingers."

"Fascinating." She started to reach out and run her fingers through his hair, but hesitated.

"Go right ahead. But be warned, there will be no reaction."

This was a very unusual situation for her. She was touching him and there was not a single response. Not so much as a twitch from his nose. "I am not sure I like seeing him like this. We have come too close to losing him too many times this last year."

"One of the reasons that we waited until now to invite you in." He began moving Charlie's injured arm in different directions, stretching it and placing it in positions that he could never get into by himself. "Now that we are far enough into it, you must be seeing progress."

She thought about that. Yes. His mood was certainly improved. He had learned how to go without his glove or prosthetic around the farm. Em and Suzanne discovered they actually liked Papa's hand because now they could hold it and it was perfect for their little fingers to wrap around his own. Now there was no pain when he did simple things like holding the hands of his little girls and they were not repulsed or afraid of him. They took his hand as soon as he offered it to them.

"If you had seen him like this before there was any real improvement, you might have tried to talk him into stopping, given the unusual nature of the treatments."

"He will be able to walk without his cane?"

"Eventually, I think so, yes. The leg wounds are serious. It may take a little time. Charlie is a good patient and he is responding quickly."

"Yes, he is." She ran her fingers through is hair again as Rex continued his work on the battered body in the bed.

"At some point, you will be able to take over the morning exercises for him if you are willing. I can teach you everything you need to know. He will be able to induce the trance. I have already implanted the command to awaken him."

"I am very willing. Thank you."

"He may not move or react to touch." Rex grinned as he began working with his leg. "But now is a good time to ask him any questions you might need answered."

She sat up straight and looked at Rex with surprise. "Really?" This was an unexpected benefit.

"Really," he nodded. "How do you think Edgar and I have managed to stay together for so long?

～

Sunday, August 5, 1866

Darby caught Richard as he was coming out of the church after the Sunday morning service. "Uncle Richard, what am I supposed to be doing for you now? I figured that with the baby just born and all, you would not need me, but I also know that the sword for Papa Charlie is expensive. I want to keep working for that, sir."

Richard looked into the face of the very earnest young man in front of him. "Darby, you have no idea how valuable the work you did for me and Aunt Elizabeth was. You have more than earned the price of the sword. I have already commissioned it, and it will be ready well before you birthday. So I suggest that you take this month and just be a boy for once. It will be good for you to get out and play before you have to settle down to lessons in September." He grinned at him. "I would wager that your friend Jeremiah would be willing to do a little fishing, and perhaps some exploring through the woods around here."

"Well, sir, I do like to do a bit of fishing. And frogging – that is lots of fun. And I think maybe there are some crawfish down in the run. So we could do that." He thought for a moment. "Do you really think that Jeremiah could take time off from his leather working?"

"That is up to Mr. Duncan and Miss Samantha, but it would not hurt to ask."

Darby thought about that for a second, then grinned, crinkling his nose. "We did have fun when he stayed over after the wedding and on the Fourth of July." He looked around and located his best friend, who was standing with his parents in a group of people having what looked like a very serious talk. He turned back to Richard. "You know, Uncle Richard, Papa Charlie has a new tutor coming in September to start teaching me and the girls. I am looking forward to it, but I am not so sure Em or Suzanne are. I think Suzanne likes to follow Aunt Charlotte around more than trying to read a book. And Emily would rather dig in the dirt."

Richard laughed at the image of Em crusted in dirt and Charlotte with her six-year-old shadow, then said, "So go find Jeremiah."

When Darby slipped into the group of people surrounding Duncan to stand beside his friend, he caught part of the conversation. Mr. Duncan was saying, "Yes, it will be finished this week."

Mr. Cooper added, "And I have all the furnishings ready to go in."

Mrs. Frazier looked strained. "So who is going to actually go tell her it is time to move? I know for a fact that Horace would rather have a tooth pulled without pain killer than face that woman."

It only took a couple of minutes for Darby to realize they were talking about moving Mrs. Williams out of the manse and into the cottage they had refurbished for her. It was a shame. It meant that Reverend Edgar and Mr. Rex would be moving into town. He liked having them around. Reverend Edgar was funny, and Mr. Rex had done so much good for Papa Charlie. But he figured they would be around a lot. It seemed that most people were.

He tugged on Jeremiah's sleeve, and indicated that they could slip away from the grownups.

With Jeremiah in tow, he sidled up to Rebecca's side. "Mama Rebecca, can Jeremiah come and stay with us for a couple of days? Please? We would like to do some fishing down on the run, and it is easier if he is staying with us."

She smiled at her oldest child, cupping his chin with her hand. "MAY Jeremiah come out to the house, Darby? Of course. Jeremiah, you are always welcome at the house. Shall we go and ask your parents?"

Shortly, very shortly, Jeremiah ran back to rejoin the Redmond clan to make the trip out to the Stables, a bundle of his clothes and his fishing gear in his arms.

For the next three days, the most anyone saw of the boys was at hurried breakfasts, requests to Sarah for packed lunches, and very grubby, muddy lads who arrived with just enough time to get cleaned up for dinner. Sarah received several strings of bass, crappies and catfish, a small box of frogs and a big bag of crawfish to fix for supper all week. They were having a wonderful time.

Monday, August 6, 1866

The two hired teamsters unloaded the crates and boxes from the train and loaded them onto their heavy dray. General Redmond and his lady had ordered almost half a train car load of assorted boxes, crates, and barrels, much of it the product of the shopping trip they had taken the previous month.

The younger of the two heavily muscled black men wiped his sweaty forehead with a bandana. It was still early, not quite eight in the morning, but the heat and humidity of summer were already in full force. Coupled with the weight of all the goods they had first unloaded from the train and were now carefully packing onto the big wagon, he was sweating profusely.

"Jimmy, what do you s'pose they need with all this stuff?"

Jimmy paused, his arms wrapped around a small keg of brandy. "I don' rightly know, but if it is stuff to help Sarah cook one of her special church dinners, I ain't gonna complain. An' don't you neither, George."

The two men worked in silence for a little longer, artfully packing the wagon so that nothing would shift, and so that there would be room at the back of the wagon for three large open slatted crates which were currently sitting in the shade of the station porch. It was clear that whatever was in those crates, they were not happy. Distressed bleats came from the crates periodically, as well as occasional muffled thumps. Finally, George loaded the last barrel and tied it down.

"Jimmy, boy. Come here and lend me a hand with the beasties."

Dutifully, he shuffled over. Each man took an end of the first of the large crate and heaved it up on the tailgate of the dray. Pitiful bleats, followed by resounding thumps came from the crate. Two more heaves, a minute or two to tie them down securely, and one last stop at the rain barrel for a drink of cool water and the two men and their load were off, headed down the road to the Redmond Stables.

Tarent was standing in the stable yard as the dray pulled in, having just walked up from the summer kitchen with a mug of coffee in his hand. "Jimmy, what are you and George doing here? That stuff goes up to the main house."

Jimmy waved to him as they pulled in. "Mr. Tarent, they's three crates of some kind of aminule in here, so we figgered you get them."

"Aminule?" He thought for a second. "Oh. Animals. Gen'l's goats, I suppose. See that little pen over there, away from the main barn? Put the crates in there, and I will have someone take care of them."

Jimmy and George hauled the bleating crates into the little isolation pen, set them down reasonably gently, and happily drove off to the kitchen yard to unload the rest of the supplies and see what they could wheedle out of Sarah.

Tarent called one of the stable boys over and issued simple instructions – some grain, alfalfa, and water in the pen, then pry open the crates and let the goats figure the rest out for themselves.

～

Charlie was sitting at his desk at the bank when Eloise knocked, then slipped in without waiting for his permission. He found that a bit distracting, but at least she gave him a little bit of warning before she entered by knocking.

"General Redmond, Mrs. Allen is here to see you. And she has a man and a large, um, demijohn full of something with her."

He looked a bit surprised. What was Mrs. Allen doing here and what was she doing with a huge jar in a wicker cradle? "Well, Miss Eloise, I suppose we should see her and find out what she is carrying with her."

She ushered Mrs. Allen in the door, with the man who did odd jobs around her house following, carrying the jug that had aroused Eloise's curiosity. Rather than returning to her desk, she took an unobtrusive position at the back of the room.

The general was on his feet right away. "Good day, Mrs. Allen. To what do I owe the pleasure of your visit?"

"Oh, General Redmond, you will never guess what I got today!" the local purveyor of prime moonshine gushed. "I received a check in today's mail. And it is for more than I even asked for. They sent me interest to make up for not paying on time! And your clerk cashed the check without asking any questions."

He smiled. "Well, it seems that my little trip to Washington did some good."

"Oh, yes, sir, thank you, sir. I am thrilled. I think I will make some additions to my house."

"Well, I will be pleased to watch your progress." He could see her house from the window at the front of his office.

"As promised, I am making some of my special brew available for you and your friend. Wat has it for you. And for you, I have a special price. Only five cents a quart."

He calculated quickly; twenty quarts at five cents each, then reached into his pocket and pulled out a silver dollar, which he handed to her. He looked at the demijohn in the big man's arms. He was sweating and five gallons plus glass and wicker could not be considered a trivial load. "Um, Mrs. Allen, could you drop that off at Jocko's tavern for me? I am not quite in a position to be able to carry it myself."

"Oh, General Redmond, I really cannot be seen making deliveries to my competition. May I just leave it here and let you handle it?"

Charlie glanced at Eloise, who was trying valiantly to not break out laughing, then said, "Of course, Mrs. Allen. I understand completely. And thank you so much for helping my friend."

She and Wat left and Eloise quietly closed the door after them, before she dissolved into a fit of giggles. When she caught her breath, she said, "General, when I go to lunch, I will find someone to carry this over to Mr. Jackson's."

"Please do, and thank you for your help. I suspect this is not the first time we will have unusual things coming through our hands here."

"Oh, no, General. You should have seen some of the things that my father's clients paid him with – or at least tried to pay him with."

CHAPTER 21

Monday, August 6, 1866

Tarent finished his rounds, then stumped up to the main house for his daily chat with Rebecca.

"Yes, ma'am, the spring foals are coming along nicely. That little boy from Jack out of Mirabelle is going to be a goer, I think."

"I told you those two lines would mate well, Tarent. The books do tell the tale."

"Yes, ma'am, they do. I believe you have the finest breed books I have ever seen – you are making a true science of it, Miss Rebecca."

"Why, thank you. A great deal of it is due to you and Albert and your impeccable taste in horseflesh."

"Well, ma'am, I should be getting back. Gen'l Charlie's goats came in this morning and I need make sure the boys have tended to them properly."

"Goats?"

He sighed. "Yes, ma'am. Goats. Some harebrained scheme that Jocko thought up – to raise goats here at the farm. Maybe for meat and milk, maybe for cashmere. I honestly do not know. But I can tell you that I am having the boys build a goat shed. I do not want those little buggers bringing in who knows what to our horses."

"Goats." She rubbed the bridge of her nose and Tarent knew that was a bad sign. "Yes, please, keep them away from the horses. I will speak with General Redmond when he comes home this afternoon."

The morning passed quickly. She finished her paperwork, checked on the children as they finished their morning lessons, consulted with Sarah about the menus for lunch and dinner, chatted with Beulah about sorting and storing the newly delivered supplies, and was finally ready to drop in at the stables and check on the rapidly growing foals for herself.

As she walked down beside the stone barn toward the practice paddocks, she could hear squealing and young girl giggles coming from the direction of the isolation pens. *Uh oh. The girls are up to something, and I will bet next spring's entire foaling that they are doing something with the new goats that will decidedly upset their father.*

She slid around the corner of the barn and gazed with horror on the scene in front of her. There were six small goats, lying splayed in the dust of the little pen, clearly dead, probably from fright, while Suzanne and Emily ran around them in circles, squealing, shrieking and giggling outrageously.

"GIRLS!" Rebecca stood at the pen gate, hands on hips and a very displeased looked on her face. "What exactly is it you think you are doing with these goats!"

Suzanne and Emily stopped dead in their tracks, looked at their mother, looked at each other, and stifled another giggle. Then they did something extremely strange. They stiffened and fell over on their sides, then lay very still.

"What in the..." Concerned for her children, she entered the pen and knelt down to each girl. She sighed when she could see impish smiles and fluttering lids. "Alright, you two. Up. You have to explain to your father why you have killed his..." Before she could finish her sentence, the little animals all got to their feet. "What in the name of the good Lord above..."

"See, Mama? They like to play. When we tease them, they fall down. Papa got us goats that like to play ring around the rosie!"

"No, no, no, my little darlings, I do not think this is what Papa planned. Come now, let us go back to the house..."

"But, Mama – they are lots of fun. Just one more time?"

More quietly, Suzanne spoke up, cajoling where Emily tended to be demanding. "Yes, Mama. They are loads of fun. Can we show you?"

Against her better judgment, with a loud sigh, she simply nodded.

The two girls grinned at one another and started running in circles around the cluster of small black and white goats, flapping their arms like demented chickens as they ran. They were singing at the top of their lungs, "Ring around the rosie, pocket full of posies, ashes, ashes, we all fall DOWN!" As they ran, the little herd of goats tried to get away from the flailing arms and raucous sounds. On the word "down," the little girls' voices rose to a piercing shriek. The girls tumbled in the dust. The goats' already protruding eyes bulged out so far they looked about to pop. With that shriek, the goats' limbs stiffened, splayed out, and down they went, clearly paralyzed with fear.

"My stars." Rebecca knelt down to the nearest little beast and gave it a pat. A second later it was on its feet scampering to the other side of the small pen. "Alright, girls. That is enough. You will give the poor things a terrible fright, then you will have to explain to your Papa how you killed his goats."

Darby came roaring at full speed around the corner of the stone barn, babbling at the same time. "Mama 'Becca! I tried to get them to stop, then I went up to the house to get you, but Sarah and Beulah said you had come down to the stables, so I...." At that point, he simply ran out of breath. He leaned over, put his hands on his knees and panted.

She smiled at her oldest son. "It is alright, Darby. I know what a handful they can be." She waved her arms to herd the children out of the pen. "Goats," she mumbled as she latched the fence. "Fainting goats. Charles Redmond, when I get my hands on you..."

~

Charlie drove down the dusty road, almost as hot and sweaty as his cart pony was in the miserable summer heat. Not a cloud in the sky, not a breath of wind to ease the burning heat of the sun, nothing but a muggy haze of dust. All he wanted to do was get home, strip out of his sweat soaked shirt, wipe off some of the sweat and dust with a cool, damp cloth, and drink about a quart of Sarah's lemonade. No one met him at the front door, which was unusual, so he wrapped the pony's reins around a hitching post in the shade of an old white oak tree and tromped into the house, shouting for Reg as he went.

Reg came hustling out of the door to the back stairs and into the main hall, slipping around the wall to the front door and mumbling "Pony…stable…Sir…"

At the same time, Rebecca appeared in the door of the back parlor. She was still in her boots and britches, and dusty and disheveled from the stable yard. Her hands were on her hips and the glint in her eye suggested that he was in for it.

"Good afternoon, dear. Have I missed lunch?"

"You will be very lucky if I ever give you another meal, Charles Redmond." She tapped her booted foot.

His brows shot to the top of his head as he looked at her carefully. He thought about his own behavior over the past couple of days. No, he had been being especially easy to get along with lately. When he left this morning, everything was fine and she had not brought out his middle name. So he decided that one of the children must have done something egregious – one of his children when they were bad, though they were always her children when they were good. "So which child do I need to talk to and what did they do this time, dear?"

"Did you buy some goats?"

"Goats?" He looked a little puzzled for a moment, then it struck him and he smiled as he gestured. "Oh, yes! The goats. Well, you see, darling. Jocko has this friend who had a small herd of goats that produced very nice coats for cashmere and were supposed to be good meat animals, so I bought a few. I just thought we could see how the goats do here. Just a little experiment. Maybe something for the smaller farmers to use for spare milk or a cash crop." He paused for a moment. "I take it they arrived?"

"Oh, yes, they arrived, much to the delight of your daughters. Did Jocko tell you the goats were defective?"

He approached his wife rather cautiously. "Defective? What do you mean defective? Are they ill?"

"No, they seem quite healthy. They are just flawed."

The two of them started moving toward the back stairs together, on their way to see the defective goats by mutual, unspoken consent. "Flawed? How can a goat be flawed? Do they have hoof problems or something?"

"Hooves are fine." She paused and called the girls from the kitchen, where they were having a cup of milk and giggling like crazy. "Girls, shall we show Papa his funny goats?"

He was totally confused by now. "Funny goats? Are they blemished somehow?" The entourage continued out the kitchen door toward the goat pen.

"Blemished? No. Just slightly faulty." She was rather enjoying keeping him in the dark. Only a man would buy goats that fainted.

As they passed the barn, Charlie was rapidly achieving a high level of confused frustration. "How can a goat be faulty?" They turned the corner and he peered at the six black and white bug-eyed beasts huddled together by the water trough. "What do you mean, faulty? They are a little small, but they look fine to me. Healthy, beautiful silky coats..." He looked from the goats to his wife's smug expression and back to the goats.

"Girls, would you please show Papa the game you play with his goats?"

The two girls looked at their mama, who nodded, then grinned and giggled at each other. Slipping through the gate, they started singing at the top of their lungs while circling the huddled herd of goats like demented banshees. "Ring around the rosie..." At the final shrieked word, the two girls and the goats hit the dust together.

Charlie just stared for a moment, and then he pointed into the pen, gesturing erratically. "They killed my goats! My brand new goats! Rebecca! Your children just killed my goats!"

She chuckled. "Now if this were going to kill your goats they would already be dead. Several times over. Just watch." Mama motioned the girls out of the pen and waited as the animals started coming to. "Your goats suffer from the vapors, General." She laughed outright as she leaned against the fence for support.

He watched as slowly his goats struggled to their feet, a little stiff for a few moments, and then began scampering around the pen, working to get as far away from the gate and the terrifying small children as possible. "They fainted. The goats fainted."

He blinked for a few seconds, then started muttering, "Jocko and his friend have a lot to answer for. Selling me defective goats. I never heard of a goat fainting." He turned around and stomped off toward the house. She could hear him mumbling, "Fainting goats. What kind of deal is this? And I paid good money for them because of the cashmere. And they faint. Defective bloody goats..."

Wednesday, August 8, 1866

Charlie had dropped Rebecca at Elizabeth's. The two women had planned on spending the afternoon together while he took care of a few errands in town. As he drove the little trap over a particularly rough spot in the road he heard the snap even before he felt the buggy lurch. He pulled the horse to a stop and looked down to his right, sure enough at least one and maybe two spokes had broken in the wheel. "Damn," he grumbled, climbing out of the trap.

He decided to lead the horse and buggy, rather than risk further damage to the wheel. A few blocks ahead he stopped in front of Duncan's shop where at least a half a dozen men were moving about working on various projects. It made him smile to see Duncan doing so well. He tied the horse off to the hitching post and wandered inside looking for his friend. The young man sat in a small office with two other men; they were engrossed over a clipboard when Charlie rapped on the jamb with his cane.

"General, w-what can I d-do for you?"

He grinned as he leaned against the door frame and gestured, "You certainly look like a proper business man now."

Duncan ducked his head and nodded, "Thank you, sir. M-mostly b-b-because of you."

"Nonsense. It is because you are a brilliant carpenter and a hard worker. I do have a job for you though. Do you have a wheelwright?"

"Well, I h-have a fella that d-does some wheel work on the s-side. He splits his t-time between w-working with me and working with Granville at the f-f-forge. He will b-be here in about a half hour or s-so. D-did you b-break a wheel, G-general?" Duncan rose from his chair and handed the clipboard to his assistant.

"The road broke my wheel, but yes." The general followed the young man outside where he inspected the buggy.

"I am p-pretty sure my man c-can f-fix this, General, but it will t-take a c-couple of h-hours."

He drew a deep breath and let it out slowly as he considered his options. "All right, Duncan. I have a few things to do. Then I am going to walk over to Dr. Walker's to let Miss Rebecca know that our buggy is here. I will see you in two hours or so."

He tapped his cane impatiently for a few seconds as he considered what to do first. He knew Rebecca would be with Elizabeth for a couple of hours at least. That would give him time to walk over to the bank and pick up anything waiting for him there and a quick stop at Cooper's store to put in an order for a few dry goods Sarah needed and a new pair of boots for Darby. The boy could grow out of footwear faster than any human being Charlie had ever seen. He was on his second pair of slippers, second pair of shoes and third pair of boots since he and Suzanne had joined the family seven months before.

He settled his hat on his head and turned toward town.

Rebecca knew she should have asked Charlie to wait, but she had not anticipated that Elizabeth would be called out to one the farms well outside of town for a broken leg. Richard had gone into town and Ruth was left taking care of the baby. She spent about a half hour holding her godson and singing him lullabies, remembering a time when her boys were so tiny.

When it became clear Elizabeth would not be returning anytime soon, she decided to walk toward town to find Charlie. Maybe she could convince him to have lunch at Jocko's. As she set off down the quiet dirt road that would take her to the heart of town, she was completely unaware she was being watched.

As she continued toward town, behind her she thought she heard footfalls, but when she turned, the road was empty. She considered that it must be a distant echo of a wagon or perhaps hammering. She was, after all, headed for the center of town where several buildings were under construction. She came to a rather disrupted spot in the road, carefully stepping over what appeared to be a purposely dug rut. She could see the splinters of more than one wagon wheel. It did seem damn strange and she reminded herself to mention it to both Charlie and Richard.

She crossed over so she could walk under the shade of a row of white oak trees that lined the right side of the little road. Then she heard the twig snap and she knew there was most certainly someone behind her. She did not turn this time. She kept walking and very slowly placed her hand in her reticule, feeling for the Derringer Charlie had demanded she not only learn how to properly load and fire, but carry when she was alone. For the first time in her life, she was actually starting to feel like she might need it. Keeping her hand tucked in her bag, the little gun clutched in her fist, she continued walking toward town.

Charlie had completed his business at the bank, quickly signing some documents Frank had left on his desk and picking up his mail.

Mr. Cooper had laughed when yet another order for boy's boots was placed. He just nodded, knowing his growing group of troopers would keep Mr. Cooper in business for the next several years all by themselves. He was assured the dry goods order would be delivered by afternoon. Charlie tipped his hat to Mrs. Cooper on his way out and headed towards Elizabeth's to meet up with Rebecca.

As he made his way down the street, he had to stop several times to avoid being run over by teamsters driving heavy wagons loaded with a wide and varied supply of goods. Wood was being delivered to both Duncan's shop and numerous building sites. Crates of goods were delivered to various businesses both established and just opening. Culpeper was starting to regrow and it made him very happy.

Crossing over the street towards Duncan's shop once again, he could see the wheel had already been removed from his buggy. He nodded his appreciation of the quick work and continued on his way.

~

Rebecca could see movement on Main Street; she knew in just another minute, she would be surrounded by people. She began to relax and removed her hand from her bag. She was making her way around a large stack of lumber, just before Duncan Nailer's carpentry shop when he appeared. She was startled when he suddenly stepped out before her, blocking both further progress around the stack of wood and her view of town.

"Alex Raeburn," she said as she tried to keep her voice calm and even.

"Rebecca Gaines." He both leered and sneered at her, taking one menacing step forward.

She tried to side step him, to get past the wood and into a position where someone, anyone might see them. He simply stepped back and put his arm up against the stack of lumber, once again blocking her attempts to get past him and the ability for any casual passerby to clearly see the small woman. He was using the accidental barricades created by Duncan's supplies and the heavy wagons moving about to his advantage.

Her heart was beating hard in her ears, feeling like it might break through her chest. She worked her hand back into her bag and fumbled for the little pistol when Alex backed her up against the wood pile and pinned her hand to her side. "Now, that is NOT nice." He growled as his face drew closer to hers. "How could you marry that bastard? How is it that his wife and his whore live under the same roof? Does she share your bed too? Or does he go back and forth?" He put his lips close to her ear and snarled, "I can show you a trick or two that might keep the Yankee bastard satisfied."

She shook her head, refusing to answer his questions or to be angered by his suggestions, as she tried to figure a way out. She knew she could scream but he had the advantage and he could most definitely hurt her and probably kill her before anyone arrived. She needed to find a way to get away and get to Duncan's shop. She turned her head sharply to the left when she realized that it was his intention to force a kiss from her. She barely had time to react to his hands on her breasts when she heard what could only be described as an ungodly roar.

Charlie had begun weaving through a corridor of wood and crates that would eventually give way to the road leading to Elizabeth's. As he turned left around one large stack of lumber, he could not believe what he was seeing.

With a howl from his lungs that sounded like it came from the deepest, fieriest pit of Hell, he grabbed Alex Raeburn by the back of the collar with the two fingers and thumb of his right hand and yanked him completely off his feet as he threw him backward in one quick motion.

Rebecca was not sure exactly what was happening as it was all so fast. It took a full five seconds for her to realize that Charlie was there now and that he had turned his back on her to focus his attention on Alex, now on his back on the ground as Charlie raised his cane. Alex put his arms up quickly trying desperately to block the violent strikes to his face and head.

"Charlie!" She screamed as she watched him beat Alex with the handle of his cane. His blows were so fast she could barely see the top of the cane as he drew it up and well above his head over and over again. "Charlie! Stop!"

Her husband was furious in a way she had never seen him. She ran past him to Duncan's shop and called for all the men to come. As they responded to her call, she pointed and they jumped from the porch of the shop and ran over to the two men. By the time they reached them, the cane lay broken in the dirt and he was using his right forearm to pin Raeburn to the ground as his good hand, balled into a tight fist continued to strike the man.

It took Duncan and three of his biggest men to pull Charlie off Alex. He continued to struggle with them as the rest of the men helped the badly beaten Raeburn sit up. Blood was pouring from his ears, nose, mouth and one eye. Both of his eyes were already turning a deep black that would last for months.

Charlie was still struggling against the men holding him when he snarled, "Touch my wife again and I will kill you!"

"A threat?" Raeburn spat blood on Charlie's boots.

"A promise!" He lunged again only to be held firmly by Duncan.

Duncan and one of his men pulled him away from the man whom, they could tell, Charlie would have killed at this very moment, if he had not been stopped. "C-c-come on, G-g-general."

Rebecca followed the men into Duncan's shop. They put Charlie in the office and made sure he was calm enough to be let loose. He was still livid, but he knew he could not strike out at Duncan and Rebecca. "Bastard," he spat as he took his handkerchief and wiped Raeburn's blood from his hands and face.

He just gave an irritated jerk of his head when one of the men opened the door and put his broken, bloody cane on the desk. As he wiped the blood from his hands, he noticed that Jeremiah's prosthetic was now damaged and stained with blood. He took a deep breath and tried, quite in vain, to wipe the sticky substance from the soft leather.

Rebecca had never seen him in a rage like that. It honestly frightened her. She had not even been sure he was physically capable of such a thing. She was waiting for him to stop shaking before she said anything or even tried to touch him. "Charlie?" she offered softly, hoping to calm him.

He looked at her and was immediately worried only for her.

"Oh, my darling, I am so sorry. Did he hurt you?" He opened his arms, inviting her in.

"No." She shook her head and gratefully accepted his embrace. "He just scared me."

He kissed the top of her head, holding her tight against his chest. The vision of another man, especially Alex Raeburn with his hands on her, had been more than he could bear. There would be no saving the next man irresponsible enough to touch her. "Do not worry, darling. He will never have that chance again."

"I thought you were going to kill him, Charlie."

"I was." He nodded.

As Duncan was pulling Charlie off Raeburn, one of the on-lookers ran to find Richard. As the official representative of the Military Government of Virginia, Richard was needed. Right now. He ran to the site as quickly as he could, finding Raeburn still sitting in the dust, dripping blood. "Can you stand up, man?"

Raeburn looked up at him. "I think so, no thanks to your damned General Redmond."

The provost looked around at the men standing and watching. He motioned to a couple of them. "Help him up. We need to get him over to Dr. Walker's infirmary."

When the men had Raeburn on his feet, with one on each side of him holding him up, Richard said, "Go on. Get him to Dr. Walker. I will meet you there shortly."

He turned to the other men still standing around. "All right, which one of you wants to tell me what the hell happened here?" One of the local teamsters who had been bringing yet another load of wood to Duncan's, stepped forward and slowly raised his hand. "Well, George. What did you see?"

"Well, as we wuz drivin' past, we saw Mr. Raeburn had Miz Rebecca cornered over yonder." He gestured to the stack of wood some thirty feet away. "It looked like he was trying to kiss her and she warn't having none of that. We wuz about to yell to her to see if she wanted our help." He ducked his head, slightly embarrassed at the thought. "You know, Miz Rebecca being a lady and all, but then Gen'l Charlie came around the corner. I swears, I never sawed a man so crippled as the gen'l move so damned fast. And the sound that came out of him, I ain't ever heard such a noise."

All the men gathered nodded immediately at the description of Charlie's initial encounter with Raeburn.

George continued, "He was possessed by the Devil hisself, I tell ya! He yanked Mr. Raeburn off Miz Rebecca, with his BAD hand, mind you! Threw him on the ground and beat the holy hell out of him with that silver handled cane of his. Mr. Duncan and some of his men came when Miz Rebecca screamed, and pulled Gen'l Charlie off him, but ... well, the gen'l sure can do some serious damage right quick." George was trying to look appropriately appalled, but somehow the grin on his face won out.

Richard had one initial thought that summed up the situation precisely. Oh, shit.

As George finished his narrative, the other men around him nodded, and murmured, "Yes, sir."

"That's what I saw."

"Aye. Yup. Raeburn had his hands on her."

Richard looked up sharply at the last statement. "Had his hands on her? What do you mean?"

"If I ain't mis-seeing, he was trying to feel," Bobby Joe paused, clearly embarrassed, "her bosoms."

Richard nodded, a grim look tightening his lips. "So in your opinion, General Redmond was protecting his wife from Mr. Raeburn, who appeared to be accosting her?"

"Yes, sir. The gen'l was just doing what any decent man would do iffin his wife was being offended, and doing a damned good job of it too."

"All right. George, Jimmy, Bobby Joe. I will be around later to get your formal statements. Do not discuss this with anyone until I do. But first, I need to go see to Mr. Raeburn."

~

Richard set off toward his house and his wife's attached infirmary. At the same time, Elizabeth was headed toward home, returning from having set a farm worker's leg out at the Dunbar farm. Raeburn and his escort had made their way slowly, with Raeburn making the most of his injuries for his audience of two. All three of them converged in front of the entrance to the infirmary. Raeburn was bloodied, black and blue, and being half carried by two burly men to her door. Richard was looking very official and very grim. *What the hell is going on here?*

Elizabeth looped her horse's lead around the hitching post, and hurried up the steps. "Bring him in here," she commanded as she opened the door to her examination rooms. "Richard, please go get Nigel and have him bring several pans of boiling water." She turned to look at Raeburn closely, gently touching his cheekbones and eye socket. "Well, nothing seems to be broken, though I see you are short a couple of teeth." He flinched as she checked the line of his jaw.

Nigel appeared at the door, bearing two large metal buckets with steam rising from the water in them. After six months as serving as Elizabeth's assistant, he had mastered all of her basic procedures. He set the buckets down and pulled out a pile of boiled cotton rags from a cabinet.

"All right, Mr. Raeburn. Let Nigel clean you up, then I will see what needs to be done to put you back together."

Raeburn snarled, "I will not let a damned nigger treat me like a baby. You are the doctor; you do it."

Silently, Nigel pulled out a pan, poured a good dose of iodine into it and filled it with steaming hot water, standing aside to hand Elizabeth the clean cotton cloths. He was used to this, unfortunately.

Elizabeth took Richard aside. "What the hell happened to him? Did he get kicked and trampled by a horse?"

Her husband looked disgusted. "Sort of. A horse's ass named Charlie Redmond. Seems Mr. Raeburn there put his hands on Rebecca."

She rolled her eyes. "Oh, my God." She glanced back at the

injured man, then turned back to Richard. "You know he is enough of a bastard to press charges."

He sighed. "I know. He wants to hurt Charlie any way he can. This may give him leverage."

She got a thoughtful look. "Of course, Rebecca could also press charges. Assault? Attempted rape?"

He considered her statement and nodded. Based on the statements he had already heard a tradeoff might possibly be negotiated. "Good thought. Fix him up and then I will have my turn at him. I will be back in a few minutes."

The doctor turned to the injured man and started cleaning him up.

Richard left, his notebook pulled out of his pocket. He took Elizabeth's trap, which was still tied to the hitching post out front, and drove back over to Duncan's shop. The teamsters, George, Jimmy and Bobby Joe, were waiting for him outside, sitting in the shade of a white oak tree and enjoying the short break on a hot day.

The teamsters had seen Raeburn cornering and manhandling Rebecca, and had seen Charlie come charging around a stack of wood. They had seen him pull Raeburn off Rebecca with his bad hand, and watched as Charlie beat Raeburn mercilessly with his cane. To the extent that they could, Duncan and his men corroborated the teamsters' story. Duncan handed Richard the broken, bloody cane. "Thank you, gentlemen. You have been very helpful."

He returned to the infirmary, where Elizabeth was finishing the last set of stitches needed to put Raeburn's face back together. She whispered to Richard as he passed her, "I am going to go check on Charlie and Rebecca. I will meet you out there."

Richard escorted Raeburn into his wife's consulting room, seated him, and pulled up another chair to sit uncomfortably close to the injured man. Raeburn started in on Charlie immediately. "So, Mr. High and Mighty Government Official? Are you going to go and arrest your precious general for assault and attempted murder, as you should? You can see what he did to me."

Richard looked him up and down; his clothes were soaked in

blood, and there were multiple places on his face that Elizabeth had needed to stitch up, including a large gash across his nose that would leave an ugly, jagged scar, even with her careful sutures. One of his earlobes had to be tacked back together as well. Anyone looking at him would say he had been run over by a team of horses with a huge wagon behind them. *Damn Charlie.*

"Yes, yes, if you decided to press charges, I certainly will. However, I still need to gather some evidence. Based on what I have learned so far, you may find yourself under arrest as well, as I believe Mrs. Redmond may be pressing charges against you for assault and attempted rape. I will point out to you that there is no jury in this country that will find a man guilty for defending his wife against a vicious assault. Especially with several reliable witnesses who say they saw you put your hands on her before her husband came to her defense."

Alex looked at Richard, a calculating look in his eyes. "So are you suggesting that if I do not press charges, neither will she?"

"Mr. Raeburn, I cannot speak for Mrs. Redmond. What she does is entirely up to her. I am simply pointing out to you what the evidence suggests and the practical and legal position that you may find yourself in. What you do with that information is up to you. However, I strongly suggest that you do not leave the area until this is completely resolved."

With that, Richard stood and escorted his battered "guest" to the door. "Good day, Mr. Raeburn. Let me know what you decide."

Charlie sat at his desk, nodding as he stirred a bit of sugar into his coffee. "I know, Rebecca. I am sorry."

She reached out and took his hand. "I understand why it happened, Charlie, I really do, but what if Alex decides to press charges? That will not be good for us. I doubt Mr. Cooke and General Grant will be thrilled you were fighting in the street like a common urchin."

"I do not know how Mr. Cooke will feel and I do not care. As for General Grant, when he discovers I was protecting my wife from a potential rapist, I suspect he will try to find a medal I am eligible for."

She smiled at that, even though she knew she should not have. This was serious. Charlie could not just go around beating the citizens of Culpeper, no matter the cause or suspected outrage. Their family was already poised to become one of, if not the leading family in the valley. He had to understand that he was not only playing with his own future here, but the future of his children.

"Charlie, my love, I have always known that you would fight like a demon if there was ever a threat to our family; I just did not expect to see it like I did today. I will not lie; you scared me."

He looked at her and saw the remnants of that fear. "I am sorry. You know I could never do that to you or the children?"

She nodded, looking into her own coffee cup before looking directly into his eyes. "I know."

"But you are still worried?" He felt absolutely horrible. The woman he had only wanted to protect and keep safe at any cost was now apparently afraid he would hurt her or their children.

She shook her head. "Not about you. I am worried that Alex will try to use this to his advantage."

Before he could respond, Elizabeth knocked on the door frame. "May I come in?"

"Please," he gestured, "anything to take my mind off of all of this."

"Yes, well," she laid a piece of paper on his desk, "I am not sure that will be possible. The bill for Mr. Raeburn's treatment. I assume you will want to cover it so he will have one less reason to file charges."

He groaned and took his checkbook out of his top drawer.

"I prefer cash from hooligans," Elizabeth chided. Even Rebecca could not contain a snicker.

He sighed heavily and put his checkbook away. He opened the bottom drawer of his desk and removed a small cash box. He retrieved a skeleton key from his pocket and opened the box, removing two ten dollars gold pieces and placing them on the corner of his desk.

"For your trouble, Doctor Walker," he offered, sounding a lot like a sullen child as he put the box away.

After a few minutes of uncomfortable silence with Charlie continually stirring his coffee, Richard walked in.

"Charlie. Rebecca." He sighed heavily. "Rebecca, could I have a word with you in private?"

"Why Richard, anything you have to say to me, or I to you, we can say in front of our spouses." She did not move a muscle.

"All right, then. I need to ask you if Raeburn touched you in any inappropriate way or place."

"Do you mean did he try to kiss me? Did he grope my breasts?" Everyone heard Charlie growl. "Yes. And I would like to bring charges against that wretched piece of pond scum."

Richard actually got a relieved look. "So would you be willing not to bring charges against him if he agreed not to bring charges against Charlie?"

She sat absolutely silent and still for a moment, then looked at Charlie, considering the situation.

"Darling, it is up to you. I can withstand any thing he brings against me, if you want him arrested."

"Richard, if I bring charges, will I have to go to court and tell everyone what he said and did?"

"Yes. Most likely you will."

"And you think he will be willing to just let this whole thing go if I do?"

"I think so."

She looked at her hands, which were attempting to wring her handkerchief into a knot. The real threat was what he had said about Charlotte. *Exposing her identity, our situation, could be disastrous.* She looked up at Richard. "I will let it go if he will. I just … scandal… gossip… I would rather avoid it if I can."

CHAPTER 22

Friday, August 10, 1866

Charlie took a deep breath and rapped on the doorframe. Jeremiah turned from his place on a stool at one of his work benches where he was working on a saddle. He tossed a cloth over the saddle and stood with a smile. "General Redmond. What can I do for you, sir?"

Sometimes it was hard for Charlie to believe that, like Darby, this was only a boy of ten in front of him. He sighed and removed the prosthetic from his pocket. "Sir, I have to ask for a repair." He offered the piece to the young man.

Jeremiah inspected the set of fingers and shook his head. "I am afraid I will have to make a new set. I could probably fix the armature for the fingers, but I think the leather is beyond help. I could try to dye or bleach it, but it would never look right." He nodded, sure of his assessment. "Yes, sir, I will have to make a new set."

"I would be very appreciative if you could, Mr. Carter. Please let me know what this replacement costs, yes?"

Jeremiah nodded his understanding. "Yes, sir. I will have to special order the leather for this. It will take at least a couple of weeks, maybe a month. You still have your glove?"

Charlie nodded.

Tuesday, August 21, 1866

The next two weeks were actually fairly peaceful at Redmond Stables. Richard had discussed his options with Raeburn and no charges were forthcoming on either side. Charlie was occupied with the bank and Rebecca was focused on the children and the horses. In fact, she had given Albert very specific instructions on finding the perfect mount for Darby's first horse. Next month was going to be quite an event, with two of her boys celebrating on the same day.

She and Charlie had reviewed a number of resumes as they searched for a tutor who would be able to manage both Darby's unquenchable curiosity and the girls' beginning efforts at the basics. They had found three candidates, all of whom looked good on paper. Over the next two weeks, each of them would be visiting Culpeper for interviews.

The most exciting event of the week was that the cottage for Mrs. Williams had been finished. The local ladies had joined together to help her pack her personal belongings, and today was the day for the big move. Edgar and Charlotte had invited Charlie and Rebecca to join them in looking over the house, while Rex had been mumbling about horrible wall paper with little pink flocked roses meeting a fitting end for a couple of days.

So immediately after lunch, the five of them climbed into the carriage and headed into town. As they pulled up to the manse, those reliable teamsters Jimmy and George were carrying the last of Mrs. Williams' furniture out of the house and loading it onto the big dray.

Rebecca poked Charlie in the ribs. "Look, darling. Her bed is a big, old mahogany four poster. Look familiar?"

He grimaced. "I did not need to be reminded."

"Neither did I. But since I was, I decided you needed to share the pain."

Edgar, Charlotte and Rex looked at the two of them with great curiosity. "You two share an old mahogany four poster?" Edgar finally inquired.

Charlie gave his best, command assessment of the situation. "Shared. Past tense. It was the bed I had in the room I rent in Washington. It was not up to having Rebecca and I utilize it one night when we were up there, and collapsed under us. It was decidedly embarrassing."

Rex bit his lower lip, Edgar snorted, while Charlotte laughed outright. "Utilize it, General Redmond?" She laughed again. "Did you do to the bed what you did to Raeburn? Try to destroy it on sight?"

Charlie and Rebecca just looked at one another, while their friends guffawed at them.

As a weeping Mrs. Williams, supported by the Misses Simms and Reynolds, left the manse for the last time as its mistress, the five watchers held back. They did not want to be seen as vultures descending on the carcass, as much as all five of them wanted to see what was left and, more importantly, what would have to be done to make it livable for Edgar and Rex.

Once Mrs. Williams and her entourage were out of sight, the friends piled out of the carriage and went inside to conduct their critical survey.

It was bad. It was very bad. Once the pictures were off the wall, one could clearly see how long it had been since the walls had been cleaned. The wood floors were badly scuffed and scratched and splintered. While one could tell where there had been rugs, even the finish under the rugs was scuffed from sand that had sifted through and been ground in. Even if the wall paper could have been cleaned, it was terrible. Rex's comments about pink flocked roses was no exaggeration. Every single room had wall paper in shades of pink and cream. Rex examined the fire places and emerged from looking up the flue with smudges of ash on his face. Based on what came falling down when he poked at the damper, the fireplaces and chimneys had not been cleaned in years. The risk of a chimney fire was very real.

The least offensive room in the house was the library. Mrs. Williams had left all of the theological books, and the built in shelves were fundamentally sound, but needed to be refinished. The most offensive room in the house was the master bedroom. There, the wall paper had large pink and red roses with green velveteen borders.

Charlie looked at the walls and then looked over his shoulder at his friend. "Oh, Edgar. I think it is you to a T."

Rex led the way to the warming kitchen, where the level of soot on the walls was enough to cause him to gag. But that was not to be the worst. Walking out to the detached kitchen, he took a deep breath before opening the door. The floor was packed dirt. There were strings of onions and garlic hanging from the rafters that had obviously been there for at least three or four years, based on the degree of desiccation. There were pots, skillets and cauldrons hanging on hooks from the ceiling beams, which were so low that Charlie and Edgar both had to duck to get past them. And then there was the range and ovens. The ovens were simply holes built into the fireplace with cast iron doors to close them. The range consisted of a sheet of iron laid in front of the open fireplace on wooden saw horses. There were several hooks and a couple of spiders that could be moved into the fireplace to hang pots. The source of water was the well outside the door. There was a dry sink. In other words, the kitchen was at least 100 years out of date and there was no hope of rescuing it. It needed to be torn down and replaced with something that at least acknowledged they were living in the nineteenth century.

Rex looked at Edgar. "I cannot cook in this place. And even if I could, I cannot guarantee that you would not die of some kind of terrible food poisoning."

Edgar stood there, looking at the pathetic excuse of a kitchen, and considered the condition of the rest of the house. He looked at Charlie and Rebecca, with a pitiful expression on his face. "Please, can we continue to stay with you? This place needs to be gutted, and I'm perfectly aware that the church does not have the money."

Rex looked at his friend and smiled. "The church may not have the money, but I do. And since I am offering my money to pay for it, I get to have it done the way I want it." He turned to their gracious hosts. "It will take a while, though."

~

Jimmy and George were covered in sweat. Mrs. Williams's furniture was bloody heavy and maneuvering it all into the cottage, which was much smaller than the manse, was a challenge. To add to that challenge, Mrs. Williams could not decide where she wanted it. She rearranged each room several times before she was satisfied. Finally, the dray was completely unloaded, all the furniture was in the little house, and they made as rapid an escape as they could before she decided to rearrange everything yet again.

Missy Frazier and the other ladies of the community had been busy, planting a lovely flower garden in front of the cottage and a kitchen garden behind it with everything Mrs. Williams could want. They had all volunteered plants from their own gardens, so that some of the plants were already maturing, and in some cases, even flowering.

Duncan and his men had been just as busy, making sure that the cottage was not only structurally sound, but that the woodwork and floors were smooth and highly polished. They wanted to make sure Mrs. Williams had nothing to complain about. A good stock of firewood was already stacked in the back yard, and the wood bins in the house had been filled.

Katherine Reynolds and Mary Simms had accompanied Mrs. Williams to the new cottage and were trying to help her in unpacking and placing her personal items around the rooms to make it as cozy and welcoming as possible. Their first efforts were to make the small winter kitchen as organized as they could, so that they could immediately offer the distraught woman a nice cup of tea to sooth her nerves. Mary also went looking for the box with the small collection of bottles. A good shot of whiskey in Mrs. Williams' tea would probably help about now. It would not hurt Mary or Katherine's strained nerves either.

As Katherine and Mary were sorting the kitchen, experiencing the same indecisiveness that had driven Jimmy and George to desperation, they heard a knock on the door. Margaret Williams bustled to the door, still dabbing her eyes with what was now a very sodden handkerchief. It was good drama, that handkerchief.

When she opened the door, she was surprised to find Alex Raeburn standing there. His face was still bandaged in a spot over his right brow, and what was not bandaged was still black and blue, but he had cleaned himself up and was nicely dressed.

"Why Mr. Raeburn! What brings you here? I would have thought you were still recovering from the beating you took from that man!"

"Good afternoon, Mrs. Williams. I know how difficult changes can be, and how hard it is for a lady like yourself to have to live alone, so I decided to come and offer my assistance. My friends and I would be happy to do things such as making sure you have enough wood and that your wood bins are filled, and your water is hauled in every day. I also thought you might find it useful to have a man around while you unpacked."

"Come in, come in, Mr. Raeburn. Your assistance is most welcome."

She escorted him into her parlor, then bustled back to the kitchen to warn Mary and Katherine that they had company and that perhaps some tea would be welcome. Mary was particularly happy that she had anticipated the need, though not for entertaining a guest. She finished loading the tea tray, adding a cup for Raeburn, and followed Mrs. Williams into the parlor.

"Thank you so much, Mrs. Williams, Miss Simms. I would not want to inconvenience you on this very busy day, though."

Mary spoke up. "No problem, Mr. Raeburn. We were just about to take a break and have a cup of tea ourselves."

Mary sat the tray down, then excused herself to rejoin Katherine in the kitchen.

"Mrs. Williams," said Raeburn after a few minutes of social chit-chat. "I wonder if you would mind if my friends and I called on you on a regular basis – you know, just to make sure you are doing alright?"

"Why, Mr. Raeburn, I would be happy to have you and your friends over. After all of the years at the manse, I am so accustomed to having guests, I was afraid I would be lonely here by myself. It would be a treat to have such handsome and noble gentlemen who believe in maintaining our southern traditions to come by regularly."

"Thank you, ma'am. We think that it is important to take care of the people who still hold to our traditions and support our cause."

∾

Saturday, September 1, 1866

Charlotte walked into the breakfast room with a slightly abashed look on her face. "Rebecca, would you happen to have a pair of britches, some boots and a shirt I could borrow? Rex and I are meeting Duncan at the manse to start looking at what will need to be done to make it livable, and, well, ah…"

"And it is so grubby that if you have to go crawling around you do not want to mess up any of your nice dresses," she finished for her with a knowing laugh.

"Exactly." Charlotte sighed with relief. "Edgar had to ride out to one of the small towns around here – I cannot for the life of me remember which one – and Rex wants to get started. Anyway, Rex is paying for it, so Edgar really does not have much say in the matter."

"Between you and me, dear, I suspect Edgar would find a way to get someone else to manage this particular issue whether he was paying for it or not. Home décor does not strike me as one of his great interests."

Rebecca took Charlotte upstairs to the storage room on the third floor with Andrew's old possessions, rummaged in the cedar chest and found old clothes she thought would fit. The contents of the cedar chest, once packed to the lid, was rather bare at this point, as she had used it to dress everyone who had needed emergency clothing.

Charlotte changed into the clothing found for her, then met Rex in the front hall. Reg had the trap brought around for them, and they climbed in and set out for town. As they went, they discussed their respective tastes in furnishing styles and colors.

Duncan was waiting for them outside the manse, along with one of the lads who ran errands for him. He had a notebook in his hand and a measuring rod in his back pocket. "Good morning. S-s-s-hhall we s-see how b-big a m-m-mess we have?"

The three of them walked in, leaving the boy with the horses. Duncan looked around the hall, sucked his teeth, made some notes in his notebook, then took his penknife and lifted the edge of the wall paper. He made a "tch-ing" sound, and made more notes. He then walked into the parlor, where "tch-ing" continued, as did note taking. He went and looked at the fireplace, and immediately pulled back. "Miss C-charlotte, w-would you ask J-jamie to come in, p-please?"

She went to the door and called, as Duncan had asked. The boy ran immediately to the door.

"J-jamie, please go and ask Mr. Hudnut to c-come over and join us as q-q-quickly as he can." Hudnut was a local brick layer. Jamie took off on his errand at a brisk trot.

Duncan looked apologetically at Rex and Charlotte. "The f-fireplace is in b-bad shape, and I t-think Hudnut is a b-better choice for l-looking at it and f-fixing it."

As they continued to walk through the house, the carpenter alternated between sucking on his teeth, and making the "tch-tch" sound, while taking copious notes. Hudnut showed up as they were finishing inspecting the bedrooms upstairs, and the sounds he made as he prodded at the chimneys were much harsher than Duncan's teeth sucking. In fact, he outright cursed like a sailor and wondered why the place had not burned down.

Hudnut led them out the front door, as he inspected the window frames and the pointing of the bricks, especially at the corners of the building. His cursing became more profound. "You realize that this damned building has had no maintenance work done in at least twenty years? How could the church elders let this go to such a terrible state of disrepair? I am amazed that the windows have stayed in their frames." He continued to grumble as they worked their way around the building.

All five of them walked out to the summer kitchen. They stood just inside the door and looked aghast at the condition of the room. Duncan pulled out his pen knife again and pressed it gently against one of the wall boards, which immediately crumbled away, showing what looked like ant trails through the wood. "W-well, in my opinion, you n-need to t-t-tear it d-down and st-st-start over."

Rex immediately nodded his agreement.

"F-f-fortunately, it w-will be easy to t-tear d-down. It has already been eaten up by t-t-termites. I am amazed it is st-still st-standing."

"Termites do not eat dirt – so that must be what is holding it together." Charlotte brushed her hair back, leaving another smudge of muck on her own cheek.

Duncan just shook his head, while Hudnut wrote some more notes of his own.

They turned to leave. Duncan inadvertently bumped one of the pans hanging from the rafter. The pan fell, bringing its hook with it. That weakened the rafter, and all of the other pots and pans hanging from hooks on that beam followed their mate to the ground.

Standing outside, where it was safer, the craftsmen talked for a few minutes. Then they turned back to Rex and Charlotte. "Well, there is a great deal of work to be done just to get this house livable. And that is before you consider how you want to decorate and furnish it. We strongly recommend you simply tear down the kitchen and build a new one. If you will allow Mr. Nailer and me a couple of days, we will get a bid together for you. It is a damned good thing that we have more than one brickyard here in Culpeper. We are going to need a lot of bricks!"

Charlotte, with Rex's permission slyly given with a wink,

looked at both men, then nodded and said, "Very good. I will send you concepts for the kitchen tomorrow."

"Very good, ma'am," said Hudnut. "A well designed kitchen is important for any household."

~

That afternoon, Charlie and Rebecca rode back into town to meet the new tutor at the train station and drive him out to the house. As they drove past Mrs. Williams's cottage, Rebecca noticed that there was a group of men surrounding Mrs. Williams on the front porch, the most obvious of which was Alex Raeburn.

"Charlie! Do you see that? What are Raeburn and his cronies doing with Mrs. Williams? Should we go and try to help her?"

He laughed, rather dryly "No, dear. That is a regular event. The weekly meeting of Culpeper's I Hate Charlie Redmond – or more accurately That Man – Club. Richard is keeping an eye on them, but since technically they are perfectly within their rights to visit and pay respects to the Widow Williams, there is nothing he can do."

Rebecca harrumphed.

They rode on to the train station. They had selected a young man, John Foxworth, who was a recent graduate from the University of Pennsylvania. He had a strong background in history, literature and languages, as well as a good record in basic mathematics and sciences – in other words, a well-rounded liberal arts education. He was qualified to teach the children French, Latin and German. He even spoke a few words of Spanish, Russian and Chinese. And he had been absolutely fantastic with the younger Redmonds when he visited for his earlier interview.

Darby had started asking him questions as soon as they got into the library, while showing him the books he had already read. Young Foxworth had handled the questions smoothly and knowledgeably. What had convinced Charlie, though, was the glowing letter of recommendation Foxworth had received from their old friend, Walt Whitman, who had specifically noted that this man was, in his opinion, worthy of Charlie and Rebecca's trust. He wondered briefly if Foxworth had been one of Whitman's lovers, but was distracted from that thought by watching Foxworth with the girls and their disputed doll house.

They picked the tutor up at the station, and the station porter loaded his trunk and a couple of boxes of books into the back of the carriage. The ride home was polite and congenial. When they got there, Darby appeared, eager to help the young man settle into his room. By the time dinner was finished, he seemed like a long-time member of the household. He announced that lessons would begin on Monday morning.

~

Monday, September 3, 1866

Immediately after breakfast, John led Darby, Suzanne and Em to the old library on the first floor, which had been converted into a proper school room for the children. They had left the nursery, where the children had been taking their hit and miss lessons up until then, to the two baby boys. Foxworth handed Darby a thick tome – a history of England from the reign of Alfred the Great to modern times. "Please, read the first chapter and we will discuss it this afternoon."

He went to the other side of the room, where a chalk board had been set up on an easel, and called the two girls to sit in front of him. He started with the alphabet, working his way through the letters to see what the girls knew and what he would need to teach them. Each girl had her own slate, on which they carefully drew each letter and a picture of something that started with that letter. Within an hour, they had worked their way through the first third of the alphabet before he let them go and play, while he went to talk with Darby, who was already full of questions.

~

Charlie sat in his office at the bank reading and rereading the most current financial news. He was actually starting to feel like he understood it the second time around. He made a few notes for the next time he spoke to Jerome. Looking out his office door he was happy to see several people in the lobby, waiting for one of the three tellers to be available. It had only been a few weeks, but so far he was pleased--the bank was busy and everyone seemed very happy to have it among the first businesses in Culpeper.

He pulled his watch from his vest pocket. It was time to start walking to Jocko's. He had promised Rebecca he would meet her there for lunch after her appointment with Elizabeth. He had been alarmed and concerned when she said it was a professional appointment until she assured him that occasionally a lady just needed to speak with her doctor and that nothing was amiss.

He fetched his new cane from the corner and headed out. As he left the bank, one man quickly stepped out of his way and touched the brim of his hat, "General Redmond, sir."

He forced a smile and nodded, then continued down the street. Even though the thoroughfare leading to Jocko's was busy, he noticed a definitive lack of foot traffic wherever he seemed to be walking. People appeared to be trying hard to blend into the woodwork or whatever convenient background they were leaning against. A few of the men made a show of saying good day and wishing him well as he made his way past.

He nodded to each one politely, knowing exactly why they were acting like this, but unable to say anything about it. It did not keep him from hating it. He made his way to Jocko's and sat at the bar. Jocko poured a coffee and placed it down in front of him. "That is a very sour face."

"Mmm." He grunted and reached for the sugar bowl.

"So what crawled up your arse and died?" Jocko leaned on the bar. He could not wait to hear this one, from the one man in town who had no reason to complain.

"You do not want to hear it."

He continued to lean against the bar, his chin resting in the palm of his right hand as he tried his best to look bored. "You are right, probably not, but unfortunately I am both your friend and a barkeep, so I have to listen. You have me over a double barrel."

"Have you noticed how everyone is acting now?"

"Oh, you mean that bowing and scraping everyone seems to be doing as Your Highness walks by? Aye, I noticed." He bowed at the waist with a great flourish of both arms.

"Stop it! This is not what I wanted." The general groused, stirring his coffee with a bit more force than necessary.

"You were complaining when everyone was outright hostile. Now half of them are impressed, and half of them are petrified, but no one is hostile, and yer still complaining! You should have been a bloody Brit."

Charlie tugged his glove off and lifted his right hand, dropping his first finger.

"Oh well, isn't that nice from the distinguished general!" Jocko snapped as he turned and stomped toward the kitchen.

When Rebecca arrived, she and Charlie sat together at a small table near the window that was her favorite. "What is for lunch?" She asked, removing her hat and gloves.

"I suspect whatever Jocko comes out here and dumps in my lap."

"Oh Charlie, what did you do to Jocko?"

"I just saluted him." He grinned as he sipped his coffee.

She noticed the cane leaning against the table. "Is that new?"

"Mmm," he nodded, handing it to her. "Had to replace the one I broke on that hard headed son of a bitch."

The thick black cane was truly beautiful, but she noticed three things immediately. It was denser and heavier than the last cane. And where his first cane had a simple, silver handle, this one was far more ornate. It was the small, elevated CHR repeated continuously around the circumference that caught her attention.

She adjusted her chair to get a better look at it in the sunlight. "Charles Huger Redmond, what exactly is this?"

"A monogrammed cane?" He raised a brow making absolutely no effort to look innocent.

She shook her head as she pointed at the silver top. "No. Charlie. This is a weapon. You have had your initials raised all around the side of this. This is a branding iron."

"Only if it needs to be."

～

Thursday, September 6, 1866

Charlie sat in the dining room chair, a bit forward toward the edge. His hands gripped the arms, rubbing them in anxious frustration.

"Relax." Rex's voice was, as always, low and calm. "When you're ready."

Charlie nodded and then pushed up from the chair. For the first time in nearly a year and a half he was standing under his own power without aid of crutch, cane or another person. He grinned when he realized he was actually very stable on his feet.

Rex stood at the opposite side of the room near the veranda doors. His arms crossed over his chest as he silently willed his friend to take the all important first step. *Come on, Charlie. Do it.*

Charlie moved his right leg and foot forward, taking his first step without excruciating pain tearing through his body. It was easy to take the second, then the third. Very shortly, he was standing in front of Rex with a very stupid grin on his face. "I can walk."

"Yes, you can. I suspect that you can do much more than that. Come with me."

The smaller man turned and led Charlie out through the French doors to the porch. Duncan, Jocko and Jeremiah stood with Black Jack and another mount, both saddled and ready to go. The big black horse threw his head and pawed the ground the second he saw his master.

The former cavalry officer felt a lump in his throat as he looked at his faithful friends. He shook his head. "I cannot possibly…"

"You can and you will." Rex took him by the arm and led him closer to his horse and friends. "Listen to them."

"General," Duncan stepped forward and handed Jack's reins to his rightful rider. "W-we have d-d-done our best to keep him h-healthy and w-well exercised, b-but he m-m-misses you."

Jack took that moment to nudge Charlie's shoulder, which was his horse's way of asking why they were still standing there.

"I am just not sure…"

"I made you a special saddle, General Charlie." Jeremiah stepped forward, proudly laying his hand on one of the most beautifully made pieces of tack Charlie had ever seen. "It will support your right leg more comfortably and a special combination on the fork at the pommel with a bit of extra horn will make it easier to grip one handed."

"And now that you can properly bend that leg, there is no reason you can't mount your horse," Rex added quietly with a nod towards the increasingly anxious animal.

Jocko stepped forward. "Aye, Charlie. Rebecca and the other ladies are actually at my place this afternoon, cataloging the books Miss Charlotte ordered for the church and school. We were thinking that if you would want to ride into town, I could ride along. I need to get back to make sure they have not hung chintz curtains in the place."

Charlie cleared his throat, willing the tears he felt in his eyes not to fall. He nodded as he took his place at Jack's side and put his hand on the horn of the saddle. None of them realized they had all been holding their breath until he actually pulled himself up and onto Jack's back. He immediately relaxed in the saddle; it was quite clear Charles Redmond was back in his element.

Black Jack tossed his head quite happily, but stood stock still. He craned his thick neck and eyed his rider, ears twitching; he was waiting for his command.

"Slow and easy, old friend. Slow and easy," he told him with a pat to his neck and twitch of the reins.

Jocko pulled himself up on his horse and the two men set off at a slow, easy pace. Jack, sensing that Charlie was not as stable on his back as he could be, was being especially careful to provide a smooth ride. Rex nodded with satisfaction. He patted Duncan and Jeremiah on the shoulders. "Well done. Well done."

Jeremiah went off to find Darby. Duncan, who had penetrated

Rex's façade to some extent while watching Rex deal with Charlie's injuries, went off to discuss the kitchen at the manse with him.

～

"I so wish it were different, but so many of these children have no opportunity to learn even the most basic things except in Sunday school." Charlotte sighed as she started to unpack the case of primers that was one of the books she had ordered and was donating to the church. "I probably spend more time teaching basic reading, writing and arithmetic than I do teaching bible stories."

Grace Cooper nodded as she opened a case of readers for slightly older children. "Yes, but they are needed on the farms, so their parents have to choose between having the help they need to bring in crops, put them up and prepare for the winter and sending them to school. At least you can work bible stories into your reading lessons."

"Perhaps with the school opening, they can spend some time in the mornings – just basics, reading, writing, arithmetic, geography, history – and do their farm work in the afternoons. All children deserve to acquire the basic skills." Rebecca stopped inspecting the small, wood framed slates she was unpacking to look up at the other ladies. "The new school teacher, Miss Reynolds' cousin, has been in town for a while. I am so glad that Andrew convinced her that Culpeper was a good community when he met her before Antietam. We can start her off at the Sunday school and see if we can get some commitments from some of the parents to send their children to the school after harvest."

Something was wrong. Grace and Charlotte were both sitting across the table from her; Missy Frazier was sitting beside her. Both of the women across from her had half risen out of their chairs, their mouths working like fish out of water, but no sound was coming forth. Wordlessly, Charlotte pointed over and past Rebecca's shoulder, shaking her finger aimed at something outside and directly behind her.

Rebecca looked confused. So did Missy Frazier. Both women rose and turned around to see what their friends were gawking at.

When she looked out the window, she found herself face to face with Black Jack. The big horse jerked his head up gently, indicating that she should look up. Her eyes travelled over the horse's very perked ears to see a face with a big toothy grin, smiling down at her. One she never expected to see on top of a horse again. Charlie was back in the saddle and leaning forward on it like an absolute rake with that silly grin on his face. His expression told her that somehow his world had righted itself.

The slate that she had been holding, slipped from her fingers, falling to the floor and cracking. Neither Rebecca nor any of the other women took any notice. She bolted out from behind the table, knocking several books to the floor, and charged through the front door of the tea room that Jocko and Esther had added to one side of the tavern. She flew across the porch, jumped the two steps down to the street and grabbed on to Jack's left stirrup and Charlie's left leg as she looked at them both in wonder. "Oh, my God! Oh, my dear God," she gasped.

"Sweetheart, I am certainly not a god. But I would like to know if the ladies can spare you for the rest of the afternoon." He grinned down at her. "So, madam, would you like a ride home on the back of your knight's gallant steed? I think Jack can carry us both even though he has gotten fat and lazy."

The horse heard his name, and nodded his head up and down again. Then as if he had realized what Charlie had said, he gave an annoyed snort and turned his head to give him a one-eyed glare. Jack's timing was, as always, impeccable. The various people witnessing this moment laughed heartily at the horse's antics.

Charlie reached down, and at the same time, bent his left leg back, offering his wife, who was a consummate horsewoman under any circumstances, a leg up. She hiked her skirts up and swung on to Jack's back, wrapping her arms around Charlie's chest. "Shall we go home, husband? How are you feeling?"

He turned his head back to look at her with yet another silly grin. "Horny."

She captured his head in her hands and quickly kissed him before wrapping them back around his waist, "Oooo, I can help you with that."

~

His grin was practically predatory and it made Rebecca tingle all the way to her toes. It had been a long time since he looked at her like that. He moved forward, pushing them both through the front door. Their lips met and they started up the stairs. She was not even completely sure a groom had been up front to take Jack back to the barn. All she knew was her husband was sweeping her off feet again after a year and a half. It felt wonderful.

Since he had come home and begun the long road to recovery, they had remained as close as his injuries would allow. He had been in so much pain that even their intimate moments had been an effort for him. He had spent every moment he had when he felt well making her feel loved, wanted and desired. Though she had tried, her efforts to reciprocate had been met with polite denials of need she knew were utter nonsense, but there was only so much he could manage and he always chose her happiness, contentment and pleasure over his own.

Now, she felt him tugging at her skirts, his breathing ragged in her ear as his lips kissed her neck making her weak in the knees. "Charlie," she gasped.

"Our. Bed. Now!" He growled his demand, even as he began working the buttons on his own vest.

She could not help but laugh at his frantic clawing of his own clothing. She grasped both his hands and said gently. "Easy there, big fella..." She led him up the stairs and down the hall by the hand, laughing all the way to the bedroom.

~

Rebecca lay draped over Charlie's body. Both of them were working hard to breathe and focus, their bodies slick and warm against each other. Rebecca wiggled with delight as his fingers grazed over her bare back.

"You," he gulped, kissing her very damp brow. "Are very good at that."

"You are not so bad yourself." She chuckled, placing a kiss on a chest still vibrating with the hard pounding of the heart under her ear and hand.

"Mmmm." Charlie just nodded, His eyes drifting closed, happy and content to be supporting almost all of Rebecca's weight.

"You are going to sleep on me?" Rebecca gave Charlie a playful poke. "Oh, I do not think so." She laughed even as she began kissing her way down her partner's lanky body…again.

～

"Rebecca!" Charlie chortled, fighting off playful hands. "Woman, we have to eat!" He laughed as he got up and put his robe on, leaving his diminutive partner lying back in their very messy bed with a rumpled sheet pulled over her reclined form. They had come home midday and no one had seen them since.

He has lost track of the number of times they had made love and then dozed in each other's arms only to wake up and do it all over again. They had truly never enjoyed each other this much and he was simply awed by it. It felt good to feel whole again. He knew he owed Rex a debt he could never repay, especially now.

"I do not know about you, but I have worked up quite an appetite." He gestured between them. "We have been busy. I am hungry."

She adjusted the pillows on the bed so they supported her as she pulled the sheet modestly over her. "Supper is long over, Charlie."

"Wife," he fetched his slippers from under the sofa. "Do you think this is the first time I have raided a kitchen?"

"In your robe? Yes." She nodded with confidence.

He laughed as he tightened the knot at his waist. "You may have me there. However, I am confident that I can successfully perform

407

this particular midnight raid without Sarah catching me in my current state."

"Mmm." His wife merely nodded, absolutely amused by his antics. This was her Charlie. Her sweet, silly Charlie. The man she had married. The man she so desperately tried to bring home. He had finally returned to her. She knew that Rex was to thank and she made a mental note to do so.

"I shall return in a flash with sustenance for our weary flesh." He kissed her on the brow.

He padded to the bedroom door pulling it open and nearly tripping over the large silver tray that sat in front of the door. He snorted as he retrieved the tray and closed the door. "Seems, my darling, that our needs have been anticipated by our dedicated staff."

He brought the tray to the bed where they found a selection of meats, cheeses, bread and fruit. The makings of a perfectly lovely dinner of finger foods. The ingredients for tea and coffee were included on the tray but not prepared. They could boil the required water in the kettle in their room if they wished.

He plucked a strawberry from a small bowl, dipped in the provided sugar and offered it to her. "Something sweet?"

"I have had you for hours so now I will live with the strawberry," she quipped before biting it from his fingers.

They sat there, quietly for a few minutes, just eating and glancing shyly at each other almost as if they had just met. Eventually the ridiculousness of the situation became too much and they finally just burst out laughing at the same time.

"I do believe, dear husband, that this is how newlyweds are truly supposed to feel."

"I am so sorry it took so long." He shook his head giving her a remorseful look.

"Do not apologize, Charlie." She laid her hand on his. "We knew it would be a long road and while I would like to think this is the end, you must know it is just the end of this particular part of our journey together. We still have five children to raise. A farm to run. A community that is relying on us to lead the way. We have lots of forks to choose from before us."

He was mostly listening to her. Rebecca had either not noticed or simply did not care the sheet had pooled around her waist. Wordlessly, he sat the tray aside and then crawled up on the bed, starting slowly at the foot and prowling his way up to her. She was now giggling again. She tugged the belt of the robe and everything serious was once again forgotten as the lovers explored each other one more time.

CHAPTER 23

Tuesday, September 11, 1866

Charlie stood on the front porch of the house, with Em at his side. She clutched the fingers of his right hand in her left and held her doll firmly against her chest with her right. She was having a Papa day and had refused to be parted from him even for a moment. Tess continued to check back regularly to make sure he was not ready to be rid of his little shadow. He just continued to smile, wave her off, and take his little girl all over the farm with him. At least he made her keep her shoes on now.

Tess had never seen a man so dedicated to his children. Usually the men handed the children off as soon as they were born and had nothing more to do with them until they could dress themselves and ride a horse. Not General Charlie. He spent time every day with every child. He was as well aware of what went on with them on a daily basis as Miss Rebecca was.

Charlie's ears perked up when he heard the transport wagon rolling up to the house. Carefully, guiding Em down the steps, he waited for the wagon to stop in front of the house. "Wait until you see this, Emily."

"What is it, Papa?" She was craning her neck now. There was a big wagon with two men on the driver's seat and two more men riding on back next to something covered by a big canvas. "Present for Em?"

"No." He smiled and scooped her up on his good hip. "A present for Papa." He moved to the wagon. "Good day, gentlemen. I assume that is my delivery from Baltimore?"

"It is indeed, General Redmond. We'll get it unloaded right quick. Want it here or closer to the barn?"

"Here is fine." He nodded. He stepped back as the men pulled the canvas off revealing a shiny new black gentleman's coach. It was beautifully trimmed in red with rich, dark leather seats. He stepped back and returned Emily to the ground, warning her to stay well back while the men rolled the new carriage off the back of the wagon.

It only took the men a few minutes to get the coach off the wagon. Charlie signed the bill of lading and they were on their way back down the drive, leaving him there to inspect the new vehicle.

"Really, Charlie?"

He had been inspecting the wheels when he heard Rebecca's voice behind him. He stood up and turned slowly, giving her a grin. "Really."

She just shook her head as she joined her husband and her daughter down by the new coach. "And we need a new coach why?"

"Well, darling, to be fair, I ordered it when I was still a cripple." He laughed as he opened the door and lifted Em inside so she could try out the new seats. "It is like the one we used in Baltimore. It was very smooth. It had a lovely ride. Remember?"

She nodded and just kissed him on the cheek. "If this is going to become a habit with you, tell me now so I can be prepared for the next thirty years."

"What?"

"This tendency you have of just buying things and having them delivered to the house."

He nodded. "Get used to it." He looked down at her less than happy smile and sighed. "Sweetheart, when I was in the army, I rarely ever spent any money on myself or anyone else for that matter. I had everything I needed and no one I loved enough to spoil. Now, I have the money. Money that we have because I spent nearly twenty years sending paychecks to Jerome. I want to enjoy life. I want you and the children to enjoy life, and if that means we spend the money, then we spend the money."

It was a beautiful fall day and there was no other way the Redmond family would prefer to spend it than with their horses, especially now that Charlie was back in the saddle. There seemed to be a new energy among the family and around the farm.

Lizbet and Tess stood keeping an eye on the boys as they tried to struggle out of the strollers that were containing their rambunctious little bodies. It was clear why they wanted to be up and out--Mama and Papa were out there with their brother and sisters and everyone was playing on a horse, but them.

Charlie was actually walking around the ring, Jack standing as patiently as he could manage near the fence. He was focused on Darby and his brown and white paint pony. "Very good, Darby. Take him to a trot." He smiled as the boy and horse immediately made the transition.

He was putting his son through all of his paces to make sure he had actually mastered the ability to ride and handle the pony. In a few days, the boy would be getting his first real horse. It was crucial that he was confident enough to take on the larger animal.

Rebecca and a groom were working with the girls and their little tan Shetlands. The girls were being taught by Mama how to appropriately sit sidesaddle. She made sure to walk with each girl, showing them how to properly balance and maintain a safe seat.

Finally, the littlest boys could stand it no more and the dual shriek at the top of their lungs made everyone, human and animal, stop and look. Charlie could only laugh as he walked over and peeked through the fence at his littlest troopers. They immediately began reaching for him, their strollers scooting forward as they tried their best to get to their papa.

He stood and whistled, Jack came immediately and he climbed up into the saddle. Each time he did it, his mount was smoother and smoother. Rebecca decided that it would not be long before he was vaulting back into the saddle.

He gestured to Tess and she handed Buddy up to him. He settled the toddler safely in front and wrapped his right arm firmly around his stomach. "Hold on," he told his son as he nudged Jack into a slow walk around the ring. Buddy was thrilled, hanging tight to the saddle horn, laughing and then clapping. Finally he looked back with a very serious look on his face and said, "Go fast, Papa. Jack go!"

He gave Jack a low whistle and the big horse immediately picked up the pace, though it seemed as if he could tell he had one of the general's foals aboard as he was being extremely careful with his footing. The faster ride with papa caused more shrieking and laughing from the little body in front of him. He took Buddy around the ring a few times, and then traded out sons. Andy's reaction was very much like Buddy's and before long he too was demanding, "Make Jack fast!"

~

Wednesday, September 19, 1866

Edgar had headed into town for the Wednesday evening gentlemen's prayer meeting. Since Charlie and Richard were intent on supporting Edgar's efforts to continue to reach out to and combine the community, they were both in attendance. It also gave Charlie a legitimate excuse to have dinner at Jocko's and enjoy Esther's outstanding pork chops. So Elizabeth had packed little Dickon up and wended her way out to Redmond Stables for dinner with Rebecca, Charlotte and Rex.

Rex had promised to teach the ladies a new game, and she was looking forward to the distraction as something to hold over the gentlemen and their weekly poker game.

Sarah served a light supper for the assembly, with chicken, a fresh salad, and a mix of the freshest vegetables she had harvested from the kitchen garden that afternoon. They ate quickly, then adjourned to the back parlor and the beautiful set of multi-colored inscribed tiles that Rex had laid out on the gaming table.

"Ladies, Mah Johng is a traditional game from my country, rather like a simple card game, but with the tiles taking the place of the cards. Like poker, we look for both runs – sets of tiles in the same suit in numerical sequence, and sets – tiles of the same type. There are four tiles of each numerical value in each suit, and there are bonus tiles." He spent a few minutes showing the ladies each suit of tiles and the various bonus tiles, then dealt the first hand. The ladies juggled their 13 tiles into the stakes provided to hold them, and started learning how to play the game. The tiles were beautiful, and had the silky quality of ivory, making them a pleasure to handle. But soon, the ladies were less attracted to the texture and more committed to the strategy of the game.

After a while, Charlotte looked up from her hand and asked, "So, what is the betting tradition for this game?"

He just smiled, a slightly wolfish smile, and explained how to bet on each hand, round, and game.

The evening progressed nicely, with the ladies struggling to master the nuances of what they had discovered looked like a simple game and was not. Finally, Rebecca sighed, as she had been losing consistently all evening. "I give up for the night. Shall I get us some coffee?"

"Certainly. On both counts. But we will have to do this again." Elizabeth, who had been winning almost as regularly as Rex, had acquired the same wolfish look that he had.

With coffee served around the table and the tiles put away, Rebecca got a thoughtful look on her face. "The three of you may be able to provide some insight into Charlie's behavior for me. From the perspective of friends who know him, very well on a variety of different levels. What Rex has done for Charlie is simply a miracle."

The other ladies nodded their agreement. "He is back to being the man he was when we first met and were married. I cannot tell if it is because he is no longer using the laudanum, or if it is because of the healing that has been facilitated in his arm and leg, or if it is because he is back on Jack, or what, but he has changed, and in a very good way. Even his nightmares have nearly stopped."

Elizabeth looked both thoughtful and somewhat guilty. "I am so sorry I allowed him to become dependent on the drugs, dear."

"Oh, you should not feel guilty. When we brought him back from Appomattox, he was a disaster. I was afraid he would not survive, let alone heal. You did what you had to do keep him alive. I will always be grateful to you for that."

Rex added to her comments. "Dr. Elizabeth, if you had not done what you did, he would not be alive, or would have at least lost that leg. I find no fault and a great deal of both courage and skill in what you did. I simply added a different approach to healing that supports what you accomplished. I would be happy to teach you some of my methods for rehabilitation, to support your skill as a surgeon."

"I would be happy to have you work with me on some of my other patients. I am sure I could learn much from you."

Charlotte grinned. "They are doctor-bonding. How sweet!"

Rex smiled gently, as Rebecca resumed her ruminations. "So I have some questions. For example, Elizabeth, if Charlie had been a real man, do you think his injuries would have affected his ability to, um… perform his husbandly duties?"

Everyone at the table paused for a moment, then Charlotte and Elizabeth both broke into nervous giggles.

Rex intervened. "Rebecca, what you have to realize about Charlie is that he is a real man. He just came in the wrong wrapper – a two spirited person, as I explained to you before. But he has always thought and acted like a man, and if you push him, he will respond like a man."

Charlotte and Elizabeth, in unison, chimed in with, "Just ask Alex Raeburn."

She thought back. That Charlie frightened her, as much as Gaines had when he was in his cups. But that Charlie was sober and defending her, so it was a very different situation, now that she really considered it.

Elizabeth looked at her, realizing she was the actual doctor in the room. "As to your question, you know I worked hard to put him back together – or as back together as I could. Given the severity of those wounds, I believe that if he had a penis and testicles, from my experience, I think they would have been severely damaged, so the answer is probably no, he probably would not be able to, um, perform?"

Rebecca thought about this for a moment, realizing that she was asking it badly, but trying to understand the evolution of his mood and behavior and very grateful that she had her Charlie back.

Charlotte looked at her friend very closely. "So tell me, Cousin, what has prompted this line of questions? Are you seeing Charlie in a different light than you used to?"

She blushed a deep red. "Well, now that you mention it, yes, I rather have. When he and I first met, I saw him as a woman in man's clothing, but over the past months, and especially as Rex started working with him to restore as much functionality as possible..." She trailed off, confused in her own mind. ●

Charlotte picked up for her. "So you mean you have started to see him as a man all the time? And this appeals to you? Or is it that now that he is feeling better, he has a libido again and that is very exciting? By the way, the walls in this house are thick, but they are not that thick."

Rex tapped the table with his coffee spoon in agreement.

Elizabeth chimed in, "And you have both been grinning like idiots for the last two weeks."

She blushed again. She should have known better than to get these three started on a subject like this.

Rex smiled. "Actually, if he was a naturally born male, and he no longer had sexual capacity, he would probably not have a libido. So consider yourself lucky that he is a two-spirited person."

"Oh, I do." She nodded with a grin as she sipped her coffee, leaving her table mates in another fit of giggles. She placed her cup back in the saucer and shook her head, "Thank you all for humoring me. I am afraid that I am not explaining myself or my questions very well, but I do appreciate your efforts."

Elizabeth nodded. "Rebecca, I am sure I can speak for our friends here," she gestured to either side of her, "when I say we understand there are very few people you can openly talk to about these things. As your physician, I am always available to you, but I understand it can be comforting to speak with friends and I am glad I am included here as well. I think you can rely on us at any time."

Rex and Charlotte nodded immediately and Rebecca smiled. "Thank you."

Charlotte sat straight in her chair and offered, "I would like to say I have known Charlie a long time, almost as long as Elizabeth."

"Perhaps even a bit longer," Elizabeth agreed with a nod.

"This Charlie," Charlotte continued, as she tapped her finger on the table, "is very different from Captain Redmond, or Major Redmond, or any incarnation of the soldier that Charlie Redmond was. His place in your world reinforces and redefines his manhood, his maleness, in a way the army never did. The," she ticked them off on her fingers as she said, "husband, father, landowner, horse breeder, banker, and leader of the community that he has become with you, is so different from the simple solider that he was when we first knew him. Especially, since it is a place in the world he never expected to achieve. It is not surprising that you are seeing him in a different light as well. I think we all are to some extent."

"Absolutely." Elizabeth nodded. "Well said, dear."

Just then, they heard the sounds of Edgar, Charlie and Richard returning. Rebecca looked at her guests, and smiled. "Thank you. You three are the only people in the world I could turn to for advice on this. And please, please, do NOT mention this conversation to Charlie – or Richard or Edgar. Please, keep my confidence." They all nodded their agreement and understanding.

All four were laughing gently when the gentlemen came into the room a few minutes later.

~

Wednesday, September 26, 1866

Charlie stood in the front hall shuffling through the thick stack of envelopes he had collected while in town that morning. As was his habit, he split them into two piles: one he had to deal with, and the other was all Rebecca's. As he sorted down to the last envelope, he was surprised to find an official letter from West Point.

He left his pile of letters on the table near the steps up to his office and made his way with Rebecca's mail to her office. She was nowhere to be found so he dropped the mail on her desk before taking a seat in her chair and plucking a letter opener from the holder on her desk.

He slit the envelope carefully and pulled out the letter.

Brigadier General Charles H. Redmond

Redmond Stables

Culpeper, Virginia

Lieutenant General Thomas Gamble Pitcher

Superintendent, United States Military Academy

West Point, New York

13 September 1866

Dear General Redmond,

As the summer encampment has ended and the fall academic year has begun at West Point, the second year, third class Corp of Cadets have requested that I inquire upon your person and invite you to come lecture the fourth week in October of this year. We would be honored to have you do a three part lecture series on your engagement and campaign at Appomattox Station as is appropriate for their Tactics of Infantry, Artillery, and Cavalry classes.

We look forward to your positive response.

Cordially,

Thomas Gamble Pitcher

Superintendent, United States Military Academy

P.S. Charlie, please, feel free to bring this beautiful wife of yours that Jerome is always going on about. Looking forward to seeing you again, old friend. – Tom

He was considering the invitation in his hand when Rebecca came through the doors. Dressed in her boots and britches, it was clear she had been in the barns. Even if her clothing had not given it away, the smell certainly would have.

"Whoa! That is a mighty odor!" He stated, waving the letter in front of his nose. Her presence was actually making his eyes water.

"Why thank you, kind sir. The manure spreader broke." She offered a little bow.

"I never would have guessed." He coughed a little as another wave assaulted his nose. He rose from the desk chair.

"I am going to need a long soak in our tub tonight."

"Yes, you are. I will be more than happy to wash your back." He wiggled his brows as he offered his wife her rightful seat at her desk.

She settled in her chair and leaned on her desk, chin in palm. "I may take you up on that, if I have the energy reserves. What brings you down here?"

"I was just dropping your mail and having a look at this." He rattled the letter. "It is an invitation to lecture at The Point the fourth week of October."

"West Point? That is wonderful! A great honor, I would think."

He nodded. "It is. I am afraid we will have to pull my uniforms out of storage and get my trousers altered to fit my new frame. Jocko has a tailor in Washington he had always trusted for my clothes."

She sat up and smiled, "Nonsense! I can alter your uniforms." She smiled, "And I can make sure that everything fits just the way it should."

Sunday, September 30, 1866

Rebecca woke early that morning so that she could artfully arrange her gift to Charlie for his birthday before he could dress in his usual clothing. For the past three months, she had been planning, designing, then knitting and stitching new undergarments for him, making sure that not only was he unaware of what she was doing, but so were all of the other inhabitants of the household.

She had made him a tightly knitted under-vest, made of the finest silk yarn she could find, that would restrain his small breasts without binding, had enough give so he could breathe easily, and was much lighter and, she considered, had to be more comfortable, than the bandages he had wrapped around himself for so many years. With the careful insertion of old pieces of whalebone stays, split and trimmed to the correct shape, the vest even gave his chest the look of lightly sculpted musculature under his shirt. It also provided him with a good excuse to wear such an undershirt with just a shirt on over it, rather than always wearing his coat and vest, no matter how hot it got. If someone noticed and inquired, he could say it was there to provide a bit of bracing and support for his injuries.

She had spent more time and care in creating new underpants for him. Again, using the small, tight rib knit stitch and the extremely fine silk yarn, fortified with elastic in appropriate places, and similarly padded in appropriate places to lend bulk and shape to the areas where muscle was missing, and in places where gentlemen normally had a bit of a bulge. His pants – even those skin tight ones that were part of his dress uniform, would look better with these light weight, but structurally enhancing garments.

Charlie looked at the new undergarments with wonder. They felt so soft and fine and light that he could not understand how they could enhance his form, but when he tried them on, and realized just what they did, he spent several minutes in front of Rebecca's full length mirror, turning this way and that, admiring himself. "Darling, they are wonderful. They are so light and cool, I almost feel like I am naked, but they make me look good – really good." He swept her into his arms and kissed her soundly. "Thank you so much, my love."

She grinned, then pulled open the top drawer of his dresser. There, carefully folded, were six more pairs. One for each day of the week. He swept her up again and kissed her thoroughly, then decided that he was overdressed for the moment.

Rebecca watched as he slid his suspenders over his shoulders. It was the farmer look that always made her smile. He rolled his sleeves to the elbow and then ran his hands over the front of his shirt. "It is amazing. I am not sure how to act now that I do to have to wear so many layers."

"I had hoped they would make you more comfortable."

"They most certainly do, darling. Thank you. You are a very clever woman. I am a lucky fellow." He picked his jacket up and gave a little grin as he placed it over the wooden rack near his wardrobe.

He sat down on the sofa and tugged on his boots as Rebecca finished getting herself together before they rounded up the family for breakfast and then church. Charlie stood and moved to the veranda doors, having a look down towards the barn.

She chuckled as she finished checking her reflection in the mirror, realizing what was going on in his head. "It arrived yesterday evening, just as planned. But please remember that even though it is your birthday, it is Sunday. Breakfast first. Services. And then birthday celebrations."

He closed the doors to the veranda and sighed. "Yes, dear." He had forgotten it was Sunday and thought he had a day off. He rolled his sleeves back down, plucked his necktie from the stand, tied it and fastened it with a stickpin, then pulled on his vest and frock coat. "I am now ready for the morning's obligations."

The trip into church that morning was interesting. Darby tried to be a gentleman, but the general excitement of having a birthday that was actually going to be celebrated was a little more than he could contain. He was halfway between bouncing and trembling with suppressed excitement. Charlie was not much better.

With the changes in the Redmond family over the past few months, their pew was rather crowded. But they settled in amicably, with the girls seated between Rebecca and Charlotte. They had chosen to leave the boys at home, since one-year-olds were not required to attend, and teething children could be decidedly disruptive. Charlie and Darby anchored the two ends of their pew.

Edgar and Mr. Cooper, both knowing it was Charlie's and Darby's birthday, had each prepared a small honor for the Redmond men. Edgar's sermon was based on the theme of "Our brother's keepers." He started with the story of Cain, who had defied God by asking sarcastically "Am I my brother's keeper," and was punished with the mark of Cain for his disobedience and his sins. But Edgar went on, to use Paul's discussion in 1st Corinthians of how the Church is like the human body, made up of many members, all of whom are important to the function and well-being of the body. He finished his sermon with Paul's great admonishment about love that begins in Chapter 13.

If I speak in the tongues of men and of angels, but have not love, I am a noisy gong or a clanging cymbal. And if I have prophetic powers, and understand all mysteries and all knowledge, and if I have all faith, so as to remove mountains, but have not love, I am nothing. If I give away all I have, and if I deliver up my body to be burned, but have not love, I gain nothing.

Love is patient and kind; love does not envy or boast; it is not arrogant or rude. It does not insist on its own way; it is not irritable or resentful; it does not rejoice at wrongdoing, but rejoices with the truth. Love bears all things, believes all things, hopes all things, endures all things.

Love never ends. As for prophecies, they will pass away; as for tongues, they will cease; as for knowledge, it will pass away. For we know in part and we prophesy in part, but when the perfect comes, the partial will pass away. When I was a child, I spoke like a child, I thought like a child, I reasoned like a child. When I became a man, I gave up childish ways. For now we see in a mirror dimly, but then face to face. Now I know in part; then I shall know fully, even as I have been fully known.

So now faith, hope, and love abide, these three; but the greatest of these is love.

"And so I admonish you all to remember, love IS the greatest of all. Love thy brother, for you are thy brother's keeper."

He spoke the last words, looking pointedly at those in the congregation who had made it clear they were not accepting of those in the community who had supported the Union cause.

Edward Cooper rose to read the weekly announcements. He called out the names of those who were ill, those who were visiting, and the events of the week. His final announcement was directed at the Redmond pew. "Finally, we wish to extend our best wishes to both General Redmond and his oldest son Darby, who share this day as the anniversary of their births."

Charlie smiled and Darby grinned.

The congregation filed out of the church, with the usual separation of pro-Unionists, who were congratulating Charlie and Darby, and the hard-core southerners pointedly snubbing them. Edgar, standing on the church steps, once again noticed the division within his congregation.

Obviously, his lecture had absolutely no impact. The anti-unionists gathered around Alex Raeburn, who was sporting a very obvious scar across his nose and a very bitter look on his face. The flesh around his eyes was still showing traces of yellow and green, where the black and blue had faded over the weeks. It particularly disturbed Edgar that Mrs. Williams was part of Raeburn's crowd.

Charlie was in a hurry to get home. He wanted to give Darby his gift and had had to wait far longer than he wanted to already. Rebecca looked at her husband as they waited for the coach to come around and tried but failed to keep the smile from her face. "I do believe that you are more excited about this than Darby is."

Darby had run off to one side of the churchyard with Jeremiah to share a few minutes before the coach came, and was bouncing like a rubber ball in anticipation of the birthday celebrations.

"Who, me? Why would you think that I am excited? Just because I am about to give my oldest son his first real horse, why would I be excited?" He grinned at his wife, knowing perfectly well that she understood the importance of this moment for him, especially as he had feared he would never be able to teach his children to ride because of his war wounds.

He had been able to start the children on their ponies, giving direction to them from the ground. But since Darby was graduating to a horse, and would soon be old enough to ride with the hunt, the things Charlie needed to teach him now could only be done on horseback.

"Albert did a splendid job of finding a horse that would meet our needs. Not only does he have a lovely temperament, but he also resembles Jack. In fact, if I did not know better, I would think Jack had sired him. I am sure Darby will be thrilled." She grinned at her overeager husband.

The coach finally arrived, and Darby came running up, breathless and impatient. The Redmonds headed home, with the usual contingent of participants in the Sunday supper to follow at their leisure. Rebecca laughed as Charlie told Tomas to make his best time. She quietly added to his instructions, telling Tomas to pull around to the stables. She then turned to her men. "Gentlemen!" she chided gently. "We will be home very shortly."

Darby, who could barely stay still, bouncing in his seat with eleven-year-old excitement, nodded enthusiastically. "Yes, ma'am. I will try to be good." He tried to be still. He knew that birthdays were special at Redmond Stables, and always included cake and good food. "But could we please hurry?" He anticipated books for his birthday. He loved getting books of his very own.

She sighed as she watched her husband and son both behave like excited eleven-year-olds. Suzanne reached over and patted her hand as she often did when she believed her mama was distressed. She smiled and caressed her daughter's cheek. "Thank you, sweetheart. Mama is fine."

Rather than pull up in front of the house, Tomas drove the coach around to the stable yard. Darby's eyes grew enormously. Both Darby and Charlie looked like they were going to jump out of the coach before it came to a stop. It was clear to the boy that books were not the only gift he was getting for his birthday.

Charlie looked to Rebecca for permission. "Ma'am, I think that your gentlemen are being called by the siren song of the paddock. May we?"

"Go," she tempered the command with a smile. "Before Darby or you combust."

Both of them, man and boy, jumped from the coach, and moved as quickly as Charlie could to the paddock. Looking closely, you could tell that he still moved with a limp, and probably always would. But the time spent in Rex's care had been an absolute miracle. It was a blessing, she thought.

Darby, who was usually a pretty self-contained little gentleman, was babbling away as he gazed at the beautiful, black Morgan gelding standing in the paddock, fully tacked up and ready to ride. "Papa Charlie, he is so beautiful! I think that he is the most beautiful horse in the stable, all black like Jack. Do you think he will be a good hunter? Can I join the hunt with you if he goes well? I know I could keep up, if you let me ride with you."

Charlie smiled and put his hand on the excited boy's shoulder. "We shall see, son, we shall see. I suppose that eleven is not too young to at least join the hill-toppers, but you must always remember to take care of your horse and obey the hunt master."

"Yes, sir. I promise. Perhaps someday I could be the hunt master?"

"Well, now, you do know that the hunt master has many obligations? You will have to learn many things – not only how to ride properly, but how to handle the hounds, how to organize the hunt, how to keep everyone up even though you ride in the front. Think you can learn all that?"

"I would like to try." The boy looked up to the tall man who was more of a father than he could remember his real father ever being. "Especially if it would make you proud."

He smiled at the boy beside him, who had tried so hard, and still did, to be a man long before his years. Very gently, he spoke, "Darby, lad. I am always proud of you. You are more mature, responsible, and honorable than many men three times your age. I think I worry more that you sometimes do not do the things that a boy should do, that you are trying to grow up too quickly."

Darby started to say something, but before he could, a groomsman led his new horse toward the paddock gate, and someone brought Jack out, also fully tacked up. Darby bolted for the fence.

As the boy ran, Charlie looked at him with a grin and shouted. "Happy birthday, son!"

Father and son mounted up, and Charlie began putting Darby through his paces. The two of them rode together, then Darby asked Charlie to make Jack do some of his fancy moves. He nudged Jack through basic dressage movements, starting with flying lead changes interspersed with half pirouettes that made the big black thoroughbred look like he was dancing.

As they played together, Charlie looked up toward the house. There were people all over the back yard, and tables loaded with food and drink. Big Ben was presiding over a smoking pit, with several other men extracting something from the ground. There was a barbeque going on without them!

"Darby!" He called. "I think we may have overstayed our time down here. We need to get up to the house. Your mother has guests up there waiting for us," he pointed. The boy looked up at the house, and flushed a deep red. He nodded his agreement, knowing the only reason Mama 'Becca would allow this lapse in good manners was because it was their birthday. They handed the horses off to Tarent, who has been watching and waiting, and hurried up the hill.

Tables were set all over the back yard. There were people roaming around the grounds, relaxed and happy, and the smell of barbecued pork and Big Ben's special sauce filled the air. Sarah had bowls of salads, vegetables and fruits, and platters of cheeses, breads, rolls, and biscuits laid out. Reg presided over the drinks table, with two large punch bowls and his usual array of bottles.

As the Redmond men came hustling up the hill, Rebecca called out to the guests, "Ah, ladies and gentlemen! Our guests of honor have decided to join us at last."

The crowd gathered around to wish them happy birthday. Edward Cooper said, in a carrying voice, "Thank God! Finally, we can eat!" This volley was greeted with laughter and agreement, as the guests queued up to serve themselves at the buffet spread before them. Charlie and Darby let everyone else be served before they got their plates, to atone for their delay down at the paddock.

Darby tried not to fidget in his chair as their birthday dinner was completed and the party adjourned to the gazebo. The girls had already presented both he and Papa Charlie with their little gifts of colored pictures of them mounted on their respective horses. Apparently, the little artistes had drawn from life when they were out together with Mama Rebecca watching them ride around the paddock together.

Finally, it was his turn to give his gift. He was very nervous and not sure how it would be received. Richard cleared his throat from the edge of the gazebo, where the box holding Charlie's new sword had been stashed before dinner. "Darby?" All of the guests stopped and turned to look at what was going on. They became very quiet, so that they could hear what was being said.

He nodded nervously and got up to accept the box. "Thank you, Uncle Richard," he said quietly. The box was long, a beautifully polished walnut with brass hinges and a plaque in the center boldly engraved with C.H.R. Darby carefully placed the box in Charlie's lap and retook his seat to his adopted father's right.

"I hope you like it, Papa Charlie. Uncle Richard helped me get it. He said that you would need this one now that all of your engagements would be ceremonial."

The general's fingers slid over the cool wood. He knew exactly what was in this box, even before he opened it. "Darby…" his voice was choked with emotion "Son…"

He realized his son had worked all summer for Richard and Elizabeth just to buy him this gift.

He slowly, reverently opened the box. Inside, laid out on a field of red velvet, was a new Cavalry Officer's dress sword along with an elaborately decorated scabbard, engraved thusly:

Brigadier General Chas. H. Redmond

United States Army (Retired)

Final command

13th Pennsylvania Cavalry

January 20, 1846

May 12, 1865

He could barely speak, as he first took Darby's hand and gave it a squeeze. As tears slipped down his cheeks he pulled the boy close into a long hug. "Thank you, son. It is beautiful."

"Are you sure you like it?" He pulled back. He was a little worried; he had never seen Papa Charlie cry before.

"I can assure you, Darby," his Mother said as she rubbed her husband's back from her seat next to him. "He loves it."

Charlie nodded, still too overcome by emotion to speak clearly; he just kept patting Darby on the head and running his fingers through his hair. Finally, he cleared his throat and managed to get out in a rather hoarse voice, "You have no idea you much this means to me, son. Thank you so much."

Darby stepped closer and again put his arms around Charlie's neck. "I am glad, Papa. I love you."

Richard and Elizabeth, Samantha, Jeremiah and Duncan Nailer, Mr. and Mrs. Cooper, Charlotte, Edgar and Rex, and the Fraziers were most closely gathered around the family table. They broke into applause as they embraced, and then Charlie proudly displayed his new dress sword to the attendees at the party.

CHAPTER 24

Saturday, October 6, 1866

When Charlie awoke, he could hear the rain pouring down on the roof. He lay there in bed, listening to the pattern of the rain and Rebecca's gentle breathing, easy and very relaxed. She was on her left side, her back to him. Slowly he rolled over and draped his arm around her waist, cuddling in behind her. This was his favorite time and place. The early mornings he spent holding her before she woke. He felt as if nothing could hurt or touch them as they lay there together, warm and content.

She took his wrist, quite by rote and pulled it tighter around her waist. "It is cold," she mumbled.

"Mmmhmm." He agreed quietly, pulling the quilt over her shoulder. "Early too."

"Why are you awake?"

"I have no idea. Maybe it is because I do this every morning."

She rolled over and tucked herself closer to him. "What do you do every morning?"

"Lie here, holding you while you sleep. Listening to you breathe in the quiet. It is very comforting to me."

"You are a hopeless romantic."

"Only when it comes to you, my darling." He held her closer.

"Well, it would seem we are awake now. Are you ready to do your exercises?"

"Which ones?" He asked with a laugh.

"The ones that Rex wants you to do. I hear the rain and feel the cold too, Charles Redmond. I know you must be stiff and a little sore."

"No, but I could be." He laughed as he began exploring her warm, soft frame. She could only laugh as she felt him lift her sleeping gown.

Rebecca came in the kitchen door. Shaking the rain off her hat and coat, she hung it on the hook, stopping dead in her tracks when she saw Charlie standing in the kitchen with a broom, making little sweeping motions at a small pile of white on the floor. She brushed the rain from her hands as she said, "This is a very interesting double standard, General Redmond."

Without a word, he just looked at the ceiling, shaking his head. She knew he was having another chat with God. Given how often he did that, she was fairly sure they were on a first name basis.

"Why is it I am not allowed to have a broom in my hand, but you are?"

"Because," Sarah's voice called from the pantry. "He broke the sugar bowl and I am making him clean it up."

Still silent, he lifted his brows at Rebecca and brushed a hand in gesture to the pantry, then continued sweeping.

"And make sure you get it all!" Sarah yelled. "If I get ants in my kitchen it will be on your head, Gen'l Charlie."

"Yes, ma'am," Charlie, the scolded boy, answered as he used a dustpan to pick up the sugar. He looked up at his wife, who looked like she was going to have to chew on her fist to keep from laughing outright. "Enjoying this, are you?"

"Mmmhmm." She nodded, her fist still tucked tight against her lips.

"You had better be nice to me or I will not give you a ride to Jocko's tonight," he warned playfully pointing his finger at her.

"I have a barn full of horses; I am not worried about getting a ride." She teasingly slapped his hand away.

He laughed as he set the broom and dustpan in the corner. "Well, there is that, seems you have gotten me on a technicality."

He was amused that the ladies had decided it was perfectly all right to play Mah Johng with Rex in the tea room on Saturday night since the men had their poker game in the bar. He was not too sure how the other gentlemen would react, but he was smart enough to just stay out of it. It did not bother him in the least that Rebecca wanted to do it. That was good enough for him.

～

The rain had finally subsided and Charlie was spending the afternoon reshelving books in the library. His son loved borrowing the books, but had a devil of the time putting then back where they belonged. He was putting the last volume away when he heard the gentle clearing of a throat.

"Yes, Darby?"

"Papa, I think Freddy needs help."

He turned and looked at his son. "What kind of help?"

"I do not know, but did you know he has no mama or papa?"

He settled in a chair and shook his head. "I did not."

"Yes, sir." Darby took a seat next to his father. "I found out by accident. I am not even sure about where he is living. I do not think he has a house. He always heads off to the south part of the property. You know, near the apples and grapes."

"So what is it you want to do?"

"I want to help my friend."

"Then let us saddle our horses and see if we can find out what kind of help he needs."

Darby smiled and nodded as he turned and ran from the room.

Twenty minutes later, they were both headed down the path toward the area Darby had seen his friend retreat to in the evenings.

⁓

Charlie saw the smoke before he saw the fire. He knew right away what he was in for. He allowed Darby and Tucker to take the lead in their little two-man rescue team.

"Freddy?" His son called quietly before dismounting.

"Darby?" Freddy called back, emerging from a small stand of trees to stand near the little fire.

Charlie dropped from Jack's back but stayed well back, allowing Darby the lead on this particular situation.

"Yes." The boy nodded, dropping Tucker's reins. "We came to check on you."

Charlie's heart sank when he saw the little campsite. That is all there was to it. A small fire and a shelter made from fallen logs and brush with no blankets or pillows made up the entirety of the boy's life. A skinny squirrel was roasting on a stick. He would have been better off in Slab town, but as an orphan, there would be no one to look out for him there either.

"It is alright, Darby. It is fine."

"No." The young man shook his head. "I do not think it is and I do not think Papa will think it is alright either."

"Gen'l Charlie?" The boy gulped.

"I am here, Freddy." Charlie walked closer to the little camp. "We came to make sure you were alright. It is getting colder at night..."

"Thank ya, sir, but I is alright."

Darby moved forward slowly toward his friend. "Freddy, this is not alright. What will you do when it snows?"

The boy smiled at his friend. "It is okay. I know where to hunker down to stay warm. I have done it for two winters now."

Darby turned to his father, the pleading in his eyes clear.

The general took a few steps forward. "I think we could offer you a room on the third floor of the house. It is important for you to be ready to light the fires for Sarah and Reg. If you are in the house it would be quicker. You would not have to travel so far in the morning."

"The big house?" He was in awe of the offer.

"Yes, the big house." He nodded. "Climb up there behind Darby and we will take you back to the house and get you settled."

∾

As they drove into town for their respective gaming sessions he told Rebecca about Freddy. "The kitchen boy, I put him on the third floor in Tomas' old room."

"Not that it matters to me, but why?"

"Well, because your son is a very astute young man, like his mama, and we discovered Freddy living in the woods near your apples."

"Oh, Charlie!"

"Exactly. Not only that, after we managed to get him to open up, we found out some truly disturbing things." He pulled the buggy to a stop and looked at her, "That boy has been digging down in the barn refuse to keep warm in the winter. He has literally been sleeping in shit to stay warm through the colder nights, then taking cold baths in the creek to wash in the morning before coming into the kitchen."

She realized in that moment she was probably about to run through the last of Andrew's old clothes.

∾

Charlie looked at his cards and shook his head. "This is terrible," he said as he tossed his hand in. "I am having no luck tonight."

"We all have those nights." Edgar nodded as he tossed a chip into the center of the table. "Last week was mine if you will remember correctly. You fine gentlemen took home about thirty dollars of my money."

"That is because it was not your money anymore," Jocko snorted. He had taken home the lion's share of winnings that night. Now he just hoped Esther would not lose it all learning to play that blasted game Rex and Rebecca had introduced her to.

All the gentlemen laughed softy as they continued around the table. "Say, Richard." Charlie lit a cigar. "You would not by any chance still have your button board, do you? I cannot find mine to save my neck and I need to polish my kit before the West Point engagement. It would not be suitable for me to show up with tarnished buttons and buckles."

"I should say not," he said with a laugh. He looked up at his old friend, his brows knitting together as he thought about it. "I suspect I do, but I have no idea where it is. Elizabeth and Ruth have packed up and put away most of my things from the army."

"You know, Charlie boy." Jocko stood up as the hand came to an end. "I think I know where your button board is. I will be right back." He headed to the back of the bar, disappearing through the door that led to his apartment. He returned quickly with a small wooden crate, which he placed on the floor to Charlie's left. "These are some odds and ends that were sent back when camp was disbanded. I have been meaning to give it to you for months and it just kept slipping my mind."

As Jocko retook his seat, Charlie indicated he would sit this hand out. Then he opened the lid on the little crate. Sure enough his button board was lying right on top. He lifted a few of the other items, sorting through the box to see exactly what was in it. He found one of his old journals, two belt buckles, a pocket knife, two ink pens and a bottle of India ink. There were also a handful of buttons, his sewing kit and a three pairs of socks.

Under the socks he found something he thought lost long ago – Rebecca's letters. They were still tied together with the blue hair ribbon he had taken with him the morning he left. He smiled as he picked up the little packet of letters and gave them a sniff. Even after all this time in a box, they still smelled of her perfume.

He put the letters inside his jacket, close to his heart, and flipped the lid closed on the box. "Thank you, Jocko." His old batman nodded without even looking up; he was too busy trying to win more of Edgar's money. Once the hand was over, Jocko looked up at Charlie, who was cleaning his fingernails with a penknife.

"Speaking of keeping you all neat and orderly." Jocko winked at Edgar before Charlie's head jerked up. "Why aren't ya taking your faithful old batman to West Point with you?"

"Well," he sputtered; it had not even occurred to him Jocko might want to go.

"I mean, I did get you through school, you know?"

Richard sat back and tried not to laugh as the Irishman began tormenting their old boss. There were things about the army he really missed. This was one of them. Everyone who knew Charlie knew he had worked damn hard to get through West Point, but it was especially fun to listen to Jocko tease him. Having been given a field promotion to second lieutenant at Buena Vista before his arrival, the academy had afforded him a few special privileges, including the company of John Jackson, his personal batman.

Charlie just nodded, knowing he was being tormented. He struck a match and lit a cigar. "Want my star too?"

"No." Jocko shook his head. "But I would not mind your pension."

~

Monday, October 8, 1866

Charlie sighed. He was having a terrible time getting anything on paper for his upcoming lectures at West Point. He had started and discarded a dozen drafts. He realized that, on an emotional level, there were still a lot of things from that place in his life that he needed to deal with. The brandy and the laudanum had numbed more than his body.

He continued to sit there, staring at the page, drumming his fingers on his desk. Sheridan lifted his head from his spot by the fire, hoping that the drumming meant there was some sort of food.

A thorough sniff of the air told him it was not to be, and he put his head back down.

When his office door opened without anyone knocking, he knew two things: it was Rebecca and he was in trouble. "Yes, dear," he offered before she even said a word.

"Come with me, General Redmond."

With a sigh, he stood and dutifully padded to the door, where he placed a kiss to the top of the stormy woman's head. "Who did what?"

"Just come with me." She led him a short way down the hall to the door that was the playroom for the children. She gestured, "You first."

When he opened the door, he immediately closed his eyes and dropped his head in resignation. There were his two little girls, standing on opposite sides of the doll house, fists on hips making some truly ugly faces at each other. He looked to the ceiling and shook his head.

"He is NOT going to help you this time," Rebecca teased as she gave him a gentle push through the door. Then she leaned on the jam to see exactly how he was going to solve this problem he had created.

Charlie moved to his little girls, taking up a position between them looking down at them. They eventually realized that their papa was in the room and two sets of fiery eyes turned in his direction. *I am in so much trouble.* "Ladies, I understand there is a problem."

Both girls immediately began pleading their case for why the doll house was theirs and theirs alone. His shoulders slumped when he heard his wife snickering behind him. She had been waiting for this. He had been set up. He nodded and took both girls by the hand, leading them to the sofa near the fireplace. He sat, keeping them apart by placing himself between them.

"Now." He looked at each one seriously. "How is it that you two cannot share this dollhouse, when you share everything else?"

Once again, the girls began begging and making their case. He gestured for them to be quiet. "So, you do not think there is any way that you two can share?" He looked to each little face and found two pouty mouths attached to heads shaking no.

"You are absolutely sure?" He asked one more time. Again, his daughters let him know there would be no truce over the doll house.

He looked to his wife, who was enjoying this immensely. She mouthed, "I tried to tell you to get two." She once again held up that visual clue. He sighed and closed his eyes for a second. Then he nodded and looked to each girl seriously. "Alright then, the two of you can stay here while I go to the barn and get a saw."

"What?" Suzanne's brows shot to the top of her head.

"Why, Papa?" Em asked while she rubbed his arm as she did when trying to beguile him. She had seen Mama do it; she knew it worked.

"Well, it seems clear to me that if you cannot share this doll house, I shall have to saw it in half."

"No!" The girls bolted from their father's side to their doll house and stood shoulder to shoulder protecting the little structure. "Daddy! Please!"

Rebecca straightened up when they called him Daddy. That was a word they only used when they really needed to wrap him around their little fingers. Any other time it was Papa.

Charlie stood and shook his head. "No, girls, I am sorry, but I fear if I do not saw your house in half, you will just keep fighting over it. This way you will both have half."

"No! Daddy!" Both girls ran and wrapped themselves around his waist, mostly in an effort to keep him from going for the saw. "We promise!"

"You do?"

They nodded earnestly.

"No more fighting over the house?"

"No more," Em said very seriously.

"No more," Suzanne agreed with a nod.

"Alright then. I supposed that I can let you try. But remember, any more fighting and I will go right to the barn for the saw."

"Yes, sir," they answered in unison. He kissed them both on top of the head and sent them back to the doll house, where they settled down together and started moving furniture from room to room.

He turned back to Rebecca and smiled. "And you said He would not help." He pointed up.

"Well done, Solomon." She had to give him his due; he had handled that masterfully. Until the next time. They were, after all, three and four.

∾

Friday, October 12, 1866

The ladies that Charlie referred to as Rebecca's Renegades met at Esther's tearoom for lunch. Every one of them had turned out for this meeting, as the critical issue of the school was the topic of the day. Rebecca and Charlotte were joined by Missy Frazier, Elizabeth, Samantha Nailer, Grace Cooper, and even Esther came out of her kitchen to join the group.

In addition to the regular lady Renegades, a couple of other women with school age children had also joined them, including Laura Granville, the blacksmith's wife, and Penelope Armistead, the lumber mill owner's wife. The guest of honor was the new school teacher, Annabelle Calvert, who preferred to be called Annie.

Esther had seen to it that the ladies were served a light lunch of grilled trout, salad, sweet tea and fresh biscuits with honey, then joined them for the repast. When the attendees were properly fed, Rebecca opened the discussion.

"We have all had the chance to meet our new school teacher, Annie Calvert, since she has joined Charlotte in teaching Sunday school."

Charlotte spoke up, "We have had more children in Sunday school than ever before, but our efforts to get children of the community to attend the regular school have been less than successful."

Annie, who had been sitting quietly with her head slightly bowed, looked up. "I have been at the school every weekday morning for a month, and have rung the school bell, but not one child has shown up so far." She sighed. "I have seen this problem before. The farmers and merchants in Antietam were so short of people, and there was so much that needed to be done to try and rebuild, that every child over about seven was needed to help with the animals, the crops, stocking and cleaning the stores and shops – you think of the thing that needed to be done, and the children were being put to work to do it."

The rest of the ladies at the table nodded, some in resignation and some in frustration.

Missy Frazier asked, "Do they not realize that to be good merchants, farmers, and citizens, these children need to know how to at least read, do ciphers, and know some history?"

"I am sure they do, but the long-term needs are not as important right now for most of these families as getting in the harvest and having food and firewood for the winter." Annie was nothing if not pragmatic.

Penelope Armistead questioned, "Do you think attendance will become possible once the harvest is in?"

"I hope so. Miss Redmond and I have been chatting with as many parents as we can reach every Sunday, and they are all happy that there is a school, but they say that they need their children right now to get ready for winter."

Rebecca listened to all of this, looking rather thoughtful. Finally, she asked, "Do you think that it would help if we limited classes to mornings only until after harvest was in? At least for the children in town?"

"It might. I can certainly ask at Church on Sunday."

"And I can help by sending you Darby in the mornings." She turned to Samantha. "Do you think you can pry Jeremiah out of his leather shop for a few hours a day?"

"I can talk to Duncan about it, but I would think so. Especially if we tell him this is something he needs to do to be a better businessman."

Penelope Armistead added, "I think I can convince James to let

Henry go for a few hours and I will send Amy as well, though I think she is a little young. She is only six, you know."

Annie laughed. "I can at least start her on her alphabet and numbers, Mrs. Armistead."

Penelope looked thoughtful. "I may be able to talk some of the other girls' mothers into sending their little ones to you as well."

Rebecca smiled. "A plan, ladies. Let us pray it works." She smiled more broadly. "I think that Esther has a dessert for us to enjoy."

As the dessert plates were being brought out, Rebecca leaned over to Samantha and whispered, "I hope Charlie understands. I mean, he is spending a small fortune to have a tutor at the house, but…" *John usually spends the mornings with the girls, so Darby will keep up with the more advanced subjects. Charlie will just have to accept it.*

"Well, dear, Duncan will just have to accept it. Jeremiah is still my son and I have a say in his education!" Samantha was adamant.

～

Friday, October 12, 1866

With over a year and a half since the end of the war, the surviving gentry of Culpeper County had returned and settled back into their homes and their various pursuits. Up until now, Charlie and Rebecca had primarily dealt with the townspeople, but with the opening of the bank, and its focus on supporting the farmers of the area as well as the merchants in the town, Charlie had come to know some of the owners of larger properties outside of town.

Prior to the war, these men had been what were referred to as gentlemen farmers; now they were starting to put their farms back together. Some, like the Redmonds, bred horses; others raised cattle, both for meat and milk; still others grew corn and wheat. But all of them had home farms to defend, and that meant, among other things, keeping the fox population under control so their chicken flocks would not be destroyed.

To do this, and to help bring the community back together, the grand Virginia tradition of the fox hunt had been reinstated. The couple and their eldest son were invited to join that fall, which they did in part because Rebecca was a well-regarded horsewoman who had ridden the hunt before the war. Charlie, as a military officer, had long ago earned his hunt colors as an honorary hunt master. Darby just wanted to be part of the hunt because it was a sign of growing up.

The closest rural neighbor to the Redmonds was the Hitt family, who bred both horses and Black Angus cattle. Sam Hitt was the local hunt master, and he had invited Charlie to join in. He also invited Edgar to ride with the hunt and was surprised when Edgar asked if Rex could join in, though neither would be able to join until the formal hunts began in November. Richard was invited but declined as Elizabeth thought fox hunting was rather barbaric. Something about cutting off the fox's tail and keeping it as a trophy offended her.

This morning was just a cub-hunt, one of the last opportunities the hunters had to train and evaluate the young fox hounds before the formal season began in November. Nevertheless, Darby was up, dressed and ready to go at dawn, and before the light had changed from pink to gold, he was knocking on his parents' door, with Freddy right behind him carrying coffee and cups on a tray.

Even though Charlie and Darby were only going to ride with the hill-toppers, who followed the hunt on a path without any jumps, it was still his first hunt and he was incredibly excited at being allowed to join the adults. He was considered too young to take the jumps that were part of the main hunt party, Tucker was not a jumper, and Charlie had not been back in the saddle long enough to risk a fall on a jump – at least that was what Rebecca thought and so made him promise 'no jumping.'

When the three were dressed, they walked down to the stable. It was part of Charlie and Rebecca's rules that all riders tacked their own horses whenever they could, caring for their horses almost as if they were children.

Jack was eager but gentle around Charlie, as if he knew that his master was still a little shaky on his feet. Rebecca had whispered to the big horse, as they started grooming, to take care of Charlie.

Shannon could tell something fun was coming and was prancing. Tucker was his usual self, calm and steady. They brushed their horses down until their coats shone, then tacked them up, mounted up and set off for the Hitt farm. Rebecca reminded her men of her one rule for riding together – especially important when they were dressed alike. They were not allowed to ride circles around her. It tended to make her nauseous.

As they arrived, it became clear that the cream of Culpeper County's rural society had turned out. In addition to several members of the Hitt family, there were representatives from the Pendletons, the Walkers, who were distant relatives of Elizabeth's, the Allcocks, and the Kirtleys, as well as several of the smaller farm holders in the area. Because this was just a cub-hunt, most of the men, except the officials of the hunt, were dressed in rat catchers like Charlie and Darby, and the women were in standard riding habits, without the colored collars and special buttons that formed their formal hunt garb.

A buffet breakfast had been laid for the hunters and the attendees who would be riding with the hill-toppers. Eggs, biscuits, ham, bacon, cinnamon rolls, and crisp apples and pears were all consumed, along with a goodly quantity of coffee and tea. Once sated, they all mounted and Hitt's servants brought out stirrup cups filled with port for the men, sherry for the ladies, and apple cider for the younger riders. At the hunt master's signal, the huntsmen and whippers-in let the dogs loose and the hunt began.

The main hunt rode at a brisk trot behind the dogs as they cast about across the fields for a fox. The hill-toppers followed the path alongside the fields. It did not take long before the dogs caught a scent and flushed a fox. The chase was on. The main hunt was off across the fields, jumping hedgerows and fences as the fox ducked and wove through whatever cover it could find to try and avoid the dogs that were hot on its tail. Somehow, Rebecca managed to stay on the side closest to the hill-toppers, who were following along to watch the progress of the dogs and the riders. It was rather unusual for her to hold back, as historically she would ride on the tails of the hunt master, but this way, she could ride with the hunt and still keep an eye on her menfolk.

Forty minutes later, the fox went to ground in the roots of an old oak tree. The dogs and riders pulled up. Every human face was pink with excitement and exertion. Every dog and horse face was coated with slobber and lather. All participants had had a great time.

They agreed to head back to the Hitt house and were joined by the hill-toppers in the ride back. As they rode, they debated the merits of various dogs and horses. Darby listened to this discourse eagerly, drinking in all of the information he could. He did not start babbling about his experience until he was on the way home with his parents and could permit himself to behave like a boy who had just had a wonderfully exciting experience, rather than the polite young man he had presented to the neighbors. He wanted to be invited back.

CHAPTER 25

Monday October 22, 1866

About a half hour before the train was due to arrive in Cold Spring, New York, Charlie took the time to change from his civilian clothing into his regular service uniform. His dress uniform and evening clothes were packed securely in a trunk in the event there were any formal engagements either military or civilian, but for his and Rebecca's arrival his everyday uniform was more than sufficient. Her handy work with his small clothes had done wonders for both the fit and feel of the uniform, and with Jeremiah's new set of prosthetic fingers in place, he looked and felt a lot like his old self.

Rebecca smiled as he ran his hands over his tunic smoothing the front before buckling his belt in place. It had been a very long time since she had seen him like this. She remembered the very first time she had seen him, dressed in the same manner. The dark blue double breasted short jacket with the shining brass buttons, the yellow shoulder straps that had sported an eagle then and was now command blue with gold braid and his gold star, the dark blue trousers with the yellow braid denoting his role as a cavalry officer, and with his hat and gloves in his hands. Piercing blue eyes and a smile that captured her heart the moment she laid eyes on them, even if she had not known it at the time.

When the train arrived at the Cold Spring station, they disembarked to find a carriage awaiting them. Behind the carriage was a wagon, also driven by a cadet, which was obviously for their servants and baggage. Two young men, cadet corporals in full dress uniform and the distinctive cadet Shako hat, sat on top the carriage box maintaining both the horses and attention in a seated position as best as they could. A third other young man stood near the carriage door at attention, snapping a crisp salute as they approached.

"Sir, Captain of Cadets Hall, sir!" The young man did not move a muscle until Charlie raised his hand to return the salute.

"At ease, Cadet Captain," he offered softly.

"Sir, thank you. It is an honor and a privilege to escort you and Mrs. Redmond to The Point, sir," the young man said sincerely to Charlie as he opened the carriage door and offered his gloved hand to Rebecca. Once she was settled, she noticed that he had returned to attention as Charlie entered the carriage, but his eyes carefully tracked the general's movements, should he require any assistance. It was clear they had been well advised of his injuries.

Are they in for a surprise... She laughed silently as Charlie settled into the seat across from her.

The cadet captain climbed up onto the box and, after waiting a few minutes for Tomas and Lizbet, with the help of the porter at the train station to load their baggage on the wagon, the carriage, followed by the wagon, set out for the short trip to the ferry, which took them across the Hudson River to the North Landing.

The ferry trip was quick and smooth, though for Charlie it brought back many memories of his first arrival at this institution and the excitement and trepidation he had felt as he approached it for the first time. This arrival was much different.

The carriage proceeded up the path to the top of the cliff overlooking the river, and around the boulevard to stop in front of the superintendent's residence. The wagon went on to the cottage that they would stay in for the next few days.

The superintendent, Thomas Pitcher, an old friend and West Point classmate of Charlie's, was standing on the parade ground side of the boulevard, waiting for them. Behind him stood the entire student population of the school, dressed in their full parade uniforms of black boots, white pants, grey short jacket with tails, white belts strap crossed over their chests, Shako hats with the stiff black feather rising from the crown, and rifles resting along their right legs. Charlie felt underdressed. Rebecca felt overwhelmed and a little regretful she had never seen him in a cadet's uniform.

Thomas, who as superintendent carried the three-star rank of Lieutenant General, walked up to greet them. Charlie, out of pure habit, snapped to attention and delivered a crisp salute to his old friend. Tom returned the salute and laughed "At ease, General. How are you, old man?" He reached out to shake hands.

"Much better than I expected to be after Appomattox Station, Tom. Much better. Allow me to introduce my wife, Rebecca."

Thomas turned to her, took her hand and lightly kissed her fingers. "Welcome to The Point, Mrs. Redmond. I hope your stay here is a pleasant one."

She smiled demurely and murmured softly, "Pleased to meet you, sir. Oh, and I have a note for you from Jerome Lord." She fished in her reticule and pulled out a small envelope, which she handed to him.

Thomas turned back to Charlie with a smile. "I know a full turn out is not standard operating procedure, old man, but the men insisted. They would love it if you conducted an inspection of the troops. You up to it?"

"I am if they are." He smiled and held his cane out to Rebecca. "Darling, do you mind?" He leaned over and whispered as she took it from him, "They are giving us a good show. I need to return the favor." He winked at her before he turned and walked to the commandant of cadets, standing at the head of the assemblage. The young man, already at attention, saluted. Charlie returned the gesture.

"General Redmond, sir! The cadets are ready for inspection, sir!"

He nodded his approval, then walked the length of the assembled young men, stopping occasionally to commend one or question another, being very careful not to suggest that any of them were out of order in their uniforms or stance.

In fact, he did not see any major faults. The only thing he could see was the odd grass cutting stuck on a boot, or smudge of dust on a jacket sleeve. How many times had he stood here hoping not to get a demerit for the same things? He returned to the commandant of cadets, saying, "The men are well turned out, Cadet."

He then turned to the assembly. "Gentlemen, thank you for the warm and genuinely reverent greeting for my wife and me. I am humbled. I hope you find what I have to say in the next few days is worthy of your outstanding reception. You have all done The Point proud in your showing today." He grinned, then in his best battlefield voice, called, "Cadets! Dissss-MISSED!"

The young men, in perfect unison, all placed the toe of their right foot behind their left heel and executed a flawless about face as they broke formation and started wandering off in various directions. There were a few who stayed back, clearly anxious to speak with their distinguished guest, but not wanting to interrupt him or their superintendent. Eventually, even they wandered away, knowing they would have plenty of time with him during his lectures.

While Charlie had been inspecting the troops, Tom took a moment to read the note that Rebecca had brought him. It was enormously brief. All it said was, 'Dear Tom, I win. – Jerome.'

He looked up at the lady in question for a moment, and thought, *Yes, yes you do, Jerome*. He then turned to her and began a polite conversation while they waited for Charlie to finish.

Tom escorted them to the cottage a bit farther along the boulevard where they would be staying. As they strolled along, Tom looked at Charlie. "From what I heard, even making this walk would be hard for you. In fact, I put you in one of the instructor's cottages rather than the hotel, specifically because of your injuries, but you seem to be gimping along just fine. Even the limp is minor. What happened?"

Rebecca jumped in. "Oh, General Pitcher, he has had the most miraculous recovery with the help of an oriental physician who has done wonders with his rehabilitation. We never thought he would walk without the aid of a crutch or a cane, but not only is he walking, he is riding again as well."

"That is amazing! I am so glad to see you back in one piece, old man. From what I heard, you were almost pushing up daisies."

"I was, but a great doctor – you remember Dr. Walker – and a devoted wife," he shifted his head toward Rebecca with a smile, "put me back together, and a brilliant Chinaman made most things work again."

"Well," said General Pitcher as they turned into the front garden of a charming cottage, "here are the quarters we assigned you. I believe your servants and baggage have already been delivered and there will always be a batman on call if you need something. I have planned an early and informal dinner for tonight, as I am sure you are tired from your trip and will want to rest up before tomorrow's interrogation."

They entered the cottage. There was a cozy sitting room, a small dining area, two comfortable bedrooms with an attached washroom between them, and rooms for Tomas and Lizbet at the back of the cottage. Stairs led up to a loft, where Rebecca assumed there were rooms for the instructor's children, if they had any. It was by no means opulent, but it was entirely livable, especially for any small family accustomed to military life.

Tomas and Lizbet had already unpacked their clothes, hanging them to let the wrinkles fall out, and Lizbet was in the small kitchen area heating up the irons. Tea and a plate of finger foods were waiting on the table.

Charlie pulled out his notebook and sat at the desk. "I still do not have a clue as to what I am going to say tomorrow, but I must make some sort of start. Do you mind, dear, if I work at this for a bit?"

"Not at all, darling. I really want to get out of these dusty clothes – train travel is so dirty – and get freshened up before dinner, and if that is not enough, I have a book. But I do have one question. Why does Tom call you 'old man'?"

He laughed. "Most of my classmates did. You see, I was older than most of them, and the superintendent gave me some special privileges because of that – especially a room of my own instead of having to share lodgings in the barracks. Usually that is only reserved for upper classmen, and then only the higher ranked ones."

She nodded. "Ah yes, that makes sense. Thank you, old man." She patted his back, kissing him on top of the head, before she turned away.

He snorted, then settled in at the desk, while Rebecca and Lizbet continued to put their clothes in order.

~

They walked up the boulevard to the superintendent's house that evening, enjoying the cool breeze of the Hudson and the fall colors on the trees.

They arrived to find Tom waiting for them on the front steps, enjoying a small cigar and the last rays of the sun. "Come in, come in. Formality is so much a part of our life that we enjoy it when we can let go of some of the stuffiness." He led them into the parlor, where a pretty, plump woman whose brown hair was just starting to show minor streaks of gray was waiting. She rose to greet her guests.

Mrs. Pitcher kissed Charlie on the cheek. "It is so good to see you again. We had heard that you were terribly injured at Appomattox, so I am thrilled to see you doing so well."

"It is good to see you too, Mary. You and Tom have done well for yourself. Allow me to introduce my wife, Rebecca."

She stepped forward. "It is a pleasure to meet you, Mrs. Pitcher."

"Oh, Lord, call me Mary. And may I call you Rebecca?"

She grinned and nodded. "By all means, Mary. And you can call him," she pointed at Charlie, "Charles when he gets into trouble."

449

The woman laughed and gave Rebecca's hand a gentle squeeze. "Spoken like a long-suffering army wife." She lifted her chin toward her husband. "The only time he is Thomas is when he has done something silly. Shall we have a sherry while we wait for dinner to be served?"

"Please," their guests answered in chorus.

As they waited for dinner to be served, Mary and Tom entertained them with tales of what it was like to live as a married army couple. Some of the stories of the housing, especially in the western territories, sent chills up Rebecca's spine. Shortly, a batman came in to announce dinner.

Dinner was pleasant, if a bit ordinary, but the conversation was lively and brisk, and they found they had much in common. Rebecca's horse breeding was a major point of discussion, as both Pitchers had a birthright of farming and horse breeding from growing up in rural Indiana.

It got a bit heated when Charlie mentioned that George Custer had just been assigned the command of Fort Riley in Western Kansas. "Well, if Johnson wants another Indian war, sending Custer out there pretty much guarantees it will happen."

Tom looked at him sharply. "Yes, you served with him under Sheridan, did you not?"

"I did, and a bigger ass I doubt I ever met."

"Even bigger than the one you put in the super's office?" Tom grinned.

He had the grace to flush as he smiled and ducked his head. Mary leaned over and asked Rebecca in a whisper, "What are they talking about?"

She answered, "Charlie played a prank on the Super when he was a fourth year. He put a donkey in his office one night. Apparently, it was quite a surprise the next morning."

The older woman chuckled. "Here's hoping that no one does that to Tom."

The gentlemen ignored the ladies side conversation and continued their discussion of Custer. Charlie recounted how Custer's battle lust and willingness to take stupid chances resulted in his having the highest casualty numbers of any officer under Sheridan's command. What he did not say was that the arrogant man's foolishness was the primary reason for him being in the shape he was.

After dinner, the gentlemen stepped out onto the front steps for a cigar, while the ladies retired to the parlor for tea.

"So, Tom, what is it that you and Jerome Lord are communicating about that my wife is carrying messages for him?"

He broke out laughing. "Jerome mentioned in a letter several months ago that within our little group of friends from our days here, you had managed to capture the most beautiful wife. Since I was going to meet her, he figured he could bring that bet home. His note simply said, 'I win.' I thought it was pretty funny, and terribly accurate."

Charlie grinned. "Well, I will give him that. She certainly is lovely. And I am enormously lucky."

"You are that, old man. In many ways."

∽

Tuesday, October 23, 1866

After about the third sharp note from the bugle, Rebecca sat straight up in bed, rubbing her eyes and running her hands through her hair. "What in the name of God is that?" She inquired in the direction of her still apparently slumbering husband.

Charlie did not even bother opening his eyes. He certainly was not going to get up. He reached out and brought her back into his warm embrace. "Reveille," he told her as he kissed her ear.

"Do they have any idea what time it is?"

This made him chuckle, shaking the whole bed. "Yes, dear. It is five thirty."

"Why are you not climbing out of bed?" She snuggled close to his chest.

"I am not a cadet. Rank and retirement have the occasional privilege," he mumbled as his arms once again wrapped firmly around her.

She lay there, as she had so many times before, her head tucked under his chin, her lips just a hairs width from his throat, feeling his pulse gently against her own. His arms wrapped around her, warm, strong and safe, as his breathing settled into the gentle rhythms of sleep once again. She smiled as her fingers grazed the silk of the knitted small clothes she had made for him. It had not taken long before he had given up his sleep shirts, preferring to sleep in the shirts and shorts she made. He explained that they did not bind against his scars in the night, the way a traditional sleep shirt always did. She knew she would be making these things for the rest of her life.

She lay there, feeling his body against hers rise and fall in easy slumber. His arms were, as always, the safest pace in the world as far as she was concerned. She slowly, gently, easily, moved her hands over his body. She was just feeling, touching, through the material of his underclothes, not trying, at least intentionally, to rouse or arouse her partner. She thought she was doing a good job until his head pulled back, one blue eye opened and staring down at her.

"Yes, wife?" He murmured. "Is there something you require of your husband this morning?" He grinned.

"Mmmm." She nodded and whispered against his neck. "Always. You know I love your attentions in the morning, General."

As he lay dozing, Rebecca watched Charlie. Her thoughts confused and jumbled in her mind. Her finger's grazed over fluid, tight, muscles--not as big as a typical man, but certainly powerful in their own right.

The chest was chiseled, hard muscled and toned. Yes, there were small breasts, but given that she had seen men bare chested, working in the summer heat who appeared to have bigger breasts than he did, she realized that this was not necessarily a giveaway to the secret either.

As her hand traveled down his stomach, his hand grasped hers quickly and he muttered. "I surrender."

She laughed and laid her head on his shoulder, his arm automatically going around her. "Charlie, may I ask you a question?"

"You know you may." He nodded, but never opened his eyes.

"When you are nude, do you suddenly have an urge to wear pantaloons and whalebone?"

Now his eyes were open. He turned his head slowly. "What?"

"I know." She shook her head as she pushed up on her elbow to look at him. "That did not come out right." She sighed and tried again, "When we are like this," she gestured to their nude forms covered by the sheet, "this," she tapped her index finger gently against his forehead, "does not spontaneously start thinking like a woman. Correct?"

He considered her question for a moment then nodded slowly. "Correct. Is something wrong?" His fears and insecurities were starting to rapidly rise to the surface. "And what has happened to my very shy wife? Are you the same woman who used to giggle when I kissed her--"

She placed a finger over his lips. "It still makes me giggle when you kiss me there. And no." She was firm in this as she placed her fingers on his chin, turning his head to make him look her in the eyes as she spoke the truth to him. "No. There is nothing wrong. As for your shy wife, she grew up. Having lived with Edgar, Rex and Charlotte all these months, it was bound to happen."

He nodded and rolled over to face her so they were lying close and could talk quietly. "Then continue sweetheart. Let us talk it out together." His smile was so gentle it made Rebecca feel truly loved. "I take it something has happened to make you question our situation?"

"No." She smiled and shook her head. "Our situation is just fine. I love you. You are not getting off that easy. I intend to spend the next forty or fifty years making you understand that." She kissed his chin. "Every." Another kiss. "Single." Another kiss. "Day. So stop it."

He sighed, very confused and a little scared by all of this, but he knew he had to trust her. He nodded. "I am sorry, love. Please, continue."

She made sure to maintain physical contact with him. The last thing she wanted was for him to assume the worst. "Tell me, what is it, in your eyes, that keeps you from being," she paused for effect, "a 'real' man?"

He drew a deep breath, not expecting that question at all. His heart pounded in his chest and ears as he tried to find the answer he hoped she wanted. "Umm..." He snorted as he tried to draw another breath. "Well." He cleared his throat gently. "I suppose the lack of, well," he ducked his head shyly, "of a usable member?"

She nodded slowly. "So, some part of you, some part of your own mind, keeps you from being wholly male because you lack the ability to get an erection?"

He scratched his forehead, brows drawn together in what was rapidly becoming serious frustration. "It would seem so."

"What if I told you, based on the best medical opinions available, that if you had been 'wholly male' when you were wounded, you would not be able to get an erection because of your wounds? Would that make you less of a man then?"

Now he sat up. He rustled and shuffled pillows until he was sitting up in bed. She followed and they sat there looking at each other as the early morning sun broke through the windows. "I suppose I have spent so long trying to be a man, that trying has become a habit," he said slowly. "If you would prefer I change my habits..."

She sighed, a deep and heartfelt sigh. She took his hand and intertwined their fingers. "Darling, in all ways that matter, you are a man, and have been one for a long time. Not only do you dress like a man, you think like one, you act like one, you talk like one, and you care for your family like one, because you are one. So perhaps you can just stop trying and just be you. Charlie Redmond. Man."

Before he could respond to this, she went on. "Yes, I know that at first I found you fascinating because you were physically a woman, and being so different from Gaines, I felt safe with you.

But believe me, dear, I have come to see you, understand you, and love you more and more each day, not because you appear at times to be a woman, but because you are truly a man – a wonderful, gentle, kind, loving man."

He sat there, listening to her, realizing she understood him better than he understood himself some days. As she returned to her normal place at his side, Charlie Redmond felt shackles fall free he had not even known bound him.

Somewhat later that morning, though still early enough to be within The Point's rigorous schedule, they rose to find Tomas and Lizbet waiting to serve them a lovely breakfast of eggs, ham, biscuits and fresh fruit. Rebecca asked, "Where did you get this?"

Lizbet responded, "A gentleman with a hot cart came by and dropped them off just a few minutes ago. He said that The Point caters meals for all guests."

After eating, they went to finish preparing for the lecture. Tomas shaved Charlie carefully, gave his hair a quick trim where needed and made sure his boots were shined so brightly you could see yourself in them, and that his uniform pants and jacket were immaculate.

Tom had warned him that some of the cadets had a serious case of hero worship, made more profound by the lecture that Sheridan had given the previous spring about the final campaign with the running battle along the James River up to Appomattox, so Charlie wanted to present himself with full military spit and polish.

Rebecca chose a dove gray day dress, demure and entirely appropriate for the wife of a general. Her hair was pulled back in a simple Phoebe Knot, looking sleek and elegant. He carried his leather notebook in one hand and his cane in the other. Rebecca carried a simple reticule. Together, they made the short walk past the cadet barracks to the academic building. Out of consideration for Charlie's injuries, they had scheduled the lectures to be presented in a ground floor lecture hall.

Before they entered the building, he stopped and looked down at his wife, gently caressing her cheek. "Are you sure you want to hear this? I suspect some things will come up that may be difficult for you."

"I know." She patted his chest. "I think it is time we both dealt with this, and I cannot think of a better place."

He gave her a tender kiss on the cheek before opening the door for her. They moved down the hall with Rebecca looking at the portraits of former students and the memorabilia that covered the walls. As Charlie opened the door to the lecture hall and they stepped into the room, they stopped dead in their tracks.

The room was packed. Every seat in the risers was taken, and cadets who could not find a seat lined the side and back walls. It was not what either of them had been expecting. Charlie took a deep breath and Rebecca patted his arm. He stepped forward and the cadets were called to attention as they walked in.

A nicely padded armchair had been set in the middle of the room, with a small table holding a glass and a water pitcher beside it. Another armchair, table and water had been set to the left side of the room, toward the front, but in an unobtrusive site, so Rebecca could see and hear everything but not intrude on the lecture unless Charlie needed her.

He escorted her toward the chair that was obviously set for her. Then he moved to stand in front of the chair set for him as he leaned his cane against the table, placing his notebook on the top.

He turned to where a large-scale map of the Appomattox area, showing both the location of Appomattox Court House and Appomattox Station, with the railway and the topology of the area filled in, had been mounted on a large easel.

Then he turned and looked around the room, more than a little overwhelmed at the turn out, and cleared his throat. "At ease, gentlemen. Please, take your seats. Thank you for coming. I did not expect such attendance."

He waited a moment as the young men got settled. He could see a few of them with notebooks and pencils in hand ready to take notes. The entire time he had been here as a cadet, he never imagined being back under these circumstances. Suddenly he felt a bit speechless. After clearing his throat one more time, he began.

"Today I am here to talk about one of the strangest actions in the recent war – the confrontation of unsupported artillery against unsupported cavalry." He limped to the map. "As you can see, the bulk of General Lee's Army of Northern Virginia was deployed here around the village of Appomattox Court House." He indicated the Confederate emplacements.

"General Grant had flanked the Confederate forces, cutting off access to the south and General Lee's hopes for an effective retreat. Because of the forces facing him, General Lee thought he was facing only cavalry forces, which he felt he could punch through by using his artillery troops as infantry."

"Because of how General Grant had us deployed, as you can see, the cavalry was facing the Confederates, with infantry support behind them, and more cavalry covering the rear of General Grant's positions. For General Lee, it was critical to cut through our cavalry to get to the rail lines and the much-needed supplies that were coming up from North Carolina via train. He knew that the trains themselves were guarded by artillery mounted on flat cars at the head and tail of the first train. Given their limited resources, and with the trains running close together, he believed that if the first train could cut through, the other two would follow fairly safely."

He stopped and took a deep breath. Talking about this was harder than he thought. After a moment, which he covered by taking a sip of water, he continued. "General Lee was wrong. General Custer and I were sent to protect Appomattox Station and prevent those supplies from reaching General Lee's western flank." Another sip of water was necessary. "By the time I got there, the Confederates had managed to pull their guns off the train, ranging them on either side of the rails, and had been pounding at Custer's troops for about an hour to keep them at bay. The situation was a stalemate."

"My troops and I had a chance to slip around behind the train, using a stand of trees as cover for most of the maneuver. The ground was muddy, slowing things, but we still wrapped our horses' feet to muffle any sound. The last thing we needed was for General Walker's troops to notice us too soon and bring those howitzers around to bear on my men. We had about one hundred fifty yards of open ground to cover before we could get to their emplacements."

"Unfortunately, the last gunner in the line caught our movement out of the corner of his eye, and swung his howitzer around, letting go with a wild canister shot. What Minié balls can do to a group of charging horses is pretty terrible. My men charged in, many of them jumping from their horses, either because their horses went down or because it was what was needed. They took on the artillery men hand to hand, taking on the enemy one emplacement at a time. It was a bloody mess. And unfortunately, it took General Custer more than a little while to realize that the Southerners were no longer firing at him."

"Gentlemen, to be perfectly honest, the battle of Appomattox Station was an act of desperate determination. Without those supplies, General Lee could not go on. So we had only one option. Stop those trains, no matter what it took. And you all know the outcome." Charlie stopped, walked to the chair they had set for him, and sat down. "So rather than try to explain the details, as this was not a well-planned assault, but was in fact a desperate action with a strategically critical objective, I think it will be easier to take your questions at this point."

"Sir, Cadet Williams, sir. Sir, why did General Grant give General Custer military lead? Your battle record is far superior to his, sir."

Charlie thought for a moment. Denigrating Custer's abilities was the last thing he wanted to do, and questioning chain of command was a major military sin. "General Sheridan was in command of our actions, under General Grant's direction. While General Custer and I are of equal rank, he had more troops under his command, as my men had taken quite a beating on the way up from Petersburg to Appomattox, so he gave Custer the lead posting."

"Sir, Cadet Younger, sir. Sir, if General Custer had more men, what kept them from supporting you when you started taking fire from the artillery positions, sir?"

The general laughed, a little nervously, and said, "Gentlemen. Everybody here knows I am a 'sir.'" He glanced over when he saw Rebecca smile and nod. "So if we are to get through this, I suggest that we drop the formalities and focus on the issues. As for your question, young man, I believe you would have to ask General Custer. I have no idea what caused him to delay in sounding the charge, as he never explained it to me. I have not seen or heard from him since that morning." He looked over at Rebecca again, and she smiled reassuringly.

"Cadet Magnus, sir. General, do you remember being hit?"

He bowed his head, and then looked up at Rebecca once again. Her face showed a mask of pain. They had never talked about this. For a brief moment he considered lying to spare her more hurt, but then he realized in the end it would do no justice to anyone in the room, especially her.

"Yes, I do." He paused. "I remember hearing the blast. I remember seeing the muzzle flash out of the corner of my eye. I remember feeling the tearing of my skin, the heat and the pain of the rocks, wood and metal embedding in my flesh. I remember my horse falling out from underneath me and for a brief moment I was very grateful I was not on my regular mount, Black Jack. I remember hitting the ground and feeling the blood leave my body, and I thought I was dying, and would never see my wife or my children again."

He looked back over at his wife. She had tears running down her face as she tried to maintain her composure; she had never heard him say these things before. Looking directly at her, he said, "I am not ashamed to admit I wanted my last word to be her name. I called out for her."

He walked over to stand beside his wife, offering her his handkerchief before looking back to the young men who were watching the general's wife dab her tears. "Fortunately, because of Dr. Elizabeth Walker's skill, Sergeant Jocko Jackson, medics Albert Samuelson and Walt Whitman's continuous care, and ultimately, my beloved wife's determination that I stay around a while longer, I am still with her." He looked around the room. "Gentlemen, if there is one piece of advice I can offer you, it is simple. Marry well. The right woman will see you through hell and back."

Every cadet in the room stood in silent tribute to Mrs. Redmond's courage. As one, they bowed to her. She blushed, holding Charlie's hand to her cheek, and nodded her silent acknowledgement.

After a few moments, Charlie cleared his throat, patted her hand, and then walked back to his chair. "Shall we continue the questions?"

For the next hour, he fielded questions about the march from Petersburg, the string of battles and skirmishes along the James River, and what little he knew of the final battle the day after Appomattox Station.

Through the course of the questions, he did mention that after hearing that Charlie had been seriously wounded, General Lee himself had come to the 13th's encampment after the surrender to see how his old friend was faring. Even though Charlie had not known it at the time, he had been told by Richard and Elizabeth well after the fact. Though it was left unsaid, the difference between General Lee's gentlemanly action and General Custer's arrogance and self-aggrandizement with his well-known declaration that he was responsible for General Lee's surrender because he had cut off access to supplies, was obvious.

Lunchtime came, and the cadets escorted their honored guests to the mess hall. As they entered, once again, the cadets came to attention. "At ease, gentlemen. Enjoy your lunch." Mary, taking pity on Rebecca's over exposure to male military conversation, came to the mess hall for lunch, something that she almost never did under normal circumstances. Charlie and Rebecca joined the instructors at the head table, and lunch was a pleasant event for all.

Charlie and the senior officers adjourned to the small garden beside the mess hall for an after-lunch cigar. A small horde of cadets quickly surrounded them, four and five deep, hoping to get a word with the guest speaker.

Mary took Rebecca's arm, and said, "Come back to my house. I have tea, some berries and cream, and an opportunity to relieve you of the over-exposure to young males trying to be important." Rebecca laughed, signaled to her husband that she would meet him at the cottage later, and escaped to the pleasant company of the only other woman in the sea of masculinity.

That evening, Tom and Mary hosted a dinner at the superintendent's house. It gave Rebecca a chance to meet the wives of the other senior officers, and to realize that there was a normal social life at The Point, or at least as normal as any higher school environment could be. What was most important was that she got a good picture of what being married to a military man on active duty was like, with the moving, the long months apart, the miserable quarters in some places, the lack of access to decent food stuffs, decent cloth, sometimes reliable mail, and a host of other things that made being the wife of an active military man a nightmare. Rebecca was intensely grateful that Charlie had retired.

CHAPTER 26

Wednesday, October 24, 1866

The second day of his lectures went very much like the first. Although he was only supposed to be lecturing to one class, it quickly became clear that every cadet at The Point wanted an opportunity to hear and question him. As a result, he got some of the same questions with each new set of audience members.

It did get easier for Rebecca to hear the response to the inevitable question as to whether he remembered being hit. Not a lot easier, but easier. Tea after lunch with Mary was a pleasant relief. They had struck up an immediate friendship and Mary was fascinated with the tales of how they had acquired and managed a household with five children in it in a little less than two years.

That afternoon, Charlie came around to collect his wife so they could prepare for dinner. The upperclassmen and cadet officers had invited them to dine with them that evening, an event that she did not entirely look forward to, but the boys were so insistent that she could not turn them down.

It turned out that she had a lovely time with them. It was reminiscent of the one dinner she had attended with Charlie and his officers in camp when they wintered over. The biggest difference was, while she had been the center of attention then, Charlie was firmly in the sights of the young men in attendance of this event. He took all their questions and comments with good humor, shaking each man's hand at least once and sometimes two or three times. She could not help but smile; if nothing else this trip had been extremely good for his ego and general outlook.

Toward the end of the festivities, Cadet Captain Hall stood and called all the men to attention. As they all stood, facing Charlie and Rebecca, Captain Hall stepped forward. "General Redmond, sir. My men and I understand that when you were injured you also lost your academy ring." He stepped forward and placed a small box on the table in front of him. "We would like to give you this ring. We know that we cannot replace your ring, but no man of The Point, no brother should be without his ring."

Charlie grinned widely and opened the box, showing the ring inside to Rebecca. She took it from the box and with the reverence due the moment, slipped it on the second finger of his right hand. The boys had done well; it was a perfect fit. She smiled as he held his hand up and the cadets broke protocol by applauding and whistling when he showed them their gift properly displayed as it should be.

After dinner, they strolled back to their cottage. At the end of the walk leading to their temporary home, Charlie saw one of the older boys harassing an underclassman. He walked up behind them to hear the older cadet viciously hazing the younger boy for his stutter. The officer in the general took over.

"Atten-shun!" he snapped. Both cadets immediately came to attention. He walked around, looking at the two boys, then addressed the older one, who had been one of the most aggressive of the young bucks jockeying for a word with him after the first lecture. "So, Cadet Mason, I think." The boy nodded quickly but did not say anything. "You think that having a stutter is a problem for a soldier? Let me tell you that one of the bravest men I have ever known has a profound stutter, but if it were not for him, I would not be here today. He saved my life under heavy fire."

He looked directly at the younger man. "At ease, Cadet." Both boys relaxed. Charlie growled at the older one. "Not you." The lad snapped to attention again.

He turned back to the younger lad. "You are?"

"Sir, S-second year C-cadet Robertson, s-sir."

"Robertson, I would guess that your stutter gets worse when you are nervous." The boy nodded. "May I suggest that you try singing? It will help you relax and learn how to speak more clearly. It has certainly helped my friend, Sergeant Nailer."

The boy relaxed a bit more. "T-thank you, s-sir. I have n-noticed I have l-less trouble singing. But my f-f-father has always t-told me that I could c-control my stuttering if I j-just tried h-harder."

Charlie shook his head. "It is a shame, but I have found that the exact opposite is true. I suspect the harder you try, the worse the stutter gets. Just try to relax, and recognize that other people simply need a little patience. I am sure that when you do talk, you actually have something to say that is worth listening to."

"Thank you, sir," the young man said without a single hitch.

"Go on. I am sure you have a pile of books waiting for you." He dismissed the younger lad, then turned back to the upperclassman. "As for you, Mason, you have a lesson to learn, young man. Each of us has different skills and abilities. If you are to be a good officer and a gentleman, you need to learn to take each man for his worth, not for his weaknesses. You can stand here at attention until such time as I release you, thinking about what it means to be a good officer." With that, he took Rebecca's arm and escorted her to their residence.

An hour later, she looked out the window. Mason was still standing at attention outside their cottage. "Charlie. What are you going to do about that boy?"

His answer was terse. "Leave him there." He turned the page on the paper he was reading. She just looked at him with a bit of disbelief in her eyes. She was really beginning to understand she did not care for military life at all.

Another hour went by. It had started to rain, and a cool breeze was blowing in off the Hudson. Rebecca was once again at the window. "Charlie, if you leave him out there, he will catch his death of a cold."

"He is wearing wool. Leave him there." Now he smoked a cigar and sipped his coffee as she looked at him.

Finally, after another hour, as she was thinking of going to bed, she growled, "You are being cruel. If you do not go out and let that boy go right now, I will go out to him."

"Go ahead if you want to get wet, but he will not move until I release him. Rebecca, he was tormenting that boy because he is exactly like Duncan. And you know if it were not for Duncan getting to me as quickly as he did, I would not have survived. So, no, I do not think I am being cruel. I am teaching a young man the consequences of being a bully. I will release him before I come to bed, I promise."

Rebecca, whose evening ritual was somewhat longer than his, nodded, kissed his head and called Lizbet to pry her out of her evening wear and help her with brushing out her hair.

Charlie pulled on his great coat and hat then walked out to Mason, who was now officially cold, wet and miserable, but still at attention. He stared into the young man's eyes. "So, boy. Have you had a chance to think?" The rain poured from his hat onto the young man's front, and down his boots, as Charlie's face was only an inch from his.

"Sir, yes, sir!"

"Let me tell you something, Mason. You are an arrogant, cocky, know-it-all young man, just like that bastard Custer, who could not manage to send his troops in when they were needed and damned near got me killed and did manage to kill a number of other good men who would not have died if Custer had been paying attention and acted as he should. I may be retired, Mason, but I am still a general. And I can still keep an eye on you and your career. So I strongly advise that you pull your head out of your ass. Dismissed." He turned and walked away before Mason had a chance to say a word.

~

Thursday, October 25, 1866

Charlie's third and final day of lecturing, or more accurately, answering questions, was even better attended than the previous two days. Rebecca used the excuse of preparing to return home the following morning and managed to avoid attending the third day of the lecture. It was all just too overwhelming. Instead, she went and spent the morning and had lunch with Mary in her garden overlooking the Hudson. It was a very pleasant and relaxed day for her.

For Charlie, the third lecture was a real challenge. The room was packed, as every cadet who had not managed to attend the previous lectures was there, as well as some repeat audience members. The presentation went as expected, and the questions and answers were fairly predictable. Until the very end, that is. He announced he had time for one more question before lunch. The same young man, Robertson, whom he had rescued from Mason's bullying, stood up and Charlie recognized him.

A slightly evil grin played around the young man's face as he asked, "Sir, General, sir. C-could you p-please tell us hh-ow you m-managed to get a g-goat into the s-superintendent's office when you w-were a c-cadet?"

Charlie ran his hand over his face and sighed. "Well, Robertson, for starters, it was not a goat. It was a donkey. And out of consideration for my good friend, Superintendent Pitcher, no, I will not tell you. All I can say is, be sure you have at least three good friends and allies. Those stairs are a real bitch."

The room exploded in laughter and applause as he bowed, gathered his cane and notebook, and made his escape. Tom met him at the door. "Charlie Redmond, you are a rat, old man. You know one of these jackdaws is now going to try and put a donkey in my office."

"Too late, Tom. They already knew the story. At least you will get a donkey, not a goat. A goat would probably eat all your papers. And for God's sake, remember to lock your office door."

The two men strolled over to Tom's house to join the ladies and get a bite to eat, laughing and joking as they went. "Like that will stop them. Will you and Rebecca join Mary and me for one more dinner? I know you have to leave early in the morning, and I will be out to see you off, but it would be nice to have another casual, non-military dinner before you go."

Charlie grinned, and said, "If Rebecca says so. She is a tougher commander than Sheridan or Grant ever was."

~

Sunday October 28, 1866

Rebecca sat at her dresser, carefully pinning and styling her hair. Lizbet had awoken this particular morning with a miserable cold. Her friend and mistress had sent her right back to bed with orders that the young woman stay put until she felt better. Not only was she concerned for her lady's maid, but she certainly did not want a cold spread around the house this early in the season.

She knew it was bound to happen. Someone would get sick. Charlie was prone to miserable colds in the winter and she knew it was only a matter of time before he or the children would come down with the first one of the season.

Charlie approached quietly from behind, bending to give her bare neck a tender kiss. "Happy anniversary," he murmured against her tender skin.

"Anniversary? Charlie, our anniversary is in January."

He nodded as he pulled something from his pocket. "You are entirely correct, my darling. He separated a delicate chain and placed it around her neck. "However, today is the anniversary of the day my life began, and I wanted you to have a reminder. It was two years ago today that we met." He glanced at the small clock on her dresser. "In about two hours or so."

He pointed to their reflection as her fingers caressed the jewels. "One birthstone for each of the children." He grinned. "And one for me too."

The necklace was a simple thing by most standards. Charlie's olive-green peridot was in the center of an X-shaped of silver filigree, with a teardrop pearl for Em suspended from the bottom, and the stones for the rest of the children on each branch of the X. There was another peridot for Darby, a pinkish-orange topaz for Suzanne, a deep purple amethyst for Buddy, and a deep green jasper with tiny red spots for Andy. He explained which stone was for which child.

"Oh darling, it is beautiful. Thank you."

∾

Tuesday, November 6, 1866

Jocko placed the plate of pork chops down even before Charlie took his regular seat at the bar. The general eyed his old batman warily. Pork chops were not supposed to be on the menu today. Service like this since leaving the army could only mean one thing.

"What have you done, and what do I need to do to bail you out this time? Not more damn goats, I hope. Rebecca will kill me."

"I am glad you asked!" Jocko piped up as he shook his finger towards his old friend, completely ignoring the goat comment. "My niece will be arriving on the train in the next hour or so. Thought you might go with me to greet her."

"Your niece? Well, of course I would. Not sure why you want me along, but I will be happy to..."

"Good, good," Jocko agreed as he managed to find something else to do at the other end of the bar.

"That was odd," Charlie mumbled as he began eating his lunch. His questions concerning Jocko's unusual behavior were quickly forgotten as he devoured Esther's pork chops and gravy.

Thirty minutes later his plate was empty, his stomach was full, and Jocko was standing before him with a grin that told him the food had been a trap. He sighed, "Jocko..."

"Walk with me, Gen'l C. The train is due any minute."

As they made their way to the station, Jocko decided to come clean. "So, since we have had all this trouble brewing, I decided to call in some help."

468

"You called in your niece?"

"Aye. Just wait, Charlie. She will scare the britches off of ya. And if she doesn't, the wee beasties she is bringing certainly will."

"Jocko!" His good hand slid down his face as the train pulled into the station. "What in the name of hell have you gotten me into this time?" Knowing his old friend as well as he did, Charlie suspected this could end up a lot like the bar fight in Kansas City in '60. It had been a painful experience all the way round. Not as bad as the Sedona hangover, but close.

Jocko stalked away, looking up and down the train waiting for some sign that his niece had arrived. Several passengers disembarked and Charlie stood by patiently waiting for Jocko to signal he had found their quarry. The Irishman continued to stomp up and down the platform, not moving near any of the ladies leaving the passenger car.

Charlie's head swung up when he heard the door to one of the cargo cars slide open and a voice call, "Aye! Uncle Jocko! Over here!"

The general watched as his friend marched toward the fourth car on the train toward the young woman standing in the rail car doorway. He shook his head as he made his way toward the pair.

The young woman was tall and thin with a mop of short dark hair sticking out from under her hat. She was dressed much like Rebecca did on the farm. The biggest difference, which he noticed right away, was the gun holstered on one hip and the twin knives sticking out of the top of each boot.

Oh, shit. Jocko, what have you done? Charlie ambled over to the car where Jocko was standing. He smiled politely as his old friend made the introductions.

"General Redmond, may I introduce my niece, Roselle Jackson, Ro to those of us who bail her out of trouble on the regular."

"Must run in the family," he grumbled at his batman as he extended his hand. "My pleasure, Miss Jackson."

"Aye, General. I suspect it is." She grinned down at the tall man. Very few women were taller than him, and it was a bit unnerving. "So, do you have someone who can help me with the dogs?"

469

Charlie's brows climbed toward his hairline as he looked between them. "Dogs?"

"Aye," she nodded as she stepped aside and revealed four slat crates. Three of them held a pair of the largest gray dogs he had ever seen in his life. Simply standing inside the crates, on all four paws, were bitches that would easily reach his mid-thigh, and the males looked a bit bigger. The fourth crate held a single bitch, heavily pregnant with pups. "Uncle Jocko said you would be needing my special brand of help."

"He did, did he?" His stare turned to the Irishman.

Jocko gave a sheepish grin and pulled him off to the side. "I did, what with all the unrest around here." He paused and swallowed hard. "I also told her you would cover her expenses."

"What?" Charlie stood up straight, glancing back at the young woman, who now sat patiently in the rail car door. "Jocko…"

"Charlie, you have always trusted me before. Trust me now."

He sighed and nodded. "Alright. Let us go figure out what we are going to do next."

Darby took a moment to brush the dust and dirt from his pants. He gave his shirt a quick look and brushed his fingers through his hair. He had no idea why Papa was calling him to the office, but it could not be good. When he heard the clocks in the house chime three o'clock, he stood straight and knocked on the door of the office.

"Come," was the clipped response. He knew from residing here now for nearly a year that meant his father was concentrating on something. He opened the door and stepped inside. He quietly and gently closed the door. Charlie sat at his desk, head down, pen in hand.

He paused briefly, looking up to see his eldest son. "Have a seat, Darby. I will be right with you. Just let me finish this letter."

The young man took a seat in one of the two chairs across from his father at the desk. The high back leather chair at the left side of Papa's desk was for Mama. No one sat in that chair but her. He tried hard not to fidget but the waiting was taking a toll on his young body.

Charlie lifted his pen. Giving the letter one last read, he used the blotter to remove the excess ink and set the letter aside to dry. Then he looked to Darby.

"Hello, Mr. Sweet." He smiled and stood, offering Darby his hand across the desk.

"Umm." The very confused boy stood and shook the general's hand. "Hello, Papa."

"Please," he gestured, as Darby had seen him do hundreds of times before with the businessmen that were always visiting. "Have a seat, sir. Thank you for agreeing to meet with me on such short notice."

Charlie settled back down into his chair and watched his son, managing to keep the smile from his face as he continued to address the young man. "Sir, I will not waste your valuable time. I have a business proposition for you."

The boy blinked. "A business proposition? For me?"

"Well, you see, Mr. Sweet." Charlie stood and poured them each a cup of tea and placed two of Sarah's best cakes on the plate next to the cup before placing one in front of Darby. "You have a piece of property I would be interested in renting from you if we can agree on a fair price."

Darby sat there confused, trying to figure out what kind of a test this was. He took a deep breath and let it out before saying, "I am sure I do not understand, Papa." He took his teacup and carefully sipped it, waiting, hoping Charlie would let him off the hook with this particular riddle.

"Your property, west of town? The little farmhouse?"

Darby thought about it. That house seemed a million miles and a million dreams away now. He had not thought about it since the night he and Suzanne had left it behind. "Y..yes, sir? What about it?"

"I have need of a property exactly like yours for a new business that has blown into town rather unexpectedly. Your property would be perfect."

471

The young man just shook his head. "Then use it, Papa."

"Well now, it is your property, Mr. Sweet. It would not be fair for me to just use it without your permission and giving you proper compensation. So I would like to offer you ten dollars a month in rent."

Darby placed his teacup and saucer on the small table between the two chairs that sat in front of his father's desk. He drew a deep breath, letting it out slowly and looked across the desk at the man before him, finally figuring out the test.

"Fifteen dollars a month," he said with serious determination.

Charlie nearly choked on the tea he has just taken a drink of. He drew a quick breath through his nose and cleared his throat. He placed his cup in the saucer on his desk. "Eleven."

Darby first nodded, and then shook his head. "Forgive me, General Redmond."

Charlie's brows crawled up his forehead; he had not expected this when he decided to play with Darby. His son was certainly turning into a proper businessman.

Darby looked directly into the eyes of the man he had come to think of as his real father. "You need my property. I do not need to rent it. Thirteen dollars a month and you are responsible for all repairs needed to get it in livable condition."

Charlie burst out laughing and quickly stood, offering his hand to the formidable opponent across from him. "You drive a hard bargain, Mr. Sweet, but I can see I have little choice." He winked at his son. "And do not tell you mother or I will be the Powder Monkey for the next month."

"Papa?"

"Yes, Darby?"

"Please, sir, think about what you just said. Based on your own comments, it is actually in my best interest to tell Mama. Perhaps you should reconsider the fifteen dollars a month."

Charlie could only stand there gaping. He had just been hoisted by his own petard.

~

Thursday, November 8, 1866

Charlie pulled the collar of his coat around his neck. The wind was absolutely biting as he made his way up the little road that would lead to Darby's property, the home of the newest transplant to Culpeper, Ro Jackson and her huge dogs.

The general had been thrilled to find out that the house actually had not been in that bad of shape. One of the chimneys needed to be cleaned, but Big Ben and a couple of the boys from Hudnut's shop had gotten it taken care of very quickly. The roof was sound, as was the floor, doors and windows. All in all, getting a few pieces of actual furniture in place had been the hardest problem and Duncan had handled that efficiently.

The good news was Rebecca still had no clue about the most current mess Jocko had gotten him into. This was so much worse than the goats.

Jocko had explained that Ro had been brought in to provide special security for the farm. The dogs she trained were known as Irish Wolf Hounds and were proven, especially with her training, to effectively guard any target she set them to. It would take a few weeks of training and working the dogs, but eventually Charlie would have a pack of dogs roaming the grounds that would be the first line of defense for everything from his family and home to his horses and barns.

He pulled Jack to a stop at the front door, remembering the first time he had been here with Rebecca. Then, the yard had been overgrown, there were weeds in the corners, and the whole place had a rundown, shabby quality.

Already the place was looking better. The yard had been tended, and there was a small flock of chickens roaming through the neatly mown grass. In one corner, a plot had been tilled, ready for spring planting. The windows had been washed. Ben was there, whitewashing the house to give it a clean, crisp look. Smoke rose from one of the two chimneys. Hudnut's men were still working on the other one, which he could tell from the man standing on the roof.

Eventually, part of the back yard would be turned into kennels and a dog run, complete with gated off areas to keep the dogs away from one another if necessary.

He walked up to the little house and rapped on the open doorframe. He was greeted with seven raised gray heads. All of Ro's dogs were lying in the middle of the floor, rather like a large, lumpy gray rug. Ro turned her head as well, and said, "Hello, General Charlie. Come in." As soon as she spoke, the dogs lay their heads down again. Their ma was happy, so they were too.

She was obviously busy putting things away and making her little home orderly. Earlier that day, Duncan and his men had brought out a new bed, a dresser, a couple of chairs, a set of bookshelves and a large kitchen table. It was not as much as Charlie had wished, but it was enough to get her started.

∼

Friday, November 9, 1866

Rebecca made her way up the steps to Charlie's office, a little box tucked under her arm. Charlie had awoken with a bit of a head cold and decided to work from home. She had decided that a trip to town would be in order for herself so she could pick a few things up at Mr. Cooper's, go to the post office to collect their mail, and to the bank to see if Frank had anything for Charlie.

She was not amused when she saw the post mark on the box. Baltimore. This could only mean one thing. More damn lead soldiers. Charlie was hiding behind a handkerchief when she came in, obviously having just survived a major sneezing attack. She sighed, knowing the little box would make him feel better.

"Your toys arrived." She laughed as she set the box down in front of him.

"What toys?"

"I have no clue, but I suspect that since this box is from Mr. Schwarz in Baltimore, it is more of your little lead soldiers."

He tried not to look excited as he eyed the box. He wanted to open it, really wanted to open it, but she was still standing there looking down at him. "I promise you I did not order any more. I have no idea what is in this box."

"Then perhaps you should open it before you explode." She handed him the knife he kept on his desk for such tasks.

"Oh, goodie!" He clapped his hands before taking the knife and carefully opening the seal on the box.

She watched with a certain degree of amusement as he unpacked a few more lead soldiers, horses and pieces of artillery in styles very different from what she knew was already in the house. Her head actually dropped to her chest when he also extracted a few new pieces of dollhouse furniture. "The man is insane," she murmured to no one in particular.

"He is a brilliant businessman." Charlie chuckled as he maneuvered a new cannon across is desk.

~

~

The dining room in Mrs. Williams' little cottage was packed with men. Alex Raeburn took the seat in the room usually reserved for the head of a household and looked around at the men before him.

Mrs. Williams flitted in and out filling and refilling coffee cups and leaving plates of food for the men to enjoy. She thought herself completely in her element--the charming hostess to the best the South had to offer.

"They just finished building a big indoor exercise ring and I heard he is planning on building a carriage house in the spring," Eddie said, as the ashes of his cigar dropped onto the rug, leaving a black scorch mark. "Then there are the little houses on the edge of the property."

"You know anything about that, Brooks?" Alex queried.

Robert Brooks raised his head and nodded. "Yeah, it has been mentioned."

Alex arched a brow as his mouth drew tight before he growled at his man. "Is that so?"

Brooks nodded again.

"Anything else 'been mentioned'?"

Brooks sat back and gave a disgusted sigh. "What in the hell do you want to know Alex? Redmond is a decent man." He heard the entire room grumble. "I know that is not what you want to hear, but it is the truth. This is the best damn job I have ever had."

"You turning on us, Brooks?" asked Eddie.

Eddie had managed to maintain a part-time job at Duncan Nailer's shop and Brooks had seen him out on the property several times with the carpenter and he was happy to tell everything he saw or thought he saw on the property.

"No, I ain't turning on anyone. Just statin' facts. You know as well as I do," Brooks shook his finger at Eddie, "I have never seen you turn down a hot meal or a cool drink from his kitchen when you have been out working for Nailer. And you've made enough money off of Redmond for a new horse which you bought from him, clothes and a fancy gold watch. So maybe you just need to be quiet."

His attention returned to the group. "Redmond pays on time, middle of the month. Like clockwork. He pays cold, hard coin and he takes care of his people. Everyone gets a meal a day. Hell, I have taken home baskets of food to my family at the end of the day. If there is a special piece of equipment or tool we need, he gets them. Damn it, I found out he covered all the feed tabs some of you boys ran up on his wife last winter." He nodded. "He's a real bastard. He is even giving each man in the barns an extra dollar next month as a Christmas bonus; now, I don't know about y'all, but my wife and daughter can sure use that extra dollar for Christmas and I am happy to work for it."

Several of the men looked like they were about to bodily throw him out the door. Alex tapped his fingers on the table and got their attention. "Easy now fellas, Mr. Brooks there is entitled to his opinion." He settled back in his chair and poured some tobacco into a paper, a very self-satisfied grin pulling at his lips as he rolled the cigarette. "We try to take that away and we ain't no damn better than the Yankees or that bastard Redmond."

Raeburn went on. "There is a different issue that I want you fellas to think about. My old commander, General Forrest, has started a new organization out in Tennessee that we want to look into. He is calling it the Ku Klux Klan. Knowing Devil Forrest, it is NOT what you would call a neighborly charitable organization. He wants to make sure the niggers stay in their rightful place, and the nigger-lovers get what they rightfully deserve. I think we should find out more about this little organization. Mebbe do something like that ourselves. What do you think?"

"Well, I sure would like to do something about them uppity niggers, who are taking jobs out at the brickworks past Sweetwater. They's taking jobs from good white folks 'cause they will work for cheap."

Raeburn looked thoughtful. "Mebbe something to scare them back into their rabbit holes." He stroked his chin. "And now that they get to vote, we sure as hell want to scare them away from the polls."

Eddie spoke up. "What about the nigger-lovers in town? Do a little something to keep them from shoving their niggers down our throats?"

The men settled down to discuss just who they wanted to strike out at first.

Mrs. Williams just kept their coffee cups full. She smiled, pleased at the thought that her boys would be taking care of that man's influence on her town.

CHAPTER 27

Tuesday, November 13, 1866

Suzanne's birthday, like all birthdays in the Redmond family, was something of an event. Buddy and Andy's birthday had been a food fight for one-year-olds. Em's third birthday had been a formal, very grown up dinner where Em was the guest of honor. Rebecca's was a picnic in the new gazebo, and Charlie and Darby's birthday was a pig roast. Suzanne was eager to see what was in store for her. A fifth birthday was a big event in her mind.

It was also a big event in her mama's mind. She needed to find something special for Suzanne's birthday. Given the child's love of Cousin Charlotte's wardrobe, she decided that her daughter deserved a dress-up party for her birthday. She had made friends with a couple of the girls of her age at Sunday school, who would no doubt be more than happy to join them for the big event.

So on the morning of the big day, Rebecca, Charlotte, Lizbet and Sissy trooped up to the third floor, where there were chests of old clothes in several of the storage rooms. The four of them went through chest after chest, pulling out clothes, hats, shoes, and ancient costume jewelry. When they were done, they had about six boxes of clothes and accessories for the girls to play with. Reg sent two of the houseboys up to carry them down to the formal parlor, which had been decorated by Beulah and her troops with pink and lace hangings for the big event.

Sarah had also outdone herself. A buffet lunch was laid in the breakfast room, along with a cake redolent with pink icing and real, edible flowers. Precisely at noon, several buggies, traps, and wagons pulled up to the front steps. The ladies, both adult and children, had arrived.

The party first had their lunch. Proper food was a necessity for any party. The beautiful cake received all of the appropriate "oooohs" and "aaahs" from the guests. Suzanne, as guest of honor, got to sit at the head of the table, where her mother usually sat, and play the hostess for the meal. She did a reasonably credible job of it too.

The gentlemen of the family had taken one look at the decorations in the parlor, and at the big, very pink cake, and huddled up in Papa's office. Charlie and Darby had no desire to spend the afternoon being overwhelmed by pink and giggles. With Darby's scheduled afternoon lessons with John Foxworth, and Charlie's never-ending supply of paperwork, it was a good excuse. The smaller boys really were not yet old enough to participate in a girl's party anyway, since the family would have a birthday dinner together that evening. They had already given Suzanne her birthday presents at breakfast that morning, including a new saddle and bridle for her pony from Mama, a set of horse statues, complete with stable and paddock from Charlie, compliments of the Schwarz brothers, and a book on horse breeds from Darby. It was a good bet that the gentlemen were safe for the afternoon.

As the ladies entered the formal parlor, there were more exclamations at the decorations that had been added to that normally very formal room. The boxes had been arranged so that one could see the fabrics, shawls, and gewgaws cascading out of them. Rebecca announced, "We thought you would enjoy an afternoon of playing dress up. So have at it, girls."

Suzanne took command, pointing a box out for each girl to rummage through. Very soon, there were young ladies draped with a wide variety of garments, all of which were too big for them, parading around the room in shoes that were also too big. It was a wonderful way for girls to play.

The adults retired to one side of the room, where a nice pot of tea had been set. They tried to carry on a reasonable conversation, but they were continuously interrupted, with girlish voices screaming, "Look, Mama. Look at what I found." The adults laughed, gave up, and turned their attention and efforts to commenting on the girls' outfits with loving encouragement.

By the time the guests had left and the family assembled for dinner, the women of the house, Suzanne, Em, Charlotte and Rebecca, were all so worn out they could barely eat. But Suzanne was one joyously happy little girl. She had just had the best day of her life.

~

Tuesday, November 27, 1866

Reg was a bit startled when he heard the knock on the front door. He was absolutely positive that all the guests had not only already arrived but had been seated for supper. Jerome Lord, his wife Amelia and their eight children, Edgar and Rex, and Richard and Elizabeth along with little Dickon were spending the week at Redmond Stables to celebrate Thanksgiving.

He pulled the door open to find a very elegant lady. She was dressed in a long soft blue dress, with matching hat and gloves to complete the ensemble. "Yes, ma'am? Welcome to Redmond Stables. How may I help you?"

"My name is Victoria Landau. I am here to see General and Mrs. Redmond."

The major domo gestured and brought her into the foyer. "May I tell the general and Mrs. Redmond why you are calling?"

Reg hurried to the dining room. He took a deep breath and slipped in quietly, immediately moving to Charlie's side. He leaned over and whispered. Rebecca could feel dread welling in her stomach as she watched her husband. When his eyes went wide and the blood drained from his face, her panic started to really set in.

He rose and offered gently, "If you will all please excuse me. Something has popped up that requires our attention. We will return shortly. Please continue and enjoy dinner. Do not let Sarah's efforts go to waste or I will pay for it."

He walked to the other end of the table and quietly invited his wife to join him by extending his hand. She took it and they left the room as quickly as possible.

"Charlie?" She queried as they walked down the hall.

"I am not really sure. Let us see." He shook his head.

They entered the foyer to find the lady sitting in one of the high back chairs nearest the windows. She rose and extended her hand as they entered. "Ah, General and Mrs. Redmond, so good to finally meet you at last. I am Victoria Landau, Darby and Suzanne's aunt."

Rebecca looked at the woman before her. She was tall and slim, rather austerely dressed in a blue travelling dress, and had Suzanne's red hair. She had come, no doubt, to tear her family apart. She wanted to kill the woman on the spot and hide the body. Her hands knotted into fists, which she had to force herself to unclench so she could shake the woman's offered hand.

Charlie spoke first, as Rebecca could not find her voice. "How can we help you, Miss Landau?"

"Why, General Redmond, I would think it is apparent. I have come to get my sister's children. I know you have cared for them, and for that I am grateful, but now that I am back in the country, I think I should be responsible for my own family."

Rebecca spoke up. "Miss Landau, perhaps we should move this conversation to a more comfortable environment. Please, come into our parlor. Have you eaten?"

"Thank you, Mrs. Redmond. Yes, I had a bite in town before I came out. I do not want to impose on you any more than our family already has."

Rebecca turned and led the way to the back parlor. If she shoved a stick up her bum, she could not possibly be any more of a stiff-necked bitch. Victoria Landau had not made a good impression on Mrs. Redmond.

As they walked up the hall to the parlor, Charlie politely asked, "You have been out of the country?"

"Yes, General. I am a horse breeder in Kentucky and I was over in North Africa looking for new Arabian stock, then in England, where I purchased a new sire for my herd from the Godolphin line."

"Taking your breed stock back to the basics? I would like to do so as well but am considering adding standardbreds to our lines just because they have more versatility." The horse breeder in Rebecca could not help but pick up the conversation.

"Yes, they are certainly good horses for a number of uses."

The three of them entered the parlor and sat. Victoria looked at them and returned to her purpose. "Chatting about horse lines is all well and good, but shall we get back to the point? I am here to collect my sister's children. The sooner we can get underway, the happier I will be."

Rebecca clenched the arms of her chair. "Miss Landau, the children have become an integral part of our family. They are as dear to us as they would be if they were conceived between us and born of my own body." Unsaid, but still obvious between them was her plea to not take the children she considered hers after all these months.

The woman looked from Rebecca to Charlie. The pain and fear of loss was obvious in both faces. "I understand you have grown attached to the children, but they are my sister's blood and I feel I must be responsible for them."

Charlie cleared his throat. "Miss Landau, have you ever met your niece and nephew?"

"Unfortunately, no, General Redmond. My sister was estranged from the family before the war. Our father did not approve of her marriage to Mr. Sweet. And what with the war and my business..." she paused. "No, I have not met them."

He sighed deeply. "Well, to be perfectly honest, my wife and I would prefer to keep the children. We would be happy to adopt them, as a matter of fact. But whether the children stay here with us or go with you, do you not think that it would be better for them to meet you and get to know you before you go hauling them off to a new place?"

Rebecca grabbed his hand. At this point, every day, every minute she could get with the two oldest of her children was precious.

"Yes, I can see where that would be a good idea. But please, let me be clear. I am determined to take my sister's children home with me."

And I am determined that you shall not, thought Rebecca. But she said nothing, and rang for Reg and a maid to make a guest room ready for Miss Landau.

~

Charlie had seen Miss Landau off with Reg to get settled in her room. Rebecca had stood by quietly until the woman left and then she simply turned and headed up the stairs towards their bedroom. He returned to the dining room. He took a deep breath and smiled, as Darby was still in the room and right now he could not let his son know there was anything wrong.

"I do apologize. Miss Rebecca has developed a severe headache and I am afraid I need to tend to her. Please everyone, continue to enjoy each other's company and I shall return as soon as I can."

As he turned to leave, Richard and Jerome were at his side. "Charlie?" They both asked, very nearly in unison.

He motioned them into the hallway, closing the door gently behind them. "Seems Darby and Suzanne's aunt from Kentucky has returned from abroad and she has come, determined to take them away."

"Is there any kind of paperwork or court orders?" Jerome asked, the lawyer in him coming out to protect his friend and his children.

He shook his head. "No. We took them in earlier this year." He just shook his head again. "I need to get to Rebecca. We will talk in the morning."

"All right." Jerome nodded. Richard gave his friend a

sympathetic pat on the back as he began climbing the steps to his distraught wife.

By the time he reached their bedroom she was sitting on the edge of their bed, sobbing.

"Oh, darling," he lamented as he sat next to her and wrapped her up in his arms. "I am so sorry."

"We cannot…" She clutched his lapel in her fist as she gasped for air. "Cannot let her take them, Charlie." She looked up at him, her face stained with tears. "Promise me you will not let her take our children!"

"I promise you I will do everything in my power to stop her."

"They are our children! We love them! She does not even know them!"

He hugged her tighter and kissed the top of her head. "I know, love. I know. Jerome is already in defensive mode. Let us try to be pleasant to her and convince her to let us adopt them while she is here."

"What if she refuses?"

"Then, my love, I am afraid we may have to let them go with her."

She collapsed into his chest, sobbing once again. For the moment, he decided to let her cry. She needed to get the anger and frustration out before they tried to convince this woman not to tear apart their family.

After several minutes, she settled into his embrace. He just rested his cheek on top of her head. "How can she do this? How can she just destroy our family like this?" She whimpered, the sound of her voice causing his heart to break all over again.

"Maybe we can change her mind," he offered softly. "Darling, why not get ready for bed? I will make sure our guests are settled and join you shortly."

She shook her head and wiped the tears from her face. "No. I need to go tuck everyone in."

"Darling, are you sure?"

She nodded and stood, moving to the wash basin to freshen up. "I will not let her steal the time I do have with them."

He gave her a moment and then they both began their nightly sojourn to each of the children's bedrooms, Charlie carefully handling the lamp to light their way from room to room. As was their habit, the toddler boys came first, both of them sound asleep in their respective cribs. Rebecca made sure they were covered and sleeping soundly before moving to the girls' room. Both of them were sound asleep in their beds, their dolls tucked in neatly beside them. Kisses from both parents, were placed on sleeping brows before heading off to Darby.

When they entered his room, he was still sitting up in bed, a book clutched in his hands, the lantern turned up so he could read.

Rebecca settled on the edge of his bed. "You should have been asleep a half hour ago."

"But this book is just so good, Mama!" His eyes were bright and his face alert. "It is The Three Musketeers!"

"Oh, that is a good one." She brushed her fingers through his hair, even as she removed the book and placed it on his night table. "Lots of adventure. The perfect thing for a young man such as yourself."

Charlie stood back and watched them, his heart cracking into small pieces as he imagined their life without this bright young man. He knew she would never get over losing them. He was not so sure he would either. He had to do something to convince this woman to leave them in peace.

Rebecca tucked Darby securely under the covers, placing a kiss on his forehead that lingered a bit longer than normal.

"Love you, Mama," Darby murmured as he snuggled under the covers.

"I love you too, son." She sat there for a long moment, brushing her fingers through his hair as he nodded off to sleep.

When she stood from his bedside, her shoulders were slumped almost as if she were already defeated. She could only shake her head as she walked to the door where Charlie waited. As she moved past him, she looked up, tears brimming in her eyes. Without a word she returned to their bedroom, leaving him at their son's bedroom door. He closed the door quietly and turned to go comfort his wife.

She was sitting on the bench at the end of their bed, staring at her hands as her fingernails picked and scraped against each other. He took her hands in his and knelt down in front of her. "I promise you I will do everything in my power to keep our family together. You know that?"

She nodded, the act causing the tears in her eyes to slide down her cheeks. He stood and moved to the brandy decanter. He sighed and poured one. Retrieving the glass, he handed it down to her. "Drink this."

"Charlie…"

"One brandy is not going to hurt you and I am not having any. So drink it."

She nodded and gratefully put the glass to her lips. After so many months, he had been right, it only took one. Between the brandy and her exhausted, emotional state, it did not take long before he put her to bed, where she slept fitfully through the night. He could only sit in a chair next to the bed, watch his wife try to sleep, and stare out into the dark night sky.

~

Wednesday, November 28, 1866

The next morning one of the upstairs maids led Miss Landau down to the dining room, where she found them seated at opposite ends of the long table. Seated between them, a small group of people, looking very much like back up, or an ambush.

She gave a knowing, but annoyed smile as she offered, "I had rather hoped to do this privately, but I can see that will not be the case."

"Well, you see Miss Landau." One of the men stood and escorted her to a seat. "I am Jerome Lord, General and Mrs. Redmond's attorney. I am here with my wife and family to celebrate Thanksgiving with them. General Redmond and I have been friends since we were both at West Point."

"I am the physician to the Redmond family, and given the general's state of health after his terrible injuries at Appomattox last

486

year…" Elizabeth tapped her coffee cup with her spoon, letting the rest of the comment die on her lips.

"I am the family minister," Edgar offered as he rose and poured the lady a cup of coffee, placing it in front of her.

"I am General Redmond's cousin," Charlotte offered with a less than sincere smile at the woman she was considering helping Rebecca kill.

Victoria looked at the table and gestured first to Richard. "And you?"

"Oh, me." He leaned back in his chair. "I am just his best friend." He pointed at Charlie. "And damn nosey. So tell me, Miss Landau, what part of Kentucky are you from?"

"I am from Lexington, Mr…?"

"Polk, Lieutenant Colonel Richard Polk, United States Army and provost of the Town of Culpeper." He looked to Charlie and grinned. "I remember Lexington, and surely you do too. What happens in Lexington, stays in Lexington."

Victoria turned to Rex, who smiled benignly before simply saying, "I am here to keep Miss Rebecca from poisoning your coffee and hiding the body."

"I did not hear that." Jerome moaned as he retook his seat.

"Miss Landau," Charlie started tentatively. "We had hoped after an evening to rest and reconsider, we might be able to come to some sort of an agreement."

"An agreement where I leave my niece and nephew with you?"

"No." Rebecca shook her head. "An agreement where our son and daughter remain with us."

"Mrs. Redmond, I do appreciate your passion and concern for the children, but the fact remains you are not their mother."

"How dare you!"

It was not the explosion anyone at the table expected, but suddenly Charlotte was on her feet, hands planted firmly on the table as she hissed in the direction of the woman across from her.

"Rebecca is a loving, doting mother! She kisses every bump and bruise! Soothes every nighttime terror! I have seen her run herself ragged to care for the children. She nearly worked herself to death a few months ago when they all came down with the measles at the same time. It was Rebecca who sat up all hours of the day and night to make sure those children were cared for. How dare you say she is not a mother to the children!"

Edgar moved quickly to calm Charlotte and help her retake her seat. "Darling, please," he whispered as he refreshed her coffee. "This will not help Charlie and Rebeca's situation."

"Please." Victoria held her hand up. "I did not mean to insult Mrs. Redmond. I am simply stating a fact. I am very grateful for the care that the children have been given by the Redmonds. We will always be indebted to them for that, but they are not Darby and Suzanne's rightful parents."

Edgar took a seat next to Charlotte, continuing to hold her hand, tightly in his own. "I think that would depend on how you define parents. Are the Redmonds the two people who came together to create these lives? No. But are they the two people who have come together to care for and love these children as any parent would? Yes. Absolutely."

"And the children have blossomed under their care," Dr. Walker added with a nod. "To take them away from here would devastate them."

"Is that a medical opinion, Doctor?" Victoria lifted a brow.

"It is my personal opinion."

"And you may keep it to yourself." Victoria stood and looked at each one of them in turn. "I have come to take my niece and nephew back to Kentucky with me. I am open to the suggestion of spending a few days here for the children and me to have a chance to get to know each other. However, I will not tolerate this hostility. It will do the children no good to try and get to know me if you all are walking around with your hackles up. So, when you have all come to your senses, and you feel the time is appropriate, I would very much like to be introduced to my niece and nephew so that we may start this process. I will be in my room. Thank you."

With that she turned and walked away, leaving the entire table stunned. These were people entirely accustomed to getting their own way and Victoria Landau had just given them a rather large, unappetizing taste of crow.

Jerome waited for just a moment before asking Charlie, "What do you want to do now?"

"Throw that bitch out of my house and forget we heard her knock."

～

Charlie and Rebecca gathered Darby and Suzanne and took them to Charlie's office. When they entered, Victoria rose from a chair near the fire where she had been asked to wait for them and smiled. Rebecca wanted to kill her, and if her derringer had not been locked in her husband's gun cabinet, she might have given it a try in that very moment.

This woman was a real threat that she could do nothing about. It was not as if she were a bandit trying to rob the bank or a marauder breaking down the door of the house. No, this was a threat far more dangerous than anything she had ever imagined protecting her family from. A woman who had every right to take the children she had grown to love from the moment she laid eyes on them.

Charlie exhaled and moved the children gently forward until they stood in front of the tall woman. "Children, this is your Aunt Victoria," he said quietly, never removing his hands from their shoulders. He was feeling every bit as possessive as his wife, just not as murderous, yet.

Darby extended his hand. Suzanne clutched Charlie's pant leg and hid her face. "It is a pleasure to meet you, Aunt Victoria," the boy offered sincerely.

She took his hand and smiled. "You look like your mother."

"Yes, ma'am." Darby nodded.

Rebecca was doing her best not to give into the urge to grab the children and run. Very quietly, she moved from her spot near the door, "Excuse me." And she was gone. A threat like this to her children could bring Rebecca, who was normally so strong and capable, to her knees. Charlie felt his heart break all over again.

They all settled into seats, Darby escorting his aunt Victoria to a chair at one side of the fireplace, then took his place beside his father in the love seat across from her. Suzanne was still attached to the tall man, now sitting so close to him she was almost melded into his side. It was a little cramped, but neither Charlie nor the children minded.

They simply waited. After a somewhat strained pause, Victoria started. "Well, children, I am happy to meet you at last. I want to be perfectly clear with you. As your mother's closest living relative, I have come to not only get to know you, but to take you home with me so you can be with your real family."

Suzanne whimpered fearfully. Darby looked at her with cool suspicion but said nothing.

Aunt Victoria continued. "I live on a lovely farm outside of Lexington in Kentucky. We raise horses."

At horses, Suzanne lifted her head a little. "What kind of horses?"

"Mostly thoroughbreds and standardbreds."

"Mama raises thoroughbreds too. I like horses."

"Well, then, Suzanne, you will like it at my house as well." She looked at Darby. "And what do you like?"

"Oh, I like to learn things. Books. Maps. History. Science. All kinds of things. Papa found us a really wonderful tutor, and we have an outstanding library here as well."

She looked around the room, which was obviously lined with very well-filled bookshelves, had maps on the walls, a large globe and a beautiful bronze orrery that showed all of the planets circling the sun, and their moons circling the planets, with a handle that you could turn and they would all move.

The young man went on. "Papa and I have a beautiful set of soldiers too. Right now, we have them laid out like the troops at Waterloo. I am reading French history as well."

This bookish boy would be a bit of a problem, as there were very few books in her house, and what few there were tended to be romantic novels. "Well, then, Darby, we will have to build you a proper library."

Darby looked skeptical.

Victoria went on. "When I heard from General Redmond, I knew I had to come and get you, rather than leave you all alone here in Virginia. I am sure we can build a lovely life together in Kentucky."

Suzanne piped up. "We are not alone. We have Mama 'Becca and Papa Charlie, and Em and Andy and Buddy, and all our friends here in Culpeper."

Victoria was growing a bit impatient with this outspoken little girl. As far as she was concerned, children were to be seen and not heard. Clearly, no one had taught the child this most fundamental aspect of childish manners. "Yes, but they are not family. I am your mother's sister. That makes me family. Little girls and boys should grow up with their family."

The response to that was a rather strained silence. Charlie sat with his hands in his lap, but still touching both of the children, one on each side of him.

Finally, Darby spoke up. "So, my mother's sister? May I ask why we have never had the opportunity to meet you before?"

Victoria was startled at the very blunt question from what she regarded as a young, naïve boy. "Uh, well, Darby. I live in Kentucky, and what with the war and all, it was not an easy thing for me to come here."

He looked disbelieving. "And before the war, ma'am? I can understand why Suzanne never met you before, but I am eleven, and yet I have never met you either."

She looked into his eyes. It was clear from the look on his face that a polite lie was going to do more damage that the truth. "Well, to be honest with you, there were problems in the family. Our father did not like your father, so the family went separate ways. But our father has died, and there is no reason why that rift should continue."

He said nothing, but the look on his face was still shuttered.

Charlie interjected. "So is it just you now, Miss Landau, or do the children have other relatives living in Lexington? Maybe you could give the children some idea of who else in the family they might meet."

"Alas, no, General Redmond. My mother died many years ago, and both of our brothers died in the war. So, yes, it is just me now, maintaining the family heritage. But Lexington is a thriving town, having survived the war with minimal damage, and there is a large horse breeding community, an active social life, and many children for Darby and Suzanne to be friends with."

Suzanne responded, "We have lots of family here. We have Mama and Papa and Aunt Elizabeth and Uncle Richard, and Cousin Charlotte, and Reverend Edgar, and Rex, and Aunt Grace and Uncle Edward and there's Miss Samantha and Mr. Duncan and Jeremiah."

Rather impatiently, Victoria broke in, "Yes, Suzanne, but they are not your family."

Rather stubbornly, Suzanne retorted, "Are, too. And we have lots of friends here. All of the girls my age from Sunday school came to my birthday party!"

"I am sure you do, and when you come with me, you will get to make new friends."

"But I like the friends I have here, ma'am."

Victoria looked frustrated. In her opinion, these two were rude, poorly mannered and unruly children. She thought she would have a time with them and was convinced that they had suffered from having the rod spared, and so were spoiled little brats.

Darby realized this was going nowhere, and just upsetting his sister. "Aunt Victoria, would you like to see our soldiers?" He got up and stood waiting to escort her over to the table in the far corner where he and Charlie had the troops laid out.

She accompanied him, where he treated her to a lecture on the battle of Waterloo, pointing out the maneuvers that the British, Prussian and Russian troops had made to defeat who some said was the greatest general of the century.

He then took her over to the orrery and told her about the planetary orbits. His lecture then moved on to the various maps, where he discussed geography, and finally to a bust of Caesar, where Roman history was the topic of his dissertation. She was well and truly bored out her mind.

Fortunately, lunch was announced just then, and they all went downstairs for a rather quiet and strained repast.

After lunch, Suzanne and Darby adjourned for their daily lessons. Victoria looked at Charlie with disdain. The man had said nothing to support her creating a relationship with the children. On the other hand, at least he had not said anything to discourage her, either. This morning had not gone as she had anticipated.

~

Thursday, November 29, 1866 (Thanksgiving)

Thanksgiving Day dawned bright and downright chilly. After a rather noisy breakfast with not only all of Charlie and Rebecca's children at the table with the adults, but with Jerome and Amelia Lord's brood as well, the children who were old enough to run did. Out into the bright morning and the fascination of a farm with horses, pigs, goats, chickens and God only knew what else. Victoria retired to her bedroom to rest, read a pot boiler of a romance novel she had brought with her, and escape the rush and bustle of a horde of rapscallions, and the silent condemnation of a mass of resentful adults.

Around three o'clock, there was a tap on her door. One of the houseboys was standing there when she opened it.

"Miss Landau, Miss Rebecca asked me to tell you that Thanksgiving Dinner is being served."

She had dressed carefully for this dinner. She needed to turn these people around, whatever it took. So when she entered the ball room, which had been set as a dining room, she was surprised.

All of the women in the room were beautifully dressed, in clothing that would have passed muster in the great salons of Europe. The gentlemen were dressed in formal suits, appropriate for an afternoon dinner.

And all of the children, even the toddler boys, were in attendance, wearing smaller versions of the same garb as the adults.

There were more people present as well, as they had been joined by the Nailers and the Coopers.

Victoria felt overwhelmed. And underdressed.

The dinner conversation around the adults' table stayed polite and socially acceptable, with no reference to the reason for Victoria's presence. Politics, horses, literature – these were the topics of discussion. To a great extent, Victoria was ignored as much as she could be and still have the afternoon remain polite. The children were fairly quiet as they ate at their own table set to the side.

After dinner, the children went off to do whatever children do after Thanksgiving dinner, and the adults enjoyed after-dinner coffee and drinks. Conversation turned to war stories. Someone finally asked Victoria how she had spent the war years. Briefly, she spoke of supplying Standardbreds to the army, and then travelling to Europe and North Africa to re-build her herds over the past few months.

It was with great relief that she could excuse herself from the group, pleading the need to get an early start the next morning.

It was also a great relief to the others in the room, as they had been stretched as thin as possible to maintain a polite front.

Rebecca then headed straight into the gentlemen's smoking room, and went for the tantalus, pouring a large brandy. "I hate her," she said to no one in particular and to all assembled.

Charlie looked at Jerome. They were gathered in his office later that night, after all of the non-residents but Elizabeth and Richard had departed. Rebecca sat to one side, supported by Charlotte, Amelia, Elizabeth and Edgar. Richard stood behind Charlie, one hand on his shoulder. Rex leaned against the wall, watching as always. However, the pain clearly registered on his face as well as the others in the room.

"All right, Jerome. What can we do?" Charlie asked from his

spot near the tantalus. It was clear he was considering pouring himself a drink.

Jerome cleared his throat. He would rather chew broken glass than have to say the next words out of his mouth. "Immediately? Nothing."

Charlie poured the brandy and threw it back quickly, recapping the decanter.

Jerome sighed. "She has the right to take them, and there is nothing we can do to stop her. You have no paper, no documentation, no court rulings. In other words, no grounds to keep Darby and Suzanne. I can and will do everything possible to get them back. I will throw every law book and every crooked judge I can find at her, both in Washington and in Lexington. But right now, you have no choice. You have to let them go with her."

Rebecca burst into tears.

Charlie's heart was breaking. "Do it. I do not care what it will cost. I will spend every damned dime I have to get those children back. Do you hear me? Get them back."

~

Friday, November 30, 1866

Darby stood between the porch and the coach watching everything. Suzanne was already in the coach, sobbing and reaching out toward Mama and Papa. All of their possessions were loaded into boxes and trunks stowed on the boot, including his and Papa's beloved lead soldiers. The woman inside was looking satisfied with herself.

Papa and Mama looked like they were about to burst into tears. He could tell Papa was actually holding Mama in place. He was not sure if it was to keep her from running to the carriage to grab Suzanne or if it was just to keep her from collapsing on the porch.

Uncle Edgar and Uncle Richard looked like they were about to punch someone or something. Mr. Jerome's face looked like a mask carved from marble as he stood there tapping his leg with his leather folder.

And they were supposed to go with this woman?

This woman, whom they had never met until two days ago? This woman, whose family had disapproved of his father; this woman, who had treated his mother, her own sister, so badly and then turned their back on her. How could you love someone and turn your back on them? He knew how hard he had worked to take care of Suzanne before Mama and Papa came into their lives. He knew he could never turn his back on his sister. How could she do that to her sister? And if she had turned her back on her sister, their mother, what was to say she would not get angry with him or Suzanne and turn her back on them?

He looked up at the woman in the carriage. He was only two steps away from joining her.

Darby looked up at his aunt, took a deep breath, shook his head and very formally said, "Miss Landau, I appreciate your offer to take my sister and me into your care. I understand that you feel it is your obligation as our blood relative, as we are your sister's children. But let me say to you that the only reason why you even knew of our mother's death was because Papa found you and told you."

"I assume you are here because you feel some kind of sense of duty toward me and Suzanne, but I believe you gave up that duty when you and your family disapproved of our father and rejected our mother. I am eleven years old, and I never met you until Wednesday. As far as I know, my mother did not receive any communication from you during my whole life. Ma'am, you owe nothing to Suzanne and me."

"Papa and Mama Redmond love us; they took us in and made us their own. I will not go with you. I will not let you take my sister. If you try to force us, I will take Suzanne and run away the first chance we get. So please, understand, I choose to stay with people who want and love me and my sister, not with someone who has forsaken my family in the past and, as far as I know, may do so again in the future."

He reached out his hand to his sister. "Come on, Suzanne. You and I are Redmonds now. We belong here." He turned to Reg, who had been standing at the head of the team; even he had tears in his eyes. "Reg, could you please get our trunks off the coach? Thank you very much."

He took his sister's hand, helped her down from the coach, and, with great dignity, walked over to stand with Charlie and Rebecca, who immediately put a protective arm over each child's shoulder, drawing them close to her skirts. Darby looked up at Charlie, "Can we please fix the name thing, Papa?"

He could only smile and nod.

"Young man, you are a disobedient child! You must come with me; it is the law." Victoria sat forward in the coach looking as if she would disembark and drag them back aboard.

Edgar walked up to stare Victoria in the face and stop her from leaving the coach. "Madam, he has obeyed a much higher law. The law of our God. The ten commandments tell us to honor our father and our mother. Darby has done exactly that. He has honored his birth parents by recognizing the relationship, or more to the point, lack of relationship, you chose to have with them. And he has honored his chosen parents, as well, by electing to not abandon them, as you abandoned his parents. I believe that his choice will stand in any court in this land."

Jerome stepped forward opening his leather folder. "Miss Landau, as the family's attorney, I believe Reverend Vile is correct. Young Master Darby is old enough to bear accurate witness in any court in this country, and his argument as to the validity of your claim of guardianship is very compelling. I would be happy to represent him and Miss Suzanne against any action you care to bring in the matter, pro bono. As will the entirety of my firm, as I am very sure we will prevail. However, we do have another option…"

Miss Landau did step out of the coach, looked from one face to another in the crowd surrounding her. Darby's face was resolutely set. Suzanne had her face buried in Rebecca's skirts. Charlie, Richard, and Edgar all looked like they were ready to strike out if she made a move toward the children. Jerome's wife Amelia and Charlotte were both supporting Rebecca, one on each side. And

Jerome was standing there with his leather folder in one hand and a pen in the other.

The attorney continued, "Well, Miss Landau, it seems that the children have made their choice. You can either make a mess of things that will cost you a great deal of money or you can surrender to the inevitable. And with Darby's testimony, it is inevitable. So I suggest you sign the papers I have here, and give up your claim to the children, authorizing formal adoption by the General and Mrs. Redmond." He took another step forward.

She looked around again and gave them all a disdainful look. "All right, if you want to keep the ill-mannered little brats, you are welcome to them." She accepted the folder from Jerome, laid it on the floor of the carriage, quickly scanned the pages, then reached out for the pen. She signed the papers, Jerome asking Edgar and Richard to both sign as witnesses to the agreement.

By the time the paperwork was completed, Reg had unloaded the children's trunks and boxes. They sat in a large pile beside the carriageway. Jerome nodded at Reg, then turned to offer Miss Landau a hand up into her carriage.

She disdained the offered hand and climbed in. Jerome shut the carriage door and she leaned out the window. "I bid you all farewell. I hope to never hear from you or yours ever again." With that, she signaled the coachman to drive on.

Charlie knelt down to embrace Darby. "Son, that was very, very brave of you. I am so proud of you I cannot begin to tell you how proud I really am. You and Suzanne are safe and sound now, with us as you should be." He reached over to embrace Suzanne as well. "Brave daughter." He kissed here temple. Finally, he looked in Rebecca's eyes. Tears were running down her face, but now tears of joy and relief. He stepped forward and gathered his wife and two oldest children in his arms. "We are a family."

As they all moved back into the house, Reg called one of the footmen, and they started returning the children's things to their rooms. They adjourned to the back parlor, where Sarah had anticipated their return and set fresh tea, coffee and sweet rolls for everyone. Em came running into the room and threw herself into Suzanne's arms. "You get to stay! I am soooo happy."

Rebecca collapsed into her chair. "Thank you all so much. I honestly have no idea how we would have survived that without you."

Before anything else could happen, Sarah appeared in the door. "Gen'l Charlie?"

"Yes, Sarah?"

"Sir, your Thanksgiving dinner was somewhat downcast, with Miss Landau and her threats. So I am preparing you and your guests a true Thanksgiving dinner for today. I would say we all have some very important things to be thankful for today."

Charlie stepped forward and embraced the woman, tears stinging his eyes. "Indeed we do, Sarah. Thank you so much."

"You are most welcome." The woman smiled at him and the rest of the family and turned to return to her kitchen to oversee the preparation of a proper Thanksgiving feast for her friends.

CHAPTER 28

Monday, December 3, 1866

Today, Ro was to bring her first dogs to guard the house and family over to meet everyone. Rebecca had been rather skeptical when Charlie had sat her down and explained that he was bringing guard dogs and a trainer to protect the horses, barns, house and family. He had argued that it was not enough to have the stablemen ride the fences, that they did not need to lose any more horses, and that he would feel better if there was a vigilant first line of protection for the stables and the family.

Her skepticism was deepened when he told her that Ro was Jocko's niece. Her experience with Jocko's bright ideas was not terribly sanguine. Charlie explained how Irish Wolf Hounds functioned as guard dogs. They had to be trained, and two of Ro's dogs were already trained specifically to guard stables and horses, but they also had to be trained to guard specific people.

Today, Ro was going to bring over three dogs; one for the barns, one for the horses, and one to meet the people. That meant that she was going to bring herself over. Charlie had no idea what kind of reaction his wife would have to this most unusual woman. Charlotte and the girls were still another issue. He was not looking forward to all of the delicate discussions he knew would have to be managed.

At about nine that morning, Ro drove the buckboard he had provided her into the stable yard. Tarent came out to meet her, having been warned that she was coming. He had also been warned that she was a bit unusual, but when Tarent met her, she was even more unusual than he anticipated. The woman was half a head taller than him, and he was no shrimp. She had short dark hair stuffed under an old felt slouch hat, a calico shirt under a canvas vest with multiple pockets, each of which was stuffed with various lumpy things, and a pair of gabardine pants stuffed into a very well-worn pair of calf-high boots, each of which also sheathed a bowie knife. A gun belt was strapped around her hips.

On the back of the buckboard were three huge crates, each of which holding a big gray dog. The dogs were lying in their crates, eyeing him suspiciously. They were not cute little puppies. In fact, when one stood up in the crate, he suspected these dogs were almost as large as a small pony.

Ro extended her hand to him. "Mr. Tarent, I assume. I am Ro Jackson. I have brought you a couple of dogs to guard the stables and horses. They have already been trained; I just have to introduce them to you and your staff so they know who are friends and who are not."

Tarent looked from her to the dogs. "Good morning, Miss Jackson. Um, can I ask what kind of dogs these things are? They are huge."

She laughed, having seen this reaction many, many times to her beloved dogs. "Please, call me Ro. And the dogs are Irish Wolf Hounds. They were originally bred to protect sheep herds from wolves, but it turns out they can be trained to protect anything you want them to. So I trained these two to guard stables and horses. I have one more that I will train to guard General Redmond's family and the house."

Tarent looked from her to the dogs and back again. Behind her, he could see his employers walking down from the house. "Well,

General Charlie and Miss Rebecca are on their way. We can get started when they get here."

The two humans turned to watch them approaching. All three dogs stood up in their crates, their hackles rising a bit, but not barking because Ro was still calm. They watched too.

Rebecca looked at the young woman standing beside the buckboard. If she had not had obvious breasts, she would have thought she was a man. She whispered to her husband, "Is she like you?"

"I do not know, and to be honest, I do not care. I suspect she is simply a free spirit, more inclined to live in whatever way is most comfortable for her. Given the life she has had and the work she does with dogs and protecting people and places, I suspect that britches, boots, and handy weapons are most comfortable for her. Just like they are for you."

"Minus the firearm and knives."

"Thank goodness."

As they drew near, Ro spoke up. "Good morning, General Redmond."

"Good morning, Miss Jackson. I would like you to meet my wife, Rebecca Redmond."

Rebecca extended her hand. "Pleased to meet you, Miss Jackson. And thank you for bringing a new level of protection to me and mine."

"My pleasure, Mrs. Redmond. And please call me Ro." She turned to the crates, opening the first one and commanding the dog down with a simple gesture. The big male immediately sat at her feet, his thick tail pounding the ground. "This is Maor Páirce. It means Ranger. He has been trained to guard horses. We will have to introduce him to you and your staff, so that he knows not to attack them, but he will attack anyone or anything that tries to bother the horses after that. His partner is Scioból Madra, which is literally Barn Dog. And it is obvious what she guards."

"The one for you and yours is Feighlí Páistí or just Feighlí. It means baby-sitter. She guards wee bairns, and I will train her to guard your house as well."

Ro snapped her fingers and Maor Páirce lifted his thick head. "Maor, this is General Redmond." She looked at Charlie and said, "Hold out your hand. Let him sniff you."

He extended his hand and Maor gently sniffed it, then licked it. He looked into his big brown eyes and saw nothing but gentleness. He stretched his fingers and scratched the big dog's chin. The dog dropped his head into his hand.

"That is very good. He knows you and likes you. Mrs. Redmond? You ready to try?"

She held out her hand, a little cautious, but willing to try. The great dog stepped to stand in front of her, sniffed, licked, and then sat down at her feet, leaning against her – Rebecca staggered a little, but Charlie caught her. She laughed, a nervous laugh, then scratched the big dog between the ears. Maor leaned a little harder.

Ro laughed. "Well, well. It seems Maor may have found a new love. The only person he has ever done that to before is me." She looked at Rebecca, who was still scratching the dog's head and now neck. "Leaning like that means he trusts you. Take it as a dog's compliment."

Ro repeated the introduction with Tarent, then let Madra out and repeated the process. She asked if she and Tarent could go and complete introductions with Madra and Maor first, and then show the dogs where they would sleep, get water, and be fed. "Once we do that, they will know this is their new home and will not wander. Oh, and Tarent, you will need to take Maor and Madra around the fence line so they learn their limits."

"I can do that. Do they follow when you are mounted?"

"Yes. Just call them. I will teach you all of their commands as we go around the grounds." She turned to Charlie and Rebecca. "Training Feighlí will take more time, as her limits are rather different. Perhaps I will keep her here until I am done with Madra and Maor, then I will bring her up to the house."

"Certainly, Ro," Rebecca replied. "I will be in my office, which is just inside that door." She pointed to the back door on the ground floor. "Just knock when you are ready."

As they headed back to the house, Ro and Tarent moved the

buckboard with the last dog still crated into the shade and got a bowl of water for her.

~

They stopped in the kitchen for a cup of coffee, and then settled into Rebecca's office for a quick chat.

"My God, Charlie! Those dogs are huge. Do you really think they will be safe with the children – especially with the boys?"

"I think so. They are still dogs, and dogs tend to want to care for children. They are certainly intimidating creatures. I would not want to face one unexpectedly, would you?"

She thought for a moment. "I am afraid the bigger problem will be introducing Ro to the townspeople. What do you think they will do with her?"

He considered it. "Darling, I think it is less a matter of what the townspeople will do with Ro and more a question of what will she do to them. That woman will take no insult or cut from anyone without a rather unpleasant response."

"So will it be Mrs. Williams or one of Alex Raeburn's crowd that experiences her first?"

"I am sure I do not know, but I truly want to be there when it happens. I suspect Culpeper is in for a shock."

"Do you think we can get her into a dress for Church?"

"I rather think it does not matter. She is Catholic. It is their problem, not ours."

She had a mental image of the local Catholic priest dealing with Miss Ro Jackson. He was a little man, with a slight Irish accent rather like Jocko's, and a soft voice that no one in town had ever heard raised to more than slightly above a whisper. The Catholic congregation in Culpeper was always small, and since the war had dwindled to tiny – no more than ten or fifteen people. Ro Jackson was going to make waves, no matter where she went.

~

504

Shortly before lunch, Rebecca heard a knock on the back door. When she opened the door, there stood Ro, with one of the huge gray dogs on a leash, sitting patiently beside her.

"Mrs. Redmond, this is Feighlí." The dog wagged its tail on hearing her name. "I have brought her up to start her training this afternoon."

She reached out to the dog as she had done with the previous two. A sniff, a lick, a pet, and some ear scratching later, and Feighlí was sitting on her feet, leaning against her as happily as Maor had earlier.

"Well, this is a good thing, ma'am. If your guard dog thinks you are a wonderful human, it makes things much easier."

"Come into my office. I have some lunch coming and I am sure you are hungry after your morning here."

"Thank you, ma'am." She walked into the office and seated herself in one of the available chairs. Feighlí settled down on the floor beside her, quiet and still.

Rebecca stepped across the hall and asked Sarah to send lunch for the two humans over to her office. She asked for a bowl of water and a bowl of chopped meat for the dog as well.

They sat chatting for a few minutes while they waited for lunch to arrive. The tale of bringing seven dogs from Belfast to New York by boat and then from New York to Culpeper by train had several funny moments that Ro recounted with a dry sense of humor.

Rebecca finally got around to asking the woman why she was so heavily armed.

She explained about the troubles in Ireland. While there had been no open warfare between Catholics and Protestants since the end of the last century, there were ongoing skirmishes between the Irish Nationalists and the Orange Order, especially in and around Ulster in Northern Ireland, Jocko and Ro's home county. For her, being armed was simply something she had to do to protect herself, her family and her dogs. Rebecca nodded, understanding all too well from her experiences with troops moving across her lands during the recent War of Northern Aggression.

Just then, Freddy knocked at the door, and then entered without waiting for permission, carrying the lunch tray. He looked at the big dog. The big dog looked at him, her hackles rising slightly. He froze, terrified.

Rebecca leapt to her feet, crossing the room in a hurry to rescue the lunch tray before it could drop from the boy's trembling hands and hit the floor.

Her sudden movement had all of Feiglí's attention and the dog rose from her position to stand at alert, clearly watching to make sure that the wonderful new lady was safe, and if she was not, to do something about it.

She took the tray and set it on a table. She reached out her hand to him, saying, "Come on, Freddy. She will not hurt you. Come make friends with the new dog."

He had cold sweat running down his face. "Miss 'Becca! Are you sure that is a dog? And that it ain't gonna eat me? Gen'l Charlie said he wouldna beat me. He ain't never said nothin' bout not getting' ate." He still could not move.

"I am very sure, Freddy, and she needs to get to know you so that she understands you belong here and that you are one of the people she should protect."

He still could not move. Rebecca looked at Ro, who nodded encouragement. So she called, "Here, Feiglí."

The dog did not move. Ro offered, softly, "The command is 'teacht.' I have not taught them English commands. That way, only a few people – you, your family and your staff, and possibly Uncle Jocko, will be able to command these dogs."

Rebecca smiled her understanding, then said, "Feiglí, teacht." Immediately, the dog walked to stand beside her.

Ro whispered, "Tell her 'suí.'"

"Feiglí, suí." The dog's butt hit the floor with a slight thump.

Rebecca reached out and took the boys hand. "Just hold your hand out. She will sniff it, then lick it. Then, if you like, you can pet her."

Hesitantly, he did as he was told; standing stock still except for the slight tremor that shook his hand. Feiglí sniffed, then, recognizing the child's fear, very gently nuzzled and licked the back of his hand. A look of wonder came over his face; he had never experienced so much gentleness from an animal. Tentatively, he reached out to pet the top of the big dog's head. Feiglí turned her head to offer her cheek for him to pet.

"You see, Freddy? She is your friend now. And you know, friends never hurt each other."

"Yes, ma'am. But Miss 'Becca, white folks don have dogs to protect niggers; they keeps dogs to hurt niggers." He ducked his head, then carefully backed out of the room.

Both women shook their heads at the boy's words. They had been very careful to not hurt his feelings, but they also appreciated the humor and the bravery he had shown.

Ro snapped her fingers; Feiglí returned to her side and settled down. The two women enjoyed their lunch, chatting about Culpeper and what Ro would have to face to get her breeding program started and to find clients in the town. Rebecca was quick to offer a word of warning about Mrs. Williams and her collection of followers.

After lunch, they and the new resident of the house went upstairs to meet the children and other members of the household, including the indoor animals, Papa Puppy and Sheridan. Darby was very matter of fact about meeting the big dog. Suzanne fell in love at first sight, a feeling that was mutual between her and the dog. Em was more hesitant, as her first doggie love was Papa Puppy.

Papa Puppy had a seriously territorial response; the little Jack Russell went after the big dog like it was an invader to be repelled at all costs. Rebecca had been afraid this would happen. Ro knew better.

Feiglí looked at the little dog bouncing and barking in front of her and did exactly what the breeder expected. She reached out with one huge paw and backhanded the smaller dog out of her way. Papa Puppy went rolling head over tail across the floor. One could almost hear the big dog thinking, 'Go away, pup. You bother me.'

When Rebecca took the big dog into the boys' nursery, they were both playing on the floor. Tess looked terrified. Feiglí took one look at the toddlers and her tail started wagging hard and fast. She crouched down and slowly crept closer to the boys. They noticed the big fuzzy thing creeping up on them, and together cried out, "OOOOHHHHH. A doggie!" They immediately flung themselves on the big dog, and Feiglí rolled onto her side, calmly letting the boys climb all over her body and even maul her ears.

Tess started breathing again. Ro and Rebecca introduced the big dog to the nanny, who found the unerring gentleness of the animal to be disarming in such a big beast. Tess, like Freddy, knew what big dogs like this usually meant, but in this case, she understood the dogs were not there to hurt her or anyone else, unless the family was threatened.

They walked out into the hall and down to Charlie's office. Papa Puppy was waiting in the hall for them. She was still not sure about the big animal, but the swat she had received made her a lot more cautious than she had been. There was no ferocious barking and jumping, but there was a low, quiet growling from her safe spot under a bench in the hall.

They entered the office, closing the door behind them. He smiled at them, knowing the routine. Rebecca walked over to his side, and called Feiglí, who came to her immediately. He introduced himself to her and was immediately accepted.

However, one occupant of the office was not so welcoming. Sheridan stood at his windowsill beside the cat door Duncan had fashioned for him in one of the window panes, ready to make a run for it if necessary.

Rebecca released Feiglí, who strolled over to meet this other resident. Sheridan's back arched, his tail lifted and turned into a perfect bottle brush, and a low hiss issued forth. Feiglí ignored this and kept coming, gently, to be sure, but she kept going toward him. The big dog got within paw reach and immediately got a slap on the nose from the annoyed cat, which then turned and bolted out of the escape hatch.

All three broke out into gales of laughter. When he could talk again, Charlie wondered, "How long do you think it will take for him to come back?"

Rebecca, knowing exactly how spoiled the cat was, replied, "He will be back as soon as he is hungry, dear."

Ro just stood there smiling and petting Feiglí.

∽

Rebecca lay with her head on Charlie's shoulder, his arm draped down her back. Their bodies molded together as usual after making love. He bent his right leg up at the knee, letting it fall out from under the sheet as he shifted a bit. She resettled immediately and began playing with the few little black hairs on his thigh.

"Why do you do that?" He asked, looking down at her picking fingers.

"What?"

"Pull the hair on my leg."

"I am not pulling the hair."

"Trust me. You are."

"I am petting you. Touching you. Caressing you. Like we always do, after. Just like your fingers are grazing the small of my back right now." She sighed contentedly.

"I am not pulling the hair on your back."

"I do not have hair on my back."

He chuckled when she managed to find two small black hairs together and yank them from his leg. "Ouch."

"That is what you get, you evil man."

"Not what you said twenty minutes ago. Then I was… What was the word? Mag--"

A finger over his lips stopped his next declaration. "I know what I said."

He smiled at her, amused by her apparent bashfulness. Hugging her a bit closer, he sighed and closed his eyes.

"Charlie?"

"Mmm?"

"I want to thank you."

"You do not have to thank me. I enjoy doing that."

"Not for that. But yes, thank you for that too." The bed shook a bit as they both laughed. "No, I mean for showing me how good this can be. There was some part of me that was afraid that I might

509

never really recover from my experiences during my first marriage. I was worried that somehow I would always be reserved, or maybe even frigid. But with you it is not a duty by any measure and something I not only look forward to but find myself thinking about a lot."

He laughed and nodded. "I agree. I think about it a lot as well."

"No, Charlie, you do not understand. There are times when I see you out in the barn and I want to close the door and do things to you that will frighten the horses."

This made him burst into uncontrollable laughter. His entire body shook and it seemed like the harder he tried to stop, the more he laughed.

She continued, "The only reason I have not done it is because I am afraid we will be caught." As an afterthought she grumbled, "Too many damn people around that barn most of the time."

Once his laughter began to subside she moved closer still and began rubbing his stomach. "It is easy to love you. You have given me more confidence and because of that, I am more comfortable with taking these things out and having a look at them now."

"You are not nearly as shy as you used to be. You have not just trotted out your desires; you threw a bridle and saddle on them and rode off at a hard gallop."

She laughed. "Oh the things I could say to that! I fear the company I keep has been a terrible influence. It is still hard to believe one of you is a minister." She shook her head. "It is good though, right?"

"Absolutely." he nodded. "It is because with you it is right every time. And it is right because we both hunger for it and each other. I have a terrible time keeping my hands off you as well, my dear. There are moments when I see you standing in front of the window in the rear parlor, the sun coming through just so and it always takes my breath away, makes my hands itch and my belly ache. It is horrible that it is usually first thing in the morning because then I suffer all day long."

"We are a pair."

He kissed her forehead before offering, "Of what, I am not sure, but since we are happy with each other and not imposing ourselves unnecessarily on anyone else, I suppose the rest of the world can just go to hell."

"Exactly." She began exploring his neck and ear with her lips. "Know what the best part is for me?"

"I would like to think I do, yes." He nodded with confidence.

"I am sure it is not what you think." Gently, she turned his face so their eyes met in the dim light. "I love watching your eyes when you go over the edge. They turn so silver they are almost translucent."

"That is because there is no blood left in my head."

"Do you know what Charlotte told me once?"

"It is hard to say knowing her."

"She told me, and I quote, 'The walls in this house are thick, but they are not that thick.'"

He groaned.

"Yes, I am sure that is exactly what she was talking about."

"I doubt it, dear. She was no doubt commenting on that long, languid moan that starts from your chest and rumbles there for a moment or two before escaping your lovely throat. It is the most sensual thing I have ever heard and it always precipitates your fall from the pedestal."

~

Saturday, December 8, 1866

It was the last Saturday poker game before the Christmas holidays, as well as the last Mah Johng gathering. They had all agreed that the holidays had so much going on that they would suspend the Saturday evening get-togethers until January.

To add to the evening, Mrs. Allen, the local source of outstanding moonshine, was closed that day for some reason. So while Alex Raeburn and his cronies usually gathered at her place, tonight they were also at Jocko's, very pleased to find that he had some of her best.

The poker players were at a table at one end of the bar. The I

Hate Charlie Redmond Club was at a table as far away as they could get and still be in the same bar. A Christmas truce had been called.

Ro walked into the bar, accompanied by her largest male dog. She stomped up to the bar and hailed her uncle. "So, Uncle, what does a girl have to do to get supper around here?"

Jocko finished serving the client in front of him, then walked over to stand in front of his niece. "Well, first, hand over your gun and knives. No one comes into this bar armed."

She looked stunned. No one ever asked her to disarm. Ever.

"You know I will not do that."

"Well, if you want to eat here, you will. Otherwise, you can go eat in the kitchen or upstairs in our rooms. The situation here is touchy enough without having someone armed for bear."

She looked around the room, seeing the obvious split between the occupants and understanding her uncle's concern. The middle of the room was totally empty.

With a sigh, she unbuckled her gun belt and handed it across the bar.

Jocko said, "The knives too."

She pulled the two bowie knives out of her boots and handed them over.

"And the derringer."

With a disgusted look, she reached into one of the pockets of her vest and pulled out a little derringer, handing it over too.

"The knuckles."

She pulled a set of brass knuckles out of her pants pocket.

"And the blackjack."

She reached behind her back and pulled the short, weighted leather baton out of her belt.

"And the wrist knife."

She sighed, rolled up her sleeve and unbuckled the sheathed poniard from her forearm.

"Anything else?" Jocko asked.

"No, unless you count Carraig." She pointed to the dog.

"All right. What do you want for supper?"

"Whatever Esther made as a special and a large lager."

She took the beer and wandered over to an empty table in the middle of the room. Her dog followed and flopped itself down at her side as soon as she sat down.

Charlie looked up, noticing what she was drinking. "Excuse me, gentlemen. I need a word with our latest resident."

He sat down beside her, speaking very quietly. "I have no say in what you do on your own time. But please do not drink beer either before or during your time at my house. Miss Rebecca cannot stand the smell of it – on anyone. She had a very bad experience with a beer drinker and I simply do not allow it on our property."

"Not a problem, Gen'l. I am not much of a beer drinker, anyway. Just using is to wash down supper without compromising my abilities."

He went back to the poker table while she sat quietly waiting for her dinner to arrive and playing with the dog's ears.

Alex Raeburn looked over at the newcomer. He called out to her, "So, what are you, and what the hell is that beastie beside you?" The dog bristled and sat staring at Alex at full attention.

She looked over at him. "Me? I am a dog breeder."

Alex snapped back, "No, I meant are you a man or a woman?"

"For what it is worth to you, little man, I am a woman. Please, do not confuse that with weakness, as I can take any one of you, if need be, with or without the tools of my trade." She indicated the dog. "And this is an Irish Wolf Hound."

The men at Alex's table all laughed. "Not many wolves around here anymore."

"Aye, but it does not matter to Carraig whether the wolf has four legs." She paused and grinned directly at the man. "Or two." Her Irish accent was very obvious.

The men at Alex's table laughed among themselves at the cut that she had just delivered. "So that monster is your defender?"

"Aye, or he will guard anyone he knows that I ask him to." She leaned over, petting and whispering to Carraig, who immediately got up and walked over to Charlie, where he sat down beside him, clearly at full alert. "Now, if any of you brave boys want to find out, go ahead and walk over to General Redmond."

Eddie, who worked part time for Duncan, got up and walked toward the poker table. As soon as he passed Ro's table, Carraig was on his feet, planted in front of Charlie, hackles up, teeth bared, and a loud warning growl emitting from his throat. Eddie stopped cold. Charlie murmured something to the dog, which immediately lay back down, but did not stop growling. Very slowly, Eddie backed up all the way to his chair, never taking his eyes off the big dog.

Ro snapped her fingers and Carraig returned to her side, positioning himself between his mistress and Alex's table, and then lying down, but clearly still on full alert.

The ladies in the other room had heard the commotion and could be seen peering through the door. Ro's meal had arrived, and Jocko unobtrusively set it in front of her while this scene was going on. Calmly, she began eating.

But the challenge was not over yet. Alex called out. "So, Redmond! What other niggers and furriners are you going to hire to take good jobs from our boys? You have that Chinaman, your hand-picked niggers, carpetbaggers, and yet another damned Mick."

Ro and Jocko both bristled.

Charlie looked at Alex sternly. "Mr. Raeburn, I do not know if you have noticed, but Redmond Stables has hired six men from town in the last three months, three of which are sitting with you. We have also hired long term Culpeper residents to work at the bank. In addition, we have helped a number of other businesses get started or restarted, which has created yet more jobs for returning soldiers. What have you done to create new opportunities?" *Starting the I Hate Charlie Redmond Club does not count,* he mused as he watched the men across the room.

Raeburn stiffened as did the men he was with.

Richard thought, *Oh, shit. One more jibe and we will have a full-fledged bar fight on our hands.*

Edgar stood and quietly walked around the edge of the room to stand by the door to the tearoom where the ladies were gathered. He motioned to Rex to do the same from his side. Then he said, "Gentlemen, there are ladies present. Please consider your manners."

Alex half rose from his seat. "I do not care!" He gestured at Charlie. "This damn scallywag has come in here, forced one of our women, turned our town upside down, brought in all kinds of carpetbaggers and furriners, and taken away our Southern heritage and our rights."

Before anyone could respond, Carraig stood, took two steps toward Alex, set his feet and growled.

Ro spoke dryly from her chair, her spoon halfway to her mouth. "Mister, if you do not want your throat torn out, I suggest you shut your mouth and sit back down. You have pissed off my dog. And once he is pissed off, he tends to stay pissed off until he kills something." The pause was uncomfortable. "Or someone." She put the spoon in her mouth and sat chewing contemplatively.

A few minutes later, Alex and his friends settled their tab with Jocko and left, staying close to the wall and as far away from the growling dog as they could.

CHAPTER 29

Thursday December 13, 1866

Charlie stood on the front porch pacing and looking at his pocket watch. The men he had sent to pick up the payroll from the bank were late and that worried him. Every fiber of his being told him something was wrong, that he needed to go to town. Just as he put his foot down to walk toward the barn to get Jack, Richard came flying down the carriageway on his horse.

"Charlie!"

He shook his head, knowing his fears were about to be confirmed. He moved to Richard and helped stop his horse by taking hold of the bridle. "What has happened?"

"Your men got waylaid. About a mile and a half from here. Got the living hell beat out of them."

"Are they alright?"

"Elizabeth and Nigel are putting them back together. Charlie, they got your payroll."

"Damn it! I knew when the boys were late getting back there was a problem. Any ideas?"

"Not at the moment. You?"

"One or two, but without evidence I cannot just go pointing my finger. Let me go tell Rebecca what has happened. I will come to town shortly. I am going to still have to cover payroll."

"Alright, I will see you there." Richard turned his horse and was headed back to town at a hard gallop.

With a huge sigh, Charlie headed back into the house to find his wife. Inside, he found Tess coming down the stairs with Andy on her hip. He kissed his son on the head and smiled to his nanny, "If you see Miss Rebecca, could you ask her to come to my office as soon as she is able?"

"Yes, General Charlie. Right away."

He mounted the stairs and made his way to his office. Opening the doors on a tall wooden gun cabinet behind the door, he looked at his display of firearms. Picking a revolver he knew he could handle with his left hand, he chose a holster from the top drawer and buckled it around his waist.

Rebecca knocked on the open door, not seeing him as he stood behind it. "Darling?"

"Come in."

She stepped in, closing the door. Her eyes went wide when she saw him put the last bullet in his gun before holstering it. "What has happened? Why are you wearing a gun?"

"I have to go into town. Our payroll has been robbed."

"What?"

"I sent a couple of the men to town like I always do at the end of the day to get the household and farm payroll from Frank before the bank closed. It is the last piece of business we do. It has worked this way for months without any problems; obviously someone has figured out my system. Apparently, they were attacked halfway between here and the bank."

"How are the boys?"

"Richard says they are pretty beat up. Elizabeth is taking care of them." He moved to the door and gave a shout for Tomas. It did not take long for the valet to appear. His eyes went wide when he saw him wearing a gun.

"Yes, sir?"

"Could you please see to it that Jack is saddled and up front in five minutes?"

"Yes, sir. Is there anything I can help with?" His eyes traveled to the gun strapped to his boss's hip.

"Well, that depends?" He reached into his gun cabinet and pulled out a shot gun. "Willing to carry this?"

The valet nodded emphatically.

"Then have a horse saddled for yourself as well. See if Big Ben is around to drive a wagon into town."

"Yes, sir. I will be right back." He made a hasty retreat and his feet could be heard pounding down the steps at double time.

"I am going with you," Rebecca said as a matter of fact. She started to turn for the bedroom.

"Oh, no! No. No, you most certainly are not!" He caught her up by the arm.

"Charlie…"

"I will not argue with you over this." He pointed a determined finger directly at her. "This is one of the more dangerous situations that we have seen and I will not have you running into the middle of it. I promise to keep you well informed and tell you what has happened down to the finest detail, but I am putting my foot down. You are not going into town."

She opened her mouth, an angry retort already rising to her lips. She looked into her husband's face. This was not the face of the man that she could convince or cajole into almost anything. This was the face of the soldier who knew when it was truly time to be prepared for battle. The angry comment died on her lips. "All right, Charlie. Please be careful."

"I will." He kissed her on the forehead and headed downstairs.

~

A mile and a half from the house, he pulled Jack to a halt and signaled for Tomas and Ben to halt their progress as well. As he dismounted, he dropped the reins and made his way carefully to what was left of his first wagon. He closed his eyes when he saw the horse lying in the grass, shot through the head. "Bastards," he growled as he began looking at the ground around the remnants of the wagon.

It looked to him as if four or five men had come from a small grove of trees, easily catching the driver and his unarmed partner by surprise as they drove past.

The wagon had been tipped on its side, and the panel that had hidden the small chest of coins easily popped from its place inside the wagon revealing the contents. The wheels had been smashed and broken, and it looked as if they had tried to set the wagon on fire, but it failed to catch. As he looked at the dead horse, he realized he was angrier over that than the loss of the wagon or the money. And he still had to tell Rebecca one of her horses was an unexpected casualty.

Climbing back up on Jack, he waved his hand and the men continued to town. He sent Ben and Tomas to wait at the bank and told them he would be there shortly. He turned the corner and headed for Elizabeth's infirmary.

Stepping inside, he found his two farm hands mostly bandaged up, but certainly looking worse for the wear.

"Gentlemen, I am very sorry this happened," he offered immediately as he took a seat in front of them. "I will make sure you are properly cared for and compensated for this attack. I promise you nothing like this will ever happen again."

Both men could only nod and murmur, "Thank you, sir."

Elizabeth stood back and could only smile as Charlie tried to ease his own guilty conscious over this incident. He had not been the one listening to these two men for the last hour; they had been terrified that General Redmond would blame them for the robbery. They both expected to be going to jail. No matter how she had tried to reassure them, she knew that he would be there to make things right and she had not been surprised when he walked through the door.

As he finished with his men, he turned to his friend as he moved toward the door. "Give them anything they need and I will be handling the bill."

"Yes, General." She gave him a smile and a casual salute as he shook his head and made his way outside to go to the bank.

Riding down the street very slowly, so slowly it was nearly painful for Jack, he looked at his pocket watch. Five thirty and he noticed that while Culpeper should still be busy with people, it looked a lot like a ghost town.

He knew damn well that people should be at Jocko's for dinner; hell, the real early birds should even be lining up at Mrs. Allen's for her weekend delivery of moonshine, but as he looked at the little house sitting across the street from the bank, the place looked abandoned.

He shook his head as he dropped from Jack's back and entered the bank. Tomas and Big Ben were sitting in chairs right inside the door looking serious and prepared for anything. Tomas was still clutching the shotgun Charlie had given him. Richard and Frank were at Frank's desk and it was clear that Richard was taking a statement.

Charlie held his hand up, letting them know he did not want to disturb them, then he unlocked and entered his office. Sitting behind his desk, he pulled his personal checkbook from a drawer and wrote a check. A moment or two later, Richard knocked on the doorjamb.

"Come in." He sat back and sighed. "Hell of an afternoon."

"To say the least. Here is what we know. Frank had your payroll ready right at three o'clock when he was getting ready to close up. Your secretary had already left for the day."

He nodded.

"He says he did not see or hear anything unusual as your men loaded the wagon. It was a perfectly normal payroll drop as far as he is concerned. Your men left and he locked up to finish his paperwork before going up to his apartment." The provost pointed up, indicating the rooms above the bank where Frank lived.

"Your men proceeded like they always do and about halfway between here and your place, five or six men ambushed them from a grove of trees."

"I counted four or five by the tracks."

"Well, it was a bit of a mess from what they say. Maybe they counted wrong."

"Maybe." Charlie was not convinced. Had he missed something? Or was someone lying?

"The men were wearing bags or hoods over their head with holes cut in them."

"How imaginative."

"Seems to have worked. The boys cannot identify them."

"Did you ask them about boots or horses?"

"What?"

"Richard, you can identify me by the boots I wear. As can I with you. Anyone would know Jack even if I had a bag over my whole body. And I would know that old nag you ride anywhere." He grinned. "I suspect if we have any chance of finding out who did this we will have to rely on the smallest of details."

Richard shook his head. "I did not, but I certainly will. Elizabeth plans to keep them overnight. I will question them again tomorrow morning before they leave."

Charlie stood and went to the door calling Frank over. "Please, cash this for me. I still must make payroll tomorrow. Just bag it up. Tomas, Ben and I will take it out to Redmond Stables."

"I will go with you." Richard stepped up and smiled as he lifted his coat, revealing his side arm, snugly tucked in a shoulder holster. "You are not as handy with a gun as you used to be."

"Even with my left hand, I can still hit something from five feet away, and trust me; no one is getting any closer. I only need to lose five hundred dollars once before I learn my lesson."

~

Saturday, December 16, 1866

Rebecca nearly laughed out loud when she entered the rear parlor. There in a perfect little line, from tallest to shortest, stood her entire family staring out the window at the falling snow. The human line was broken between Darby and Suzanne by Feiglí, who was also sitting and staring out the window, her tail thumping frantically. The storm had come on hard and fast the night before, dumping about three inches of snow between supper and bedtime. Her husband and her children were grumpy when they discovered snow was still falling in the morning and they thought that meant being stuck in the house all day. Now they were all standing there next to him; even Buddy and Andy were in on this particular act. Buddy was banging on the window while Andy licked it.

"Charlie, really!" She went to the rescue of her youngest sons; obviously their father was not paying attention.

"What?" He turned to find her scooping both boys into her arms. "They were fine."

"Andy was licking the glass, Charles Redmond."

"The window is clean," he protested.

"Keep digging," the blonde warned as she wiped drool from Andy's mouth and chin. "Why is it you four," she gestured to her husband and three eldest children, "cannot find something to do? I happen to know there is at least fifty dollars' worth of little toy soldiers in your father's library and another hundred dollars' worth of toys in the playroom."

"We are bored." The tall man pouted. "We have already played with the toys."

The actual children in the room giggled.

She fingered the necklace he had given her. She had not removed it since the day he put it around her neck, but now it was perfectly clear she had a birthstone for all her children, including the big one.

"Charles... Huger... Redmond," she growled, rubbing the bridge of her nose.

He blinked; all three of his names were bad. All three with that pause was very bad. He was now the Powder Monkey and there was no way to pass the charge to Darby because he was already in the room and that was against the rules of the game. He began rounding up children so they could make a hasty escape. "I think we can find something to do." With that, the four of them and the dog were out the door.

She looked at her two youngest sons, who were now happily sucking their fists as they looked to their mama. "How about some apples before your nap?"

"Apple, Mama!" Buddy bounced happily.

"Mmmmmm. Please." Andy agreed as he buried his head in his mama's shoulder.

The boys had been settled down for their naps for about thirty minutes when Rebecca was once again in search of her family. After checking every possible location in the house, she realized that they had managed to slip outside.

"Charles Redmond..." She grumbled as she made her way around to the kitchen. She found Sarah busily making a big pot of hot tea and she could hear the screams and giggles of children through the back door. "He took them out?"

"Yes, Miz Rebecca. He did. But he did have them bundled up nice and warm. Even put the girls in their britches and boots."

"Thank goodness for small miracles." She huffed as she tossed on her coat and stepped out onto the back porch.

There they were. All four of them and the damned dog too. Charlie was up to his knees in snow trying to chase his eldest son. Darby found the nearly thigh deep snow a bit difficult to get through as he tried to get away from his father.

The dog was having a glorious time snowplowing through, nose first. The girls were screaming and laughing as they tried their best to plow through the ruts made by their brother, father, and Feiglí. They were all covered in white, their faces red with the chill and wet, but they were having a wonderful time. Rebecca could only smile as she watched Charlie fall back into the snow as Darby nailed him quite squarely in the chest with a snowball to stop his forward advance. The girls piled on top of him, continuing their fit of screaming giggles. The dog came bounding over and started licking snow from Charlie's face.

"Sarah," she called through the door. "I think we will need a nice hot pot of soup too."

Friday, December 21, 1866

It was close to midnight when Albert finally trudged up the driveway to Redmond Stables. He was scheduled to arrive the following day after having been away for several weeks, just in time for the holiday celebrations, but had managed to catch a ride on a freight train with one of the trainmen he had befriended when shipping horses.

He had then caught one of his old friends coming out of Jocko's after the normal Friday night activities and had ridden back to his house, about two miles down the road from the Redmond place. He walked the last two miles and then quietly let himself in the back door, as he knew where the emergency key was kept.

He crept up the back stairs to the first floor, carefully avoiding the squeaky step. He then started up the main stairs to the second floor, but only got about three steps up when he was confronted by a great gray shadow standing at the top of the stairs, alternately barking and growling. In the moonlight through the front windows, Albert could see the great beast's bared fangs. He dropped his valise, froze in place, and had the uncomfortable feeling of his boots filling with warm fluid.

Charlie leapt out of bed when he heard Feiglí barking and snarling. He grabbed his service revolver and headed for the door to the hall. Rebecca was right behind him, though he pushed her back. The last thing he wanted was for Rebecca to tangle with an intruder.

Feiglí had taken to sleeping in the hall right outside of Rebecca's rooms. In that position, the dog could guard everything in the upper hall and anything coming up the stairs, while remaining as close as possible to her beloved lady. In every way, Feiglí was Rebecca's dog. And right now, it was clear, she was protecting her person.

He went out into the hall, calling, "If you know my voice, you know my name. Say it."

Albert choked out, "It is Albert here...Cousin Charlie"

He could tell Albert was scared out of his boots. He tucked his pistol behind his back, hoping the children had not seen it as everyone suddenly seemed to clamor into the hall like a great wave of ants. He commanded Feiglí to relax and sit. She would not obey his command, and stayed right where she was, on full alert, growling and snarling. Rebecca, having heard Albert's voice, came into the hall. "Feiglí. Teacht." Obediently, the dog moved over to her side, but kept an alert eye on Albert.

"Come on up, Albert. You need to meet the newest member of the household."

"If you mean that monster." He shook his head at his dear cousin.

"Albert," she warned.

"Promise it will leave me intact?"

She nodded.

He grabbed his satchel and trudged up the stairs. "I was going to try and surprise you by getting home early. Guess it was not such a good idea."

"Here, Albert. Stretch out your hand." She introduced Albert and Feiglí, at which point the big dog dutifully wagged her tail and licked Albert's hand.

Charlie looked up and down the hall. The children, Rex and Edgar, and Charlotte were all peering out their doors, trying to see what was going on. "It is all right, everyone. Albert just got in a little early, or a little late, depending on your point of view." Heads withdrew, doors closed, and Albert trudged off to his room to get cleaned up. "Welcome home. See you in the morning, Cousin Albert," he called after him.

~

Monday, December 24, 1866

Charlie was trying to complete some last-minute correspondence before Rebecca came up to box his ears for working on Christmas Eve. He gave his last letter a glance and set it aside in the tray to dry when Tomas entered the office with a handful of envelopes and papers and a small wooden box on top.

"General, Miss Rebecca asked me to relay the following message." He took a deep breath and let it out quickly before saying. "If she finds any more of your messes around this house before the New Year, you will find yourself living in the barn with Jack."

Charlie winced, then nodded with a smile. "I am sorry you got the brunt of that."

Tomas just smiled and put the pile in the center of his desk. "I am used to it by now, sir. I was wondering if you are done for the evening? I have been invited to Lizbet's for supper."

Charlie sat back and smiled at the young man he had grown very fond of in the last few months. "Very nearly. I do have one more thing." He pulled a few papers from his desk and stood moving to the chairs by the fireplace. He gestured for Tomas to join him.

"Is there a problem, sir?" Tomas unbuttoned his jacket as he sat, on the very edge of his chair.

He nodded seriously. "Sort of."

The young man swallowed hard; he could not for the life of him think what might have his employer sitting him down like this. "Yes, sir?"

"You see, Tomas, we have been working together for several months now and you have been very open and forthcoming about everything but your military service."

"Yes, sir. You know how it is, General. Some things are just easier not to talk about."

He nodded. "Indeed I do. However, I am also a lot like my eldest son, insatiably curious." He smiled and leaned forward in his chair. "Old Generals are allowed to look up records. You were a medic."

"Yes, sir."

"You wanted to be a doctor and now you are here folding my shirts."

"Yes, sir."

"Young man, we must rectify that situation." He sat back in his chair. "I am releasing you from my employ."

"But, General." He was about to go into full blown panic. "Sir, I need this job!"

"You cannot do this job and study."

"Study? Sir, I am afraid I do not understand."

"Yes, Tomas, study. Any man who wants to be a doctor must study. You told me when I hired you that you wanted to do something good. This is your chance."

He handed him the papers he had retrieved from his desk. "The first five are letters of recommendation from me, Miss Rebecca, Reverend Vile, Colonel Polk and Dr. Walker. The sixth page is your acceptance to the newly established Howard University for the fall semester of next year. They open officially this coming March and have just started accepting applications, but Doctor Walker had a few well-placed contacts that expedited your paperwork. You will be part of the first fall class. The seventh page is my personal letter of guarantee. Miss Rebecca and I will be covering all of your costs while you are at university studying. Mr. Lord has already been notified and is setting up the appropriate accounts. All the information you need is there." Charlie lifted his chin at the papers the man clutched in his fists.

Tomas stared at the papers in his hands and could only shake. Charlie put his hand on his friend's shoulder and offered softly, "You are a noble young man. I want to make sure you get a chance to do that something good."

He just shook his head, tears falling on the papers in his hands.

"I want you to take the next few months off to be with your family. Settle your affairs here. Because once you are off to school, you will not have time to do it then. I will continue to pay you your salary while you do so. I expect great things from you, Tomas."

"I will make you very proud, sir." He offered his hand to the man before him. "Thank you so much."

"Merry Christmas. Miss Rebecca and I cannot wait to get an invitation to your graduation."

∾

Tuesday, December 25, 1866

They had decided this Christmas would be a small, private

family affair. They had come too close to having the family torn asunder by Victoria Landau; they simply wanted quiet family time with just their children.

Most of the presents had been opened and the children were spread out all over the parlor, playing with new dolls, hobby horses, blocks and of course for Darby, books. He had his nose stuck firmly in the newest tome, Mr. Verne's Journey to the Center of the Earth, provided by his parents. Charlie just shook his head as he pulled an envelope from the top drawer of his desk. "Darby, there is one more thing for you and Suzanne."

When Darby looked up from his book, he handed him the envelope. He took it and opened it, removing the thick bunch of papers. He read slowly and smiled. "Thank you, Papa."

"It was our pleasure, Mr. Redmond," Charlie said with a wink.

EPILOGUE

Monday, December 31, 1866, and Tuesday, January 1, 1867

New Year's Eve/Day

The New Year's Eve gala at Redmond Stables was in full swing. A wonderful supper had been consumed and after a couple of hours of rest and relaxation, those gathered had reassembled in the ballroom where they would dance until a late dinner was served around eleven, to sustain them until midnight and the arrival of the new year.

The room was filled with gentlemen, dressed in their best evening wear, black waistcoats with tails, heavily starched white shirts, white ties and vests. The look of the proper gentleman was completed with the white gloves each man either wore or held gripped in his hand. No gentleman could dance with the ladies without his gloves on to protect both her dress and modesty.

The women broke up the wall of black and white with their gowns of every seeming color. Charlie had considered that when the room was in motion with couples dancing a beautiful waltz, it was as if a tornado and a rainbow were moving through the room at the same time.

Rebecca was looking especially radiant in her deep maroon and gold trimmed ball gown. All the gentlemen gathered, making sure to pay their proper respects to their hostess, without going so far that they received a thrashing from her husband, who was looking better and more fit than anyone had remembered seeing him in a long while.

As the musicians took their place in the alcove, Rebecca looked around, waiting for some eligible gentleman to request her companionship on the dance floor. As all the men around her paired off with the ladies of their choice, there was a quick look of disappointment or perhaps frustration on her face as she found herself unaccompanied when the music began.

The gentle tap on her shoulder was all she needed to turn with her most charming smile to face – Charlie.

He chortled at the look on her face. She had not expected him. While a husband and wife dancing together was considered unusual in most social circles, their friends and family had learned that these two embraced the unusual, generally with great gusto.

Charlie was determined. He had even gone so far as to ask the musicians to begin the evening with a waltz so that he and his wife might start the festivities properly. They obliged with Johannes Brahms, Waltz for Violin, a beautiful and very gentle piece of music for the general and his wife to dance to.

He offered her his left hand, placing his right on the small of her back, took her in his arms and waited momentarily to catch the beat. He smiled as he guided her around the dance floor. For the longest time they could only smile at each other as they moved to the music.

It was completely lost on them that there was not one other couple on the dance floor. As soon as he had taken her into his arms, the other participants took notice. They stepped back and cleared the floor. Everyone in the room, whether they were family, friend or neighbor would not have encroached on this moment between the general and his lady. They had never expected to see Charlie dancing again.

They all stood around the fringes of the dance floor, drinking and happily watching the couple before them step and move to the beat and tempo of the music. It was truly a beautiful thing to see them this way and not one among them would have considered intruding.

With every crescendo, he swept her around the dance floor causing her skirts to flare and a laugh to erupt as she tried to catch her breath.

"I may not be able to dance a reel, but all your waltzes are mine, Mrs. Redmond," he whispered in her ear.

She looked at him, with a happy smile and tears in her eyes. "Absolutely, General Redmond."

And with that they were off for the last circuit of the floor before their first dance in nearly two years ended with a round of applause from all those gathered.

They both had the grace to look embarrassed.

~

Just after midnight, as the last toast for a calm and prosperous new year had been delivered by one of the many attendees, Edgar slowly made his way over to Charlie and took him off to the side for a private chat.

Rebecca watched from near the fireplace. The rapidly changing expressions on Charlie's face were making her very curious as to what was being said. Eventually, he grinned, nodded and shook Edgar's hand while giving him a pat on his other shoulder.

The hostess of Redmond Stables, like the rest of the gathered entourage, did not have long to wait. Edgar stepped into the center of the room and cleared his throat, and everyone turned immediately to their minister, expecting that he would be offering some sort of new year prayer or blessing.

"Ladies and gentlemen." He smiled as he turned to find Charlotte in the crowd. "I have indeed been very blessed with my posting here in Culpeper. I have made wonderful new friends. I have been given the opportunity to lead a magnificent congregation and," he paused as he walked closer to where she stood, "I have fallen madly, deeply in love."

Charlotte's eyes were the size of dinner plates as he took her hand and dropped to one knee.

"Charlotte Redmond, there is nothing that would make me happier than to be able to start this new year with you agreeing to be my wife. Will you marry me?"

She stood there, gawking at him kneeling in front of her, her mouth working, but no sound coming out. She raised her free hand to her face, tears forming in her eyes, but still no sound emerged. From the side of the room, someone laughed and offered, "You are supposed to say something, Miss Charlotte."

With a very nervous giggle, she reached out to pull him to his feet. She looked around with a look that was very reminiscent of a startled deer, searching for three faces. Charlie was smiling an encouraging smile. Rebecca was smirking. Rex was grinning like a cat who had found an enormous pitcher of cream. She looked into Edgar's rather anxious eyes. This was taking longer than he had expected. She smiled at him, and finally managed to say, "Yes, yes, I rather think I will."

He pulled a ring box from his pocket. Inside was an elegant ring--platinum set with diamonds. He whispered, "For the purity of your soul, my dear." He slipped it on her left hand ring finger.

He laughed and swept her into his arms. Everyone else – or at least most of the rest of the assembly – broke into applause. Some of the single women turned to one another, grumbling because they had not managed to capture the eligible, handsome, single young minister. The musicians started playing a flowing rendition of Mr. Strauss's new waltz, From the Mountains, a beautiful and graceful tune. The tune built to a very celebratory crescendo as Edgar whirled Charlotte around the room.

As the musicians finished the evening with a lovely rendition of Wilde Rosen, all of the party guests who could dance did, including Rebecca and Charlie.

For a number of guests, packing up to go home was a little more time consuming than usual, as each stopped to congratulate Edgar and Charlotte. As the last person headed home, Charlotte, Edgar, Rebecca, Charlie and Rex retired to the back parlor for a quick night cap. Rebecca pulled Rex aside for a moment. "Are you alright with this?"

He grinned. "Of course I am. Edgar and I have discussed this at length. It serves a number of purposes, maintaining both Edgar and I beautifully. She gives him something I cannot; I give him something she cannot, and together, we have formed a very healthy alliance that provides the perfect support system for him. What could be better? I also care for Charlotte a great deal," he assured her with a smile.

Rebecca shook her head. She could not envision sharing Charlie with anyone else, but Rex, Edgar and Charlotte had been introducing her to new ideas for a while now. "Then I am glad for the three of you," she leaned in and gave him a kiss on the cheek. "I hope you are very happy."

The End

(The Redmond Saga Continues in Book 3: Enemies In The Gate)

Thank you for taking the time to read **Paths of Peace**. If you enjoyed it, please consider telling your friends or posting a short review. Word of mouth is an author's best friend and much appreciated.

Thank you,
T. Novan & Taylor Rickard

Also By T. Novan & Taylor Rickard

Redmond Civil War Romance Series

- Words Heard in Silence
- Paths of Peace
- Enemies In The Gates
- Honor They Father

Other Fiction by T. Novan

- Madam President (with Advocate)
- First Lady (with Advocate)
- The Claiming of Ford

Made in the USA
Monee, IL
26 April 2020